GOOD BOYS

Unleashed

WORKS BY JEREMY ROBINSON

The Didymus Contingency
Raising The Past
Beneath
Antarktos Rising
Kronos
Pulse
Instinct
Threshold
Callsign: King
Callsign: Queen
Callsign: Rook
Callsign: King 2 – Underworld
Callsign: Bishop
Callsign: Knight
Callsign: Deep Blue
Callsign: King 3 – Blackout
Torment
The Sentinel
The Last Hunter – Descent
The Last Hunter – Pursuit
The Last Hunter – Ascent
The Last Hunter – Lament
The Last Hunter – Onslaught
The Last Hunter – Collected Edition
Insomnia
SecondWorld
Project Nemesis
Ragnarok
Island 731
The Raven
Nazi Hunter: Atlantis
Prime
Omega
Project Maigo
Refuge
Guardian
Human After All
Savage
Flood Rising
Project 731
Cannibal
Endgame
MirrorWorld
Herculean
Project Hyperion
Patriot
Apocalypse Machine
Empire
Unity
Project Legion
The Distance
The Last Valkyrie
Centurion
Infinite
Helios
Viking Tomorrow
Forbidden Island
The Divide
The Others
Space Force
Alter
Flux
Tether
Tribe
NPC
Exo-Hunter
Infinite²
The Dark
Mind Bullet
The Order
Khaos
Singularity
Hunger – The Complete Trilogy
Nemesis
Point Nemo
Good Boys – The Lost Tribe
Good Boys - Unleashed

GOOD BOYS

– UNLEASHED –

JEREMY ROBINSON

Breakneck Media

Cover design and title page art by Jeremy Robinson, and Midjourney AI.

Visit Jeremy Robinson on the World Wide Web at: www.bewareofmonsters.com.

For Mom and Dad,
who made sure we had a dog
every day of the twenty years
I lived at home.

1

MICAH

Winter came early, with the first snow falling on Halloween night. Hasn't really stopped since. Fine by me. Keeps people indoors, hunkered up by fires, making Jiffy Pop, and drinking hot cocoa. It's the time of year, between leaf-peepers and ski bunnies, when this part of the world goes quiet.

The season between seasons.

Not that there are tourists anymore. Travel has all but shut down. Borders, too. Countries are on high alert for any kind of monkey business. Paranoia is rampant, and I don't blame anyone for it.

Unlike the people and the Kynolari living in my house, the rest of the world has little clue as to what's going on. All they know is that a surge of information tore through the minds of every human on the planet. Hundreds of millions were transformed into a different kind of person—more violent, ambitious, and powered. 'Psychic Psychosis' became a popular term for it.

We just call them the Draun—an alien species that co-mingled with humanity a hundred thousand years ago, genetically altering our species and leaving us susceptible to their influence generations later. The signal that was sent out awakened an army that congregated in—and conquered—Japan. The island nation has since gone dark. Every attempt to reach its shores has ended in death. Any satellite that turns its gaze in the nation's direction sees only bright white light. The world is blind to what's going on there.

For a time, it was all anyone could talk about. Japan had become a specter more frightening than Cold War nuclear Russia. But then the world had other problems. While the roughly five hundred million dog owners around the world were largely protected from the Draun transmission, billions were susceptible. And over time, they're changing.

While the early adopters of the Draun heritage gained their powers and new memories immediately, far more people were a work in progress. The more the world fell into chaos, the more powerful the urge to leave humanity behind became. As a result, there's a constant flow of migrants setting out for Japan.

No one knows if they're making it or not. It's a long journey to an island nation. They could all be drowning on the way.

But I doubt it.

Snow crunches beneath my feet. It sticks in my boot treads, making me feel an inch taller. The screen door creaks shut behind me, clicking into place. Five feet from the front steps, I stand still.

And listen.

Snow falls from a windless sky. The trees are still. The world is frozen. All I can hear is the gentle ticking of thick snowflakes landing.

For a few minutes, it's magical.

Another world.

Still at peace.

The illusion is shattered by a rumbling engine, and the clang of a loose metal bumper. I open my eyes to see an old red pickup truck with chains around its wheels, rolling up my driveway.

I sigh out a cloud of frozen breath and walk to the unplowed drive. Marie-Michelle Pelletier never misses a delivery. She's more reliable than the USPS, which, along with every other service in the United States, has become almost non-existent. Life and death utilities and infrastructure are being maintained. But it seems like everything else, including the Internet, is beginning to fail. More and more people are either setting off for the Land of the Rising Draun or deciding to hunker down at home and prepare for the apocalypse.

Marie-Michelle rolls down her window and unleashes a 'New Hampsha' accent that makes me smile every time. "Hey they'a, Micah. What're you doing outside this early?"

It's 6am.

"Habit," I say.

"Right, from the military."

"Early morning cartoons, actually," I say, getting a smile as she slides out of the front seat and wades through the snow, headed for the truck bed.

Truth is, excluding my connection with Earth-dogs, I'm an introvert, and rising with the sun is really the only way to get a moment alone these days.

"Tell me the truth," she says, unlatching the tailgate and lowering it. She reaches beneath a dirty white canvas tarp strapped down over the bed and pulls out two six packs of glass milk bottles, filled to the brim. "What in the hell do you need all this milk for?"

I force a laugh. "World is falling to shit, Marie."

She raises an eyebrow at me. "Marie-Michelle."

I wave my hand at her. "Fuck your French-Canadian bullshit."

She mock gasps at me. "I'm liable to piss in your next delivery."

We've known each other for a long time. She babysat me when I was a kid. Picked me up in Concord when I came home from deployments. We have the same sense of humor, which mostly includes pretending to say horrible things to each other. She's pushing sixty but hasn't slowed down yet. Still works the dairy farm, mostly by herself, and could probably beat the German Shepherd-looking Gruunlokar at arm wrestling.

"Now quit pussyfooting around and answer the question," she says, handing me the heavy, metal milk carriers.

"Some people deal with chaos by getting drunk, some by getting violent, some by putting their heads in the sand. Me? I have chocolate frappes."

She grins and nods. "Good on you. You got New Hampshah blood, boy. Cold and sweet. Just make sure Grover doesn't get any. You know what chocolate does to the pooches? Where is he, anyway? Don't normally see you two apart."

"Still sleeping," I say. "Late night."

"Looking at the shooting stars?" she asks.

"Didn't know there were any."

"Oh, yeah," she says. "The Orionids. Come every year around this time. Was outside for ten minutes last night. Saw three of them before the clouds rolled in. They were something else, I tell you. Bright blue. Looked like they'd crash into the ground and then...nothing. Just *poof.* No crash. No boom. Just slid behind the Whites and gone. You should watch tonight. They'll be back."

"Might do that," I say with a nod, thinking her description sounds a little more ominous than a regular meteor shower. But I'm not going to tell her that. Most humans barely know the Kynolari are on Earth.

That will eventually change.

It will have to.

But we can't risk revealing ourselves until we have backup, or a plan beyond, 'More milk!'

Marie closes the tailgate. "Don't be letting Grover have any vanilla frappes, either, on account of his diabetes. Sugar's not good for a dog anyway, and it's not much better for you. You'll get a gut, if you're not careful."

"A gut is the least of my worries," I say, looking toward the truck's cab. "Where's Betsy today?"

"Being lazy," she says, and raps on the door. "Betsy, come say hi to Micah."

At the sound of my name, the black Labrador Retriever raises her tired head, eyes wide, panting with feeble excitement. She's fourteen years old, showing some gray in her muzzle, and age in her joints. But she's still loving life. Hope I'm as positive when I'm her age in human years.

I place the milk in the snow, pet her head, and get licked in return. Then she's sniffing my sleeves. "You smell Grove? Yes, you do. Who's a good girl?"

Betsy's tail wags hard enough to gong off the rear window.

"Think she smells a lot more than Grover," Marie says, eyeing the house. "Who you got in there with you?" Her eyes widen. "I heard you and that Bender girl were a thing. Is she—"

I smile and nod. "She is."

Marie's jaw drops and she swats my shoulder. "Good on you, Micah. Always thought she was a good girl. Whole world falling to pieces and you're still making a life for yourself. Your folks would be proud."

I pick up the milk and notice the snow around them is melted. "Thanks..."

Marie waves her hand toward the milk. "Don't mind the milk. It's fresh from Lucille this morning. Still warm. Why I came early: to leave it in the snow. Let it chill before you found it. Might want to, still."

She climbs up into the truck and Betsy leaps into the passenger's seat, sitting up, ready for the next delivery.

"Appreciate you coming out in this weather," I say, giving a nod.

"We're Yankees," she says. "It's what we do."

Then she's backing up, turning around, and driving back the way she came. Most days I wake up feeling the weight of the world on my shoulders, but something about this very real, very down-to-earth interaction with Marie has left me feeling centered. And her parting words have inspired me.

We're Yankees.

New Englanders.

Resisting domination is in our blood.

"I peeing."

I turn around to find Grover, the world's best Golden Retriever, crouching down despite being chest deep in snow. His tail is curled up. He's intensely focused on the task, but his eyes are on me.

Smile on my face, I wait for him to finish.

His whole body relaxes, then he stands taller and trots toward me, his happy voice coming from the regulators attached to his head, allowing him to speak like that dog in *Up*. "Love Micah." But Grover seems to be evolving, his understanding and vocabulary slowly expanding. And along with that, the connection between us is growing stronger. We can see through each other's eyes, and maybe even delve into each other's minds—something we'll find out later today, if Torel gives us the all-clear.

I crouch down for our morning hug, and he slips his chin over my shoulder while I wrap my arms around him. "Hey, Grove."

"Love Micah."

"Love you, too, buddy."

"Micah..."

"Yes, Grover."

He leans back to make side eye contact. "Smell milk."

"That's because I *have* milk."

I watch his eyes slowly shift to the left where he spots one of the two milk carriers. His eyebrows shift. His glance flicks back to me, full of manic energy. He's barely containing himself.

I place a finger to my lips. "Shh, everyone is still asleep."

"But..."

"Easy," I say. "Let's go inside, and I'll give you some—"

He bounds into the air like Superman lifting off. "Milk! Yes! *Milk!*"

Then he's off and sprinting, plowing tunnels through the snow as the zoomies overtake him. I walk back to the house, milk carriers in my hands, while he does circles around me, leaping up out of the snow on occasion and looking my way, ears flopping, tongue waggling. What I wouldn't give for a high-speed camera. Photos of this would be ridiculous.

As I approach the door, it opens from the inside, and I'm greeted by four of our six Kynolari allies wearing a variety of human clothing that we've adapted to fit them. Each and every one of them looks eager and thirsty.

They're good house guests, but they're also anthropomorphic alien dogs from another world, who came to Earth in search of their Lost Tribe, but found their ancient enemy, the Draun, instead. So now we're in hiding, and every day is like Thanksgiving, except six of the people sitting around the dinner table wag their tails when the food is good, right along with Grover. It's surreal.

Chirk, who resembles an armored Chihuahua, is just about hopping. "Did I hear someone say, 'milk'?"

2

PRAXION

In all the universe I have traversed during my career as a Kyno Corps operator, I have never come across a beverage as satiating as Earth's cow milk. It somehow quenches my thirst while filling my belly. It is both savory and sweet, leaving me feeling content.

Until I remember why we're on this planet.

When we watch the news and see updates on the state of this world, which is not yet under complete Draun rule, but no doubt will be soon.

Until I face the reality of our situation; we are marooned on a planet containing hundreds of millions of Draun, with billions more potential converts slowly making the change. We defeated the powerful Draun known as Jenna, but she was not the architect of this nefarious plan. That was the Visionary, Lumen Sok, whose twisted machinations nearly brought the universe to ruin and required an alliance of planets to defeat.

And what do we have? My five Kynolari fire team, a Kynolari historian, a heavily armed but badly damaged gravity skipper, three humans, and a very happy Earth dog. The only real hope our resistance has is that one of those humans—Micah—is the Axiom, able to fully access our gauntlets' capabilities and prophesied about long ago, when my people still believed in such things.

Since our landing on this world, things have been...chaotic. Gruunlokar was captured and interrogated. Chirk was on the run, pursued by biologics and Helions, but managed to befriend Sean on the way. They saved each other, and eventually the rest of us, who were lucky enough to touch down at this farm, where we met Micah, Jess, and Grover—our hosts. In the end, we all came together and managed to finish the battle alive, but we failed to prevent Lumen Sok's signal from being sent out to the world, altering human DNA on a massive scale.

And now, we're all in danger.

"Ahh!" Chirk says, placing his empty bottle on the table. Despite being the smallest of us, he manages to drink a bottle of milk faster than anyone. "Eat it, slow pokes."

Gruunlokar places his empty bottle down next. "How do you do it?"

"I might be short," he says, standing on his chair and patting his now distended belly, "but I have room to expand."

"Milk was made to be savored," Harth says. He is our largest team member, and I heard Micah describe him as a mix between the Terminator and a Great Dane. Harth is sipping from his mostly full bottle. "Ahh." He relaxes with the swallow and holds the bottle out to me. I tap my bottle against his and take a drink. I understand the temptation to just swallow it all down. The smell of it awakens something primal in all of us, urging us to consume. But like everything, I prefer a more disciplined approach. I drink fast enough to satiate my thirst and my desire for more, but slow enough to appreciate the experience.

"Is it just me," Jess says, stretching as she enters the kitchen, dressed in what the humans call a flannel onesie. She is what Micah calls his 'girlfriend.' Like him, her brainwaves are Kynolari, and she has perfectly adjusted to the regulators behind her ears, and the gauntlet on her right arm. "Or are they, like, a bunch of old dudes sipping beers?"

"Yeah," Micah says, standing over the stove, cooking our next favorite food—a lot of it. Chirk introduced us to it. *Bacon.* "Except they don't have to pretend that they like milk."

If war were not impending, I would be enjoying this congregation of friends and food. But today begins our first step toward resistance—through Micah and Grover. The journey they undertake will guide us forward. The big breakfast is meant to calm our nerves, to distract us from the schedule we've set. Ten in the morning. That's when the journey begins. It's an arbitrary time set by Micah.

Not too late, not too early.

'Long enough to take a nervous shit if I need to,' he had said.

He's been cooking since he came in with the milk, distracting his mind, or perhaps mentally preparing for what comes next. I'm not sure how such a thing could be done. None of us knows what will happen when the mind of a human is shunted into the mind of an Earth dog. It has never been done before. Not even Torel can predict the outcome.

Where is Torel?

I scan the kitchen and don't find her.

Ears up, I listen for her in the house.

Beyond the kitchen, I hear Sean. He's in the shower singing a song, belting out, "We are the champions...of the world!" I appreciate his optimism, but realism and cold hard logic disagree with his assessment. Then I hear her, gently snoring. She has been sleeping later and later the past weeks, almost as if the winter chill is triggering a need to den.

I cap my milk and return it to the fridge.

"Where you going, boss?" Chirk asks.

"Bacon's almost ready," Micah adds.

"Bacon's *always* ready. Know what I'm saying?" Chirk moves to elbow Sean, who is generally at his side, but is currently showering. "Damnit. Where's your human when you need 'em?"

"I am going to check on Torel," I say, and exit the room.

As I approach the stairs, I hear Jess whisper to Micah, "What's up with Prax? He seems…softer."

"He's anything but soft," Micah says, and I am pleased by his assessment. "I think he's concerned about…well, everything."

"Mmm," she says. "More concerned about some than others."

I'm not sure what she means by that. Is she under the impression that I am more concerned about Torel than my other teammates? It's true, I am checking on her, but that's because she has overslept, and that is unlike her. It's my job to pay attention to the wellbeing of the people under me.

Below me, the hum of a leap node announces Baarfolir's arrival. It's immediately followed by the wizened old fellow himself, who resembles Earth's Bearded Collie breed, shouting, "Bacon! Milk?! I'm glad I decided to break for the night."

"It's morning," Chirk says.

I smile. This motley crew of beings from different worlds has adapted and come together in surprising ways. Kynolari and human. Though, if Baarfolir's brain scans are to be believed, all humans are Kynolari at heart—well, in their minds—despite our different appearances.

The upstairs hallway is a maze of creaking boards, which I've memorized, allowing me to navigate the second floor without making a sound. I pause outside Torel's door, listening to her sleep. While the rest of us sleep aboard the *Prowler*, Torel has begun sleeping in the house. She said it was to keep an eye on Grover, but I suspect she is feeling protective of the humans and their Earth dog. A maternal instinct perhaps.

The well-oiled door opens without a sound.

The room is dark and frigid. She had the window open a crack, letting the cold clean mountain air sift into her room. The furless humans keep their dwellings warm. Hot by our standards. For six months out of an Earth year, humans would die at night without clothing in this part of the world. It's a wonder their species evolved to become dominant on this planet. Though we now know they had help, thanks to an infusion of Draun DNA a hundred thousand years ago.

Perhaps they had fur long ago?

I make a mental note to ask.

"Praxion." I flinch at the sound of Torel's voice. "You're letting my cold air out."

"Sorry," I say and start closing the door.

"Wait," she says. "Come in."

I do as I'm told and close the door behind me. The room's only light comes from a sliver of sunlight sneaking beneath the shades. It's enough to see by, so I head for the bundle of blankets curled up into a nest of sorts, in the middle of which lies Torel, our Kynolari medic, who Micah assures me bears a striking resemblance to a Bernese Mountain Dog.

"Are you alright?" I ask.

"Are any of us?" she responds.

I smile. "You know what I'm asking."

"Fine," she says. "Just...thinking."

"About?"

"Humans."

I sit in the room's only chair, an antique that creaks under my weight. Seems like everything in this house is old, fashioned in a time before people had automobiles, computers, or reliable plumbing. Just a hundred years ago, if that can be believed. "What about them?"

"It seems like we've been fighting all our adult lives. We still are...as are they. But they are different. They make time for other things, and for each other. Their experience of life is vivid, full of emotion, and complex. While we remain on a narrow path, focused solely on leveling our weapons toward the heads of our enemies."

"And on bacon," I say. "And milk."

She laughs. "I hear them, too. I'm glad they're having fun. But that's not what I'm talking about."

"What are you talking about?" I ask and then follow it up with, "*Who* are you talking about?"

"Micah," she says. "And Jess."

"Oh," I say, reevaluating her words through this new lens. My eyes widen. "*Oh.*"

She laughs. "You're frightened."

"Nonsense," I say.

I flinch a second time when she places her hand on my chest. Physical contact with Torel is not uncommon. We often spar. But her touch is, for the first time, gentle. "I can hear your heartbeat. The quickness of it. The pounding. And I just think it would be worth at least acknowledging that my heart beats the same."

She takes my hand and puts it on her chest. Her fur is soft. All her features leap out at me. Her brown eyes. Her smooth black, brown, and white coat. The pheromones emanating from her forehead.

I withdraw my hand, close my eyes, and turn my head down.

"We are soldiers in the Kyno Corps, behind enemy lines, attempting to prevent a second Great War, and we are losing. It would be...inappropriate to... It would be a distraction. From the mission."

She sits up and stretches. She's not wearing any clothing. Torturing me with her form, and the smile on her face that says she knows I feel differently than my words would suggest.

"Have it your way," she says. "But I wonder... Have you considered that the real difference between the Axiom and the Kynolari isn't biological or mental?"

"What are you suggesting?" I ask.

"The humans don't fight for a cause, or a creed. They fight for each other. For love. Is it possible that the Axiom's power comes from the heart, and that's what we are missing?"

She places her hand on mine. "It might be...a worthwhile experiment. We could call it 'weapons development.'"

I smile, pat her hand, and then remove it before standing. "I will...consider it."

Then I leave the room, close the door behind me, and before I can exhale the breath I've been holding, I'm greeted by Sean. "Praxion, my man. How's it hanging?"

He's dripping wet in a towel, and when he lifts his hand to 'slap me five,' as he's prone to do, the towel falls to the floor. I glance down to his exposed genitals and say, "Huh...a little bit of fur."

3

CHIRK

"Are you ready for this?" I ask, standing in snow that's up to my chest, trying not to shiver. Unlike my thickly furred, oversized compatriots, I have a fine coat and not an ounce of fat on my toned body. So instead of walking around, strutting my stuff in the cold, I'm wearing a combination of Kynolari and human layers, rubbing my arms, and sharing a blunt with Sean.

"Yeah, man," he says, taking a hit, holding it, and letting it out slowly, like a pro. Like people are judging how expertly he gets high. "It's like the ultimate sign of friendship."

"You two finally getting married?" Jess asks, walking past with a bag of trash slung over her shoulder.

"Ha. Ha." I take the joint from Sean and take a much smaller puff. Have to. On account of my size. Doesn't take much to make me useless, and that's something I need to avoid. Because who knows when we might be discovered. Micah mentioned the milk lady seeing 'shooting stars.' Bright and blue. Sounds a lot like Helions, but who the hell really knows. Could have just been shooting stars. Point is, I'm just looking to take the edge off, not spend the next six hours debating the nature of the universe and our feeble place in it. No one wants a repeat of the Great Nacho Night Deliberation.

"I'm getting a tattoo," Sean says, full of pride. "Of the Kyno Corps sigil."

"Ahh," she says, somewhat condescending.

"Hey," I say, "it's a great honor! Usually only bestowed on those of us who graduated from the Kyno Academy and then survived a battle. Sean might not have graduated, and probably wouldn't have the mental capacity to attempt it, but I think it's safe to say I wouldn't be alive without him, and that means none of you would either."

She raises her hands, smiling. "Wow. You really are a Chihuahua, aren't you?"

I stand still.

"I don't know if you're complimenting me or insulting me."

She shrugs. "Take your pick." She smiles up at Sean. "So, is this, like, a tramp stamp or something?"

"Ahuh, ahuh," he laughs. "Naw, man. On my shoulder. I already got myself a stamp. Check it."

Sean turns around, lifts up his jacket, and pulls down the back of his pants. The first thing I see is a slight mist of steam emanating from his ass crack. Then I spot the image above his crack. It features a shouting woman riding a winged horse. She has a spear in her hand. It's impressive artwork.

"God," Jess says, shielding her eyes.

"Right?" Sean says, "But for the full experience, you need to take a photo of the code at the top."

He lifts the shirt higher, revealing a circle followed by a series of vertical lines. It's some kind of code.

"I am *not* taking a photo of your ass," Jess says, "No matter what kind of Da Vinci Code shit it reveals."

"C'monnn," he says. "It'll be worth it."

Jess raises her eyebrows about as far as they can go. "You're not the first man to say that to me and not deliver."

"Just. Do. It." Sean says. "My ass hairs are starting to freeze." He looks down at me. "Man, I should have dried off better after my shower. A moist crack in zero degrees is going to give me a chapped ass."

Jess sighs and takes out her phone. She aims the camera at Sean's ass and moves closer.

"How close you need to get?" I ask.

"It's not focusing," she grumbles.

"Tap the screen," Sean says. "Just tap it."

"Do I want to know?" Micah asks. He's standing at the corner of the house, a big grin on his face.

"Hold on!" Jess shouts. "I'm taking a photo of his god damned tramp stamp."

Micah can't stop himself from having a look. He nods in appreciation. Approves. "That's a nice tat."

"Thanks, man," Sean says.

"Finally," Jess says, taking a picture and then leaning back. "Now wha—"

Music starts playing from her phone. It's exhilarating. Almost swirling through the air, stirring something deep inside—riding into battle, like the bitch drawn on his back.

"Is...is that 'Ride of the Valkyries?'" Jess asks.

"Check it!" Sean says and then starts flexing his ass cheeks. The wings on the horse start flapping in time with the music. "Fucking epic, right?"

Micah bursts out laughing. "That is the most beautiful thing I've ever seen."

"Got a tear in my eye, man," I say.

Jess looks at the three of us, one at a time. Then she just sighs, rubs her face, and says, "Men...are weird."

"If you could only see inside our minds," I say. "Then you'd really know how—"

Both Sean and Micah glance down at me, eyes wide, transmitting 'What the fuck?!' in guy code. It occurs to me then that the next order of business in our day is the merging of intellects. Micah will literally visit Grover's subconscious, and if that's possible, it means that it could work between any of us—that women could plumb the darkest depths of the male psyche.

My eyes widen.

Oh shit.

Oh *fuck*.

We're going to need to keep this under wraps or every civilization in the universe might implode.

I pretend to choke. "Anyway..." I look up at Sean and take out the imprinter from inside my jacket. "You ready for this?"

"Is it going to hurt?" he asks.

"Won't take long," I tell him. "Only takes a second. Advanced technology, remember? Nothing to worry about. And it's way smaller than that tattoo on your back."

Sean peels off his layers until he's just wearing a T-shirt. He rolls one sleeve up, exposing his shoulder. "This good?"

"Yep," I say, activating the imprinter and giving it a moment to warm up. It looks like a gun with a wide, square muzzle. The size is adjustable from one inch square all the way up to an Imperial foot, though that's not recommended. "You're gonna have to come to me, though."

He kneels down in the snow. Then I place the imprinter against his skin.

"Last chance to be a pussy," I say.

He chuckles and says, "Just do it, man." Then his forehead furrows a bit. "Hey, why are we doing this outside? Couldn't we have—"

I pull the trigger.

The image is finished before the dulled nerves in Sean's body transmit the pain. Then he shouts, flinches back, and looks at his still sizzling shoulder. Eyes wide, he shouts, "You said it was a tattoo!"

"That's what it is," I say.

"You branded him," Jess says.

I shrug. "Brand, tattoo, same thing. It's body art." I point to the snow. "And that's why we're outside."

Sean scoops up a handful of snow and presses it against the fresh laser etching. The snow drips away from his warm skin.

"Hold it until it all melts."

It's just a few seconds. His breathing slows. His look of agony and betrayal fades. Then he pulls his hand away to reveal a perfectly placed Kyno Corps sigil.

"There," I say. "Now it's official. You're one of us."

"Hey," Micah says, and he catches me off guard when he peels off his sweater and rolls up his sleeve.

"Seriously?" I ask.

"Awesome," Sean says, smiling at Micah's willingness to go through the same pain. I'm doing the same.

"We're a team," Micah says, showing his arm, on the side of which is a tattoo of a banner that reads '75th Ranger Rgt' Beneath it is a skull wearing some kind of floppy hat, a knife clutched in its teeth. "Not my first rodeo."

"Don't know what that is," I say, "but I appreciate the sentiment. Where do you want it?"

He pats his shoulder above the tattoo. "Same as Sean's."

"Sick," Sean says.

Micah takes the pain a hell of a lot better. He just winces, picks up some snow, and holds it in place until it melts. Then he reveals the fresh brand, marking him for all to see, as one of us.

"You guys are assholes," Jess says, and I'm even more surprised to see her pulling off her flannel shirt, revealing her upper body, clothed only in what humans call a bra, which is necessary given their ample mammary glands.

"Oh my," Sean says, turning away.

"Make it quick," she says, leaning down.

I smile and nod.

She grunts loudly, but it morphs into a laugh. Micah is there with a handful of snow, which he holds against the fresh brand.

"Great," I say, clapping and rubbing my hands together. "Now you're all my property."

Jess gives me a look that quickly undoes the camaraderie vibe we've got going on.

"What'd I say?" I ask.

Sean leans down and whispers about how her people were brought to this nation as slaves and have been systematically held back by 'the man' ever since. It's a sore subject.

"Ahh, shit," I say. "Sorry."

Before she can accept my apology, Baarfolir approaches, a human smoking pipe in his hands—Micah's father's—immune to the snow's effects. "Excellent, you're all here. Wonderful, wonderful."

"Hey," I say. "You don't have one of these yet, right?"

He looks at the three fresh brands and shakes his head. "I will not mar my flesh, thank you very much."

"He's afraid," I say.

Baarfolir huffs and turns to Micah. "Are you ready?"

His forehead scrunches. Glances down at his brand. "I already got one."

"Not for that," he says. "For the merger. With Grover."

"Ah," Micah says. "Right." He and Jess share a look.

She gives him a nod.

Weird, dangerous, or foolish, it's our only lead and needs to be done, before the rest of world becomes Draun and we're hunted down like Slimps during the Scardovian Skin Festival on Bington Seven.

Micah slips his sweater on while Jess and Sean pull on their layers. Then he plucks the roach from Sean's hand, takes a long drag, flicks the remnants into the snow, and says, "Let's do it."

4

MICAH

"So...warm..." Jess says, peeling off her jacket after making the quick trip from the house to the *Prowler* via leap node. We could walk the distance, even in the snow, but we'd leave an obvious trail and don't really want anyone to know there's an alien spaceship parked in New Hampshire's White Mountain region. The world is messy enough right now.

More and more people are becoming Draun every day, reborn with twisted memories and disdain for the Kynolari. Incognito is the best way forward. For now. Maybe for a long time.

The *Prowler* is warm, but not uncomfortably so. Back in the house, we're constantly changing the thermostat up and down, trying to accommodate those with fur and those without. But the Kynolari have perfected heat and humidity control. Feels like a fresh spring day. Seventy degrees without the dry needly feeling that comes from the house's old, forced, hot-water radiator system.

"This way, this way," Baarfolir says, waddling out of the node chamber, his stubby tail wagging, short legs shuffling.

Jess squeezes my arm and whispers, "He is *so* adorable."

"My grandkids think so, too," he says, looking back to wink. "I might be older than the rest of the crew, but my ears are still good. Thank you, though. I know well enough to take a compliment." He waves us on again. "Now, come, come. I am eager to begin our first attempt."

"First attempt?" I ask, following the short Kynolari historian.

"Well, yes. Obviously. This has never been attempted before."

"Anything I should be worried about?" I ask.

"Couldn't tell you," he says. "Maybe nothing will happen. Maybe you'll both be lobotomized. Maybe your minds will switch places. That would be exciting."

I lean closer to Jess. "And I'd finally be able to lick—"

"No," she says. "*Nnnno.* Bad."

"Short of *Freaky Friday*-ing me, what are the odds it will work?" I ask. "Scale of one to ten, ten being success and one being lobotomization?"

Baarfolir leads us around a corner and into a white hallway with organic looking walls that match the rest of the ship's strange and impeccably designed interior.

I'm not sure what it's made from, but it almost looks like it came out of a mold. No bolts. No seams. "I'm optimistic, so let's say…six."

"Six is optimistic?" Jess says.

"I've been on a few missions that were fours," I say with a shrug. "Six isn't bad."

"I think just living on this planet right now is a four," Baarfolir says. "Maybe even a three."

He's not wrong. Especially for the Kynolari. "Well, hopefully we can change that number today."

He gives me a nod and then places his hand on the wall. The organic mesh peels apart, splits, and reveals an entryway. On the other side is Grover, seated on a chair that has a hole for his tail. He's wearing a white helmet with a tube running out of the top and into the ceiling. An empty chair, with a second helmet hanging above it, is just a few feet in front of Grover. Torel is with him, buckling his helmet in place.

"There you go," she says to him. "Nice and snug."

Grover wags his tail, tongue hanging out, happy as can be.

Torel gives his shoulder a pat. "Good boy."

Despite being offended at the way humans talk to dogs, the longer the Kynolari stay with us, the more they've adopted our language and tone when communicating with Grover. It's been shown that dogs prefer the higher-pitched cutesy voice people use with them, and I think they sense that. Talk to one of the Kynolari that way and you're liable to get an incinerator round to the face. But they now understand why and how Earth dogs became different from them. I'm sure they're still irked by it, but they're no longer repelled and offended by the idea.

And they adore Grover.

I cup Grover's jowls and rub his cheeks, squishing his loose skin around. "How's my handsome man doing?"

"Love Micah," he says. "Love Torel." He's taken to the Kynolari like he did Jess, and I trust each and every one of them with him. They'd die for him if it came to that, and Torel has already saved his life twice.

"Stay here," I say when Grover stands up.

"But…Jess." He taps his feet back and forth, eager to jump down and then up on Jess, who he's side-eyeing.

"Chill, dude," Jess says, leaning down to accept several licks to her cheek. She rubs his back, defusing his spin up toward perpetual motion.

"I'll be right over here." I step back and sit beneath the second dangling helmet. "I'm coming to visit you. In here." I tap my head. "Do you remember?"

"Yes. Remem…remem… Big word."

"Great," I say. "So just relax, and then we'll get to play in our dreams."

"My dream," he says.

"Yes."

"Scare dream?"

"I hope not."

"Chase dream?"

I smile. Grover is known for breaking into a sudden full-on sprint when he's lying sideways and asleep. It's funny to see. But he also goes through bouts of twitching and whimpering—even before the traumatic events he went through when the Draun came for us. "I hope I can keep up."

"Micah slow. I sorry. Love Micah."

"Don't apologize for that," Jess says, giving his fur a shake. "Make fun of him as much as you want."

"Okay," Torel says, lowering the second helmet down onto my head. Before I can fasten it, she's doing it for me. "You just relax. I don't want you to think, worry, or imagine anything. Just try to clear your mind. We want the virtual world you'll both be inhabiting to come fully from Grover, or we won't be able to trust the results."

"And if any of me sneaks in?" I ask.

"You mean, would it be dangerous?" She shrugs. "First time in, let's just try to keep it simple. Like you're on a..." She looks at Jess. "What did you call it? The ride with the screaming people?"

"Roller coaster," Jess says.

"That. Pretend you're on a roller coaster but try not to scream...or influence anything around you. Okay?"

I give two thumbs up and ease myself back, trying to get comfortable in the chair that was ergonomically designed for dog-people.

"That goes for you, too, Grover," Torel says. "I need you to lie down, okay?"

Instead of listening, he just looks up at her, panting like he's smitten, drool dangling from his right jowl.

"Hey," I say. His eyes lock onto me. I snap my fingers. "Listen to her."

He smacks his lips a few times, does an awkward 360 spin in the chair and then lies down all curled up. He gives me a funny glance, like I'm going to get it later for bossing him around in front of the ladies. When I squint back at him, the tip of his tail wags a little bit, confirming our silent challenge. Later tonight, it's on.

"Right," Baarfolir says, furry little fingers tapping on a tablet as he walks around the room.

Jess moves back and leans against the wall, arms crossed. She doesn't need to be here. Won't be much help if something goes wrong, but we're her boys. Her words, not mine. She insisted on being here.

"Brainwaves are clear and in sync."

"Bye, bye, bye," I say, waving my hand at Jess, while moving it across my face.

Baarfolir stops, glances at me.

"NSYNC," I say. "You haven't been introduced to boy bands yet?"

Baarfolir raises a single brow and just looks at me. Feels like I'm back in basic and have just insulted the drill sergeant. Baarfolir comes across as a gentle little hermit, but I can see him now. Lurking just beneath the surface is a Kynolari who has seen some shit. Maybe even things the others don't know about.

I clear my throat. "Sorry."

Jess shakes her head. "Idiot."

"It appears the subjects are ready for the first integration," Baarfolir says to Torel. "Can you confirm all systems orange?"

"Orange," she says. "We're as ready as we'll ever be."

"Very well," Baarfolir says. "Begin the procedure."

"Don't we need to be asleep or somethuuuaaaggg."

The world disappears. And it's not like falling asleep. I don't lose consciousness. The world around me just ceases to exist, like I've been transported to a sensory deprivation tank.

"Hello?" I can feel my body, but it doesn't exist.

Nothing exists.

Holy shit. Is this what a lobotomy feels like? Is my consciousness going to be trapped in this black void for the rest of my life while Jess tube feeds me and changes my diapers?

"Hello?" I say again, louder. "Grover? You there, buddy?"

I'm starting to freak out now, thinking Baarfolir's 'six' was too generous.

"Hey!" I shout, voice cracking. "I think I want to—"

The world flicks to life around me. I'm whole again, looking down at my hands, but I'm no longer on the *Prowler*. I look up with wide eyes and a smile, taking in the view. "Well, hump my leg and call me a bitch. I'll be damned."

5

PRAXION

I do not enjoy sitting idly by while others are working hard. It makes me feel lazy, even though there is nothing I can do to help—something Torel made clear, several times. So now I'm sitting in a reclining chair, staring at the TV, across from Sean, who has his feet up and a bowl of Frosted Flakes in his lap. He sips loudly with each mouthful and chews with his mouth open.

It's almost more than I can bear.

On the TV is a program Sean calls *Adventures of the Gummi Bears*. He sang the entire theme song and then regaled me with stories of Gruffi, Sunni, Tummi, Zummi, and Grammi Gummi. His favorite is Cubbi Gummi because, 'he's just a little guy.'

I fail to understand why anyone would watch a program like this. It paints conflict and hardship in a colorful, almost whimsical light. Sean said it was a program for children, but I do not see what lesson young ones would learn from the Gummi Bears, other than to have false expectations of how overcoming an evil enemy bent on your destruction is enjoyable.

Reality is far darker.

Then again, Sean doesn't see it that way. When he tells us stories of himself and Chirk outrunning and outwitting biologics, or blowing up a bridge, or of Chirk's... conquests...he's always laughing. He speaks of those harrowing moments like they were the finest of his life.

I sometimes wish I shared his enthusiasm, but someone needs to be stoic. Someone needs to think logically. And yet, I find it impossible to conjure a single useful thought while Toadwart's grating voice tears at my ears.

"I would like Harth to incinerate that creature," I grumble.

"You see?" Sean says, between sloppy chews. "I knew you would get into this show. I mean, they're just like you guys. Walking, talking animals, except without the bouncing."

"You are a 'walking, talking animal,'" I point out.

His eyes widen. A smile spreads. "Whoa... You're right. Holy shit. I'm like a Gummi Bear!"

He's far happier about the news than he should be.

"Can we change the channel?" I ask. "I would like to see if there is any news."

"About what?"

"About anything," I say, "other than alcoholic cartoon bears."

"Alcoholic?" His brow furrows like it does when he thinks he's having a world reshaping realization. "Are you saying that Gummi Berry Juice is...wine? And that the bears are drinking because they're addicts, and that bouncing is a...a metaphor for being wasted? Oh my god, this show has more dimensions to it than I thought."

"Sean," I say. "Change the channel."

He picks up what the humans call a 'clicker,' points it at the TV, and changes the channel. "Right."

Programs flick by until a news reporter appears on the screen. And the terrain looks familiar. Green pine mountains.

"That looks like here," he says, turning up the volume, even though it was already too loud. Humans have horrible hearing.

"It was here that, last night, several unidentified lights were seen in the sky. Let's talk to one of the residents of Libson, New Hampshire who reported the lights. A Mr. Mike Vedral." The camera pulls back to reveal an old man with a white beard. Like most people in this world under siege, he looks tired and a bit rattled. "Can you tell us what you saw?"

"Ayuh," Vedral says. "They ahh, they came out of the North, real slow like. Methodical. 'Bout three hundred feet above the tree line. Just shining their lights back and forth like they was looking for something. Ain't nothing out there but trees. Anyone in town could have told them that. Not sure what they were looking for, but it ain't here."

"You're sure they were looking for something?" the reporter asks.

"Unless you can think of another use for spotlights, pretty sure."

The reporter nods. "Of course."

The old man gives the reporter a squinty gaze. "Not the first time, you know. Been sightings like this all over the region. Every night. It's just the first time someone has come out to report on them. Not saying I blame you. Lots of crazy things happening in the world, what with the state of Japan and all these people jumping ship on the human race. Bunch of scared rats, if you ask me. Point is, these fellas out here—maybe the government, maybe something else—they're determined to find whatever it is they think is hunkered down in these woods." He looks directly into the camera. "Whoever you are, I recommend getting the hell out of the White Mountains, while you still can. Won't be long before you're found out."

"Is..." Sean says, wide-eyed. "Is he talking to us?"

I grunt.

"Like, not *to us* to us, but *to* us. Like, *about* us."

"I believe so," I say.

Harth thumps into the living room from the kitchen. "I heard."

Chirk slides down the railing from the second floor. "Same."

While they weren't watching the television, they had no trouble hearing it. At the volume Sean prefers, we'd probably hear it a mile away.

Harth crosses his arms. "I haven't seen anything local during the night watch, but we're in the mountains. They could be just over the ridgeline, and we'd never know it. It might be tonight, or in a month, but they will eventually find us."

"Question is," Chirk says, "who is 'they?' The Twilight Directorate doesn't exist anymore. That Alton guy was turned to jelly, the base in Denver was flattened, and that Jenna chick is dead."

"The Visionary still lives," I point out.

"Yeah," Sean says, "but wasn't Jenna on the outs with him? Wanted him dead, too? And since the Draun haven't shown up with a telekinetic army, I don't think he had access to their info before it was destroyed."

"My boy's wicked smaht," Chirk says, imitating the accent in this region. Then he fist-bumps Sean. "Which leaves, who?"

"The government," Sean says. "Of the United States."

"Perhaps," I say. From what Micah has told me, the United States is the most powerful and sophisticated country on the planet. It's not surprising, seeing as they had access to reverse engineered Draun and Kynolari technologies.

"This country, like all others on this planet, is in disarray," Harth says. "On the verge of collapse."

Sean shrugs. "The Twilight Directorate wasn't the only black op in the world that knew about aliens or had access to alien technology."

All eyes turn to him.

"What? Everyone knows about Area 51. Men in Black. The AOIMSG. Don't ask me what that stands for, but they are part of the DoD. Department of Defense." He extends fingers, catching up his count to four, then tacks on several more. "Project Bluebook. Grudge. Serpo. Sign. Then there's AARO, who now call UFOs 'UAPs,' like that's going to make everyone take them seriously. Of course, everyone takes them seriously now. Even NASA did a study. They're, like, really smart people. Got us to the moon."

"To the moon?" Chirk says with a sarcastic gasp. "Wow. That's impressive."

Sean plucks a large Frosted Flake from his bowl and flicks it at Chirk. "Douche."

Chirk catches the flake with his mouth and eats it. "You know it."

Back on TV, the reporter asks another question, "And when they left, which direction did they go?"

Vedral points toward a mountainside. "Thatta way. East. Up and over the ridge. If they're following some kind of grid, they'll be back." He picks up a telephoto camera and gives it a pat. "And I'll be ready for 'em."

The reporter turns to the screen, looking and sounding exhausted. When I first saw TV news, the reporters were full of bravado and exaggeration. News was meant to be a spectacle as much as it was informative. Now, it's just the opposite. "Okay, so, you heard him. If you're in the Lisbon area, think about staying indoors for a few days. Be sure to report any sightings to your local Sheriff's office or the UAP hotline." The number flashes on the screen.

I turn to Sean. "Is there a map of the area?"

Sean pulls out his phone, flicks it on, and opens an app. "Lisbon..." he says to himself, tapping in the letters. "New...Hampshire... Okay, there we are. And I'm assuming we want to see what's to the East, yeah?"

"Please," I say.

He swipes the map to the right. "Okay... Green forest... More green forest. And more—"

"What?" Chirk asks.

Sean turns the device around so we can see its small screen. The map is mostly green with a single jagged gray line cutting through the center of it, representing a road. In the middle of the road is a label.

I read it aloud. "Sugar Hill."

"That's us," Sean says.

"Right, Chirk says. "I don't know about the rest of you, but I'm both bored as fuck and I don't feel like getting caught with my pants down. Again. And since I think we'd all like to know who's gunning for us, I propose we get ready to blow shit up while the team members with fewer destructive instincts are helping Micah and Grover have a 'la-la land' pow wow."

All eyes turn to me. I smile. "Agreed."

6

MICAH

I'm standing in a field. It's vast and full of grass. Yellow grass. The blue sky above it is full of gray clouds, but not rain clouds. They're fluffy, like they should be bright white, but I'm only seeing yellow and blue and shades of gray.

It's disorienting, like I'm looking through a pair of glasses that filter out most wavelengths of light.

Because I am, I realize.

This is how Grover sees the world.

How all dogs see the world.

But not the Kynolari. Their eyes have evolved to see all light spectrums, and more, if their vision has been enhanced—like Praxion's.

I find my altered vision disconcerting and a bit sad. Grover is missing out. And I've been duped into buying all kinds of colored toys for him when he can't see the colors at all.

Distraction comes in the form of a smell. A hundred smells. All at once. Grass. Flowers. Trees—Oaks, Maples, Birches—I can tell them all apart. Those are the basics. I'm able to pinpoint and identify so much more. A lone bee. An ant hill. A dead bird. Grover's subconscious is full of all the things he finds interesting in the real world. Including deer shit. I detect a mound of it not far away, and I find myself salivating for it.

Before I sniff out the fecal pellets, I refocus myself on the task at hand—finding Grover, not becoming him.

"Grover!" I call, my voice far louder than I remember.

A moment later, I hear the approach of a torpedo moving through the tall grass. A doppler wave of Grover's voice grows louder. "Micah here. Micah here. Micah here!" Grover bounds into the air, clears the grass, and lands in my arms. "Love Micah!" He licks, thrashes, and rubs the side of his face against mine, coating my cheek in jowl slobber, just like he does in the real world.

"Okay, buddy," I say. "Okay. Love you, too."

I put him on the ground and say, "Sit."

He does, and then looks to my hand.

"Sorry, Gro, this isn't real. I don't have—"

"Treats," he says, glancing at my hand, tail wagging.

I look down at my hand and find it full of treats. I laugh. "Of course there are treats. We're in your head." I toss him a mental treat and he gobbles it down. Doesn't matter if it's real or not.

I smooth down the fur atop his head with a pat and crouch. "Do you remember why I'm here? What you need to show me?"

"Scary things," he says.

"Right."

"Anbu," he says.

"I don't know how long we have, so we should probably do that first, okay?"

"Ball," he says, nodding his head toward my feet, where a tennis ball rests.

"Not right now, bud. We need to focus."

"Ball help...not afraid..."

I squint at him, wondering if I'm being had. But this is his mind, not an actual place. Any direction could lead us where we need to go. There is no south or north here. Anywhere we go could be the right direction, but Grover needs to feel comfortable to get us there. And right now, he's asking for some distraction. Some tennis ball courage.

So, I give in, pick up the ball, and give it a throw.

I can hear the air whooshing over the ball's little fibers. When it lands, it bounces like a tribal drumbeat, calling me toward it. I find myself running with Grover, excited by the prospect of finding the ball once more.

And when we do, a celebration. We jump and cheer.

Then he drops it again, and I throw it.

The chase begins anew. And then again, and again, and again.

I'm out of breath, but I don't mind it. Feels good. My pounding heart doesn't conjure fears of pushing myself too hard. It just is, and I don't mind it.

I pick up the ball and put everything I've got into it.

This time, it clears the field, bounces off the trunk of a towering pine tree, and disappears into the dark forest behind. Grover and I stop at the tree line, peering into dimly lit woods. The ball is gone, replaced by a path made of yellow sunlight slipping through the canopy, illuminating the golden pine needles on the forest floor.

"This is the way," I whisper.

"Yes."

"You good?" I ask.

He looks up at me. "*You* good?"

"Hey, I asked you first."

His mouth opens as he starts to pant, his lips turned up in a smile.

"Are you screwing with me? This isn't the time for screwing with me."

"Hump leg time?"

"Hump...are you serious?"

He closes his mouth for a moment, holds his breath for a moment, then he meets my eyes again, opens his mouth, and starts smile-panting once more.

Screwing with me.

"I see how it is. We'll see how funny you are when we find Anbu."

His mouth closes again, humor lost.

"That's what I thought," I say, and step onto the sunlit path. When he lingers, I snap my fingers and give a "Kck, kck." He trots after me, head low, tongue hanging out. He's nervous.

Hell, *I'm* nervous.

So far, this has been something like a dream, but I'm pretty sure it's just a prelude to a nightmare. To Anbu...Anubis. The Egyptian God of Death. He might be a Kynolari, but he predates our alien friends by thirty-seven *thousand* years, and if the historical record is right, he spent most of that time both alive, and living among primitive human beings. And in that time, he managed to leave some kind of message, imprinted on the minds of the Lost Tribe's descendants. A message that can only be retrieved by a Kynolari that has a close connection to a member of the Lost Tribe.

Right now, that's just me.

So, after a whirlwind we nearly didn't survive, I'm off to see the Wizard with Toto by my side. Except Oz is a doggy dreamworld that's even more surreal than anything L. Frank Baum dreamed up.

Forest smells jump out at me. I recognize them—moss, mushrooms, leaf decay—but they're far more potent, and I can pinpoint where the scents are coming from. I can almost see them.

"How you doing?" I ask Grover after what feels like a few minutes.

"Love Micah," he says, voice sweet, but a little quieter than usual.

His nose twitches, and then mine does, too.

We pause, smelling the air. I close my eyes and tilt my head. To the left, I detect dry air. I can hear a whipping wind. And sand. Like the beach, without the salt. To the right, I sense water. A lot of it. Even more organic decay. And something primal. Old, but alive.

When I open my eyes, there's a fork in the path.

"You know where we're going?" I ask.

"Anbu," he says.

"You know which way is Anbu?"

"Both ways."

"Do they go to the same place?"

His furry brow lowers, scrunching together a tuft of hair between his eyes that makes him look more serious and contemplative than he ever could be. He turns to the left. "Anbu." Then he turns to the right. "Xolotl."

"That like a cough medicine or something?"

The joke is lost on my dog. "No Xolotl. Too afraid."

"Is Xolotl a place?" I ask.

"Is Anbu."

"Huh..." I look back and forth between the paths. Sounds like we could go either way, but I don't want to fuck this up, so I decide to head left, toward the Anbu that's Anbu, rather than the Anbu that's Xolotl. I point to the left path. "So, this way then?"

"Still afraid," Grover says, but then he starts down the path. Just a few feet onto the new path, the fork disappears behind us and the warm pine needles dissolve into sand.

"You know," I say to Grover, feeling proud of him. "Being afraid and still heading toward something scary isn't fear."

He glances up at me.

"It's brave," I tell him.

He likes that. Smiles and pants. But then quickly stops and lifts his head.

The sand opens up ahead of us, rising into a windswept dune. The trees and forest are gone, in front and behind us. It's like we just strolled into another world, still cast in yellow and blue. The sky is now cloudless. And poking up over the sand is a small, gleaming golden triangle.

We head toward the luminous aberration at the dune's peak. It grows larger and brighter the closer we get. Then we clear the top, and I'm dropped to my knees by the view. "Holy shit."

We're in Egypt.

In Giza.

As it looked forty-five hundred years ago, before empires and thieves had their way with the region. The Great Pyramid, the tomb of Khufu, stands at the center of our view, flanked by the Pyramid of Khafre, and the Pyramid of Menkaure. Surrounding the massive triangular trio is an expansive necropolis, which no longer exists today, full of mastabas and rectangular mausoleums. The buildings glow so bright in the midday sun that they're impossible to look at. And yet, our path is clear. Directly ahead is a white limestone causeway that leads to the Great Pyramid's base, where a dark tunnel waits. It's not marked, but it might as well have a pink neon sign reading 'Anbu: this way.'

I sigh. "Okay, Grover McRover, let's get this over." Then we step onto the causeway and head for the tunnel containing a message from a long dead Kynolari that either has something important to tell us or is just wasting our time. Finding a message from the past that can help our current dire situation would be good, but I suspect it won't be pleasant. I'm secretly hoping we just find a chamber full of tennis balls we can Scrooge McDuck into. I share a look with Grover. He's thinking the same thing.

Then he says, "You...try...no scream."

He gives me a wide-eyed side eye.

"Did...did you just trash-talk me?" His eyes widen farther. "You little bitch!" I reach for him, but he's off, running and bounding, confirming that he was teasing while rubbing it in, because he knows I can't catch him.

I chase him anyway and we're off, running straight toward a nightmare, but doing it together. Two brave, good boys, about to be in the shit, way over their heads.

7

CHIRK

Earthlings don't respect short things, especially males of the species, even more so if you're aggressive. They have a term for it. Napoleon Complex. I did some research after Jess used the term on me when I protectively hoarded a bag of potato chips, claiming that they belonged to me until I deemed otherwise.

First of all, the guy wasn't even short. He was average height. Five foot seven in modern terms. It's just that the French inch was longer than the British, so history remembered him as five foot two.

Me?

I'm actually short.

Standing just over two feet tall. And yeah, I'm rough around the edges, but I'm not about to go conquering a swath of Europe or anywhere else. I'm a freedom fighter. A rogue, like Han Solo. An ace, like Maverick.

I've been watching Sean's favorite movies, which have given me a greater appreciation for this world. Humanity might be the most creative species in the galaxy. Combined with the knowledge and ambition of the Draun, imagination could make the newest incarnation of our enemy even more dangerous.

Unless we can do something about it.

Which means surviving until we know what we *can* do about it—if anything.

Hence the defensive perimeter being set up in and around Micah's property. We've been at it for hours now. No word about Micah and Grover's mental vacation, but the time has been well spent.

We've got anti-armor incinerator batteries, anti-personnel rail turrets and a defensive anti-air laser array. Enough to hold off a small army of biologics for days. Or a large army for hours. Either way, it's long enough for us to board the *Prowler* and skedaddle to some other remote spot on this tainted world.

Skedaddle. I like that word. Need to introduce it in Kynolari when we get home. "Skedaddle," I say, lying on my back, eyes on the blue sky, hands behind my head. "Skedaddle."

"C'mon, man," Sean says, hauling a quantum battery that will power the laser array for the next thousand years. "You're just lying there."

"Benefit of being the short guy," I say, kicking one leg over the other, letting it bounce. "And the pilot."

"He is right," Gruunlokar says, taking the battery from Sean and heaving it up over his shoulder. "If Chirk injured himself doing manual labor, and we needed to evacuate under fire, his performance could be affected."

"My *performance* is at its peak," I say, "but the point is valid." I turn to Sean and shrug. "See? I work hard at what I like, so I don't have to work hard doing things I don't like. Such as lifting heavy things and walking long distances."

"You could calibrate the laser array, so we don't inadvertently shoot down a satellite," Harth says, arriving with more gear.

"Has it occurred to any of you that the right move might be to just blow up all the satellites orbiting this world?"

"It would expose our position," Praxion says, drinking from his canteen.

"Yeah, but for how long?" I ask and then answer the question. "Until they were all destroyed, that's how long. Without satellites, we could move around this world undetected. The *Prowler* is invisible to their primitive radar and sonar systems."

"There are too many satellites to destroy them all," Harth says.

"How many could there be?" I ask.

"Fifteen thousand," the big man says, towering over me. "The Visionary calls the network 'SkyLink,' and he's convinced everyone that their only function is Internet connectivity."

"You're blocking my sun," I say.

He sighs and steps to the side. "We don't even know where to start or who our enemy is. SkyLink has already done its damage. And we don't know if they have surveillance packages. If the U.S. government is compromised, and we target them first, we very quickly make a new enemy and will be set upon by this world's military. Primitive though they may be, they are also formidable. And once exposed, the Draun will come for us—en masse next time."

"You," I say, "are no fun anymore."

"When was he ever fun?" Gruunlokar asks with a chuckle.

"Oh, right. I forgot. He's a Snarp."

Harth looks down at me, eyes squinted, jowls twitching.

"Go ahead," I say. "Bare your teeth. Give in to your Earth instincts."

"Hrmph," he says, and then smiles. "Only one among us has trouble with that. You don't think we hear you traipsing off into the woods to urinate?"

"Hey," I say. "Two things. First, peeing outside, in the woods, is invigorating. Second, 'traipsing?'"

"Is that not an appropriate word?" he asks.

We all turn to Sean.

"It's...a weird choice, but appropriate." Sean smiles at Harth.

"Oh, c'mon, bro, you're just saying that because you're afraid of him."

Harth puffs out his chest a little. "He *should* be afraid of me."

Sean's eyes widen a bit, but Gruunlokar puts him at ease with a casual shake of his head. Sean hit it off with the team, becoming friends with everyone, not just me.

Praxion clears his throat. He's standing at the laser array. "I've finished calibrating. The defensive perimeter is set."

I roll backward and up onto my feet. Then I clap the dust from my hands, like I've been doing hard labor. "There. All in a day's—"

A chime sounds in my ear. It's calm and pleasant, but it means nothing good.

"What was that?" Sean asks, hand to the regulator we installed at his insistence. The process was a little more uncomfortable for him than it was for Jess and Micah, but he's spent a lot of time with Kynolari now and his brainwaves are almost entirely in sync. It was a risk, but even Torel thought it would be worthwhile to know how far from a Kynolari a person could be and still be compatible with a set of regulators. "Was that in my ears or from these things?"

"Those things," I say, drawing a railgun from my hip.

Harth, Gruunlokar, and Praxion activate their gauntlets and charge them up.

"What does the sound mean?" Sean whispers.

"Proximity alert," I say. "Means someone is here."

"Means someone was here already," Gruunlokar says.

"How come the system isn't, you know, blasting them up?" Sean asks.

"Blasting them up?" Harth says, shaking his head.

"Line of sight," I say. "We don't want to be shooting innocents."

"Or, like, bears and deer," he says, nodding. "Got it."

"Talon-Actual, Prowler-One." It's Torel over the comms. "Why am I hearing a proximity alert?"

"We set up a perimeter defense," Praxion says. "Just went active. Already have a hit."

"Anything I need to worry about?" she asks.

"We're on it," he says. "Talon-Actual, out." The bossman breaks contact and turns to Gruunlokar. "Get high."

Sean's mouth drops open and he's about to make some kind of exclamation. I lift my hand at him and clamp my fingers shut. "Uh-uh. Not that kind of high."

Gruunlokar strikes out, heading uphill. The region is pocked with tall mountains and rolling landscape, but we're already halfway up the mountain overlooking Micah's property. Won't take him long to reach the top, even in the snow.

Praxion looks at the screen embedded in his gauntlet. Shows the surrounding topography being monitored, and every target in the area, including us.

"Contact is due north. Half mile out. I'll flank right." He turns to me and Sean. "Left."

"And I'll go straight down the middle," Harth says, nodding in approval. Big guy prefers the direct approach.

I holster my weapon, clap my hands together, and give them a vigorous rub. "Okay, Seany-boy, Björn me!"

Sean unclips the carrier strapped to his back and chest. Apparently, they're meant for holding human children when they're small and useless. Kynolari pups are on their feet in days. But it can take baby humans more than a year.

Pitiful.

"BabyBjörn prepped and ready!" he says.

I leap at him. In one fluid movement, I spin myself around and insert my legs into the carrier as Sean pulls it up on both sides, clipping it in place and yanking the straps. I'm secured with weapons drawn a moment later. "Let's do this."

Sean breaks into an enthusiastic run.

In the wrong direction.

"Left is downhill," I say.

We slide to a stop, and he reverses course. "Right. I knew that." He gives Praxion a salute as we charge past him for a second time.

For a moment, I close my eyes and enjoy the breeze. Sean is surprisingly fleet-footed. The slope is helping, but I've been putting him through the wringer. Said he couldn't do field ops until he was in good shape. He's been putting himself through hell to get there, and he isn't doing too bad. He's breathing like a clogged exhaust, but at least he's moving.

"Right here," I say, pointing.

He follows my instructions through the woods. I'm guided by my connection to the defensive perimeter, and by my link to the others via regulators. They don't just allow us to communicate and connect with technology, but they give us a kind of sixth sense as to where the others are…within a certain range. Kind of like Micah and Grover, but a lot less powerful and intrusive. Telling you right now, I'd be off the team if they could see my thoughts, most of which have been about Bacon, capital B. That saucy little bitch stole my seed, and my heart.

"We're getting close," I say.

"Target sighted," Gruunlokar says. "Looks human. Average build."

"Could be a local," Sean says.

"Negative," Gruunlokar says. "Target is dressed in white tactical gear, and armed."

"Armed with what?" Praxion asks.

"Looks human," Gruunlokar says. "Like Micah's weaponry."

"We might be dealing with the U.S. military," Praxion says.

"Should I eliminate the threat?" Gruunlokar asks. "I can make him a sneeze in a tissue."

"Gross," Sean whispers.

"Negative," Praxion says. "I want to evaluate the threat first. We don't want to make an enemy of the United States...even if they are on the verge of collapse."

We arrive at a break in the trees, crouching low behind a thick pine. I catch a glimpse of the man, kneeling down in front of a patch of yellow snow.

My yellow snow.

He's armed, but I don't think he's here to pick a fight. The weapon is held loosely while he scrapes some of the tarnished snow into a glass vial and stoppers the top.

"Bruh," Sean says, recognizing the area as the place we sometimes walk, and piss. "He's collecting our pee."

We lean out together and linger this time. Looks like he means business at first glance, but then I zoom in with my optical implants and get a clearer look at him—and his helmet. "The hell?"

We lean back. "Talon-Actual, Talon-Four, we have visual on target. He might be here for us, but he's *not* military. Unlikely to be Draun."

"Recommendation?" Praxion asks.

I look up at Sean and give him an upside-down grin. "Send in Beefcake."

8

MICAH

We stop short of the tunnel's entrance, all the fun from our chase down the causeway drained by the ominous darkness within. I glance back at the necropolis, and it occurs to me that this is all in Grover's head. A perfect representation of the ancient pyramids, how they looked when they were new…inside my dog's head. I might as well actually be there. And instead of gawking as we approached the Great Pyramid, the tomb of Khufu, sometimes called Cheops, I chose to run and chase my dog. My priorities would probably confuse a lot of people. Then again, those people are probably already Draun.

"Okay, Grove. That was the easy part." I look down at my pup, whose nose is twitching. "What're you smelling?"

"People," he says. "Stinky."

"People aren't the stinky ones, tennis ball breath." He looks up at me smiling.

"Not…these people."

Well, that's god damn ominous. Grover is drawn to the world's most foul scented objects. Dirty socks. Deer shit. Rotting mushrooms. And he doesn't just sniff them out, he tries to eat them. Often succeeds. If something is too gross for his olfactory palate, then I'm really not looking forward to what comes next.

But I've never been one to avoid dire circumstances. "Let's get this over with." I step inside, half expecting to step on a loose stone block, triggering a fusillade of poison darts. I make it ten eventless steps and glance down to Grover—who isn't there.

I turn around. "Hey!"

He wags his tail. "Love Micah."

"I'm not doing this without you."

"No like."

"There's nothing *to* like, but we need to do this for our friends."

"For Jess?"

"Yes."

"And Torel?"

I don't miss that he's more attached to the female members of the team, which seems to be a trait in most Golden males. They're basically chick magnets.

"And Uncle Praxion?"

I smile at that. Grover sees Praxion as a literal family member, despite the fact that their lineages are separated by thirty-seven thousand years and even more light years. According to Baarfolir, it's likely that the pair could share some ancient ancestor, but not nearly close enough to consider them family, let alone uncle and nephew. But Praxion hasn't complained, so I never addressed it. I think the bossman might enjoy the title.

"All of them," I say. "And our home."

Grover lowers his head and tail. Steps into the darkness. Hustles until he's at my side.

"Now," I say, "we're in your head, right? Any chance you can give us some light to see by?"

"This place...outside." He's struggling to explain with his limited vocabulary, but I don't have any trouble understanding.

I nod. "Not a part of you."

He just looks forward, his silence confirmation.

"With me," I say, and step into the gloom. He walks close enough that I can feel his body against my leg. It's reassuring for both of us, that even here in this ancient tomb, we have each other.

It's not long before the tunnel turns downward, leading us into the depths below the pyramid's actual structure. The air chills, giving me goosebumps. My breath echoes off the stone surrounding us as the corridor shrinks. Feels like we're in the Death Star's trash compactor, every step bringing the walls and ceiling closer. It's not long before Grover is forced to take the lead.

Just when I think I'm going to have to turn sideways to continue, the floor levels out. A few steps later, I faceplant into a solid stone wall blocking my path. I sprawl backward with a shout, clutching my face.

Grover is by my side before I've fully registered what happened.

"Okay? Micah hurt? Love Micah."

I reach out for him, knowing that my injury isn't real, but his anxiety is. He sits between my legs and leans forward. I huff a laugh and wrap my arms around his back. "It's okay, buddy." The weight of his chin is heavy on my shoulder. He's leaning in hard. Terrified. "I got you. We're okay. This is all okay."

"You hurt?"

"It's not real, remember?" I'm not sure he fully comprehends the reality of our situation. For him, this might be as real as the conscious world. "I'm fine." I give his back five slow, soothing rubs, and it helps center us both. "I just ran into the wall."

"Ran into wall..."

"Right into it," I say.

"Micah...stupid?"

I laugh and say, "Hey!"

His body waggles back and forth. He's pretty pleased with himself. Gives my ear a few slobbery licks.

"Okay, okay," I say, moving his head to the side and getting up onto my knees. "Let's see what we're working with." I search with my hands, feeling along the walls until I reach the one that introduced itself to my face. The tunnel drops down to a three foot square, big enough for Grover to move through without noticing a difference, but small enough to stop me in my tracks.

It's a tunnel for dogs, I think, which, being inside Grover's mind, makes sense. I get on my hands and knees. "Lead the way."

Grover's claws clack over the stone floor as he continues forward.

"And don't you dare fart," I say, following him.

Crawling through a rough limestone tunnel on my hands and knees is about as comfortable as it sounds. If I have to do this much longer, I might need to pull myself along with my arms. Then the tunnel takes away the choice, shrinking on all sides, forcing us down to our bellies.

Seems like every subterranean movie I've seen features a sequence where someone in a tunnel gets wedged in place, unable to move, each breath straining ribs, conjuring fears of being stuck underground for eternity. The moment that fear starts settling in my psyche, it's peeled away by the sudden relief of exiting the tunnel.

I'm not sure what's on the other side. All I can say for sure is that it's large—every sound we make echoes—and full of unseen horrors. Because I can now smell what Grover detected at the entrance.

The stink of humans. Dead humans.

I remember a diagram of the great temple. The Queen's chamber at the pyramid's core. The King's chamber above it. The grand gallery connecting it to the ascending passageway. But we've just *descended,* and I suspect we've reached what we now call the 'subterranean chamber.' Not exactly an inspirational name, but no one knows the chamber's original purpose. What it might have contained. Or where it was supposed to lead.

And I'm not sure how we're supposed to figure any of that out in the dark. Then I remember that we're also dealing with an ancient Kynolari intelligence that somehow embedded all this mental imagery into the DNA and mind of every descendent of the Lost Tribe. Means the message is important. That there's a way to uncover it.

"Anbu?" I say. "You there, buddy?"

I realize I'm talking to the once-god-dog the way I do Grover, all cutesy and shit. I lower my voice, and with a bit more authority, say, "Anbu, we're here to talk. About your descendants. The lives of every Kynolari on the planet are under grave threat."

"Show yourself." The voice booms, making me shrink back a step.

"Uhh," I say. "Don't know if you have eyes to see with, but it's dark as a motherfucker in here."

A torch flares to life in front of us. It illuminates Grover and me, along with forty other people, all in various stages of mummified death.

I clear my throat.

"Why have you come to this sacred place?" the voice asks.

"Are you Anbu?" I ask. "Because I don't want to—"

"I am he."

"Cool. Cool. Great. I'll just get right to the point."

A shape moves in the darkness beyond the torch's light. I choke on my own words as a figure stands. It's a foot taller than me, wiry, and ominous. With a single stride, it steps into the light, revealing the withered visage of a long-snouted, pointy-eared Egyptian jackal—or whatever species of Kynolari looks like a jackal. It's dressed in a simple beige tunic. There's a gold belt around his waist and gold cuffs on his arms. His head is encased in a gold and black striped headpiece, bejeweled with three rubies. None of it really matters, because *this*...this is Anubis, and he is far more horrific than I'd imagined.

He stands above me, looking down past his snarling nose. "No."

"No...what?" I ask.

"I will not speak with you..." He pulls out a sekhem scepter with a broad, flat head covered in hieroglyphs. Looks capable of inverting my skull. And he tries to do just that, swinging it in a wide arch. "Be gone from this place, Draun!"

9

PRAXION

Beefcake...

Sean insisted on having a codename while on field missions. Since I didn't imagine many futures where Sean would play an active role in engaging the enemy, I agreed, only to find out that his preferred name was 'Beefcake.'

"Talon-Actual, Talon-One, I'm not sure sending in...*Beefcake* is a good idea," Harth says over comms. "He is untested and undisciplined."

"Talon-Douche, Talon-Four, Beefcake also has ears and comms," Chirk grumbles.

The relationship between Chirk and Sean is a bit of a mystery to me. In some ways it resembles the connection between Grover and Micah, with their roles being somewhat reversed—Chirk the dominant force, Sean the subservient, but both willing to defend and even die for the other.

"Talon-Four," I say, "Talon-Actual. If you think he's up to it, I'm in agreement, but if this goes sideways, Beefcake will—"

"I get it," Sean says, "if I screw it up, I'm benched. But I got this."

"'I got this' is what he said before attempting to 'sled' off the roof into a mound of snow," Harth reminds me.

"One," Chirk says, "that was *amazing*. And two, he was blazed at the time."

I hear Harth's sigh. It helps conceal my own. This is a risk I would have never taken before. I prefer controlling situations, well thought out plans, and a team of operators in whom I have absolute and unwavering faith. But we are on Earth, where, according to Micah, 'No plan survives contact with the enemy.' That was not my experience before arriving on this planet, but since...

This world seems to seep chaos into all who set foot upon it. A theory which is supported by me saying, "Beefcake, you are go for contact, but...I will observe personally. Give me a moment to join you."

"I will remain here," Harth says.

"And I still have you all covered," Gruunlokar says. "Anything goes wrong, I'll put a hole in the tinfoil hat."

"Talon-Four, hold until my arrival," I say.

"Copy that," Chirk says, "Talon-Four out."

"Beefcake out," Sean adds.

After which I hear Chirk whisper, "We don't both need to say it."

Can't help but smile. Sean has been yanked out of a lackadaisical and simple life and thrown into the midst of a rekindled interstellar war. He is out of his element but trying his best to not just fit in with a team of seasoned operators, but also to impress Chirk.

Stepping back, I find a clear shot through the woods downhill from my position. Then I focus on Chirk and get a sense of his direction and distance. Not far, but in the name of expediency, I decide to take the express route.

I point my Sonizer gauntlet at the foot deep snow, adjust the power setting with a thought, and then unleash a low power sonic wave that compresses the snow into ice and creates a curved path. I developed the technique on Efnick, a mineral-rich, frozen world populated by Kynolari with the thickest fur. I was younger then, and creating the ice slide was for fun, but it has been a helpful skill a few times since.

Sonizer extended in front of me, I throw myself onto the frozen track, head-first and belly down. I quickly pass my full running speed, gravity assisting my acceleration down the nearly frictionless path. I weave in and out of trees and around granite boulders, leaning back and forth to control my direction.

When I sense Chirk off to my right, I sweep the Sonizer up and around, creating a tall ninety-degree turn, that drops off halfway around. I slide high around the corner and I'm sent flying when the track ends. I flip over and land on my feet, sliding to a stop just a few feet from Chirk and Sean.

Sean's jaw drops. "Did you... Holy shit... I mean... He just..."

Chirk raises a hand from below, where he's strapped to Sean's chest. Pushes the man's jaw closed. "Control yourself, Beefcake."

Sean purses his lips so hard they turn white.

Chirk smiles at me. "Show off."

I shrug. "Side effect of being on Earth."

His grin goes wry. "Been sliding down any other slopes lately? Going to blame that on Earth, too?"

I ignore him. This is not the time to talk about relationships or...her slopes. Case in point, I'm now distracted. "Has the target moved?"

"Not really," Chirk says. "He's just out there, fascinated by my piss. Or maybe Sean's. Kind of hard to tell whose is whose."

"What?" Sean says. "You wrote your name, dude."

I can't hide my glower. Pissing in the snow is dumb enough. It leaves traces of DNA and is easily tracked, thanks to being bright yellow on a white canvas, especially if you're dehydrated. But writing his name? It's a foolish risk. Torel has confirmed that Earth's air is influencing all of us, making us less risk averse, less predictable, more…primal. More like humans. Because of Chirk's size, he's more profoundly affected. Things that might have driven him to put a rail shard through someone's kneecap, like calling him, 'A sex-crazed, reckless, homo-sapidoggy,'—Jess's assessment—no longer offends him. Because it's accurate. Hence his plan to activate 'Captain Beefcake' for an active mission role beyond transportation.

"You know what to do?" I ask Sean.

"I'm a local," he says. "Out for a walk. Make conversation—I'm good at that—and assess their intentions."

"And you understand what all that means?" I ask.

It's Chirk's turn to glower at me.

"Means I try to figure out if they're cool or want to kill us all," Sean says. "Piece of cake."

"Why don't you seem nervous?" I ask. Experience has taught me that the most confident warriors on a battlefield are often the first to die.

He looks at me like I've got what Micah calls, 'dingleberries.' "Tin. Foil. Hat."

"I don't understand," I say.

"It's okay, dude. You still have a lot to learn. Check this out." He steps out from behind the tree, tromping his way toward the person who appears to be hunting us. Chirk, still strapped to his chest, pulls his arms and legs inside the baby carrier.

"Hey!" Sean shouts, sounding friendly. "Yo! How's it going?"

The target stands up from the yellow-stained snow, stumbling back a step. More than that, the person doesn't raise their rifle. Given how casually it's being held, they either have no idea how to use it, or are actually so dangerous they don't need it. Could all be a ruse.

I activate my comms and leave them open so I can hear the conversation.

"Holy shit," Sean says. "That's a lot of piss!" He laughs. "You think it was a moose or something? They're all over the place up here."

His ability to speak to a total stranger like they're lifelong friends is impressive, but if the target turns out to be a Draun after all, we'll quickly discover how good he is at having his body torn in two.

"Oh, hey," the target responds. Sounds like a female. "Am I on your land or something? I didn't mean to—I mean, I *did* mean to—I just… Nothing is marked up here, you know? I'm kind of out of my element. Oh! I love your dog. He's *adorable!*"

"Oh, this little guy? This is Chirk. He's just a friendly little dude. Nothing unusual about him."

"Do you mind if I pet him?" she asks.

Allowing the stranger, female or not, to approach Chirk could be a deadly mistake. The most powerful Draun we've faced on this world was a woman, and she could have easily slain both of them.

"Talon-Actual, Talon-Two," Gruunlokar says. "Just give me the word."

"Copy that," I say, watching and listening to the interaction.

"Hold up," Sean says. "Little dude is afraid of people whose faces he can't see."

Good, I think.

"Oh, right, of course," the woman says, lifting her reflective goggles away from her eyes and unwrapping a scarf around her neck. Her face is revealed. Black hair, tan skin, brown epicanthal eyes, marking her as being from one of Earth's Asian countries. I didn't detect an accent, so I suspect she is an American, born to immigrant parents.

Sean staggers back a step. I hear him whisper, "Whoa..." and can smell his sudden burst of pheromones from here. It's said that human women take three months to fall in love, and eight seconds for the men. I suspect it is even faster than that.

The woman smiles and asks, "Okay, now?"

"All the time. Yes. Anything you want." Sean is undone by the sudden appearance of an attractive woman.

She laughs at his response. Does she find it charming? Humans confuse me. Then she reaches out and gives Chirk's head a friendly scratch. He leans into it.

"Who's a good boy?" the woman asks, leaning closer.

"I am," Sean says. "I'm a super good boy."

The woman laughs again. "Well, you'd have to be, to have a little guy *this* sweet."

Okay, so, she's basically harmless. Doesn't mean we have time for Sean to preen his feathers and put on a mating display.

"Get to the point," I grumble in Sean's ear.

"Right," he says, and then to the woman. "Can you, ahh, why were you collecting frozen moose pee?"

The woman pulls back but seems more embarrassed than concerned. "Saw that, did you?" She laughs again, this time muted. "Well, that's kind of an embarrassing story."

"I'm full of embarrassing stories," Sean says. "Here's one... That pee you collected? It's not from a moose... It's mine. And this guy's." He gives Chirk a pat.

The woman's eyes spring open. "Oh, god, seriously? That's—I'm sorry. Oh. That's gross, right? You must think I'm—"

"Amazing," Sean whispers.

"What?"

"Adventurous," he says. "Or...something else that rhymes with amazing..."

She smiles. Sean's total lack of charm seems to be working on her.

"Okay," she says. "Promise you won't laugh?"

"Cross my heart," Sean says.

"My uncle. He lived in Japan when, you know, that thing happened with the signal and the Draun awakening or whatever. He asked me to come here and find his friends." She sighs. "He's hiding underground on an island with a lot of other people and for some reason, he thinks his friends can actually help them escape, even though no one can even get close to Japan."

"That's why you were collecting pee?" Sean asks.

"To test," she says. "For DNA. I'm a biologist."

"DNA of what?"

She sighs. "Okay, this is the crazy part. My uncle, he says his friends..." She sighs again. "He said his friends are dogs. The ones from the vision we all had. The Kynolari. Enemy of the Draun. All that."

"Hold on," Chirk says.

The woman yelps, drops her gear, and falls on her back. She pushes herself away from Sean, terrified by Chirk. Definitely not a threat.

"It's okay," Sean insists, "He's cool. He's one of them."

"W-what?" she says. "They're real? The Kynolari?"

Sean turns to the woods behind him and shouts, "It's okay, dudes. You can come out. She's cool."

I would have preferred to stay hidden, but I now suspect this woman might indeed have been sent to us by an ally. She gasps upon seeing me, and then again, when Harth steps out of the woods. Gruunlokar maintains his overwatch position.

We stop on either side of Sean.

Sean shows the woman his open palms. "It's okay. They're chill. They *are* the good guys."

"Okay..." The woman says. "Talking...alien dogs are real."

"World's gone crazy," Chirk says, "Am I right? Now, what is your name?"

"Uh," she says. "Lucy Sandall."

"Lucy Sandall?" Sean says. "If your uncle is in Japan, your parents were probably born there, right?"

She sighs. "Fine. It's not my real name."

"Hold on," Sean says. "Is...is it an anagram?"

The woman smiles wide. "Yeah, but—"

"Dana Scully," Sean says. "*Awesome.*"

"Do you know what they are talking about?" Harth asks Chirk.

Chirk shakes his head. "Not a clue."

"Real name this time," Chirk says to her.

"Gemma... Gemma Watanabe."

"And who is your uncle?" I ask.

She looks up at me, studies my eyes for a moment, and then says, "Haruto Watanabe."

"Haruto," Harth says, grunting in recognition. "The driver of the panda bus."

Before I can process this news, a second proximity alert sounds.

10

MICAH

The broad-topped scepter's passage through the air just over my head creates a pressure wave as it passes, shifting my hair about like I'm standing over a cliff-side's updraft.

Had I not ducked, my head would look like a backward C. And even though none of this is real, I get the feeling that it still would have hurt and had an impact on my psyche. Maybe enough to kill my real self, or at least leave me with crippling anxiety and PTSD triggered by cricket bats.

I jump back a step. "Whoa, whoa, whoa. I'm not—"

Momentum from the missed strike carries him around, but he's prepared for it, backhand swinging a khopesh, which looks like the love child of Conan the Barbarian's sword and some kind of battle axe from Middle Earth, shaped like a sickle.

To avoid being eviscerated in front of Grover, I fall flat on my back, coughing the air from my lungs. The blade whooshes over me as Anbu continues his spin, raising the scepter for a downward strike.

You're better than this, I tell myself, and then I hear the words of Morpheus to Neo echoing from some recess of my mind, 'You think that's air you're breathing, now?'

It's not real. None of this is real. I don't need to breathe at all.

Freed from the limitations of my physical self, I manage a quick roll to the side. The scepter clangs off the stone floor where my head had been. Before he can follow up with another strike, I get to my feet and activate my dual gauntlets.

Except nothing happens.

In Grover's mind, I'm just Micah.

Not the Axiom. Not a Kynolari warrior.

I'm just a guy that throws tennis balls and occasionally serves as a dry hump post.

"Seriously?" I say, completely exposed and in range of Anbu's next strike, which I had planned on blocking. As the blade swoops in, I can see its arc to completion. He's not just going to spill my guts on the floor, he's going to cut me clean in half.

Just before the blade bites into my flesh, it stops with a loud metallic cling.

"What the fuck?" I whisper, voice shaky. I look down to where my side should be split open. "What the—Grover?"

My gentle, loving Golden Retriever has caught the massive blade between his jaws like it was a stick. He snarls and growls at Anbu, who is profoundly offended by the interruption.

"You dare—"

Grover clenches his jaws and the khopesh blade *shatters*.

That's right, bitch, you're in Grover's mind!

Anbu releases the broken weapon, takes a step back, and assumes a defensive position. "Have our people descended so far into madness that you now defend a Draun?"

"*Not* Draun," Grover says.

Anbu shakes his head, disappointed. "Despite my best efforts, the Draun infection on humanity could not be rooted out. Humanity became the enemy. You must know this. I left the knowledge embedded within the minds of every Kynolari, along with..." He looks down at his hands. "Myself..."

He lowers his guard.

"Am I all that remains of that ancient knowledge? Have you forgotten who you are? Where you are from?"

"Forget," Grover says, "but now know. Kynolari return."

"We have been found?" Anbu says, staggered by the news.

"In a sense," I say.

He raises his scepter toward me. "Silence, mongrel!"

I look down at Grover. "You know, I thought he'd be nicer, but he's kind of living up to the whole God of the Dead thing."

"He is," Grover says.

"How dare you—"

"Seriously, I think it went to his head," I say, and then smash a dose of reality pie straight into the ancient dog-god's face. "Look. I'm sure this act frightened people a long time ago, but times have changed. We know who you are, what you are, and where you come from. Your bravado and booming voice are impressive, but they're not nearly enough to make us quiver in fright. You're not a god. You're a dog. Well, not really a dog. A Kynolari. An alien to this planet who crash landed on Earth thirty-seven thousand years ago. You lived among humanity, and somehow managed to prolong your life in a way that elevated you to the position of a deity. But then...even *you* died."

"I did not die," he grumbles.

"Put a pin in that," I say. "What I'm trying to tell you is that it's been a long time, and your people—the Kynolari—they have returned. They found Earth. Found your people, what they now call the 'Lost Tribe.' And yes, they found the Draun living among us, using our manipulated DNA to turn our people into monsters. But not all of us."

"I sense the Draun in you," he says, snarling.

"You sense it in my biology," I say. "You need to look deeper."

He squints at me. Don't blame him. His experience with the Draun isn't the same as Praxion's. He doesn't know about the war. The genocides. But he clearly interacted with them, here on Earth, suggesting that direct Draun influence on the human race lasted far longer than we believed.

I raise my hands. "Look." I step out from behind Grover. "I'll give myself to you. Access my mind if you—"

"No," Grover says. "I talk."

Grove stands between me and Anbu, then does his best to form complete sentences. "Grover love Micah. Kynolari…love Micah. Micah is good. Not Draun."

He's not exactly selling it, but then he ends with an exclamation point that dick slaps Anbu in the face, shocking him with both surprise and revulsion. "Micah is Axiom."

"Lies," Anbu whispers. "You are as corrupt as him." He staggers back a step. "The Axiom is Kynolari."

"I am Kynolari," I say.

"How dare you!" He clutches his scepter in both hands, about to throw himself into another round of ancient jaw-snapping zoomies.

I look down at Grover. "Let me show him. I think it's the only way."

"No hurt," Grover says.

"No hurt." I say, and I see my gauntlets appear on my arms.

"Rawr!" Anbu shouts, coming in with a juiced Jose Canseco swing. I activate both gauntlets, direct power to the laser claws, and raise my hands. Instead of blocking the swing, I use the blades to slice through the scepter. It falls apart around me, pieces hitting the floor.

"I hope that wasn't important," I say, and then fire a full-strength laser blast with both hands, straight up. The energy vaporizes the ceiling and everything above it, including five hundred feet of the Great Pyramid. When I'm done, a column of sunlight shines down upon me like a spotlight.

Now that I've got Anbu's undivided attention, I hold up the depleted gauntlets, and, through sheer force of will, I fully recharge them as I would in the real world. They're ready to fire again, something that can only be achieved by—

"The Axiom…" Anbu says. "…is human?"

"Not human," I say. "Not fully human. A portion of my DNA is human. A portion is Draun. But here…" I pat my heart. "And here…" I place a hand upon my head.

"I am Kynolari. As much as you. As much as Grover. As much as the team that came to find you. The Draun are our enemy as much as they are yours. And that's why we are here. We need your help, to stop them."

He takes a step back, head lowering. "If you are here to find me, inside this one's feeble mind, then I am—"

"Dead," I say. "But it seems like it took a while."

"I prolonged my life via science, extending my telomeres and remaining in stasis for millennia."

"Do you know how you died?" I ask.

He shakes his head. "My last memory is of the moment I transferred a portion of my consciousness into a virus that would spread through the Kynolari population on Earth, ensuring that my knowledge would not be lost to the sands of time." He looks me in the eyes, and it's hard to not look away. He's an intimidating son of a bitch. Literally. Ha. "How long have I been missing?"

"Best guess," I say, "somewhere between two and three thousand years."

He sighs. "You are sure? That I have passed?"

"I haven't seen your corpse, if that's what you're asking, but there haven't been reports of any dog-gods walking around the planet since then."

He leans forward a bit. "Are you sure? I lived in many places before Egypt. It is possible I relocated."

"I'll keep that in mind, but right now, we have more pressing issues."

"The Draun," he says.

I nod. "They've used a signal to awaken the Draun DNA in humanity and, like you in Grover's mind, it contained a message—propaganda really—declaring Kynolari as the enemy. It also restored the Draun's latent telekinetic abilities."

He sits back on his throne. "How many?" He looks up. "The Draun. How many?"

"Two hundred and fifty million. At least. And the number is increasing every day."

He's staggered by the number. "That is more than the entire population of the planet in my time. What is Earth's population now?"

"Eight billion," I say.

He blinks at me. "I always said humans enjoyed copulation too much."

"Most of that was in the past hundred years," I say. "Technology improved. People live longer. More babies survive. There's more food than ever. Electricity. Plumbing. Heat. Winterized homes."

He huffs. "And humanity thought it was a good idea to kill itself as a result?"

"Humanity didn't really discuss it. We are still a decentralized world."

He shakes his head. "The perfect breeding ground for corruption, hubris, and greed. The Draun's impact on this world has grown more powerful since my apparent demise." He scratches his chin, mumbling to himself before coming to some kind of internal consensus. He leans forward, elbows on his knees. "Tell me everything you know about this Draun signal."

11

CHIRK

"Ahh, what now?" I grumble. "We can't go running any time someone with a penchant for pee collecting wanders into the perimeter."

"Talon-Actual, Talon-Two," Gruunlokar says. "Active threat is not a pee collector, I repeat, not a pee collector."

"Then what the hell is it?" I ask, breaking protocol by answering for Praxion and not using codenames.

Gruunlokar's reply comes as a whisper, which means he's aiming at the same time. "Straub Hunt Squad. Three Furies and four Hounds."

"Well," I say, "Shit. Looks like we've been found."

"Not yet," Praxion says. "Talon-Two, what are they doing? Exactly."

"Mountaintop due north. They're on the peak. Doing what I'm doing."

"Then they haven't found us yet," Praxion says. "Hunt squads don't hold back if they've located their target."

"Umm," Gemma says. "Hello. I'm sorry. Should I go?"

Sean and Harth answer simultaneously. "Yes." "No."

"If they see her leaving the territory they've marked, they will kill her." Praxion's addition to the conversation leaves little doubt about Gemma's limited choices. "Everyone, into the trees. Slowly."

Once we're in the shadows of the trees, Praxion gives his next order. "Drop anything reflective."

As we shed the small amount of shiny gear, Gemma says, "Does this count?" and turns around to reveal a bright orange reflective X on her back. "I didn't want to get shot by a hunter or something."

"Looks a lot like you just put a target on your back," I say.

"Lose it," Harth says. "And anything else like it."

Gemma sheds the jacket and Sean does the same, offering his to her. *Oh, you slick bastard,* I think. *Look at you go.*

She accepts the jacket with a smile, until she smells it. She waves a hand in front of her face. "Wow. You guys smoke a lot of dope?"

"Uh," Sean says, embarrassed. "You could say that. Me and the little guy, at least."

Gemma takes a deep breath. "Blueberry Headband?"

Sean's eyes light up. "Glitterbomb. But it hails from Blueberry Headband and Grape Gas. You have a good nose."

"Great," I say, "that's great, you two. You can compliment each other's noses later. Right now, we're trying to not get staked to a tree and have our bones slowly extracted and reassembled on the ground in front of us while we're still alive.

"Wait, for real? Is that a thing?" Sean looks to Harth for the straight up honest truth and gets it.

Harth nods. "Under Draun influence, they are savages delighting in the agony of others. Those may be biologic recreations, but they will have been instilled with the same instincts, knowledge, and carnal desires of the original species. *If* we were to be overcome by them, our ends would be agonizing." He faces Praxion. "If. We have faced far worse, though."

Praxion nods in agreement. "And yet...they are most certainly not alone. How long before those who sent them arrive with forces beyond our capability to repel?"

I raise my hand. "Are you taking our newly assembled defensive perimeter into account? Because not much of anything is going to get through there, including those Straub assholes."

"Two hundred fifty million soldiers," Praxion says. "Unlimited resources. Time to plan. We are not facing a Straub Hunt Squad, we are staring down the tip of a spear far greater than any we have faced before. To charge it head on would end in our destruction."

Harth grunts. "You plan to retreat."

"Retreat," Praxion says. "And then abandon this temporary home."

"When?" Sean asks.

Praxion turns to him, dead serious. "Now. Talon-Two, Talon-Actual, rendezvous at the *Prowler*. Double time." To the rest of us he points, two fingers extended, back down the mountain's slope.

"Includes you, sweetheart," I say to Gemma. "Unless getting speared to a tree is your idea of a good time."

She's horrified.

And that's a good thing.

Means she won't complain or do anything stupid, which would likely lead to Sean doing something stupid, and then me doing something even more stupid. Then it's just a whole chain of *stupid* likely to get someone, or everyone, killed.

"Talon-Three," Praxion says, and then breaks protocol. "Torel, are you there?"

"Here," she says over comms.

"Almost done?" he asks.

"No way to know. They're connected. Their subconsciouses are entwined. Based on when and how their muscles are twitching, I'd say it's working. Whatever they're experiencing, Micah and Grover are doing it together."

"Can you pull them out of it?" he asks, following the rest of us downhill.

"I would not recommend attempting it. Best case scenario, Micah slips back into his own mind. Worst case, he becomes a vegetable while his consciousness lives on inside Grover's mind. Forever."

"Is there any way to communicate with them?" he asks. "Ask them to come out on their own?"

"No. Prax—Talon-Actual, what's happening?"

"Straub Hunt Squad," he says. "We are en route to the Prowler. Have Baarfolir prep for immediate evac."

"Copy that," she says, back to sounding like a seasoned operator. "ETA?"

"Ten minutes," he says, a moment before one of our rail cannons detects the Straub and lets loose a barrage of tungsten shards. "Give or take."

The rail cannon isn't loud, but in the silent snowy mountains, it's a beacon. We can't see the effect it has on its target, but it's safe to say one of the eight-member hunt squad is dead.

And then, so is the cannon. An explosion shakes the mountain. The Straub live up to their reputation, striking without fear. And they'll come running now that they've confirmed our presence.

"Talon-One," Praxion says over comms, despite Harth being right beside him. "Retask anti-armor and anti-air batteries to ground targets. I want them chasing anything that moves."

Normally, Harth would delight in such a suggestion, but this is the mother of all danger-close situations. "Sir, that will be—"

"Chaos," Praxion says. "It's our best hope of reaching the *Prowler* in one piece."

"Or in, like, a thousand little pieces," I say.

"I prefer being in one piece," Sean adds, and then to Gemma, he says, "But don't sweat it. We do crazy stuff like this, like, all the time. You're totes safe." He looks down at me with wide eyes, silently asking if he sold the lie.

"The regulators will prevent us from being targeted." Praxion isn't wrong, but we're experienced enough to know that splash damage is a real threat.

"What's a regulator?" Gemma asks.

All eyes turn to her.

"Shit," Praxion says, and then he waves her over to him. "Proximity to me should keep you from being targeted." He holds out his hands. "Quickly."

"Quickly," she says. "Quickly what?"

Praxion scoops her off her feet and into his arms.

"I could have done that," Sean grumbles.

"You're already carrying me, Beefcake, and if you're jealous, think about this, I've got a boner right now and I have no god damn idea why."

"Revolting," Harth says, and then follows after Praxion, adjusting the proximity defense system as he goes.

"Just wait until it happens to you, big guy," I shout at his back. "Going to be hard to hide that third leg when it's sliding down your inner thigh."

When I catch Sean looking down at me, concern on his face, I say, "Don't get all weird on me, man! It ain't from you. Just happens on occasion. On this world, at least. My hormones are going bonkers. Just be glad I'm facing forward, or you'd have a few bruised ribs."

"Chirk," Harth calls. "They're thirty feet away and picking up speed."

"You heard the man," I say, and kick my heels into Sean's sides. "Mush!"

"Targets approaching your position," Gruunlokar says, no time for codenames. "Moving fast."

I glance left and then right. A black blur catches my attention, moving between the trees. Its long angular body, rigid spiky mane, and front-heavy build are impossible to mistake. It's a Hound, powerful primal beasts used to take down prey five times their size. The bucktoothed daggers it has for teeth are a pretty good indicator, too. Then, there's the howl. A high-pitched, warbling cry that alerts the rest of the hunt squad to our position.

"Mush!" I repeat. "Mush!"

"Danger close!' Harth shouts, letting us know that all systems are now active.

"Sean," I say. "My man. You know that movie we watched with that guy who could dodge bullets? Because he's *The One* and lives in a simulation?"

"Neo, yeah."

"If you can do any of that shit, now is the time to surprise me with it."

He looks down at me, head bobbing around as he runs after the others. "Huh?!"

Motion on both sides of my periphery catches my attention at the same time. I focus on the object that's going to reach us first. "Incoming left!"

"Wha!" Sean shouts, looking left to see the rocket twisting through the trees on a collision course with the Hound. The beast moves on four legs, somewhat reminiscent of an Earth dog, only four times the size, covered in muscle, and so black that its various parts are nearly impossible to make out—until it's running. "Dodge and weave!" Sean leaps into the air, twisting and contorting his body like his puppeteer just spilled Craglian Pincer Stew on his exposed genitals.

Somehow, despite his flailing limbs, the rocket passes beneath us, close enough for me to reach out and touch.

The ensuing explosion takes place just a second after passing us.

Already airborne, the shockwave propels us downhill, the mountain falling away beneath us. We sail over the others, pinwheeling, as we shout in near perfect harmony. With each spin, I take a look back, watching as the now three-legged Hound limps along after us, and is quickly overtaken by three more.

Before the injured beast can pick up speed, a single shard cuts silently through the forest, punching through a tree before doing the same to the Hound's head. In one side, out the other, taking all the skull's contents along for the ride. While the rest of us run, Gruunlokar is still on overwatch.

But his services are no longer required, because the defense system is up and running, unleashing hell on the forest directly behind us. Lasers cut through trees, rockets weave in and out, and shards eat up everything left standing. No way to know if our enemies are being mowed down, too, but I assume they look something like the forest now: obliterated.

I look forward and realize I'm about to be pancaked in a foot of snow, beneath Sean. "Flip over!" I shout. "Flip over!" I throw my weight to the side, and we start rolling. Sean twists and we touch down on a slope so steep the impact is barely noticeable.

Headfirst, on his back, Sean becomes a sled. I slip out of my baby carrier, stand on his chest, and draw my mini-railguns, ready for whatever might come our way. "Ha-ha!"

And that's when the glowing blue Helion drops from the sky, landing on the mountainside directly ahead of us.

12

MICAH

"I see," Anbu says, sitting in deep stoic thought, chin perched on elbow, leaning on a knee. He's a relic of the past, reborn in Grover's mind. And yet, he feels very much present and alive. "Reality TV may indeed be a tool of the Draun, to dull the minds of the masses and leave humanity more susceptible to the mind-altering signal."

"Actually, I think we might be on a tangent, here," I say.

"But this man... The Situation. His title is ominous, suggesting—"

"It's a nickname," I say. "Not his real name, and trust me, other than a few unwanted pregnancies, he's probably not a threat."

He gives a slow nod. "Perhaps you are right. You said that humans are still embracing the Draun ways, over time?"

"More every day."

"And the signal?"

"I heard it just the once," I say, "but I'm also Kynolari."

"Mm..." He mulls it over for a moment. "You must destroy the signal's source, to prevent further spread of the Draun madness."

"And then..."

He leans back, snout lifted toward the ceiling, deep in thought. Then he says, "I do not know. The Draun are far more powerful than altered human beings."

"I know."

"And human beings are...frail," he continues.

"Not news."

"And you already tried—" he starts to ask.

"Nuclear weapons," I say. "Yes. Our most powerful weapons. I thought the point of this message was to contain your knowledge, of how to fix a world gone wrong, of how to defeat the Draun."

"This...is true," he says, sounding somewhat defeated. "But things have progressed farther and faster than even I had imagined. Humanity's development had been slow by any planet's standards. Advances came and went along with empires. Tribal warfare kept technological development from progressing too far, too fast, before being lost entirely. It happened again and again.

"But the history of your past hundred years has defied that trend. Instead of holding people back, wars advanced humanity. Scientific advancement is now prized instead of feared. The spoils of war." He mutters to himself for a moment and then declares, "You must destroy the satellites in orbit."

"How are we supposed to—"

"The Kynolari ship," he says. "You have one."

"One," I say. "And the last time it faced the Draun head-on it almost didn't survive. The moment we hit the atmosphere, they'll know where we are."

"Sekhtem!" It's the first word he's spoken that I don't understand. Has an Egyptian vibe, and the way he spoke it feels like a curse.

Anubis isn't exactly living up to our historical view of the jackal-man. He's just an average Kynolari who managed to extend his life. He might have been brilliant once, but he's no tactician and was completely unprepared for this scenario.

"I'm going to need access to more information. Direct access to your world."

"Okay, how do we do that?" I ask.

His brow furrows like I've just asked what color the sky is.

Then he says, "Ahh," like the answer has just come to him. "You don't fully comprehend... My mind...all of it, is contained in the mind of this canine. While I would prefer not to be awakened inside the mind of a primitive body such as this, I'm afraid we have no other choice. His sacrifice will be honored for generations, and his body will be the vessel of humanity's salvation."

His eyes turn down to Grover, leaving no doubt that his plan is to replace my dog's mind with his own.

When he looks back to me, I unleash a, "Fffffuck no."

He looks like he's just stepped in wet shit, barefoot, so it's all squishing up through his toes. It's a visceral expression of disgust. Probably not accustomed to humans shooting down his ideas.

"You defy *me?*"

"Look," I say. "You might hold a lot of weight with the Kynolari who grew up hearing tales of the great Anbu, but to me, you're Anubis, a pretend god of the dead. And it sounds like all those years scaring the shit out of people to achieve your goals—I'm assuming—might have gone to your head. You are no different than me, or the Kynolari who came to Earth. And honestly, you have yet to tell me anything that makes you more valuable than the rest of us. And you sure as shit haven't proven yourself more valuable than Grover."

He clenches his fists, and I think he's about to have another go at me. Then he turns away and lowers his head. "Leave me."

I look down at Grover. "I don't think he gets it."

"Him doggu," Grover says. "Be slow."

By 'slow' he means 'patient,' and he's not wrong. Given enough time and gentle prodding, dogs are pretty good at communicating their needs. But we have no idea how much time the world has before the Draun signal becomes too hard to resist.

"Look, Anbu," I say. "This might be your only chance to impart some wisdom that could save humanity and prevent a second Great War."

He turns his long snout toward me, ears perked.

"Is that one of humanity's modern wars?"

"We did have a war sometimes referred to as 'the Great War,' but this was bigger... A war between an alliance of species, led by the Kynolari, against the Draun, who had conquered and enslaved or eradicated several species. Your people won, at great cost, and believed the war over."

"Until they arrived on Earth," he says.

"And found the Visionary."

He squints.

"You don't know about him?"

"The Draun presence on Earth was a corruption at the genetic level. There was no guiding force. I only know who they are thanks to a craft I discovered during my journeys. The same craft that allowed me to extend my life."

"The Visionary led the war against the Kynolari, kind of their own Hitler and Himmler rolled into one."

His brow furrows.

"Never mind. Point is, he's a bad guy. A mastermind of intergalactic war and a propagator of genocide. He's been living on Earth for some time now. And not hiding in the shadows. We know him as Lumen Sok, the richest man on Earth. He's an eccentric and powerful man capable of influencing wars and elections, and he can basically buy whatever he wants."

"The weakness of a currency-based system," he says.

"So I've been told," I say, remembering a few late night lectures from Harth. "Not that money matters much anymore. To him anyway. He controls an entire nation."

That news seems to sink the old god into a depressive state. For all his bravado and planning, he now finds himself totally unprepared for a battle he knew was coming. But he had no way of knowing just how grave it would be.

Reminds me of that time Brian Brown challenged me to a fight after school. We had a crush on the same girl, which at the time—sixth grade—didn't bother me at all, but fuck me, Brian Brown was a possessive little dick. He was half my size, so I figured, why not teach him a lesson? I spent the day pondering all the different and humiliating ways I would deal with Brian. I could throw him in a bush. Atomic wedgie him into the side of a dumpster. Maybe just sit on him until he begged to be released. My friends and I drew pictures of the future event, came up with every ridiculous scenario we could think of. Except one. Brian Brown was a mean son of a bitch who'd scrapped his way through life before winding up at our school. Never saw the first two punches. He landed fifteen more, I was told, but I didn't see them either. Didn't even feel them. Because I was unconscious. Felt them later, though, and the sting of defeat.

I was a pariah for the rest of that year, *and* Brian got the girl.

When I snap back to the present, both Anbu and Grover are staring at me.

"What?" I ask.

"No like Brian," Grover says.

"You could see that?"

"In *my* head," Grover says. "No secret."

"Cool," I say, guarding my thoughts. "So glad I shared that with Anubis..."

"I thought I was no different than any other—"

"Don't give me attitude, Anubis," I say, "or I will smack you back to the ship that..." I slow turn to the ancient god. "Where is it? Your ship?"

"Shattered. Now part of a temple complex, south of the land I called Tenochtitlan," he says.

"That sounds made up."

Grover catches me off guard, saying, "Xolotl."

"Yes," Anbu says. "That was my name in that part of the world... Perhaps it still is. The culture was quite primitive when I left them." Anbu approaches me, lifting his hand.

I flinch away.

"I will imprint its location on your mind," he says.

I stand my ground and allow him to put his hand on my forehead. I'm immediately filled with the knowledge of where to go. I can't picture it, or say where in the world it is, but I can feel it like an instinct. I'll know it when I see it.

"But I had no plans to return. You need to seek me out, here."

"We're here now," I point out.

"Out there," he says. "In the world."

"In Egypt," I say, dubious. "Under the Great Pyramid?"

"In the event of my death, that was my intended burial place, deep beneath the pyramid in a secret chamber. Only my most trusted servants knew about it. If there is information garnered after I imprinted myself on the DNA of my fellow Kynolari, it will be found there."

"Then I guess that's where we're going," I say. I look down at Grover. "Ready to go?"

Grover opens his mouth and pants with a smile. That's a solid 'yes' in Golden Retriever.

"Wasn't so bad, right?" I ask him as we head for the tunnel exit.

"He not scary," Grover says.

"Right? Kind of like visiting someone in the hospital."

Anbu clears his throat. When I look back, he's standing right behind us, looking big and menacing once more. "You cannot exit back to your conscious selves by walking."

"How do we—"

Before I can finish the question, he pulls a Brian Brown and swings his fist into the side of my head.

13

PRAXION

A trio of rockets twist through the air, headed for the Helion's flank, but they won't reach the biologic recreation in time to prevent Chirk and Sean from being crushed. And with Gemma in my hands, I can't do much to help.

But Sean isn't as incapable as he lets people think. He spreads his arms and legs, adding drag to his body, slowing their descent. It's not a lot, but it's enough.

The Helion slams into the granite mountainside, shaking snow loose from tree branches for five hundred feet in every direction. The shockwave slows Sean and Chirk a little bit more, and nearly knocks me off my feet. If not for Harth's steadying hand on my back, I might have fallen.

The Helion recovers from the hard landing quickly, rising onto its six stubby legs, its back to us. A moment later, Chirk lies down on Sean's chest, mini-railguns aimed toward the sky. "Full speed ahead! Let's unzip this asshole!"

Sean pulls his arms and legs in again and the pair quickly gain speed, sliding between the Helion's limbs and beneath its several-ton body. Had it known they were there, it would have crushed them, but the beast is in its most vulnerable state in the seconds after an atmospheric insertion.

I'm struck by a thought. This isn't the first Helion we've faced since arriving on Earth, including several biologics and a single member of their original species. But we have yet to question where they're coming from. Helions are dropped from orbit, capable of landing in a battlefield like a meteor. We've been efficient at destroying them thus far. They learn and adapt from each attack, but we are never short of novel ways to destroy things. If we could discover where the Helions are being deployed, and take it out, we wouldn't have to worry about them suddenly arriving in the middle of a fight...or a retreat.

Chirk and Sean disappear beneath the Helion. I hold my breath for a moment and then sigh with relief as a line of shrapnel explodes up out of the Helion. Chirk is unloading a full-auto line of high-power shards straight through the beast's core.

A moment later, the trio of rockets strike.

The Helion cracks open like an egg, each side falling away to reveal the metallic insides of a biologic beast. While unliving, the biomechanical creation is full of slick internal components that fill the air with a rancid stink.

"Oh, god," Gemma says in my ear, "I think I'm going to puke."

I run straight through the middle of the two halves, blue sparks showering all around us, Harth directly on my heels. "Please don't."

When I clear the Helion's corpse, I'm able to see down the slope once more and find Sean and Chirk still sliding, nearly at the bottom. I slide to a stop at the slope's precipice. When I look back at the shredded panels hanging from the Helion's body, Harth tracks my line of thinking and extends one of his Incinerator blades.

With a quick swipe, he severs a panel large enough for the three of us and lets it fall on the snow.

"Seriously?" Gemma asks. "We're sledding?"

"Improvisation has saved more lives on the battlefield than direct confrontation," Harth says. "Get on."

I motion for Gemma to do as he says, and she climbs onto the sled. When she's in place, I climb on behind her, wrapping my legs around her hips.

Behind us, the ruined Helion starts to crackle. The blue sparking increases. Arcs of electricity flow between the two halves. "It's going to explode."

Harth thumps down onto the makeshift sled, his weightlifting both Gemma and I slightly off the ground. Then he tries to shove us forward. We wiggle, but don't move.

"We're stuck," he says.

"Together," I say, pushing my body forward rhythmically. If Chirk were here, he'd have a joke to make. Gemma joins in like she's done this before. Sledding is a human winter pastime introduced to us by Sean. They do it for fun. For Kynolari, it is a necessary tool for frigid mountainous regions—though our sleds are generally covered by a protective shell and can be stopped on command.

Harth grunts and digs in, pulling us forward as we shove our weight forward. Again. And again.

Behind us, a high-pitched whirring builds in volume, drowning out the crack of trees falling, the boom of rockets, and the twang of lasers cutting through the mountainside.

We reach a tipping point where the sled is wobbling. "Now!" I shout, pushing forward with Gemma. Harth pushes hard, and we're free, plummeting three feet—before the Helion explodes.

The mountainside protects us from the debris and the white-hot flames that erupt from the body, but the shockwave still slaps into us from behind. We're propelled like a rail shard, streaking down the mountainside.

To our right, a lone Fury and Hound emerge from the forest. While the Hound's charge will fall far short, the Fury pauses to take aim. He's calm. They're always calm. They stride with eternal confidence, unconcerned about their own mortality. Usually cloaked in black, their humanoid bodies hidden from view. Their pale, hairless faces are concealed by shadow beneath the hood. They are notorious marksmen, rarely missing a shot, stationary or plummeting downhill.

But I don't worry.

The Fury and Hound have exposed themselves, and no matter how fast the hunter can take aim and pull his trigger, it will never be faster than the speed of light.

A powerful beam scorches the terrain behind us, leaving a streak of rising steam in its wake. A blink later, the Fury has a clean-cut, fist-sized hole where his heart used to be. He faceplants into the snow, and slides downhill behind the Hound, which finds itself on the receiving end of a railgun fusillade. The creature is shredding apart, its body folding in on itself on one side and emerging from the far side as tiny, slivered particles. In an instant, there is almost nothing left of it.

Clear of the danger, I start to feel a very human sense of the thrill. The close call has my adrenaline rushing, my senses heightened. It feels…amazing. A smile creeps onto my face as we build speed and start gaining on Chirk and Sean, who are now on foot and running through the snow covered forest ahead.

We enter the trees at a breakneck pace, foliage passing by as a blur.

And then, directly ahead, a tree. A powerful pine that will not move, nor notice us collide with it.

"Lean to steer!" Gemma shouts. "Left!"

We all lean left, and the makeshift sled veers away from the tree.

"Right!" she shouts, pulling us back on track.

A moment later, we cruise past Chirk and Sean.

"What the!" Chirk shouts. "Hey, get bac…" His voice fades behind us.

Harth finds the momentary encounter so funny he lets out a booming laugh that becomes a genuine howl. He clamps his mouth shut, embarrassed by the momentary lack of stoicism.

We slide to a casual stop after covering half the distance to the *Prowler*, which should be nearly ready for lift off.

"Talon-Actual, Talon-Two, report," I say, sensing Gruunlokar nearby, but unable to peg his exact position. He's so practiced at stealth that even our connection via the regulators isn't enough for me to find him.

When he clears his throat, it's not through the comms, it's from above. I look up to find him near the top of a hundred-foot pine that's seen better days. He's aiming back the way we came, from which Chirk and Sean are still approaching.

"Recommend immediate evac," he says.

"What are you seeing?"

"Helions inbound. Too many to fight. More Furies and Hounds. And a man. Top of the mountain to the north. Staying out of range. Looks like he's wearing a torn black cape...and the snow isn't hitting him."

That last bit was all I needed to hear. Draun often use their telekinetic abilities to keep the elements at bay. He's probably dry and warm inside his little bubble. "Put a hole in him."

"Copy that," Gruunlokar says, taking aim. His gauntlet is connected to his eyes via his regulators. There's no need to look down a gun scope. He sees what the 1H1K Void Sniper gauntlet does.

His arm twitches when the long-range shard leaves the barrel at three thousand miles per second. A moment later, Gruunlokar grunts. Then he slides down the limbless tree, slowing his descent using his claws. When he lands in the snow beside us, he says, "I missed."

"You *don't* miss," Harth says.

"I do when there is a strong enough repelling force," he says. "Whoever that is, he's powerful. And I think he's offended. He's en route now."

"The Visionary?" I ask.

He shakes his head. "I know *his* face. Put a hole in it. I'll know him when I see him again."

"I've said it before," Chirk says, running toward us all fours. He's leaping up and back into the snow, vaulting each step forward. Looks like a lot of work. "And I'll say it again, I hate snow."

Sean arrives next, winded. He leans against a tree. "Guys..." Deep breath. "Guys... that...was awesome. You were, like...so fast."

"It was," Harth says. "Awesome."

"Yeah, yeah, yeah," Chirk says. "I pilot a spaceship across the universe in the same amount of time. Let's get moving." He hops into Sean's arms and then slides into the carrier. "*¡Date prisa, vete!*"

"I don't know how fast I can go," Sean says, still trying to catch his breath.

Harth lifts Sean by the back of his jacket like he's a suitcase. "I will carry them both."

I give a nod and scoop up Gemma. Then we're off, sprinting through the forest, pursued by a superior force bent on our destruction. And if the Draun man reaches us before we're halfway to orbit, the start of this new Great War might end on the same land on which it began.

"Prowler-One," I say into my comms, trying to sound calm. "Have the ship hovering in the next thirty seconds. Draun incoming."

"Oh," Baarfolir says. "Oh, dear. That is dreadful."

"Just do it," I say.

"Yes, sir," he says. "Antigrav drive is coming online now. Hatch is open. We are prepared to receive you and ready to leave."

"Any word on Micah and Grover?" I ask.

"Nothing yet, but I—" In the background I hear a scream. Human. Male. *Micah.* A moment later, Baarfolir's comms go silent.

"Faster!" I shout, digging my claws into the snow and the frozen earth beneath it. "The *Prowler* is under attack!"

14

MICAH

I scream, loud and feral, in a way that would normally embarrass me, but I've just been cudgeled by an ancient Egyptian god and sent to some hellish abyss that propels me toward a burning-hot, white light.

Muscles contract as I slam back into my body, launching me upward, still blinded and confused. Claws dig into my shoulders and shove me back, pinning me down as I fight for freedom.

A voice shouts at me, distorted and vague.

Is it angry?

Come to drag me into the depths?

I won't go down without a fight.

Then a word slips through.

"Micah!"

My name. And the voice: "J-Jess?"

"I'm here." I feel her hand on my arm.

"Just relax, Micah. You're back. Confused, but back." Torel. She's holding me down. It's her claws I can feel.

"Grover?" I ask.

"Waking," she says. "Slower than you."

I blink and my vision starts to return. Torel is a fuzzy black, white, and brown blur leaning over me. She shines a pen light in both of my eyes. "Bet you can't see shit," she says. "I'll see what I can do."

She tilts my head to the side, adjusting the regulator on the side of my head. A brown blob comes into view. I smile at Jess and say, "You look like a blurry poop."

"You see?" Jess says to Torel. "I told you. A true romantic, this one. Always knows exactly how to get me to drop my pants."

I chuckle. Torel puts pressure on my head. "Hold still."

"So, you guys were talking romance, huh?" There's a surge of energy from the side of my head, a lance of pain, and then my vision clears.

"No," Torel says, leaving no wiggle room to continue my line of questioning. "Can you see now?"

I turn my gaze toward her, noting the raised eyebrows, wrinkled forehead, and unflinching eye contact that says, 'Not another word about romance.'

"Perfectly," I say.

"Good." She disconnects a cable attached to my regulator that was hooked up to a Kynolari tablet before stepping over to Grover, who's lying still on the table beside me.

I try pushing myself up, but don't make it very far. Jess catches me, carrying the weight that I, for some reason, am struggling to lift. "Take it easy."

"Did I wrestle an elephant while I was sleeping?" I ask.

"It looked like it," Torel says. "Your body was reacting to whatever you experienced while you were under. Your muscles contracted and spasmed. Your heart rate increased. Had I just been watching your vitals, I'd have assumed you were in combat."

"Kind of was," I say, pushing my hands into the tableside, trying to support my weight on my own. I twist my neck back and forth. Lean back to stretch. And yawn. Mouth agape, I notice both women silently watching me. "Oh, sorry." I finish the yawn. "Right. Yeah, Anbu. Kind of an ass. But we found him. Trouble is, he didn't really foresee this potential future at the time his consciousness was transferred into doggy DNA. He recommended we find him...again. In the real world."

"Did he give you a location?" Torel asks.

"Two," I say. "But both are guesses. He had no knowledge of his life past his time in Egypt as Anubis. If he remained there, he would have been buried in a secret chamber beneath the Great Pyramid. The good news is that Grover and I just met with him there. Shouldn't be hard to find. The second location is a little more... vague. But I should be able to point it out on a map."

"Good," Torel says, with a curt nod. "Later."

"Something wrong?" I ask.

Before anyone can answer, Baarfolir dive rolls into the lab and comes up with some kind of weapon in his hand. He aims it back and forth, gasping with each movement. Then he stops, realizes there is no one to shoot, and says, "I'm sorry. I heard screaming. It sounded like—"

"Like I got my head bashed in?" I ask.

"Well, yes. Just like that."

"Apparently," Torel says. "Humans scream upon waking up from a bad dream."

"It was more than a dream," I grumble.

"Whereas Kynolari..." She motions to Grover as he calmly lifts his head, looks around the room, and parts his lips to calmly pant.

He looks over at me. "Love Micah."

"Love you, too, bud. Thanks for having my back in there." I hobble my way over to him and hold his head over his ears and place my forehead against his.

My body relaxes and my frazzled nerves, twanging like a banjo, smooth out. He leans back and gives my chin a lick.

"Uhh," Baarfolir says. "Sorry to interrupt, but we, ahh, we are still under assault. The *Prowler* is now hovering and prepped for evac. Hatch is open to receive—"

"Where is Praxion?" Torel asks.

"En route," Baarfolir says.

"Back to the controls," she barks at the small Kynolari. "Do *not* lift off until I tell you."

"O-ok," he says, backtracking out of the room.

Torel turns to me, her doctor's eyes replaced by those of a warrior. "Can you fight, Axiom?"

Using my prophetic title is meant to be a reminder that they have put their hopes in me, that I'm expected to rise above and beyond…even if I did just wake from some kind of near death experience.

The mental connection provided by my regulators allows me to activate my twin gauntlets with a thought. A moment later, they charge to full power. I still feel unsteady on my legs, but if I have to sit down and shoot, I will.

She turns to Jess. "Ready to earn your gauntlet?"

"Haven't been practicing for nothing," Jess says, her gauntlet extending out over her arm. "Also, it's called a Stinger." When Torel raises a skeptical eyebrow, Jess adds, "Hey, if Micah gets to name his 'Hell Hounds'…"

Torel concedes by raising her hands and shaking her head. "Humans."

At the time, I thought Jess's choice in gauntlet was strange, but having seen her use it in the forest, I understand the appeal. Her primary weapon is a grappling hook. It has an impressive range—three hundred feet—and can yank her all around like Spiderman, but its offensive capabilities caught me off guard. She can electrocute with the power of Torel's Lancer or heat the cable to the temperature of Harth's Incinerator. But she can also retract the cable, violently, creating enough friction to cut through anything it might be wrapped around, or yank a target off its feet. She's only fought against trees so far, but she has a lot of potential, especially since Harth built her some shock absorbent boots that allow her to survive more fall damage than the average squirrel.

Which is a lot.

But only if she lands feet first.

"You good, bud?" I ask Grover.

He scrambles to his feet, panting. "Okay."

"I want you in the cockpit with Baarfolir."

He holds his breath for a moment, protesting the request.

"There's a treat in it for you, if you do."

His ears perk up. He holds his breath. The mental debate of a genius plays out before us like an epic heraldic adventure. Then he starts panting again.

"Okay."

I help him down from the table and give him two quick pats that send him on his way. We've spent enough time on the *Prowler* for him to know his way. We follow him out of the lab, and when he turns left, we go right, toward a hatch to the frozen outdoors.

Distant explosions rock the mountainside. The crack of falling trees is mixed in. Sounds like the drum section of a marching band made up of two-year-olds on sugar highs.

"The hell is happening out there?" I ask.

"Draun," Torel says.

"How many attackers?" I ask.

"Enough to scare Praxion."

I'm not exactly sure what it takes to frighten the Kynolari team leader, but I've seen him face down what seemed like insurmountable odds without flinching. There's either an army on the way, or—I glance at Torel—his stakes have been raised and he's feeling fear in a way he's not yet accustomed to.

At the bottom of the hatch, we hop down into the foot deep snow, and wait.

"ETA?" Torel asks through her comms.

"Thirty seconds," a breathless Praxion says.

"Direction?" I ask.

"From the west," Praxion says.

"Wait here," I tell Jess and Torel, stepping into the trees.

"This is not the time for human male bravado," Torel says.

"It's not bravado," I tell her and then give her a smile. "I'm the Axiom."

She frowns but knows she can't argue the point. And she won't, because Praxion's life is on the line. Jess doesn't bother, either. She's either okay with me going or knows she can't stop me.

I break into a run. Should reach the others in ten seconds.

I hear them in five, their feet crunching in the snow. Just three sets of footsteps, though. Should be five, or four, if Sean is carrying Chirk. When they come into view, it all becomes clear. Sean is carrying Chirk, but Sean is being carried by Harth. And Praxion has a woman I don't recognize. She's not a neighbor. Not a local either. Small town means I know just about everyone.

I skid to a stop, thick snow rolling up and over my boots. "Which direction?"

Praxion glances at my charged gauntlets and understands the purpose of my request. "West. Not far behind."

"Any friendlies?" I ask.

"None," Praxion says.

"What about deer?" Sean asks, his voice bouncing with each of Harth's long strides. "Or moose?"

"Collateral damage is unavoidable," Harth says.

I build power as they pass. The woman watches me with wide eyes, staring at the orange light blooming from my arms. I see her mouth the words, "What…the… fuck…" and then they're past.

"Here we go," I say. "Sorry mom and dad."

A wave of orange laser light blasts from both hands, the sustained beam cutting through the forest. The twin arcs slice through trees, boil snow, and dig troughs in the mountainside as I sweep my arms back and forth, hoping to cut down whatever is close, and anything that might be coming behind it.

Trees topple all around, swooshing and crashing down. I cut through them at the speed of light, from my position to a mile away. The sound of a thousand falling pines breaks my heart and clears my view.

From here to the mountainside, I see nothing.

Then a shadow falls over me.

I look up in time to see a man falling from the sky, but I don't have time to get out of his way.

15

MICAH

I'm struck, but it's not by a fist or a foot or anything easily recognizable. It's a force, like an explosion's pressure wave, but directed toward me. I'm lifted off the ground and tossed.

The good news is that I'm still conscious. The bad news is that I've been flung toward a portion of forest that's still standing. With each flip, I see a thick pine tree growing closer. I do what I can to control the spin and reach out with my claws.

My body misses the trunk.

Gauntlet claws dig deep into jagged bark.

For a moment, I think I might survive the attack largely unscathed. Then physics does its thing. As the gauntlets yank the top of my body to a stop, momentum carries my lower half around the tree. My gut slaps against the trunk, knocking the air from my lungs. I hit hard enough that the impact wrenches my claws free.

I'm flung back the way I came, spinning away from the tree like a helicopter blade that's come loose. The snow on the ground softens my landing, but I'm already in so much pain I don't realize I've landed until the snow starts stinging my face.

I force my head up. The Draun stands with his back to me, ripped cape flowing in the wind. He stands with confidence. Like a soldier. His hands are outstretched toward the *Prowler*—holding the ship in place.

Still catching my breath, I activate my comms and say, "Talon-Actual, Badass-One, when I hit back, take the *Prowler* and get the hell out of here."

"Dumbass-One, Badass-Two," Jess says. "The hell we will."

"If we lose the *Prowler*," I say, "We lose everything."

"He's right," Harth adds.

"Praxion," I say, breaking comms protocols with everyone else. "Site 1. Grover can show you the way. Site 2…" With a thought, I activate the small screen on my forearm, bring up a digital world map, and focus on the instinct implanted by Anbu. I swipe across America to the west, and then south, past Mexico City. I stop, staring at a part of the world that I've never been to, but feel intimately connected to. I zoom in to what is now known as Parque Nacional Cumbres del Ajusco. When I reach the base of a single mountain, I capture the coordinates and send them to Praxion.

"Site 2, coming to you now."

"Received," Praxion says. "Are you sure?"

"I'll take care of this guy and find my way back to you at the location I've just sent." I push myself up onto my knees. "When I get his attention, you go. Copy?"

"I'm not..." Praxion is hesitating. His short time on Earth has softened his willingness to make sacrifices. Might not be a bad thing in general, but right now it's the necessary thing.

"If I'm what you think I am, I can handle this," I say. "You either believe I'm the Axiom or you don't. Time to test that faith, big guy."

"Micah," Jess says, less confident about this Axiom stuff, "don't."

"Don't worry, babe," I say. "I got this."

I try to put a lot of confidence behind the statement, but it still comes out sounding forced.

"Talon-Actual, Prowler-One," Praxion says, "full thrust on my mark."

I push myself up onto my feet, the snow around me reflecting the bright orange glow emanating from my fully charged gauntlets.

Since I'm not above hitting an asshole from behind, I extend both arms and unleash a full-strength blast from both hands. Visually, it's a little like Cyclops's 'Mega Optic Blast' move in *Marvel vs. Capcom*, except orange. Normally, it leaves a swath of destruction in its wake. This time, it strikes an invisible sphere that reflects the energy up and around my target.

Above, the *Prowler*'s thrusters roar as the ship attempts to break free from the Draun's telekinetic grasp.

C'mon, I think, growing tired. I can recharge my gauntlets at will, but that doesn't mean the effort doesn't take a lot out of me. And I'm still human. Still need to eat, sleep, and breathe. And while I don't have any broken bones from my wrap-around-tree maneuver, I'm going to be aching for weeks.

I double my efforts, screaming as I keep the gauntlets at full charge by sheer force of will. No way this guy is stronger than Jenna. She was next in line behind the Visionary, and I don't think this is him.

The wall of telekinetic energy holding back my blast wavers.

The *Prowler* lifts off, streaking into the sky, far out of reach in the blink of an eye.

My target is flung, cracking through several trees before striking the mountainside, where a cloud of pulverized dust explodes into the air.

Okay, if that didn't kill him...

The swirling dust parts around an invisible sphere.

Inside, the man floats casually toward me, his cape slightly more tattered, but he's otherwise uninjured. His features become clearer as he approaches.

Long black hair. Thick, but trimmed beard. Weathered skin. His expression is grim, but he lacks emotion. He's on a mission. Nothing personal. An operator.

And that's when I recognize him, past the beard and hair.

"Kern?"

His approach stalls.

"Isaac Kern?"

He squints for a moment. Then his eyes widen with recognition. "*Taylor?* There you are."

It's been four years since I last saw Sergeant Isaac Kern, during what would become my last deployment. He was a good soldier. A quality leader. Didn't mind getting his hands dirty. A solid operator.

But now...

"I'll be damned," he says, landing on the ground, his guard down. "The hell you hit me with?" He glances at the gauntlets on my arms and huffs a laugh. "Gone are the days of reloading magazines, huh?"

"Yeah..."

"Sorry to see you joined the wrong side of this," he says. "Would have been fun working together again."

"At least I had a choice," I say.

"Why is that?" he asks. "We've been trying to figure it out. What makes some of you different? I mean, *you* I get. Always were stubborn, and now that I see who you're hanging out with? Makes all kinds of..."

He's figuring it out.

He grins. "No... C'mon, it can't be that simple. You were always a dog-guy. Had photos of them on deployment. Your mother sent you dog-shaped cookies once. How is the old lady? Not on the losing side, I hope."

"Dead," I say.

He shrugs. "Meh. Lot of that going around. Sure you don't want to be on the side doing the killing? I know you don't like losing."

"Don't know how," I say, which gets a laugh out of him and gives me a few extra seconds to figure out how I'm going to beat him.

How I'm going to kill him.

Not sure how to get past his telekinetic shield, but it's got to take energy to maintain. Just like my gauntlets take a toll when I use them a lot. But we could level a few mountains and a nearby town or two before that happens. And from what I've heard—and seen—there's not a whole lot I can do to shield myself from getting my head burst open. Kern hasn't been a Draun that long, though. Maybe he hasn't learned all the tricks yet.

Head on tactics aren't going to work, I decide.

Subterfuge it is.

"But you're right…I don't like to lose. As much as I like dogs, these…aliens, man. I don't trust them. I saw what you saw. But I didn't know…I didn't know who to believe. You're the first person I've seen that I trust."

He sizes me up, eyes narrowed. "Still time to be born again, brother. Really don't want to kill you."

"How do I do that?" I ask, letting my fully charged gauntlets drain of energy. The orange band on the outside is a very clear indicator that I'm standing down.

He smiles. "Just open your mind and heart. If you're capable of the change, he'll find you."

"Lumen Sok," I say. "The Visionary."

"Crazy, right? Here all this time. Thought the guy was a loon. But now…hell, his people *made* us. And once we're done here? On Earth? We're going out there. Fuck, man. Telekinetic, intergalactic space marines."

"And what are you?" I ask. "To him? Still a grunt?"

He chuckles. "General, actually. This was my first solo gig, though. And you kind of fucked that up. Not going to look good. But if I can bring *you* back, on the right side of this, I think he'll forgive me."

"He knows who I am?"

"Brother, we *all* know who you are. After Denver? After what you did to Commander Flood? She was important to him. Was meant to be our future leader. The mind dump on the day of awakening was followed up by an update about you, and those Kynolari assholes. Honestly, I wasn't that upset about it. Jenna was in my way. Won't be long before I'm second in line. And then…who knows? Maybe I'll be top dog—ha! Top dog. Hysterical. Anyway, get on your knees, close your eyes, and say a prayer to Lumen Sok. If he hears you…and accepts you, we're cool. If not, well, I'll make it quick."

16

CHIRK

"Lie back in your seats and hold on to your teats!" I say before throwing the *Prowler* into a roll that keeps us from crashing into an oncoming winged biologic.

"Was that a pterodactyl?" Sean shouts as we narrowly miss a head on collision.

The winged creature is unfamiliar to me, but it has massive, outstretched wings and a head shaped like...well, I don't know. I can't conceive of any other creature in the universe with such a ridiculously shaped head. Probably a counterbalance of some kind...or evolution gone awry. It happens.

A second bizarre beast swoops around and comes in for a head on collision. "Holy shit, they're kamikaze pterodactyls!"

"I don't know what a pterodactyl is," I say, "but feel free to take a gunner's station and shoot the shit out of them."

Harth has just finished buckling himself in at the first station. Sean stumbles to the second but manages to strap himself down just moments before I roll the other way.

Gruunlokar steps onto the bridge, catches himself, and looks toward his gunner's station, currently occupied by Sean. "The fuck is this?" he asks.

"Sean's working on becoming a competent gunner," I say.

"Sup, dude!" Sean extends a hand to the side and gives a thumbs up.

"Wonderful," Gruunlokar says, deadpan. "I'm taking a nap. Someone wake me up when there is someone to kill or we're dead."

He exits the bridge just as calmly as he entered.

"He didn't say 'yes,'" Sean whispers at me.

"But he didn't say 'no!'" I respond. "That's basically a 'yes' in Gruunlokar. Just shoot some shit, okay? And no puking this time! Took a month to get your stink out."

"You said it didn't bother you," he says.

"It didn't!" I shout, "*That's* what bothers me!"

I put us into a steep climb that will take us out of the valley and into the open sky. The moment we rise above the forest canopy, all hell breaks loose. Biologics come streaming from every direction. Our perimeter lights them up but makes flying low to the ground impossible. Rockets, lasers, shards, and god damn pterodactyls in every direction.

"Sean," I say. "Do pterodactyls usually fire a barrage of rockets?"

Sean fires a fusillade. "Naw, man. They're extinct. Like, for millions of years."

"Like *Jurassic Park* extinct?" I ask.

"Yeah, dude," Sean says. "Exactly. They were dinosaurs."

"I do not remember these creatures in that movie," Harth says, firing away.

"That's because we still need to watch the sequels," Sean says. "Got one! What are you up to, Harth?"

"Seventeen," Harth says. "But...good job."

Harth used to be harder on Sean. Big guy has high standards for who we let fire our weapons, but he's made an exception with Sean. I know he's doing it for me, but that I didn't need to ask him means a lot.

"Deploying countermeasure," I say, watching the number of targets directly behind us suddenly blossom from five to thirty. Five rockets from each. *At least they're not lasers,* I think, before all twenty-five projectiles explode in a hail of oxium chaff ejected from the *Prowler*'s ass end.

Praxion drags himself into the cockpit and takes a seat beside me.

"Everyone locked down?" I ask.

He looks unsure about it, but then gives the order I've been waiting for. "Go for Nautilus."

The name comes from some kind of book that Praxion read during his downtime. Involved some kind of submersible vessel, which is funny, because where we're from, all vessels are transmedium, meaning they can operate in multiple environments, pressure and friction be damned. A vacuum, an atmosphere, an ocean—doesn't really matter to the *Prowler*.

But biologics...they're not that advanced.

We already know the oceans of this world are the best places to hide. They are vast and deep and largely impenetrable. Even if the Visionary has access to Earth's most powerful submarines, we'll be invisible, and far too deep. Their torpedoes would implode long before reaching us, and we'd have to be sitting still, and asleep, for them to have any chance of that.

So, I bank up and toward the coast, which I can already see. Behind us, the cloud of pterodactyls fades into the distance as I accelerate. But the attack is far from over. Lumen Sok once again employs his most powerful weaponry—his orbiting array of satellites, deployed under the guise of Internet for everyone, but which are also capable of redirecting ground-based laser systems.

I take an erratic and hopefully unpredictable path toward the coast. No idea how many laser blasts I'm avoiding, but I'm fully aware of how many times we've been hit. Twenty-three and counting. Each strike is recorded. Its location, its power level, and the damage caused—even if it's just a scratch. Luckily, we've been preparing for this eventuality, applying a mirror finish to the hull above the ship's most vital systems.

The *Prowler* is taking a beating, but she's going to keep on flying. The number of strikes suggests that the Visionary has been bolstering his orbital array. I don't know if that means more satellites or more laser arrays. Probably both. But we're going to need to keep our exposure time at a minimum or we're going to have a few new skylights that will absolutely let some high-pressure water in through the cracks.

I dive down to the surface as we approach a small city called Portsmouth. I cruise low, between tall brick hotels that shield us from the lasers. The buildings burst apart behind us.

Sean sees it and says, "Whoa," before looking forward and seeing the next building we're set to fly past. "Not the church!"

But it's too late to change course. A beam of energy slices through the steeple atop the house of worship. It topples to the side in front of us. I dip down, scraping the street beneath us. The steeple crashes down behind us, filling the street and smashing storefronts on the road's far side.

I feel bad about the mess we're leaving in our wake. There's going to be a body count behind us, and if someone yanked out a smartphone, there could be video of the 'accursed Kynolari' leveling a town full of innocents. Pure propaganda fodder. Might even speed up conversion rates.

We clear the city a blink later, take two more hard hits, and then plunge into the Atlantic Ocean. The grade is casual, taking some time to get significantly deep, but the water protects us from the Visionary's weapons—orbital and pterodactyl.

"Nice flying," Praxion says, unbuckling and patting my shoulder.

"Should have been better," I grumble. "I'm out of practice."

"We all are," he says.

Sean spins around from his gunner's terminal and says, "Right, so, when are we going to pick up Micah?"

"Can't go back," Praxion says.

"The hell we can't," Sean says. "We just need to be sneaky and shit, or at least ready for the fight. They caught us with our pants to our ankles, bent over a barrel, like a back-alley strumpet."

We just stare at him for a moment.

"Right," I say. "But...buddy...if we go back there, we're dead."

"But Micah..."

"Can take care of himself," Praxion says, eyes downcast. "He made his choice and, if he is the Axiom, he will survive."

"And if he doesn't?" Sean asks.

"Then we've already lost." Praxion sighs, looking like he's holding the moon on his shoulders. "Take us deep and set a course for Mexico. I want everyone in ops in five minutes."

"What's the plan?" Harth asks.

"Two strike teams. One in Mexico. One in Egypt. Find Anbu and hope he can help...or that he left something behind that can."

"On it," I say with a nod, turning back to the controls and laying in a course that will take us to the Mexican coastline without ever coming up for air.

Praxion departs without another word, leaving the scent of angst in the cockpit. Micah made the request to stay, but it was Praxion who allowed it. Who ordered us to leave. If Micah doesn't make it, Prax will take the blame. There was a time when he made calls like this and it didn't faze him. Soldiers died. Sometimes because he put them in harm's way. But this feels different. And not just because we don't have a million more soldiers to replace Micah if he doesn't make it.

He's not just an ally. He's a friend. Part of the team. And from what I've seen, he's an example of what makes humanity's enslavement of the Lost Tribe forgivable.

"Have you done this before?" Sean asks, voice quiet.

"Done what?" I ask. "We just did a lot."

"Leave someone."

"It happens," Harth says, "but...this is different." He turns to face Sean. "In combat, a soldier might be left behind for several reasons. First and most obvious: he's dead. Second, he's been captured with no hope of immediate rescue. Third, he's *injured* with no hope of immediate rescue. Fourth, he is incompetent and not worth saving."

Sean stares, in shock.

Harth cracks a grin.

"Ahaa!" I point at Sean. "He got you! You should have seen your face." I do what I hope is a very insulting impression of Sean's shocked face, eyes wide, mouth hanging stupidly open.

Sean chuckles. "Yeah, you did."

"There is no need for a fourth category. Incompetent soldiers usually die before a battle is over." Harth says, and Sean laughs a little more.

Harth raises a single brow. "That...wasn't a joke."

"Oh," Sean says. "Right." He looks up, putting on what he calls 'puppy eyes.' I guess I can see it. "But Micah..."

"Is powerful," Harth says, and he's not lying. "A soldier of the highest order. If anyone can prevail in that dire situation, it is him."

Sean shakes his head. "All by himself?"

Harth raises his second brow, and then squints. "Micah is *not* alone."

17

MICAH

When I was ten, my best friend was Zach Mohr. He had a traditional family that did traditional things. Every holiday was decorated and celebrated. Barbeque pool parties were common. Basically, they were a good time, all the time. So, when I was invited to something called, 'VBS' I said 'yes' without even asking what it was. All I knew was that there were other kids going, it was supposed to be fun, and it was two hours a day for two weeks.

The only moment of doubt about attending came when my mother scrunched her nose at the idea and asked, "Are you sure?"

My faith in Zach was severely tested, starting on day one, when I was welcomed to Vacation Bible School, three words that do not belong together. The next two weeks were spent in a hot, dusty garage, working on Bible-themed arts and crafts, being told stories about old, dead people—or not, if you believe it—and being sustained on Nilla Wafers, Freeze Pops, and penny flavored water. By the end of two weeks, I had a completed popsicle-stick bird house and a new definition of torture.

That was my first experience with any real kind of faith. My impression was that some people loved that Jesus guy so much that they'd endure summertime torture for weeks on end.

What I've asked of Praxion is a lot more severe. The consequences of failure to live up to his belief could result in the end of humanity as we know it. But to pull it off, I need to have faith—real faith, in the impossible, and in myself.

Starting with surviving Kern, my former teammate turned Draun.

Destroyer of worlds.

I pluck some freshly returned memories from VBS, bow my head, and spew a phony prayer to Lumen Sok. "Dear Visionary, hear my prayer. Great is thy power. Give me the wisdom to make good decisions, and please…forgive me for my transgressions. For the…violence in Denver."

Kern fake coughs signifying that this isn't nearly enough.

"For the…murder…slaughter…uh, war crimes I committed in the name of thine enemy, the filthy Kynolari."

I feel a little awkward saying all of this. Not only am I bullshitting, I'm really just filling the air with sounds to buy time.

Because in the recesses of my mind, I'm running through various tactics, attacks, and contingencies that might help me survive this mess. Kern is protected by his telekinetic shield. I can feel it between us, like a wall of static. Anything I manage to fire his way is just going to ricochet.

And then my head will burst.

Or he'll break my limbs, crush my gauntlets, and take his time.

The old Kern would have followed through on his promise to make it quick. He was honorable. But now that he's Draun, I can't even trust that he'd kill me well. The Draun take pleasure in pain—their own and that of others. They seek to dominate. To rule. To subjugate. They long for it the way a teenage boy in the 80s does a JiggleJuggs titty magazine. You know the kind. Kept in the woods. Buried in a metal lock box. Far from prying eyes. Irresistible.

That's my way out, I think. Not the titty mag, but the adulation.

I gasp and open my eyes.

Kern flinches. "What? Did you hear something?"

"Nothing," I say.

"Honestly, I didn't think you would, but it was fun to hear you tr... What are you doing?"

I shift my body around, facing Kern, still on my knees. "Realized I was praying to the wrong person." I bow my head and clasp my hands. "Almighty Kern, forgive my doubt. I turned to what I thought was a higher power when the true future of the Draun empire stands before me."

"What are you doing?" he says, sounding uncomfortable.

"You said it yourself," I say. "Top dog. The Visionary is great, but he's like..." I reach back through time and pull a nugget from VBS. "He's like John the Baptist, who said, 'He who is coming after me is mightier than I, whose, ahh, sandals I am not worthy to carry.' That's you. You are coming after. I don't need to be by *Lumen Sok's* side. I need to be by *yours.* To help usher in the future of the Draun empire."

He chuckles. Can't tell if he's buying it. If so, it means his hubris has overtaken his common sense and tactical discernment.

He waggles a finger toward me. "That's good. And I like it. But I see what you're doing, and it's not going to work."

"It could," I say.

"It's out of character for you, you know? On your knees, begging for forgiveness. For mercy. In fact, the Micah Taylor I knew would only do that for a solitary reason—to buy time. In the service of a con. To make some kind of play. Go out fighting, like some kind of Klingon or Viking, dying in combat, weapon in hand, ready to be whisked away to Valhalla or wherever the fuck Klingons go."

He cracks his neck one way, then the other. Raises his hands toward me. "Had me going for a second, but men like us don't beg. We either die on the battlefield, or we bide our time and take power. So, what will it be? You going to get to your feet and fight to live, or are you just going to sit there and let me build the pressure inside your head until it explodes?"

A stabbing headache behind my eyes punctuates the threat.

I run through my last-ditch options.

Direct attack.

Won't work because of the shield.

Indirect attack.

Cut down a tree and hope it falls on him. Shield is still a problem...unless he's just guarding his front. The Draun's telekinetic abilities have the same kinds of limitations as Kynolari gauntlets. Their energy is not infinite. They get tired. To conserve energy, he might only be shielding the space between us.

Tree won't work.

He'll hear it coming...and there aren't that many left standing.

Hole in the ground, I think. Directly beneath him and straight down as deep as I can dig. He falls in, I make a run for it. I'd like to think the pressure would crush him as he fell miles into the ground, but the same telekinesis that allows him to burst skulls also allows him to move through the air. He'd have no trouble surviving the fall.

I might only get a few seconds, but it will be enough. Propelled by the gauntlets, I can make good time. Get back to the house. To the truck and get the hell out of dodge the old-fashioned way. Would be tricky, given all the biologics swarming the property, but the sound of ongoing battle suggests that they're still dealing with the perimeter defenses that must have been assembled while I was visiting ancient Egypt inside Grover's head.

I lift my head to make a sarcastic last request, shifting my hands toward the ground at Kern's feet. In my head, I mentally count down from three, two, one... "I think I'll just—"

Hot, tacky wetness sprays across my face.

For a moment, I think he's preemptively popped my head, but the fact that I'm still thinking says otherwise. But I can taste blood in my mouth. Can feel it covering my face, dripping down my cheeks and over my eyes.

"The fuck?" I say, driving my hands into the snow and mashing it against my face. I scrub it around, feeling the burn as it melts to water and scours away the gore. Leaning to the side, I take a mouthful of snow, swish it around, and then spit the liquid and taste away.

I blink and look up at Kern.

He's still standing but staring down with a look of shock on his face, choking on his blood. His chest has been pierced from behind by what looks like an oversized arrowhead. I recognize the weapon and feel both dread and relief.

I lean to the side again, looking around him to find Jess, grappling cable stretched out between her Stinger and Kern's back. She has a disgusted look on her face. She's never killed somebody—that I know of. Never felt the guilt and shame that comes with it, even when it's a righteous kill. And this qualifies. When our eyes meet, she forces a smile and gives an apologetic wave.

"I'm sorry," she says. "I didn't know what else to do."

"Should have left with the others," I say, getting to my feet.

"You know what I mean," she says, letting me know she has no intention of apologizing for staying with me.

"I…will kill…you both," Kern says, blood oozing from the side of his mouth.

With a casual flick of the wrist, I attempt to Spider-Man a laser through the center of his forehead.

But it's deflected.

His telekinetic shield is still up.

I take a step back. "Hey, Chunks," I say, using one of my many pet names I have for her, 'Chunks' coming from her chunky bits. Sounds like an insult, I know, but she and I both know exactly which bits are chunky, and it's only the ones people like that way. "He's not dead…and I can't get to him."

I inspect the wound in his chest. It's coming out at an angle. Missed his spine. It's beneath his heart, between his lungs. Hell, with the right medical equipment, it could be survivable. It's the best worst shot in history. With his telekinetic abilities, he might even be able to hold his blood in. Plug the wound.

This fight isn't over.

"What can I do about it?" she asks, feeling the pressure of active combat.

"Give him everything you got," I say. "Don't hold back."

Her eyes widen with realization, then her face contorts with a mixture of hope and disgust—because we aren't defenseless, and because she has to kill him. Again.

Pressure builds behind my eyes.

She grunts in pain, too, holding her head with her free hand.

"Do it!" I shout, running away. "Do it now!"

My head feels ready to burst. Then I'm lifted off the ground and flung fifteen feet as a crackle fills the air. It's followed by a wave of intense heat and a muffled whump.

I hit the snow, slide a few feet, and roll over onto my back. "He dead?"

"Very," she says, sounding like she might puke.

I sit up and have a look for myself.

Surrounding a still-standing pair of smoldering boots is a paint spinner design in chunky dark red, the liquid already melting in and blending into the frozen terrain like Dracula's favorite snowcone.

"Gross," I say, and get to my feet.

The grappling hook's thin cable, which has super-heated itself clean, retracts into Jess's gauntlet. Stunned by what she's seen, she staggers over to me. I wrap my arms around her and say, "Thanks."

"He would have killed you," she says, and I can tell she's trying to justify what she just did.

"He would've," I say, admitting to myself that my escape plan wasn't going to work. Axiom or not, I am far from invincible. "And not in a fun way. You saved my life. I'm glad you stayed."

She sniffs and leans back, keeping her eyes diverted away from the gore. "Now what?"

"Now," I say. "We run."

18

PRAXION

I'm alone, and for the first time in a long time, I don't like it. I normally enjoy solitude. Time to reflect. To plot. But recent events have shifted my preferences toward communal living. To sharing space. Maybe a life.

It might just be the air on this world, but I find myself longing for comradery, comfort...and love.

I find it distracting, and rejuvenating. Throughout my career, I fought for the Kynolari. To protect and save my people from a horrible fate. My team has been with me throughout, but we were fighting beside each other then. Now, I fight for my friends. To protect them.

The bigger picture still exists. The human race. The Kynolari. But they are secondary motivators. Distant second and third place in a race for my attention.

The door to Ops melts away. Torel enters, looking tired.

She sits beside me and sighs, her body relaxing. "Been a day."

"A few," I say.

She casually places her hand atop mine, like it's something we do all the time. "We'll make it."

Something long dormant stirs in my gut.

I'm...nervous.

I don't get nervous. While others might soil themselves when standing on the precipice of a battle, I remain stoic. And yet, Torel has undone me with a touch.

"You okay?" she asks. "You look unwell."

"Not unwell," I say, and glance down at her hand. She follows my gaze and starts withdrawing her hand. "Sorry, I—"

I grab her hand, holding it in place, staring into her brown eyes. I smile. "It's like I've never seen you before."

She nods. "It is...strange."

"What if it is the air?" I ask.

"Then we should not leave this world."

My chest constricts. I have never spoken so plainly or intimately with anyone in my life. Before arriving on Earth, coupling with Torel never occurred to me. Sure, I admired her form. She is strong. Well-built. I could get lost in her coat...

I lean across the table's corner and kiss her, the way humans do, pressing my lips against hers. Our noses compress against each other, making us both laugh. We smile and separate.

"Perhaps kissing is best left to people with large lips?" I say.

She shrugs, "I kind of liked it."

Our noses are an inch apart when—

"Ahem."

It's Chirk.

I slow-turn toward the open door. It's everybody, including Gemma and Grover. Harth looks the most surprised. Chirk is a bit unfazed. Sean looks about ready to cheer, and I hope he doesn't.

Baarfolir raises a hand to his mouth. "Oh, my."

"This a bad time?" Chirk asks. "If there's some actual non-dry-humping about to go down, we can come back in, what? Thirty seconds?"

Torel grins and leans back, playing it off like a seasoned pro. "Thirty seconds? Isn't that the average time for your breed?"

"I'll have you know," he says, strutting into the room and hopping up into a chair beside Torel, "I went a full one-thirty-two with Bacon."

"One-thirty-two," Torel says. "Wow. I'm sure she was satisfied."

Chirk's jaw drops. "Are you suggesting that *I* don't know how to satisfy a woman? You know what?" He waves his hands in front of him. "No more hanky-panky talk about Bacon. I've already had one inappropriate erection today. I don't need to have another."

"Dude," Sean says, pulling out a chair for Gemma. "It's okay. I told you, it happens to all of us on this planet."

"I think I'm beginning to understand now why humans have so much trouble advancing as a civilization." Harth sits to my right. "They are preoccupied by matters of the flesh."

"Oh, yes," Baarfolir says, hopping up onto a seat and shuffling back into it. "The human preoccupation with copulation is evident in every culture going back to the very beginning of their historical records. It has caused wars, resulted in countless murders, and spawned endless violence. They are comparable to the Throngs of the Midragar Plains in that regard. They have *evolved* as sexual beings. Just look at the size of the female mammary glands." He leans forward and looks to Gemma. "Perhaps you could demonst—"

"Unnecessary," I say, knowing how earthlings feel about exposed breasts. Sean looks like he might pass out at the suggestion of seeing a pair. I don't understand the attraction, but then again, I didn't evolve on a sex-crazed planet. "And off topic."

"Of course, of course." Baarfolir folds his hands over his lap and settles in.

Grover sits between Torel and me, tongue hanging from the side of his mouth. He's relaxed but concerned. "Where Micah? Love Micah."

"He's...home," I say, hoping the simple answer will quash his line of questioning.

His ears perk up a little and his head angles to the side. "Micah safe?"

"Micah..."

"Micah is safe, honey." Torel takes Grover by the cheeks and scruffs up his face. He breathes heavily and gets wide excited eyes for a moment before chewing on Torel's hand. She leans in close and says, "Micah is strong. We will see him again soon. But right now, we need your help. Remember?"

"Anbu," he says. "Anbu, grumpy."

"We'll handle Anbu," I tell him. "We just need you to show us where he is," I turn to the gathered crew, "which is why we're all here."

A hand rises.

Gemma. "Who is Anbu?"

"Anubis," Sean blurts out. "But he's also known as Xylitol."

"Xolotl," Chirk corrects, "but you were close."

Gemma leans toward Sean and whispers, "Xylitol is sugar alcohol."

"You don't have to bother whispering," he says. "They can all hear you."

"Right," she says. "Because they're all dogs... Sorry, Kynolari. From space. Look, you all seem like you're in a rush, but can someone take like thirty seconds to break this all down for me...from your perspective? I wasn't sure what to think of the Draun message, other than it just felt wrong. But when I set out for answers, I really didn't expect to find...well, you."

"Okay, check it..." Sean's introduction is followed by a several minute long dramatic retelling by him and Chirk, covering the events that brought us to this point. By the end, Harth's patience has waned.

"We are halfway to our destination," he says, "and we have yet to discuss a plan."

"Anyway," Sean says. "The point is, Chirk and I are not just best buds, but we have kind of a symbiotic relationship. We each make the other better."

Gemma grins and says, "That's sweet."

Sean is thrilled by her response, but Chirk is not impressed. "Ain't nothing sweet about me, bitch."

"Uh, uh, uh!" Sean says, holding out his hands and turns to Gemma. "That's a literal word on their world. It's not derogatory."

Gemma squints at Chirk. "You sure about that? Because his tone was a little more like, 'Go make me a sandwich, woman!'"

"Enough!" Harth says, pounding a fist on the table. "No more talk of sandwiches. I am hungry enough as it is." He composes himself. "Please. Let's discuss our plans. Then you can talk all you want, and I can eat."

Since we are now short on time, and I could use a bite to eat myself, I lay it out as simply as possible.

"Harth, Chirk, Gruunlokar..." I scan the table. "Where is Gruunlokar?"

"Last I saw him he said he was taking a nap," Chirk says. "Said he didn't want to be woken up until we were dead or there was someone to kill. So, I ain't waking him up."

"And he was okay with me being a gunner," Sean adds, proud of himself.

"Did you hit anything?" I ask.

"One," he says.

I grunt.

"I will brief Gruunlokar when we arrive at our destination," Harth says, still eager to wrap this up.

I nod. "I want the three of you—"

Sean's hand goes up. I try to hide my burgeoning annoyance.

"What about us?" he asks, pointing at Gemma and himself.

"I think it would be wise for you to remain on board the *Prowler*," I say. "You have survived a lot, Sean, but I would feel—"

"He's coming," Chirk says. "He goes where I go."

"You see?" Sean whispers to Gemma. "Symbiotic."

Gemma raises her hand, and I can't help but lower my head and pinch the bridge of my nose. "Yes?"

"*Where* are we going?" she asks.

"Parque Nacional Cumbres del Ajusco," I say, using the park's original language.

"Just south of Mexico City," she says. "I've been. Two weeks hiking. Exploring ruins and the wildlife...wow. Hold on... *Xolotl*. The Aztec Xolotl? It makes sense, I guess. He was half dog, right? Was he one of you? Oh, and Teotihuacan, the heart of the Aztec empire was just north of the park." Her eyes widen. "Hold. On. *Anubis* was half dog. Well, jackal. But that's like potato-*potahto*."

Baarfolir turns to me, nodding. "All of that is correct. Perhaps her arrival was fortuitous."

"Right," Chirk says, pointing to Gemma, "she's coming with us."

I nod.

"Sean and Gemma, you will join Chirk, Harth, and Gruunlokar in search of...well, we're not exactly sure.

"Over the past decades, a number of ancient temples have been uncovered in Middle and South America. Pyramids as impressive as those in Egypt. After local populations were wiped out by war or plague, the structures were forgotten and overgrown. Now they just look like hills. I suspect Micah's coordinates will lead you to something similar."

"This...is awesome," Gemma says.

"Right?" Sean adds.

Their mutual enthusiasm is both endearing and nauseating.

"If Micah and Jess were able to—" Torel kicks me under the table. "*When* Micah and Jess...complete their task, they will attempt to rendezvous with you there."

"Aren't we all connected?" Sean says, activating his comms. "Yo, Micah. Dude. Sorry, Badass-One. You there?"

We wait a moment, but I already know there won't be a reply. "There was a comms blackout soon after we left, a common tactic of the Draun. Break up communication; sow chaos. Training and regulators help compensate for it. Hopefully, a local attack that will clear up as they head south. But there is no way to know for sure. The range depends on how many satellites the Visionary controls."

I clear my throat and continue. "Torel, Baarfolir, Grover, and I will venture to the Great Pyramid in Egypt to find out if Anbu's burial site matches what was seen in Grover's embedded knowledge. Our goal is to find something—anything—that will aid our fight against the Draun on this world. Understood?"

Nods all around. Even from Grover.

"Any questions?"

It's Harth's turn to raise his hand. He looks painfully serious. "Do we have mayonnaise on board?"

19

GRUUNLOKAR

The dream starts like all the rest. I'm standing on a small, curved beach framed by towering megalithic cliffs. The water ripples, reflecting the cosmos in the night sky above. Countless stars mingle with luminous pink nebula. The scene puts me at peace.

As it was meant to do.

I made this place years ago. A lucid sleep construction designed to relax and rejuvenate me far more than the average unconstrained dream.

Nightmares plagued my sleep for years.

Of battles.

Of the dead, both friend and foe.

But mostly I saw life through a scope, watching as a target's head burst like overripe fruit. Usually, their bodies would rag-doll to the ground, as those nearby screamed, or ran, or wiped the gore from their eyes. Sometimes the target's body would remain standing for a few seconds. On rare occasions, the body would continue with whatever task it was set to before the head was erased. Firing a weapon. Running a few steps. Giving a salute.

Those are the terrors that filled my nights.

A slide show of memories, twisted and distorted.

Pursued by the headless.

Covered in their blood.

Watching their babies cry.

That's why I learned how to control my dreams. How to rein them in. Mental discipline isn't just for the awake.

I sit in the sand, admiring the view. The air is cool and sweet. Water laps against the shoreline, sifting through the smooth stones.

Before I can lie on my back in meditation, an aberration swims into view.

Paddles, really.

A duck?

What is an Earth creature doing in my lucid dream? I am in control of this place. It contains only what I allow.

So how did this Earth creature find its way to my shore?

I watch it, both curious and annoyed.

It steps onto shore, waddles a few steps, and then shakes itself off and lets out a little quack. If it nestles down, I will ignore it. The aberration will not keep me from—

"Quack."

Irritating...

"Quack, quack."

It's looking at me now. Making eye contact. Is it trying to speak to me?

"Ducks do not speak," I tell it. "Leave this place. Now."

"Quack?"

"Ducks do not ask questions," I grumble, as it pads its way toward me.

I lie back, hands behind my head, eyes closed. If I ignore it, the duck should fade. The point of having a lucid dream is that you know you are dreaming and you have absolute control of the environment and—

"Quack."

I open my eyes.

It's standing above me. Staring.

"Who are you?" I ask it.

A whisper flows over my fur, carried by the breeze. "You know my name."

I sit up, forcing the duck to scramble away. The voice was distinctly not me. Meaning it did not come from my mind.

There is another consciousness in my dream.

"Quack."

I growl at the duck. "Is it you?"

"Quack, quack."

With a thought, a sword appears in my hand. "Show your true form!" I don't bother making a threat. The sword does that for me.

"Say my name." The voice is ethereal. From nowhere and everywhere.

It's not possible. Regulators protect the minds of all Kyno Corps operators. I might be asleep, but no one can get inside my mind.

Unless I allow it.

"Yes."

"No..." I backstep away from the duck. "You're dead."

"My name..."

Wake up, I tell myself. The command will rouse me from sleep and end this. Then Harth can run a diagnostic on my regulators.

Except, he can't.

Because the command failed.

I am trapped in my dream.

"MY. NAME."

"No!"

"RELEASE ME!"

"NO!" I scream, rolling out of my cot and falling to the floor. On my hands and knees, I gasp for air.

Harth arrives in the doorway, his Incinerator gauntlet charged and ready to reduce someone to slag. But there is no enemy to be found.

"I heard you scream," he says. "Is all well?"

"A dream," I say.

"You lost control?" he asks, fully aware of how I mitigate the negative effects of extended combat on the psyche.

"Someone took control."

"Are you yourself?" he asks.

I push myself up to the cot and nod. "I am unaffected. The dream state gave her strength."

"Her?" Harth asks.

I nod again and look him in the eyes so there is no doubt about my seriousness. "Jenna Flood."

"She is dead," he says. "We were all there to see it."

"But not her body."

He grunts.

I squeeze my fists. "As with the Visionary, we were unable to confirm the death."

"Accurate, but it seems unlikely—"

"I put a hypersonic shard through the Visionary's skull," I say. "Yet, here we are."

"Mm." Harth furrows his brow. "I'll run a full diagnostic on your regulators. If there is an aberration in your mind, or a malfunction, we will sniff it out. But, that will have to wait. We will arrive at our destination in three minutes and will be dropping at high speed."

"With?" I ask.

"Chirk," he says, and then frowns, "And the two humans. Sean and Gemma."

"Interesting," I say.

"That is a word for it," he says and then starts ticking off fingers. "As are foolish, mistake, doom, and unnecessary peril."

"That last one was two words," I point out.

He shrugs. "Had two fingers left." He holds out his hand. "Whatever comes our way, we will handle it together, as we always do."

I take his hand and allow him to pull me up off the cot. Without another word, we head toward whatever mystery awaits us next. Every step takes me a little farther from the disturbing dream, but I just want to run. A dark sense of foreboding has overtaken me.

Is Jenna alive?

Did she leave something behind when I allowed her access to my mind?

Is she confined *to my mind?*

Will she come for us again?

For me?

I take a deep breath and steel myself against the intrusive thoughts. If Jenna Flood dares to show her face again, dead or alive, I will watch it implode through the sight of my weapon. Then I will erase the memory of her demise, along with hundreds of others.

20

MICAH

"You okay?" Jess asks about three seconds after waking up from a nap she attempted to resist. She's in the passenger seat of a big ass pickup truck we stole in Franconia. Felt bad about taking someone's ride in the middle of winter until I saw the truck nuts dangling from the back. Whoever owns this beast is a douchebag. Hell, they might already be Draun and living in Japan.

Besides, we earned this ride. Played Fox and the Hound with a bunch of biologics while the defense system wreaked havoc on the enemy and everything around them. It was full-on shock and awe overkill. But it allowed us to reach the snowmobiles hidden under a white tarp not far from where the *Prowler* had been parked. We used them to escape the madness, making it to town using paths I've been riding since I was a kid and finding old Bertha here.

"Fine," I say.

She sits up straight, widening her eyes like it will help fend off sleep again. "Bullshit."

"Okay, mind reader, why am I sad? You tell me." I hold up a hand. "That came out a little feistier than I meant it to. Sorry. Just tired."

"And sad," she says, eyeing me.

"Pish," I say, wiping dust out of my eye, trying to ensure my view of I-81 South isn't obstructed. The roads aren't great right now. Snow is falling. The truck shouted a warning about slippery roads about two minutes after we started driving. But this tank with a flatbed and four-wheel drive should handle it fine. What I'm worried about is everyone else on the road. That's not a lot of people, but if one of them does something stupid, we could all end up on the side of the road. "Real men don't cry."

"Good thing you're a sorry excuse for a man," she says, getting a laugh out of me. "Okay, fine, I'll guess." She thinks about it for a moment, and then comes to a conclusion. "Ah. Yeah, that makes sense."

I glance over at her, and she looks sad enough herself that I think she might have actually read my mind. "What?"

"Your home," she says. "Your parents' land. They left you two things to take care of. You told me that. Their property and Grover."

I clench my teeth, resisting my emotions.

"And now," she says. "The land is...well, fucked up. And the house, well, we have no idea, right? Could be in shambles. Could be fine. The fighting wasn't near the house, but maybe the biologics are dicks?"

"Or all those fucking lasers cut through it along with the trees," I grumble. "Or a stray rocket blew it to bits."

"Ahh," she says. "Angry, too."

"Not at anyone. Just...what the fuck?"

She nods. "Astronomical what the fuck? Fucking dog aliens. Fucking Lumen Sok is a Draun. We've both got fucking weapon systems drilled into our fucking bones. And your fucking dog can fucking talk. More 'what the fucks' than Nick Nolte becoming president and riding to his inauguration on a giraffe."

I laugh. "Can you picture it?"

"Just standing up there, clacking his teeth together, nipping at little kids that get too close? And the first order of business? Point Break Two starring Nick Nolte as...a recluse and very handsome president who must save Johnny Wick from a hot air balloon before the wind stops blowing and a bomb on a school bus explodes."

I laugh harder. "I think you're mixing up a few movies."

She shrugs. "As long as they CGI a shirtless Patrick Swayze in, I'll be happy. Oh, maybe a scene with Nolte and some clay."

"Oh god," I say, picturing the pair of them, forming a clay phallus together, the smooth, wet– "Nope," I say, laughing hard now. "Fuck no. Don't need that image in my head."

"You're welcome," she says. "Feel better?"

"Maybe worse," I say, "but different, so...thanks? I think."

"But seriously," she says. "I think your folks would understand. Earth is our home, too, and we're doing more than anyone else to save it. If they were here, they'd be proud, right? Focus on that. And we still have Grover. Well, maybe not us, but he's safe with Praxion and the others. He adores Torel. She won't let anything happen to him."

I nod, knowing that both, like me, would give their lives to protect Grover. It might not be the soundest choice, but he is innocent and pure. Worth saving because, without him, we might be lost. He's what we're fighting for. Humanity. The Lost Tribe.

He's the best of both rolled into a fluffy, happy, drooling love-muffin.

"If the house is ruined, we'll rebuild," I say. If I have a plan, I'll feel better about it. "The forest will regrow. It has before."

"And a pack of coyotes will eat all the little bits left of that guy," Jess says.

I smile, but it fades quickly when the memory of his splattered remains snaps back into my mind. "Kern."

"You knew him," she says. We didn't get a chance to talk about him before she all but passed out.

"Served with him," I say. "He was a good man. Well, good soldier at least."

"Do you think... Do you think becoming Draun right away is a reflection on your moral compass? Like, does it mean he was never *actually* a good guy? Do people with weaker morals transition right away?"

"I'm convinced they're all cat people," I say.

She swats my shoulders. "I like cats. C'mon, seriously."

"I don't know," I admit. "It would be nice if that were true, but... I knew Kern pretty well. He had kids. Carried their photos around. Talked about them and his wife all the time. Loved them. *Really* loved them. He saved my life once. I repaid the favor. Guys like that, it's hard to imagine that they've got some kind of secret darkness inside of them, just waiting to be woken up. But...maybe that's how it works, even if the person doesn't know about it, or show it on the outside. And who knows what happened in his life since I last saw him. Maybe his wife left. Maybe his kids drowned. If I lost you, or Grover, maybe my own darkness would come out."

"Well," she says, "Don't let the bad guys know that little tidbit or me and Grove will end up on a hit list."

"I shall look at you with disdain from hence forth," I say.

"Was that like old English or old school Norse Thor?" she asks.

"I don't think Thor spoke English."

"Not the actual Thor," she says. "Marvel Comics Thor."

"He doesn't talk like that in the mov—"

She grunts and sighs. "Not in the movies. In the comics. The older ones, at least. You know, like, 'Verily, I say thee nay, frost giant!' Things like that."

"You've lost me," I say. "And I didn't know you were a comic book nerd."

"Been a while, but yeah. I was raised on them. My father. He's got thousands of them hidden away in his office. Nothing new, though. Sixties. Seventies. Eighties. Stopped collecting in the 90s. Said they became all about tits and ass and less about what it really means to be a hero."

"Huh," I say. "Did you ever learn? What it means to be a hero?"

She shakes her head. "That's more your thing."

"Maybe," I say, and let the subject drop.

Jess settles back into her seat, and I sense sleep might claim her once more. Then she perks up a little and asks, "Where are we, anyway?"

"Just south of Harrisburg."

"*Pennsylvania?* How long was I asleep?"

"Long enough that it's almost your turn to drive," I say. "Been through the shit enough times to know that a lack of sleep does not help someone be heroic.

Neither does chivalry. We can trade seats when we reach the next state border. Snow should clear up down in Virginia."

"And after that?" she asks.

I pat the GPS on the dash. "Owner might have been an asshole, but he paid for all the bells and whistles."

"Probably knows where we are," she says.

"Yeah, but he's not going to come looking," I say. "First of all, he doesn't have a truck anymore. Second, it's not exactly safe crossing the country these days. Third, police don't give a shit."

With people becoming Draun all the time, the police are focused primarily on emergency services. No one is enforcing smaller crimes like theft, speeding, or even acts of violence that don't end in death. The world has become a colder, more violent place as a result. But someone needs to handle the Draun when they emerge and almost always throw a series of temper tantrums as they move west across the country.

"Oh, look at that," I say as we pass a large sign reading, "Welcome to Maryland."

"Asshole," she says as I pull over. "You knew we were at the border."

I put the truck in park. "It's called situational awareness, Chunks. You gotta work on it."

We get out, passing each other around the truck bed. I go to swat her ass, but she knows me too well, catching my hand without looking and throwing a fake punch at me while making a "fwapish," sound effect. "How's that for situational awareness?"

"Disappointing," I say. "For me, at least."

Back in the truck on opposite sides, she adjusts the seat and asks, "So fill me in. What's the plan?"

"Follow the GPS all the way past Mexico City," I say.

"Border could be an issue," she says.

Most countries are locked down, but some traffic still flows between countries that share workforces. "We'll tackle that problem when the time comes. For now, just drive. And when the snow clears, pedal to the metal. Find out how fast Bertha can move. Total drive time is supposed to be forty five hours. I think we can do it in thirty."

"No snow, go plaid. Check. Get to Mexico, find the park, find the dog-squad. Check."

"Micah sleeps for eight hours," I say. "Check."

"Can Micah sleep through music?" she asks.

"If I can sleep through gunfire, I can sleep through music." I close my eyes.

"Deal," she says. I hear her going through the steps of connecting her phone to the sound system, and then the speakers start playing the hauntingly familiar tune of "Take My Breath Away" by Berlin.

She's playing god-awful music on purpose. I'm sure of it, but my resolve is like fuckin' tungsten. I'm not going to give her the pleasure of complaining. Though, I'm sure I'm already frowning, and I think I can hear her having a giggle at my expense. Despite all that, exhaustion slams into me like a panicked rhinoceros rudely awakened by a park ranger giving it a suppository. I fall asleep before the second chorus begins.

I wake up, in what feels like minutes later, to the sound of Jess shouting while looking in the rear view with wide eyes.

21

CHIRK

"Take care of my baby," I tell Praxion. It's less of a question and more of a veiled threat.

"I promise nothing," he says, "except that I will do my best."

"Yeah, yeah. You always do." I take a deep breath and steel myself for the bumpy ride to come. We're flying low, hugging the ground to avoid radar detection. Our course isn't direct. Not even close. We're weaving our way across Mexico to avoid any densely populated areas between the Gulf and the wilderness just south of the capital. It's a circuitous route, but worthwhile seeing as we have yet to be attacked.

All of that is fine and dandy. I plotted the course and know that the *Prowler* will follow it exactly, flying past our destination at supersonic speeds before dropping us off and making a beeline for Egypt. I asked Sean what that meant. Beeline. He said, "It's like if you're going directly from one place to another, as quick as you can." He didn't know where the phrase originated, though. Seems to be the case with him. Has all kinds of weird turns of phrase that aren't part of our translation services, but he has no idea about their origin. He did, however, remember the origin of, 'Express elevator to hell. Going down!' which is what he said when he learned how I was getting to the ground.

I step inside the node and turn around to face Praxion. We're alone in the node chamber, and I'm feeling unusually nervous. I've dropped onto dozens of worlds, riding nodes through space and rough atmospheres. But every one of those planetary insertions were smooth sailing thanks to our gravity bridge tech, which allows us to tap into the invisible bands of gravitational energy that connect all things—from black holes to molecules.

My last trip in a node didn't end so smoothly. Gruunlokar and I were both knocked off course by laser fire from Lumen Sok's satellite network. I escaped, but Gruunlokar was captured. The ordeal has made me skeptical about how clandestine we really are, and about how smooth my landing will be.

Mostly because what we're attempting now—an insertion sans a gravity bridge—has never been done before. I'm going to be dropped out of the *Prowler*, traveling somewhere around three thousand miles per hour, just a hundred feet from the ground. The pod will then either manage to slow itself and touchdown as usual, or I'll go splat. When they recover my body, it will just be a meaty smear coating the inside of the clear bubble. They might as well bury me in it at that point because my bits and pieces will be so integrated with the node's interior, they'll never get all of me out.

"You orange?" Praxion asks.

"Orange," I say.

"Don't look orange," he says.

I grimace. "Can you blame me?"

"It will work," he says, confident as always. And not because he's self-assured. He had nothing to do with the prep for this drop. That was all Harth and me. And he believes we're competent. Which we are. So, I suppose I shouldn't be concerned.

"Unless I get shot down," I point out.

"Always a risk," he says.

"Amazing pep talk." I strap myself in and tug the belt snug.

He smiles. "Never needed to give you a pep talk before."

"Don't need to now," I say, crossing my arms. "I'll get the job done. Doesn't matter if I shit myself doing it. Some dogs on this world eat their own turds, and the people still let them lick their faces."

"Love makes people do strange things," he says.

I squint at him. "What about Kynolari?"

"I have no idea what you're talking about," he says, but he does. We all do.

"No point in waiting, boss. War is a bitch. No way of knowing when your time is up. If one of you goes, the other is going to live the rest of their life full of regret."

"Sage advice from the man who philanders with every Lost Tribe member bold enough to sniff his ass." He grins.

"First of all, have you ever had a lady get right down there and give you a long sniff? It's fucking erogenous, man. It's like they're taking a long snort of the worst you've got and saying, 'Smells like god-damn flowers to me.' Tell me that doesn't get you all kinds of excited in a primal kind of way."

"Not remotely," he says, and then activates the node, which seals around me.

"Hey," I shout, tapping the glass. "I wasn't done mocking you yeeee—"

The node drops out from the *Prowler*. The sudden drop shoves my body against the restraints. Before I can fully adjust to the G-forces, they reverse as the node's thrusters fire almost immediately, slowing my descent in just a few feet. I grit my teeth, fighting the crushing force with everything I've got, happy that no one is around to hear my grunts of pain and gasping breaths.

The node touches down with a heavier than normal thump, but nothing close to life threatening. The base does its job, drilling into the ground as the node folds back, opening to a wave of hot, dry air. It's not exactly what I would call comfortable, but it's light years better than the frozen hellscape Micah calls home.

I step out of the node, which is now just a smooth metal disc on the ground. Dust swirls into the air as I use my feet to kick dirt and leaf litter over the device. It's hidden from view, but still fully functional, allowing us to leap back to the *Prowler* when the time comes, and for my team to join me without having to go through the rigors of insertion.

The sound of worried voices reaches me from outside the tree line behind which I've landed. They're speaking Spanish, but I can understand the language just as easily as I can English.

I creep up to the forest's edge, peering through a stand of foliage. There's a small village on the other side. A lot of ramshackle buildings. Nothing permanent. Looks like part time settlers…or immigrants.

Hard to say.

My eyes widen as a dozen members of the Lost Tribe skitter out of the collection of buildings. They bound on their four little legs, running and barking together. A happy little tribe. Of my people. What the humans call Chihuahuas.

"What the…" I step out of the trees. It's a really dumb thing to do, but the presence of so many members of the Lost Tribe puts me at ease.

Can't say the same for the small number of humans watching. I can hear them whispering to each other. They're worried about what my presence means. About whether they're in danger. They don't seem afraid of me, but they are afraid trouble will follow me.

The greeting party reaches me as a mass of sniffing noses and wagging tails. "Hola," I say. "How's everybody doing? Nice to meet you." One gets right up in my ass crack. "Whoa there! Okay, okay. Look, I know I smell good. Probably all exotic and shit to you guys, but let's try to be civilized."

I'm saying the words, but my loins have already been awakened. Eight of these dogs are female and at least one of them is what humans call 'in heat.' Weird way to say 'ovulating,' but terminology has no effect on biology. Pheromones are powerful, and I…

I need to resist. I can't start every mission with an impromptu romp in…the… "Good Lord," I say when my nose leads me to the bitch. She's quivering with excitement, already impressed by my obvious prowess. And while she might not be as sleek and well-groomed as Bacon, she's got hips for light years and the brownest eyes I've ever—

"Chirk."

Gruunlokar's voice snaps me back to reality, reminding me that he, Harth, and Sean were following me through the leap node. I find myself about two steps away from mounting the bitch right here and now, in plain view of everyone, including the humans, who have all fallen silent.

"I've made contact with the locals," I say.

"I can see that," he says from behind me in the trees, almost containing a laugh.

"Hey, you get out here and have a sniff. See if you don't black out and find yourself a father three months later."

"Are they a threat?" Harth asks.

"What?" I say, patting some of the dogs on their little heads. "Of course not."

"Not the Lost Tribe," Harth says. "The *humans*."

"Naw, man," Sean says, "they're cool. Look at all the doggos. No way these peeps are Draun. Heck, way the hell out here, they might not even know what's going on in the world."

"They would have seen the transmission," Gruunlokar says.

"Seeing ain't believing," Sean says.

I've found his instincts about people to be reliable, so I walk my way over to the people, lift my hand in greeting and say, "*Hola, mi nombre es Chirk. No venimos a hacer daño. ¿Supongo que ninguno de ustedes ha visto un templo grande por aquí? ¿Quizás algo con Xolotl?*"

An old woman steps to the front of the gathered humans. Her skin is wrinkled and leathery. Her gait is a shuffle. Gray hair hangs in wisps over her face. Standing in front of the dozen humans—all adults—she clears her throat and says, "Welcome, brethren of the ancient one..." in perfect Kynolari.

"Did you guys hear that?" I stage whisper.

"Heard it," Harth says. "Not sure I believe it. But I heard it."

"I think it's safe to come out," I say.

A moment later, Harth, Gruunlokar, Sean, and Gemma step out of the trees behind me. The villagers seem delighted by our presence but are still cautious.

They know the risk of hosting us, I think, *because they've done it before.*

22

PRAXION

"Are you positive?" Baarfolir paces back and forth in his library. Grover, sitting at my feet, follows his progress, moving his head side to side. "I'll be a liability, I'm sure of it."

"There is no one better suited for the task at hand," I say.

"I can observe and advise virtually," he says. "It will be just like being there. And Grover will be with you. He's been there before. Has keen senses. I'm sure he will lead you right where you need to be. Afterall, who will pilot the *Prowler* if I'm not–"

"MIMIR," I say.

"Yes, sir?" The A.I.'s voice asks. "How may I help you today?"

"Just wanted to remind our friend that you exist."

"I exist in a nontangible sense. I am without a physical body...unless you hold a loose definition of what constitutes a body. Then you could argue that the *Prowler* is my body. However, then you must answer the question: Am I MIMIR? Or am I the *Prowler*? If I am not one or the other, am I both? And if I am both, who am I really?"

"That's...thank you, MIMIR. That is all."

"Are you positive?" During our time on Earth, staying with Micah, we've not only been on the ship less, but our need to interact with MIMIR significantly decreased. When traveling through space, slipping between gravity bridges, the A.I. is invaluable. But things have been quiet up until today. It seems that MIMIR is having some kind of existential crisis. Too much time to self-reflect can leave most sentient beings all twisted up, but it happens to A.I. far less regularly and is almost always resolved by refocusing on tasks. 'Get out of yourself,' was my mother's advice when I felt sorry for myself. I wasn't sure what she meant at first. Didn't make physical sense. But I get it now.

"Actually, MIMIR," I say. "Can you access Earth's networks? See if you can track down the satellites redirecting the landbased laser arrays. If we can take them out, we'll be able to move around the globe without having to worry about being attacked at the speed of light."

We're currently moving safely beneath the Atlantic Ocean again, after dropping off Chirk's team, but I would prefer to be in the air with a nicer view and fewer large animals with the potential for collisions. The *Prowler* would sustain no damage from the impact, but I do not want to kill this world's struggling megafauna.

"Absolutely, sir," MIMIR says. "It will be done."

"Could you also inform Torel to meet me in the library, and keep us on our course to Giza?"

"Of course," the A.I. says. It's not programed to feel or express emotion, but I swear I hear a sigh of relief.

"Now," I say, turning back to Baarfolir. "I understand that you are not a soldier. No one expects you to be. But you have been studying this world and its history since our arrival."

"Well, yes," he says, "that is true, but—"

"And you have been studying the Lost Tribe for more than a decade."

"Yes, and I—"

"And there is no one better suited, on this world or any other, to connect our two disparate cultures and histories in a way that makes sense to modern Kynolari and an ancient, like Anbu. You don't need to agree or disagree. I am simply stating facts. Even if a hundred other Kynolari historians were present, you would be the one and only qualified to uncover Anbu's tomb and decipher whatever it is we might find."

He sits, arms crossed.

"When you joined this mission, you knew there would be danger. You knew you might be called upon to risk your life."

"I did not know there would be Draun involved."

"And that is the very reason why it is even more important that you bury your fears and put your knowledge to good use. Not everyone is born to fight. I know that, and I do not judge you for it. But if we do not fight... If you do not help us... You will die at the hands of the Draun. That is a certainty. Whatever your concerns are, they are mere possibilities, conjured by fears and your potent imagination."

I place a hand on his shoulder. "You have two paths in front of you. One leads to certain death, the other...the unknown. You know which is which, and I trust you will choose correctly."

Grover, ever the empath, trots over to Baarfolir and lowers his chin onto the smaller Kynolari's lap, looking up at him with big brown eyes.

It takes just a moment for Baarfolir to grin and stroke Grover's head. It is unusual for members of a Kyno Corps team to show or feel affection beyond a brutal ribbing, but that has been changing as of late. Grover has set an example for us all—love, kindness, and empathy. He might not be a genius, but he excels where most fall short. He represents an ideal that war scoured from our lives, and I fear it could happen to Baarfolir as well. I don't make this request of him lightly. I know he is fearful.

The truth is, he should be.

But we also need him. I cannot risk our mission's success by not bringing our greatest asset.

The wall parts, stretching to thin white strands before slipping to either side, revealing the doorway and Torel.

"We arrive at our destination in ten minutes." I head for the door. "Keep him company, Grover. I'll be back soon."

Torel steps back, allowing me to exit. As the door seals behind me, I hear Grover say, "It okay. I scared, too."

My heart breaks over his sweet innocence and is immediately pulled back together by rage toward the Draun for putting the world and that sweet Earth Kynolari through the tortures of war and corruption.

"You called for me?" Torel asks.

I nod, taking her by the hand. War has taken a lot from us, and I will not wait any longer to live what little life I might have left.

"We have ten minutes," I tell her.

She's silent for a moment, following me. For a second, I worry I've miscalculated her feelings for me. Then she shoves my back, hurrying me along. "We'll only need nine."

Five minutes later, I'm putting my clothing back on. Feel like a new man. Like…I don't know. This was better than anything I have felt before. Kynolari have intercourse for pleasure. All species do. But not like this. From what I understand, and know of this world, what we just experienced was more…human. Or perhaps more dog-like.

Torel lies in her bed, body relaxed. We've seen each other naked before. When you're waist deep in the shit, modesty is not a concern. But I feel like I'm seeing her—the real her—for the first time.

She smiles at me. "You look befuddled."

"I'm sure there's a word for how I feel, but I doubt it's 'befuddled.'"

She sits up, her hair sliding with her movements, the smell of her intoxicating. Somewhere deep down in my psyche is another me, shouting about the mission. But here and now, the conscious me doesn't care about anything beyond this moment.

"Overpowered?" she asks.

I hike my pants up. "Closer."

She stands up and slides her arms around my neck. "Dominated?"

I laugh. "Maybe next time."

"Next time, huh?"

I kiss her and she releases me. Picks up her pants. Fully dressed, I step toward the door. It untangles and opens. I pause and look back. "Loved."

She looks up. "What?"

"Loved," I say. "That's the word."

Her jaw opens, but no words come out.

I give her a wink and say, "Now who's befuddled?"

The door reseals behind me, and I walk down the hallway toward the cockpit. We have just minutes before we reach the coast. I'm feeling pretty good about myself.

For about ten steps.

Then doubt creeps up on me.

Prowls around me, low and stalking.

Ten more steps and it pounces.

What have I done?

There is a reason Kyno Corps operators don't have relationships with each other. It could cloud my judgment. Lead to mistakes.

Is that what this is? A mistake?

It doesn't feel like it. Feels like the rightest thing I've ever done. As bad as I feel about the breach in protocol, I feel uplifted, reinforced, and for the first time in a while—hopeful. Not that we can overcome the Draun, but that I have the most powerful motivator urging me to fight. For her. It's stronger than my concern for the entire planet.

And therein lies the weakness.

We will need to guard this relationship. The Draun cannot learn of it.

I step into the cockpit and am surprised to find both Baarfolir and Grover sitting in the command chairs, watching the sun's light shimmer as we pass through the Mediterranean Sea. From here, we will enter the Nile River and follow it as far as we can.

"Hello," I say, feeling a little awkward.

When I notice both of their noses twitching, I feel even more awkward. There is no hiding the relationship, or what has been done, from these two. The pair look at each other, and then return their gaze to the viewscreen without ever looking back at me.

"Hello," Baarfolir says, a squeak in his voice.

Grover turns his head and side-eyes me as I sit behind them. His mouth parts and he starts panting, a slow smile spreading. His tails twitches. Then wags at the tip. Then the whole thing moves.

"Ask him," Grover says.

"I'm asking nothing," Baarfolir says. "What adults do in private is their own business."

"Not...pri...vate," Grover says, trying out a new word. "Am sniff."

Baarfolir just grumbles and keeps his eyes forward.

"Grover," I say. His eyes snap toward me, head cocked to the side, ears perked. "Ask."

"Did sex?" Grover asks, painfully direct and unfiltered.

"Yes."

"Torel sex?"

"Yes."

His tail is going so fast he might break it. "Prax...*love*...Torel?" he asks.

Baarfolir's head tilts to the side. It's subtle, but he would like the answer, too.

"Yes," I say.

"I *knew* it!" Baarfolir says, holding out his hand to Grover, who taps it with his paw. He looks back at me finally. "We all knew it. Were just waiting for you to figure it out. You might be a competent war hero, but you're not exactly what humans call, 'emotionally mature.'"

"This needs to stay quiet," I say. "There was no hiding it from you two, but this information needs to stay between us. If the enemy knew, they could use it against me."

"Wrong," Grover says. "Prax wrong. Love Micah."

"We know," I say.

"Love Prax. Love Torel. Love Baar. Love *all*. Micah love Jess. Jess love Micah. All love." He looks at me with an intensity I haven't seen before, like he's laying some sage wisdom on me, and I better listen. "*All. Love.*"

I smile and pet his head. He leans into it, panting, tongue hanging out the side of his mouth.

The door opens and Torel steps in, dressed and ready for action. "What did I miss?"

"All love!" Grover says, leaping at her, paws up, tail wagging.

She laughs and says, "There's a lot of that going around."

"And sex," Grover says.

"Oh goodness," Baarfolir says, facing forward again. He stammers for a moment and then says, "Approaching the Nile Delta."

"MIMIR," I say.

"Yes, Captain?"

"Take us in. Follow the preplanned route. Keep us deep. Keep us hidden but try not to hit anything on the way."

"Understood."

Grover leaps back into the chair beside Baarfolir. I glance at Torel and pat the seat next to me.

She sits and puts her hand on mine. "We never do know where a mission is going to lead us, do we?"

MIMIR lets out a *bing* sound and says, "Welcome to Egypt."

23

MICAH

I spin around in my seat, gauntlet at full and ready to unleash Kynolari laser hell on whatever might be charging toward us from behind. I'm expecting a Helion at least. Maybe a horde of biologics. But what I find catches me off guard. I turn to Jess, "All that for a cop?"

"I thought we could speed," she says. "I thought they weren't watching the roads. I've never been pulled over before."

I smile and place a hand on her shoulder. "But you have fought against a telekinetic alien species trying to take over the planet. I think you can handle it."

She pulls to the side of the road. Puts us in park. "I guess. I'm just not comfortable with people having authority over me, you know?"

"We have nothing to worry about."

"You know we stole this truck, right?"

I nod. "And I know that police really aren't giving out tickets or chasing down stolen cars. If he's stopping us, it's for some other reason. Maybe something's going on up ahead."

"Or," she says, motioning at herself up and down.

"He's a harsh critic of warm color plaid?" I ask.

"I'm impressed that you're even aware of what warm colors are—"

"Hey, I'm a fashionista. And *you*, are a Fall. That's your palette. Orange, red, yellow. Looks good on you. Brings out your natural brown skin and eyes."

She stares at me for a moment. "You're serious?"

"I mean, you *are* a Fall."

"I'm not talking about my clothing, Micah." She gestures at just her face this time.

"I know what you're saying, but...look... What state are we in?"

Her eyes go wide, and she motions her hand out the windshield where a large green roadside shows the number of miles to Birmingham.

"Alabama," I say. "Right. Well...too late to trade seats now."

"Why?" she asks.

I glance at the driver's side window just before a large man with thick knuckles gives the glass a triple knock.

He gestures for the window to be rolled down.

Jess closes her eyes, swallows, and sucks in a quick breath. Then she rolls down the window, smiles and says, "Howdy."

"Howdy, to you, too," he says, his accent thick, "but I'd appreciate it if you didn't try winning me over with a phony Southern accent. Ain't blind, you know. I seen your New Hampshire plates."

"Sorry, sir," she says. "What, uh, what can I do for you?"

"Well, seein' as I don't know who you all is, I'd appreciate your I.D.s and the registration for this here beauty of a truck." He leans down to get a look at me. Allows me to do the same. He's pushing forty five—in age and belt size. We could take off running and he'd get twenty feet before collapsing. Still has some chocolate smeared on his chin. Remnants of some kind of pastry. Doesn't mean he can't draw a pistol quickly, though.

"The truck is mine," I say, opening the glove box so I can recover the registration and find out what my name should be. "But I'm afraid I don't have my license on me. Forgot it up North. That's why she's driving."

"Uh-huh… Up North…"

"Hold on," Jess says, stopping me from handing him the registration. "Doesn't he need to tell us why he pulled us over first?"

She's not wrong, but now might not be the time to take a stand on the reality of persistent racism in the Deep South.

"'Scuse me?" the officer says.

"Why did you pull us over?" I ask.

"You were speeding," he says.

"No one is getting pulled over for speeding anymore," she says. "And we're not the only ones out here doing it."

Accurate points, but I don't think facts matter now.

"Like I said, I don't know neither of you." He takes a step back from the door. His right hand moves back to his pistol but stops shy of taking hold of it. "And I don't take kindly to strangers, less now than before. I don't know you. Right now, I don't like you."

"You don't need to," Jess says.

"Ma'am, step out of the car."

"Like hell I will. Not until you tell the truth about why you pulled us over."

"The truth about—lady, are you trying to make this a race thing?"

"Isn't that what it is?" she asks.

The officer deflates a little. Leans down again so he can see us both. "Look, we got aliens invading the planet, taking over our brains. My aunt Florence is one of them. Sipping on her sweet tea one moment, blowing up the god damn house the next. Haven't seen her since. People are going missing all over the place. And

I'm just trying to keep things in my little patch of the world from breaking down into chaos. That means maintaining the status quo. Helping people feel normal. And that means, when someone comes through my neck of the woods pushing one thirty on the highway, you better believe I'm going to pull them over."

I lean over so I can clearly see his face. "Hello, officer…" I read his name badge. "Milne."

"Gregory Milne," the officer says with a tip of his hat.

"Micah Taylor, sir. U.S. Army Rangers." I leave out the 'former.' Sounds more impressive. My military service doesn't and shouldn't get me any leeway with the police, but there is a kind of unspoken camaraderie between men who carry guns for a living. "Pleasure to meet you. Listen, we're sorry about the speed. We're just trying to head south as fast as possible. Some friends of ours are in trouble and we need to help them."

"Mm," he says. "Lot of that going around."

"Yes, sir. Can I ask you a strange question?"

He just squints at me and waits.

"You own a dog?"

His brow furrows. "Now why would you—"

"You saw the message in your head, heard the offer, just like everyone else. You know who they're fighting against, and you know the kind of people who turned against us first. So, let me ask again. Do you own a dog?"

He gets it. I can see it in his eyes. This is a test.

His guard lowers a touch. "I got three. Little terrors each of them, but since Lucy passed, they're all I got in the world."

"And the Kynolari?" I ask. "What do you think of them?"

"You know I'm the one supposed to be asking the questions?"

"I know that the world is being divided into sides. Good…and evil. And I suspect that we are on the same side."

He squints a little further. "That so?"

I'm about to answer when a loud klaxon winds up in the distance.

"What's that?" Jess asks. "Tornado warning?"

Milne draws his pistol and scans the area. "Draun warning."

"Draun?" Jess says.

"Yeah, you know, the psychos who become sudden powerhouses and make their way to Japan. Those guys. And girls. The alarm is to let people know one is around and that they should get out of the way." He looks at us. "Look, I'm sorry for the confusion. You folks should be on your way. Just…watch how you're driving and—shit…"

His full attention diverts to the east side of the road.

"What is it?" I ask.

"It's coming!"

I climb out of the cab and run around the truck to join the officer.

"The hell are you doing?" he asks.

"Your bullets aren't going to help." I lift my arm revealing the gauntlet as it snaps to life and glows orange with a full charge. "But this..."

"What..." He blinks in surprise, looking me over again. "You're *him.* The one they warned us about. In the second broadcast."

"Guilty as charged," I say. "Now get behind the truck."

"What are you going to do?" he asks, stumbling around to the truck's far side, stopping beside Jess, who has climbed out the passenger's side door.

I watch the approaching Draun. It's moving fast, hovering a foot off the ground. The pressure wave in front of it carves a path through a field of tall grass that will one day be harvested as hay. It's a man. Maybe twenties. And he's laughing. Full of himself and his newfound power, delighted by what the Draun life has to offer.

But he's new to his powers.

Hasn't made contact with others like him.

Might not even know how to use his telekinetic abilities beyond levitating himself off the ground. That he's not flying higher suggests he's afraid of heights. A new convert...and like a baby sea turtle, he's scrambling toward the ocean and then beyond to Japan.

Given the amount of blood covering him, he's killed everyone he's passed on the way. And his eyes are firmly locked on me, Jess, and Milne.

I charge my second gauntlet. No way to really know how much power is required, so I opt for all of it.

In the military, I was taught to strike hard and first. If the enemy can't recover from your first attack, then it's not a battle. It's a victory.

Hard and fast, I think, imagining what I'm going to try and trying not to imagine what the results will be.

The Draun angles toward me. He's screaming, but he's outrunning the sound. He wants to plow straight through me and smash the truck into the other two, instantly killing us all.

I have other plans.

It happens in a blur. He's just twenty feet away when I trigger the gauntlets. He's moving faster than the speed of sound, but the gauntlets' laser energy travels at the speed of light and is controlled by the speed of thought. Torel taught me how to focus and bend the laser light using the regulators that connect my mind to the weapon. Not only can I bend light, but I can also shape it. It's some awesome Green Lantern shit, except that if you touch it...

Well...

The Draun is traveling so fast he can't even register the glowing snowplow-shaped wall that snaps to life in front of him, curving to a razor sharp blade in the middle. He strikes it traveling at full speed and is quickly severed in two. Each half of his body follows the laser light's curve, sizzling as it slides around in both directions and launches away, trailing smoke. When the two halves thump down in the grass behind us, my wall disappears. The gauntlets are drained of power, but I can refill them when I need, or let them recharge naturally.

"I'll be gift wrapped and laid at the feet of baby Jesus." Milne stumbles out into the road. "That was sumthin'."

"That was gross," Jess says, stepping into the road.

"Would have been a lot worse if I'd just made a wall," I point out.

"So," Milne says. "These friends of yours..."

"The Kynolari," I say.

He nods. "They're the good guys?"

"How long have you owned dogs, Milne?"

"All my life," he says.

I smile. "Then you're a Kynolari, too."

He steps back. "You're shitting me."

"Not at all. Those of us who spend a lot of time with dogs—the descendants of Kynolari who were marooned on Earth thirty-seven thousand years ago, have the same brain wave patterns. We might have Draun DNA in our bodies—the broadcast told the truth about that—but our minds? Our hearts? They are Kynolari. So go be with your pups. Keep them safe and they'll do the same for you. In the meantime..." I open the truck door and reclaim the driver's seat.

"Right," he says. "Of course. Sorry to have held you up."

I close the door and lean out the window. "Any other road warriors I should worry about between here and the border?"

"Which border?" he asks. "We got Mississippi up ahead, but it's a quick trip through, followed by Louisiana."

"Mexico," I say.

"*Mexico?* Is there trouble south of the border?"

"Hope," I tell him, and after getting a promise from Milne that he will radio ahead and ask for the white pickup hauling ass across the South be allowed through unmarred, I give him a nod of thanks and step on the gas as we pull away from the curb. "See? No problem. You just need to sweet talk them a little bit."

Jess rolls her eyes and then closes them before leaning her head back for a snooze. I connect my phone to the Bluetooth, scroll through my stations, and land on Thomas Dolby's "She Blinded Me With Science."

As the synth open begins, Jess has the opposite reaction to what I'd hoped for.

She grins. "Joke's on you. I love this song."

Since I do, too, I leave it playing, roll down the windows, and enjoy the warmer drive through the South. Might be the last moment of peace either of us get for a long time…or until we die.

24

CHIRK

"Come, come," the old woman says, waving us along behind her as the gathered humans fall back into their small village, where even more people gather, including children. I thought this might be a temporary camp at first, but they've definitely been here for a while. Maybe generations. "Do not be afraid."

"Afraid?" Gruunlokar says under his breath. "What do *we* have to be afraid of in a place like this?"

We round a shack and enter a circular clearing surrounded by open huts. In the center of it all is a stone sculpture, worn by time and erosion, but impossible to misidentify.

"Xylitol..." Sean says, proving me wrong. I don't bother correcting him.

Gemma smiles at him, trying to figure out if he was joking or seriously messed up the name again.

I decide to strike up a conversation, so she won't figure out that Sean's a big dummy. Hand on my hips, I stop before the statue and look up at Xolotl's stately visage, noble jawline, and pointed ears. The style is very different from the Egyptian statues of Anubis, but they're clearly the same Kynolari. "How long have you been here?"

The old woman leading us turns around, standing beside the statue. "Our people have been the protectors of Xolotl's resting place since the fall of Teotihuacan."

"And when was that?" I ask.

"Fifteen hundred years ago," Gemma says. "Give or take."

"That's a long time to live like this," Harth says.

"You believe there is something inherently wrong with the way we live?" the old woman asks, raising an eyebrow.

"No," Harth says, lowering his head. "I meant no disrespect. A simple life is often a life at peace, which is a very difficult thing to come by."

"Very true," she says. "Now... I am Citlali, elder of the Cuextecatl Ankh-Mesa." She opens her arms as though enveloping the entire village. "We are protectors of sacred knowledge passed down from our ancestors who cohabitated with the great and mighty Xolotl."

"He really did make them worship him," Gruunlokar mutters.

He's not a fan of any kind of deity worship, especially when someone claims to be a deity—and isn't. Xolotl, Anbu, Anubis, call him what you want, he was a Kynolari. Like us. Not a god. Not worthy of worship. Even if he did crack the code to immortality.

"I hate to be rude," I say, "but time is short and if you could just point us in the right direction—"

Citlali holds up her hand, silencing me. "As directed by the Magnificent, we must first perform a confirmation ritual."

"Yo," Sean says. "Confirmation is a Catholic thing. Like a...a sacrament. Confirms a person's faith. I did it when I was, like, thirteen."

"I think this might be different," Gemma says.

Won't be long before she realizes Sean's braincells are in a permanent state of 'Brah!' It's why I love the guy, but I suspect human females—especially smart ones like Gemma—are attracted more to mentally competent male specimens.

And here I am, in a village established by an ancient Kynolari that might hold the key to undoing the Draun invasion of this world, and countless more, and I'm thinking about my friend's love life.

The hell is this planet doing to me?

Citlali approaches Sean, gives him a smile, and a pat on the cheek. I can't tell if she appreciates his addition to the conversation or is just amused by him. Then she says, "Your friend is not wrong. It's not too dissimilar from the Catholic right of Confirmation. But we will be testing your purity."

"Don't like the sound of that," Gemma says to Sean.

"There is nothing sinister about it," she says. The old woman's ears are good. "We simply must verify that you are, in fact, who you claim to be. As we all know, there are creatures in this universe capable of taking the form of another."

"Shapeshifters," Sean says, almost giddy. "Like Changelings on DS9. Like Odo!" Sean changes his voice, doing an impression of the character. "'To become a thing is to know a thing.' So rad."

"Uh-uh," I say. "Not rad. These guys...they're *ferocious*. Not even the Draun messed with them." I turn to Citlali. "But we are *not* them. You saw the transmission like everyone else. You know the Draun fear us."

"Xolotl, the ever-wise, did not conceive of this test without reason. There are many on this world, and on others, that would benefit from the knowledge he uncovered during his lifetime..." She glances at her fellow tribesmen and women. "Including the human race. The knowledge he retains is meant for Kynolari eyes only."

"A prudent safety protocol," Harth says. "What must we do?"

"An offering of blood," she says.

"How very Aztec," Gemma says.

Citlali smiles. "And...of seed."

"I will give my blood," Gruunlokar says, stepping forward.

I sigh and step forward. "Looks like it's my time to take another one for the team. It's hard work, but I'll do what needs doing." I turn to Citlali. "Now, are we talking like all the ladies in the village? Because I might need a breather, or a snack, but I think I can—"

"Not you," she says, and then points to Harth. "Him."

I look Harth up and down, jaw dropping. "Can you *see* him? He will break them."

"He leaves his seed in a sterile receptacle so that we might artificially inseminate our bitches and increase the size and protective ability of Xolotl's guardians."

I step back feeling emasculated.

"I'm not sure how I feel about this," Harth says.

I look up at the big guy. "Sometimes you gotta blow a load for the team, man. I've done it. Now it's your turn. All of humanity, and maybe the universe, hangs in the balance. Now go crank one out and let's get moving."

"If I were a dog," Sean says, "I'd do it."

"See?" I say. "Even Sean would null the void for the mission."

"I can help you," says a young woman who seems to have magically materialized. She takes Harth's hand and pulls him from our group. He still looks unsure but follows the woman.

"Aww, man," Sean says. "Now I *really* wish I was a dog!"

"He will...*survive* the process," Citlali says with a grin, and turns to Gruunlokar. "Follow me."

"I'm coming, too," I say. "This is my op. No one is cutting open my people without me there to supervise."

"I am fine," Gruunlokar says, following after Citlali, who's leading us toward a ramshackle structure built around what looks like a metal shipping crate.

"Fine, my ass." I scurry after him and have to double time it to keep up. "If at any point I think this is going in an uncouth direction, I'm pulling the plug." I look up at the grim-faced Gruunlokar. He's been willing to take unnecessary risks since we recovered him from the Draun facility in Denver. As if the drop node being shot down and his subsequent capture at sea was his fault. Like he's got something to make up for. Could have been any one of us, and I'm not sure I could have endured the way he did. While I was inseminating a flurry of bitches, he was strapped down, having his mind probed. If anything, we failed him by not getting there sooner.

He looks down at me. "Uncouth?"

"It's a human term," I say.

"I know what it is," he says. "We have the same translation services. Just not sure why you expect a blood offering to be delicate."

"That's exactly what it will be," Citlali says, pausing by the closed shipping crate. It's red and rusted. Looking like it might crumble apart while we're inside.

"Sure as shit won't be sterile," I grumble.

Gruunlokar gives me a kick with the side of his foot. Probably doesn't want to offend the woman that's about to take some of his blood through unknown means. If I see some kind of sword in here, we're out.

Citlali undoes a padlock. "The Great One's texts said nothing about his people being funny."

"I've been working on it for a while," I say.

She pauses, hand on the door. Looks back and makes eye contact. With a subtle grin, she says, "Keep working." Then she opens the door and steps inside the dark container.

I look up at Gruunlokar, slack-jawed. "Wha…she just…"

"I've been meaning to tell you, you're not very funny," he says, and then follows her inside.

"You know, Sean would throw himself on a grenade if it would stop someone from insulting me like that."

Gruunlokar chuckles. "Now *that* would be funny."

"Motherfucker," I mutter, and follow him into the dark.

The container is empty. It's dark but the sunlight from the open door behind us makes it easy to see. Citlali stands at the far end, her back to the wall. "We're clear," she says, and the door behind us slams shut.

I leap toward it, shoving with everything I have, but it's been locked from the outside. When I spin around, I've got both mini-railguns drawn and ready to fire. "Listen, woman, I don't know what you do or don't know about us, or the old great one, but I do *not* like having traps sprung on me. Open the door before I—"

Gruunlokar holds his palm out in front of me. "Smell her."

"I was in the middle of making a threat," I say.

He just waits.

Then I sigh and give the air a triple sniff. Dirt. Dust. Decay filtering from the jungle outside. Something Gruunlokar ate. And then I find her. She was cooking when we arrived. Meat. Something sweet. Fruit of some kind. Past the obvious, I catch the scent of her intentions. The chemical markers when someone is being deceitful aren't present. But empathy and comfort are.

She means us no harm, and has no fear of us, even with my half-a-threat.

"Fine," I say. "Okay, lady, what's with the metal coffin routine?"

"Coffin?" she says. "Haven't you ever been through a decontamination chamber before?"

Ultraviolet lights hidden in the corners of the crate come to life, blanketing us in germ killing light. At the far end of the room, two vents snap open, one sucking, the other blowing. A fog descends around us from the ceiling, whipping around in a torrent.

I shield my face and wait it out...because I *have* been through decontamination before, though this seems low tech compared to current Kynolari standards. Probably high tech for a middle of nowhere encampment.

One of the fans reverses course and the mist is sucked from the chamber. The lights wink out, plunging us back into darkness, but only for a moment. The far end of the container splits in the middle and slides apart, revealing a laboratory that definitely was not constructed by human beings fifteen hundred years ago...or any time recently.

"Well," I say, eyes wide. "Shit."

"Follow me," Citlali say, leading the way into the lab, "and we'll get that blood drawn. But please be aware, if you are not who you claim to be, neither you nor your friends outside will leave this camp alive."

25

PRAXION

As MIMIR guides the *Prowler* through the depths of the Nile River, one of the most famous waterways in the world, a strange kind of awkward vibe settles over what's left of the team. I'm not entirely sure why, but I suspect a few things are to blame, starting with what happened between Torel and me.

Because Baarfolir knows, and Torel and I know he knows. But no one has addressed the situation yet. On top of that, I've never had to deal with this kind of social discomfort before. It is far beyond an average breach of protocol, and that's not something I take lightly. During all my time in the Kyno Corps, this is my first infraction since I was in training.

Not that Baarfolir cares about such things. As a historian, he is both ignorant to Kyno Corps protocols, and not bound to them. But Torel and I took the same oaths, and my actions might have tarnished both of our careers.

The worst part about that is...I don't care.

I would do it again.

Fairly certain I will.

Because this world has unlocked a part of me I never knew existed. For the first time in my life, I feel a strange kind of peace. In my core. And it somehow offsets the anxiety that comes with war.

But right now, as we approach the Great Pyramid of Giza under the cover of water, and the night, it is a distraction that must be handled the only way I know how—directly.

"Baarfolir," I say.

"Yes sir?" he says without looking back.

Grover turns around, tongue hanging from the side of his mouth, his perpetual smile locked in place. "Hi, Praxion."

"Hello, Grover," I say.

"Love Praxion."

His simple expression chips away at my discomfort. "Love Grover."

"Love Torel," Grover says. He's always concerned about people feeling left out, and I know what's coming next, so I just let it happen.

"Love Grover," Torel says.

"Love Baar—fo—lir," Grover says.

Baarfolir reaches out and scratches the top of Grover's head. "Love you, too, you big beast."

Grover is thrilled by the completion of what we've come to call the Grover Love Circle. He pants and looks forward at the viewscreen, which is displaying a virtual recreation of the Nile River's bottom.

"Did you have something to say?" Baarfolir asks.

I straighten myself up and say, "I just wanted to confirm what you no doubt suspect."

"You really don't ne—"

"Torel and I are in a relationship," I say.

"That's gre—"

"And before the mission commenced, we engaged in coital activi—"

"Prax," Torel says, backhanding my shoulder. "He doesn't want to know."

"He already knows. I'm just confirming his suspicions so there are no secrets between—"

"You might all be mighty warriors," Baarfolir says, "but I am still your elder, and I dare say, the wisest among us. And I have learned much during my years as a historian and a father. When it comes to matters of love, and the flesh, it is often best to keep the more...intimate details to yourself. Even the Earthlings have an expression for this. 'Don't kiss and tell.' We don't need to know. I appreciate you telling me about the seriousness of your relationship, but what you do behind closed doors can remain there."

"I do not remember if the door was closed," I admit.

He chuckles, and the tension I've been feeling breaks.

"The things this world is doing to us. It's fascinating. The liberation we all feel. I do not recall ever experiencing this kind of excited interest in all aspects of life. Intellectually, sure. But I find myself desiring experience as much as knowledge, even if it terrifies me."

"It's as though our societal limitations have been lifted," Torel says.

"And those of the Corps," I say.

"We will deal with the repercussions later." She places her hands on mine. "And together."

"Lovely," Baarfolir says, and he means it. Says it like he's proud.

"Is love," Grover adds. "All love."

And I think he might be right. While Kynolari are as free as humans to choose our lives, speak our minds, and do as we please, there are powerful expectations, social limitations and, for our generation, a presumption of excellence achieved through victory over the Draun. It has guided our lives up until this moment and, despite our recent rebellions, still guides us now.

MIMIR chimes and says, "Approaching the Insertion Zone. ETA, two minutes. I suggest preparing to disembark. There are just a few hours remaining before the dawn in this part of the world."

I stand. "All right, people. Let's get this done."

Two minutes later, the four of us are gathered in the cargo bay, waiting for MIMIR to breach the surface and open the hatch.

"This is embarrassing," Baarfolir says, looking down at himself.

"For all of us," I say, holding out my arms.

"I think it's quite comfortable," Torel says, turning back and forth to admire her flowing black burqa. It covers her from head to toe, leaving just a slit for the eyes. "And I look mysterious."

I feel far less enthusiastic about the Middle Eastern garb. While burqas are far less common in Egypt, they're not completely foreign. They're our best chance of making the nine mile journey without prompting a panicked response from the locals, or an attack from the Draun.

"You don't think anyone will notice our snouts?" Baarfolir asks, tapping his nose. "If we're supposed to pass as human, we'd be awfully disfigured."

"Even better," Torel says. "Humans have a natural impulse to avoid people who might be suffering from some sort of overt illness, not because it disgusts them, but because it creates a strong sense of social discomfort. What do you say to someone in constant suffering? Most people do not know."

"Our only real challenge is the one of us who doesn't need a disguise and whose appearance invites contact from strangers." I look down at Grover.

His panting mouth clamps shut. "Grover idea." He then begins breathing heavily, forcing exhalations through his jowls. Drool begins to drip.

"What are you doing?" Torel asks.

"Think about ball," Grover replies, still heaving his breaths.

A moment later, his plan becomes clear. He opens his mouth to reveal globs of white, frothy drool on the sides of his mouth, dripping down to the floor. He then opens his eyes wide and looks very much like a dog you might want to avoid.

"Ready to disembark," MIMIR says. "On your go."

I reach out for Baarfolir with both hands.

"Humiliating," he grumbles, and lifts his arms up.

"Don't worry," I say, lifting him into my arms like a small child. "We won't tell the others."

"I would never hear the end of it," he groans, and he's right.

"It's our secret," Torel says, and then tickles him. "Look at this little guy. Such a cutie."

We have a chuckle and then I say, "MIMIR, we are orange."

The cargo bay door opens to reveal a rocky shoreline beneath a bridge. It's early in the morning, but the roadway above us is still alive with vehicles. Like all major Earth cities, there are people who never seem to sleep. But no one can see into the gloom beneath the bridge. We step out on the stone and head for the bridge's side.

The hatch closes behind us and the *Prowler* sinks back beneath the surface without a sound. MIMIR will wait there, ready to receive us again, or swing in for a rapid pickup.

A staircase leads us to street level. There are many vehicles moving about, but almost no pedestrians on the street. From here, it's a straight shot down the roadway known as Al Haram, which will take us directly to the Giza Necropolis where the tomb of Anbu awaits.

We will have to move quickly and then double-time it back to the bridge—hopefully without raising suspicions. I'm about to start the journey, which will take nearly half the time we have before the sun rises. But before I make it to the first intersection, Torel breaks away and waves her covered hand toward an approaching white vehicle with checkered patterns on either side.

At first, I think she's lost her mind. Then I see the yellow light on its roof, reading 'Taxi' in English.

The vehicle pulls over. Torel opens the front door, rattles off an address in Arabic and climbs inside when the driver agrees. I open the back and climb inside with Grover, still holding Baarfolir in my arms.

"Okay," the driver says in Arabic. "Please buckle yourself and the baby and then we will—"

He glances toward Torel. His bushy brow furrows. He's seen her snout.

Torel turns toward the man and holds his gaze until he grows uncomfortable and looks away. He clears his throat, puts the car in drive, and pulls away from the curb. Torel continues staring at the man for a moment, daring him to say something. When she finally looks away, the man sags in relief and doesn't glance toward her for the rest of the drive, which ends just twenty minutes later.

I pay from the back seat using a currency card created by Harth. It basically generates money on demand, accessing an account he created for us in a global bank. Micah and Jess were astounded but, to a mind like Harth's, it was easy. The man doesn't thank us or speak. He just waits for us to exit and then speeds away.

"I gave him an address a half mile from our destination," she says.

I nod. "Smart. But next time tell me first."

"Yes, sir," she says, looking at me in a way that tells me we both know she could do whatever she wanted to, and I'd let her get away with it. After a brief walk, we stop beside a chain-link fence with a clear view of the well-lit Giza Necropolis and all three pyramids. I've seen photos of the site, but none of them did this justice. The sense of history is powerful here, and Baarfolir feels it most of all.

"Astounding," he says. "Reminiscent of our people's earliest megalithic structures. Far larger than I expected." He looks up at me. "Did you know that after the construction of these pyramids, they remained the tallest human structures for over three and a half thousand years when the Old St. Paul Cathedral in England was completed in 1240? Sadly, it was destroyed in the Great Fire of London."

"Fascinating," I say, "but it won't help our current conundrum."

"Conundrum?" he asks, revealing that he has the situational awareness of a Contrelian Cave Snog.

I point to the large number of heavily armed guards with spotlights, fencing, and high-tech alarm systems. Being one of the most valued sites in the world, it's not surprising, but it's also something we failed to plan on. I don't want to attack the humans, but I don't see any other way to the Pyramid other than straight through them.

"We'll approach the front gate in costume. Get as close as we can. Using controlled bursts of my Sonizer and Torel's Lancer, we'll disable the guards in groups." I turn to Torel. "Avoid casualties at all costs."

She nods.

"But—but, they're armed," Baarfolir says. "Won't they be shooting at us?"

"Yes," I say. "But—"

"Plan dumb," Grover says.

We all turn toward the pooch, and I'm a little annoyed. Grover is a lot of wonderful things, but tactician is not among them.

"Other way," he says, turning north and trotting along the fence. "*Secret* way." When no one follows after him, he pauses, turns around and says, "Trust Grover. Anbu scary. But. Anbu smart."

Then he trots away, giving us little choice but to follow him, trusting in the plan of a Lost Tribe dog with the memory of Anbu speaking to him through his DNA. As a soldier, I would have been much more comfortable with my frontal assault, but if Grover can get us inside without starting a war...then it's worth a try.

26

MICAH

"I don't like this," Jess says as we approach the U.S./Mexico border. I've crossed here before. It's been a while, but it didn't look anything like this. What was once a glorified toll booth manned by border agents is now something closer to a fortress. The border crossing is manned by a platoon of Marines and a half dozen tanks. Walls of sandbags protect machine gun nests. Separating all that from Mexico is a new chain link fence topped with some serious looking razor wire.

"I don't think we have anything to worry about," I say.

"Have you *seen* the tanks?" She thrusts her hands out toward the nearest M1 Abrams, painted beige to match the desert.

"There's a lot of firepower," I say, "but look at the direction they're facing."

She takes a moment to reassess the situation. "Ah. They're aiming at Mexico."

"Border is closed," I say.

"Then how can we get through?"

"Just because the U.S. isn't letting people in, doesn't mean they won't let people out."

"How do we know the difference?" Her voice is rising a little. "We can't just drive up and ask."

I scrunch my eyebrows.

"Why not?"

"They're *soldiers*," she says. "With *guns*."

I grin. "*I'm* a soldier. And we both have alien weapon systems attached to our arms that are powerful enough to handle all those tanks and then some. But first, how about we just play nice?" I pull up to the first station, stop the truck, and wait for the soldier inside to notice us.

He doesn't. I glance around. All eyes are facing Mexico.

"What's happening?" Jess whispers.

"Nothing good," I say, rolling down the window.

I knock on the station's window. The man inside flinches and leans away. He quickly disguises his embarrassment and opens the window. "Sorry. Didn't see you there."

"Don't worry about it, Private," I say with as much authority as I can muster. "Give me a sitrep? What's going on here?"

He doesn't miss a beat. He's so trained to answer quickly and directly that he doesn't think twice. "Something going on in Mexico, sir. We lost contact ten minutes ago. Heard some explosions."

"Anyone gone over to check?" I ask.

"Our orders are to remain at our posts and guard the border," he says.

"Could be a Draun," I say. "Could be that all of you will be next."

"Do you think?" he says, fear creeping into his voice.

"What I *think* is that our brothers in Mexico might need a helping hand."

He gives a nod, but he's just a Private. He has zero power beyond keeping people from crossing the border.

"Sorry," I say. "Not trying to give you a hard time. Just...there's a lot at stake."

"I know," he says.

"I'll make you a deal," I say. "Give me a radio, let me through, and I'll check out the situation. Report back."

"Why would you go over there?" he asks.

"Reasons," I say. "And like I said, our brothers across the border might need support."

"You're just one guy," he says.

Jess leans over into my lap so he can see her. "And woman, thank you."

"Sorry, ma'am," he says, giving her a sheepish wave. "Didn't see you there."

I extend my hand to the man. "Corporal Micah Taylor, U.S. Army Ranger, 75th regiment."

He shakes my hand. "Private Alexander Chedrawe, sir." He blinks in surprise. "Wait...Seventy-fifth? Really?"

The 75th regiment is a special operations unit that handles a wide range of anti-terror missions in the world's most dangerous places. They're the tip of the spear and are highly regarded by all branches of the U.S. military, even if the regular Army is not.

"Rangers lead the way, kid," I say. "Let me have a look."

He frets over the decision for a moment and says, "Sir...if you leave, they're not going to let you back in. Doesn't matter if you're a U.S. citizen, Army Ranger, or a Senator. Border is locked down...but I won't stop you from leaving. Problem is that Mexico might not let you in, either. Then you'll be stuck between border stations."

"My own personal DMZ," I say, getting a chuckle out of him.

"Yes, sir."

"I'll roll the dice," I say. "How about that radio?"

He thinks twice and then plucks a radio from its charger and holds it out to me.

I give him a nod of thanks. "Soon as I pull away, you report this. Tell them who I am. What I'm doing. Odds are good you won't get in trouble."

"Get in trouble?" he says, eyes wide. Before he can second guess his decision, I tap the gas and drive through the station. Ten seconds later, we pull back onto the road headed toward the bridge that connects the U.S. and Mexico, after which we'll reach our second border check.

I spot Chedrawe in the rearview, double-timing it to the admin building, where he'll hopefully do what I told him to do, and remember my name.

"So, I guess that went well," Jess says.

"Well enough."

"And if we get stuck between the border crossings, what then?"

I look at her. "You can swim, right?"

She raises her eyebrows. "Swim..."

"Rio Grande," I say. "Just need to go with the flow until the fence on the Mexican border opens up. Then we keep going."

"On foot..."

"Civilization isn't far away," I say. "We'll find a ride. Or take one."

She's quiet for a moment and then says, "How did someone so dumb become an Army Ranger?"

I huff. "Not always about being the smartest. Sometimes you just need to be willing."

"Wow," she says, deadpan. "Inspirational. You sure you didn't get discharged from the military?"

After passing a closed duty-free shop, we cross the bridge over the Rio Grande. From here, we can't see the military behind us, or what might lie ahead. I slow down, window down and, for a moment, I enjoy the warm air, the chirping birds, and the smell of water. Then the moment passes, and the Mexican border station comes into view.

I stop the car in the road, taking in the scene. Smoke rises from several buildings, a few of which are in ruins. Several Mexican border patrol agents lie on the ground.

Jess leans forward to look out the windshield, lowering her sunglasses. "What the hell? Is it a Draun?"

"One way to find out." I put the car in drive and head for the border station. As we approach, gunshots ring out from behind a building off to our right. It's followed by a thunderous crack and a scream.

"Okay, so I'm thinking Draun," Jess says.

"Uh-huh." After pulling past the border station, I claim a parking space in front of the offices and climb out of the vehicle.

I take the radio, turn it on, and call it in. "Chedrawe, you copy? Over."

"This is Staff Sergeant Jason Crim. To whom do I have the pleasure of speaking? Over." The voice is older, Southern, gruff, and pissed.

"Corporal Micah Taylor, U.S. Army Ranger, 75th regiment. Over."

"Micah Taylor," he says, far less impressed with my resume. Then he reveals why. "*Retired.* Over."

"Still a Ranger, Sergeant, and the Mexican border patrol station is under attack. Several men down. I'm hearing shots…and possibly a Draun. Over."

"Well, son," he says, "you done fucked yourself directly in the ass, didn't you?"

"I fail to see how, Sergeant," I say, knowing exactly what he's going to tell me. The world is terrified of the Draun. Has seen what they can do. And Crim isn't in a hurry to pick a fight with one. "You know what. Never mind. Follow your orders. I'll do your job for you, Staff Sergeant. You can go back to hiding at Pussies-R-Us."

When I release the call button, I catch a moment of a screamed tirade. Then I shut the radio off.

"Are you allowed to talk to him like that?" Jess says.

"Retired, remember? I can talk to him however the hell I want. Now, let's—" I squint my eyes, looking in the distance. "What is that?"

The small creature is leaping, flipping, and rolling between and over cars in a large parking lot. It's like if Simone Biles had a baby with a ninja and it never grew. It's a pug being pursued by four armed men taking potshots. They're not even aiming. They have no hope of hitting the small, mobile target.

"Is…" Jess leans forward. "Is that a pug?"

The moment she says the word, I see it for what it is. It's not just a pug, it's a Kynolari pug. And it's wearing what I think must be an infant-sized short-sleeved onesie and a pair of tiny jeans. Hell, they might even be Cabbage Patch Kid's clothes.

"Holy shit."

I race toward the parking lot, charging both my Hell Hounds. I have no intention of hurting the men, or the pug, but I need to separate the two. With a quick, concentrated blast, I put a laser through a line of parked cars. All at once, they explode, creating a wall of fire between the men and the fleeing Kynolari.

"Let's go!" I say to Jess, then launch myself forward by shooting the laser at the ground. Jess keeps up, using her Stinger's grappling hook to move between vehicles. A regular Spider-Woman.

We both drop down at the end of the parking lot, just before the pug exits the cars, looking over its shoulder. I get a look at its onesie top, which reads, 'PUG LIFE,' beneath a pair of pixel art sunglasses and a little puppy nose.

"Hey," I say, before it runs headlong into us.

The two foot tall pug slides to a stop, looks up at us, and raises its small gauntlet. "Whoa, whoa, whoa! Stay back, or I will stuff your meaty bits inside your stomach and cook your insides in a way that will horrify ninety percent of people on this backwoods planet!"

"He's feisty," Jess says.

"*She's* feisty and—wait...wait, wait, wait. Hold up. Did you understand me?"

I power down my gauntlets and watch the pug's eyes widen when she sees them. Jess does the same.

"We're not here to hurt you," I say. "We want to help."

She stares at me for a moment and then starts pacing. "What the shit? I'm hallucinating. Has to be it. Ate too many old sardines again. Wait a second...I haven't eaten any sardines!" She stops and aims her gauntlet toward me. "And who the hell are you?"

"First, your Lancer is out of power," I say, "so you can stop pointing it at us."

She looks at the power gauge, sees it's empty, and lowers the weapon.

"Second, we should get the hell out of here while we still can."

"Not until you tell me who you are," she growls. "I don't need my Lancer to take you two down. I've got teeth for days and I sharpened my claws just yesterday."

"Look," I say, turning my head to reveal the regulators. Jess does the same.

"Impossible," the pug whispers. "How?"

"I...we...are Kynolari," I say. "*And* human. We are allies with your people, and are fighting the Draun together. And...I...this is weird. I...am the Axiom."

She glares at me for a moment, sneers a bit, and then says, "Bullshit," before raising her partially recharged Lancer in my direction.

27

GRUUNLOKAR

The laboratory appears more sophisticated than anything I've seen on this planet, but it's still primitive by modern Kynolari standards. The equipment, most of which I can't identify, looks well maintained, but also antique.

Because it's thirty-seven thousand years old, I realize.

"We're in part of the lost ship," I tell Chirk.

He's on edge, hands by his mini-railguns, ready to chew up anything that so much as passes an offensive gas. It's admirable that he's protective of me, but we both know I don't need it.

And I sense no deception from Citlali. She means us no harm. A blood test will confirm who we are, and she will reveal the location of Xolotl, and anything he might have left behind for future generations.

"I think you're right," he says, looking around, body relaxing. Being inside an ancient migratory ship is an honor beyond description. The rest of them were either destroyed or used for scrap during the great war. "This must have been the med bay."

"There are pieces of this ship scattered across the world," Citlali says. "Xolotl, in his infinite wisdom, divided the ship into six sections, hoping that if some failed to survive the crash, others still might live. His decision proved to be wise. Three sections were lost. Two survived. And one remains hidden to this day."

"Let me guess," Chirk says. "The second surviving section landed in Egypt."

She nods. "Under Xolotl's direct command."

"They were fortunate to have such a decisive commander," I say, garnering a look from Chirk. It's unlike me to praise anyone. When I return his glance with a slight grin, he understands.

"Right," he says. "Don't get me wrong, Praxion is great. A real war hero. But wow, Xolotl. The Lost Tribe was fortunate."

"Lost Tribe," Citlali says. "Is that what you call them?"

I can't discern whether she is offended by the title, so I say, "Only to mean that they were lost to us, not to themselves. It is clear that the Kynolari thrived on this world and their influence here might very well turn the tide against the Draun."

"It's almost like he knew," Citlali says.

Chirk and I share another glance.

"How could he?" Chirk asks. "The Draun weren't discovered until—"

"A vision," she says. "Of a coming darkness. Of a hero who will rise, and a second who will perish. He spent his life preparing for it. Also, the Draun weren't known to you, but their influence on this world predates Xolotl's arrival by millennia."

"Right, right," Chirk says. "Thirty-seven thousand years."

She glances back at Chirk. "You know a lot about this world."

"We've made friends," he says.

"Good," she says with a nod, pausing beside a long white, wall-mounted counter. "You'll need them."

She plucks a device from the counter and opens it up. Looks like a set of Earth headphones. Micah let me use his father's record player, listening to classic Earth music. It was relaxing, but the headphones did not fit well. "This is a simple device. If you don't recognize it, that's because it was created on this world. It will test your brainwaves and your DNA."

The device hovers in front of me in her hands. She leans around them to look me in the eyes. "Do I have your permission?"

I nod. "You do."

She slides the device over my head. The band on top is comfortable. The band across my forehead pricks, drawing blood. The circular pads on each side slip over my temples. "Why not connect directly to regulators?"

"Because humans don't have regulators," she says. "It's not possible."

"Wasn't possible," Chirk says. "Past tense."

She looks at him, curious. "Explain."

"Humans that spent their lives in the company of Kynolari share our unique brainwave patterns." I take a seat while she adjusts the device on my head. "In a sense, they are as Kynolari as we are, allowing them to receive regulators and gauntlets."

"Fascinating," she says. "Do you think—"

"If you've been living with that tiny horde of—"

"Watch it," Chirk grumbles at me.

"They're quite sensitive about their size, too," Citlali says to me. "Makes them a little—"

"Savage," I say.

We share a laugh at Chirk's expense.

"I was going to say, 'short tempered,' but yes, they can be savage. When they need to be."

"You're god-damned right we can be," Chirk grumbles.

"Shush," Citlali says, giving Chirk a pat on his head.

He pinches his snout and steps away, muttering to himself.

"Now then," Citlali says, "this should only take a moment."

She activates the device. A surge of energy flows through my mind, expanding slowly outward through my body and then ricochets back to my head like a tidal wave. The last thing I see before plummeting into an abyss, is a worried look on Citlali's face.

I awake with a gasp.

"Down, down, down!" Before I can see who shouted, I'm tackled to the ground. Explosions rock the landscape all around. Then the weight lifts and I'm dragged by the collar. All around, Kyno Corps soldiers charge through a barrage of enemy fire, bravely facing death while I am dragged along like a—

I'm tossed to the side, rolling to a stop inside a cave.

That's when I feel the pain in my side. I'm wounded. Blood seeps through my armor.

I should be worried, but this isn't real.

It's a memory.

And the soldier by my side... I turn toward the Kyno Corps Captain. Still new to the job, but no less effective or brave. This was how Praxion and I met. He's got his back to me, helmet on his head, firing at the enemy ranks closing in on our position.

In a few minutes, he'll turn to me and ask if I can walk. I'll lie and say yes. He sees through my deception, and we enter the cave together and spend the night fighting in the darkness of an alien cave system. A hundred soldiers entered those caves. Only two emerged, and we have been together since.

Why am I here?

"Praxion." He doesn't respond. Just keeps on firing. Playing out the distant past.

"Gruunlokar..." A voice whispers from the cave.

"Who's there?" I ask.

I peer into the darkness but see nothing.

"Show yourself!"

I wait, tuning out the battlefield's violent thrum, the smell of blood and the grit stinging my eyes.

A gentle slap of flesh on stone grows louder.

Something is approaching.

Something small.

The impossibility emerges from the shadows, lit in the orange glow of a distant city being obliterated.

It stops a foot short of me, looks up with its small black eyes and says, "Quack!"

A duck.

The duck. From my dream.

This is not part of my memory. This is real. This is happening now. In the present. The battlefield is just a setting plucked from one of my most powerful memories.

"This is you," I say to the duck.

"Quack." It waddles in front of me, shakes its feathers, and then faces me again. Then it opens its mouth and speaks, "My. Name."

"Go to Velshnap," I say, wishing the being really would be sent to the fiery world populated by conscious, very hungry, acid.

"Say it!" the duck screams, sounding desperate.

"Why?" I ask.

"So you can know," the duck says.

"Know *what?*"

The duck takes a few steps forward, standing within pecking distance of my genitals. Then it leans forward, glaring. "Everything."

"I don't trust you."

"I don't care." The small creature lowers its head and sighs. "You are not in danger. Not from me. Not anymore. If I am here, awake, then I am not there, alive. I cannot take your mind. Your regulators make it impossible. So, say my damn name, and the door to my knowledge, hidden inside your mind when you granted me access, will be unlocked. Do with it what you will, but do not let my death result in the Visionary's victory."

The duck sits. "This sliver of myself is fading. I will not get another chance, nor will you." It meets my eyes again. "*Please.*"

I look back to Praxion, at the desperate situation we found ourselves in, at the battlefield that claimed the lives of so many of our brethren. I would do anything to prevent that desperate time from repeating.

Including the duck's request.

I turn back to the web-footed bird and say, "Jenna Flood."

28

PRAXION

We're on the outskirts of the security perimeter surrounding the Gaza Pyramid complex. Won't be long before the guards inside start paying attention to the strange female duo, their baby, and their dog on the outside. The burqas cloaking our bodies in black from head to toe conceal us from bare eyeballs but given the value of what's beyond the perimeter fencing, there must be night vision cameras watching the area.

Torel senses the danger, too. "Should we act inebriated?"

"Egypt isn't the most conservative nation in the Middle East," Baarfolir says, "but two women with a baby, acting drunk will stand out. And the burqas you are wearing suggest you hail from a more conservative country, such as Iran or Afghanistan. You might be better off pretending to be stargazing. Or just confused and hoping to get a look at the pyramids. After all, a lie that skirts closely to the truth is the easiest to believe."

"Mm," I say, looking back to Grover, still leading the way. Nose to the ground, tail wagging, he plods ahead with rare confidence. "Grover—"

"Almost," he says. "Al-most..." He stops, presses his nose into the sand, takes three quick sniffs and then blows it out hard, creating a small divot in the grit. "Here."

"Here what?" Torel asks.

"Here dig," he says.

"You want us to dig? Out here? In the open?"

"Yes," he says, panting happily. "Dig."

"I suppose we should have brought shovels," Baarfolir says.

"Use hands," Grover says and sets to work, digging with his front feet, flinging the sand out between his back legs.

"Uh-uh," Torel says. "Not a chance, and not in these full body blankets."

I scan the area and move to Grover's front. "Keep going," I tell him.

"Grover not do all work," he says, sounding outraged despite his ever-present smile. His sentence structure is improving.

"No-no," I say. "Grover is decoy. I will do all the work."

"Good," Grover says. "Love Torel. Love Baarfolir. Love Praxion. No love digging. Except mud. Love mud."

I take a seat and Torel joins me. Beneath the burqa, I activate my Sonizer and adjust its settings with a thought, watching the it shift in the HUD displayed in my vision. After making the appropriate adjustments, I do a quick multispectrum scan of the vicinity, looking for anyone who might already be approaching. We're in the clear, so I point my gauntlet toward the desert floor and unleash a concentrated burst of inaudible sound waves.

The vibrating particles separate and flow away like water under pressure. To a distant observer it will look like Grover is the fastest digging dog on Earth. It will still raise suspicions, but hopefully after a few minutes of amusement.

"How deep do I need to go?" I ask.

"I look like Anbu?" Grover says.

I turn to Torel. "Did he just— Was that sarcasm?"

"I believe it was," Baarfolir says.

"Micah will be so sad he missed it," Torel says. "His first sarcastic remark. He really is becoming more like us, isn't he?"

"And us more like him," Baarfolir says. "I have been experiencing lapses in judgment similar to Chirk's. Our size makes us more susceptible, you know."

"We know," I say, not really wanting to hear about Baarfolir's judgment issues if they are anything remotely like Chirk's. I focus on the dig, making a hole that is deep, but also stable. I don't want to empty a pit that just keeps refilling and growing wider.

"For example," he says. "The other day, I snuck an extra strip of bacon. Me! A thief!"

"That doesn't sound too—"

"It was *Gruunlokar's*!" he whispers.

That gets a chuckle out of Torel. "You risked your life for a piece of—"

"I marked my territory," he blurts out.

"Excuse me?" Torel says.

"I walked around the house. The wood surrounding the house. Even the *Prowler*." He lowers his head in shame. "And…I marked my territory the way Earth dogs do."

I can see Torel's brows raise, even beneath the burqa. "You *peed* on the *Prowler*?"

"Discreetly," he says. "But…yes. I don't know what came over me. It was like… instinct overrode my inhibitions and reason. It felt more like a—a necessity."

"Feel no shame about it," I tell him. "The air in this atmosphere is having effects on us all. Best to embrace it and focus on what's important."

Torel places her hand on my arm. "We are."

"You," Grover says to me. "Look. Now."

"Huh?" I say, and then notice Grover's attention is on the pit I'm still digging without watching. An angular shape emerges from the sand five feet below. A structure. I increase the power, doubling the output while Grover continues his masquerade. But it's more sand now than the volume of snow when Micah snowblows. Hardly believable, and too outrageous to be funny.

The sand is scoured away in smooth waves, revealing an eight-foot tall, limestone obelisk covered in Egyptian hieroglyphs.

"Fascinating," Baarfolir says, sliding down into the pit, even as I continue to shift sand away. He scans the ancient writings. "Targong's Genitals...this is it! The pictographs depict Anbu in various stages of life, ending with him residing beneath the Great Pyramid, where he will... 'count and weigh the hearts of the dead against ma'at—the feather of a large land bird.'"

He continues reading. "But... Oh dear. The rest of this is a warning, against those whose souls are heavier than a ma'at entering this tomb. It then goes on to graphically describe various deaths in detail. Perhaps this is why this entryway has been hidden all this time."

"That," Torel says, "along with the fact that it was positioned far away from the actual pyramid."

I deactivate the Sonizer and slide down into the pit with the others. I can feel the history radiating from the obelisk. It's both intimidating and intriguing.

"How do we get inside?" Torel asks.

"You can't see it?" Baarfolir asks. "Anbu might have been living here for thousands of years, but he was still Kynolari—and if I'm correct, he left this message for us—not humans. Those whose souls are light as feathers." He reaches up and places his hand atop a carving shaped like a hand, each fingertip ending with a claw. Baarfolir's hand is much smaller, but that doesn't seem to matter.

The obelisk grinds as it lowers into the ground, crushing sand to powder. The sound shakes the pit's edges. Loose sand slides into the opening that's forming around the shrinking obelisk.

"Could have designed it to open faster," Torel says, crossing her arms.

A klaxon sounds, rising into the night sky. Spotlights swivel through the haze overhead. In the distance, I hear engines roar. Our disappearance into the sand finally triggered a response.

Grover barks at the slowly descending obelisk, growing as impatient as the rest of us. I place my hands on its top and try to push it faster, but whatever mechanism is lowering the stone won't be influenced by the strength of my arms, or Grover's voice.

Baarfolir has a go at it, kicking the stone and saying, "Move it!"

And that's when it stops.

Baarfolir raises his hands. "I didn't do it!"

His kick was comparable to that of a Gornokian house-targ. "It wasn't you," I tell him, trying to push it down again. No luck.

I take a step back and raise my Sonizer toward the obelisk. "Everyone back."

"You're not going to destroy it!" Baarfolir protests.

"Kicking it didn't work, and we're out of time." The sound of roaring engines is getting louder. We have thirty seconds, tops. I adjust the settings to the limestone's resonant frequency, ready to turn stone into dust.

And that's when it drops away.

We gather around the hole and look down. The now-large opening reveals a tunnel eight feet below, four feet if you count the obelisk, which has tilted to its side, forming a nice ramp to the floor.

"Everyone in!" I shout, helping Baarfolir drop down before he can voice any concerns. Torel drops down next, taking Grover from my hands as I lower him in. I jump down last and can hear the sound of tires tearing through sand. Shouting voices. They're close.

"Torel," I say, motioning to the open hole. She gives a nod, understanding my intentions from years of combat side by side, the regulators connecting us, and whatever this new connection between us is called on Earth.

I reverse the flow of my Sonizer, aiming it at the pit above and triggering a broad, sweeping pulse that drags a mound of sand over the hole, plummeting like a tidal wave of gritty stone. Before it can fill the tunnel, Torel unleashes a blast of electricity that crackles around the hole above us, striking every grain of sand at the speed of light, forming a barrier of jagged glass that caps the entrance, and keeps the sand from falling.

Above, the sand will fall. It might look disturbed, but there will be no trace of a pit.

"Well," Baarfolir says in the now complete darkness. "That was...that was something. Are all missions like this? The tension? The risk? The relief? Oh, my heart! It's beating so fast. Whew."

Switching to night vision, I find Baarfolir leaning forward, hands on knees, breathing deeply. I put my hand on his back.

"Not always, but sometimes."

"How do you deal with it?" he asks.

"By being the best," I say, full of bravado and confidence.

He smiles, and then laughs, his tension coming out with loud whoops that make Torel and I chuckle along with him.

"Ohh," he says. "Oh my. Well, I suppose I see the appeal, but I'd still rather be reading a book in my study."

"You sure about that?" Torel asks before turning on blazing bright lights mounted on her shoulders. The tunnel ahead is lit, all its secrets revealed.

Baarfolir stumbles a step, face in shock as we lay eyes on a piece of Earth—and Kynolari history—that's been hidden for three thousand years. "Well, I'll be a hoof wanking thunder twatapotomus."

Torel and I look at him in unison.

He sees our confusion. "An Earth colloquialism I learned from our new friend, Sean."

"Sounds like it could be offensive." Torel says and looks at me.

I shrug. "Twatapotomus sounds like a fun word to me."

"Twat," Grover says. "Apot...omus..."

Baarfolir motions to Grover with his two short arms. "You see? Even the Earth dog knows the word. It *must* be common. Like the other words Sean taught me. Douche dumpster. Dick splash... Umm, cuntasaurus."

"Okay, I'm *sure* that one is offensive," Torel says.

"It's a reference to Earth dinosaurs. How offensive could it be?" Baarfolir waves a hand at Torel. "We shouldn't be discussing Earth terminology, anyway." He looks down the tunnel, covered in hieroglyphs, still as colorful as they were when they were first created. "The past awaits."

Baarfolir leads the way, his small stature casting a long shadow deep into the tunnel where only Anbu knows what waits for us.

29

MICAH

I raise an eyebrow at the pug Kynolari. "Really? I could have killed you already if that's what we wanted."

"Pssh," she says. "You're talking out of your human ass. I saw what you did to those cars." She glances back at the wall of fire keeping the border guards at bay. "Your gauntlets are drained, too, which means this fight is mano e doggo, and I've got a couple of canines itching to punch through your pasty dermis. So, hold on to your ass cheeks, things are about to get—"

I hold up both gauntlets and charge them to full power, which is revealed on the outside by the glowing orange bands of light that slide from the bottom to the top. I sprinkle jimmies on top of the sundae of doom by extending my claws and letting them radiate orange power.

"Also," Jess says, holding up her own fully charged gauntlet. "I'm right here."

The pug waves Jess away. "Get real, sweet teats, you're just eye candy." She points at me. "This guy is the fighter."

"And the Axiom," I remind her.

She squints at me. "Who are your Kynolari contacts?"

"We really shouldn't stay here," I say. "We can talk when it's safe."

"I don't know if it's safe to be with you now," she says, and I can see she means it.

She didn't arrive here with the others and, given her gruff mannerisms and knowledge of this planet, I'd say she's been here for a while. Whatever atmospheric anomaly is affecting the others has been working on her for a while now. I decide to give her a name.

"Praxion," I say. "That's the only name I'm giving you. And if you don't know who that is, then I'm not sure—"

"*Praxion*," she says. "Praxion is here? On Earth?" She turns away for a moment. "If he's lying, I'm going to kill him. Yes. That. But—" She spins back to me. "If Praxion is here, then the fleet must be right behind him, yes?"

"No," I say, and her small body deflates. "The Great War ended years ago. Praxion was leading a team in search of the Lost Tribe."

"Of course he was. Why wouldn't the greatest hero of the war spend his time looking for long lost poochies." She sighs. "Then the fleet is what? On its way?

Don't tell me they decommissioned the warships, because I swear to you, I will lose. My. Shit. Literally. I will just shit all over the damn place."

"The fleet is intact," I say. "But the *Prowler*—Praxion's ship—is damaged. We can't yet access the gravity web. Now, can we skip right past the shitting ourselves and get the hell out of here?"

She glances back at the dwindling flames and smoke. Several guards are working their way around, ready for a fight.

"Fine," she says. "With me."

She breaks into a run with a flip, then redirects toward an SUV with a cartwheel that ends in a backflip. She hits the door with an electric jolt from her Lancer and the doors unlock. With a single bound, she's up in the seat, using her gauntlet once more to start the vehicle. She turns to me. "You're driving. Your woman can look pretty in the passenger's seat."

Jess opens the door and slides in, grumbling, "I heard that."

"As was intended," the pug says, then slaps my shoulder. "Drive, human! Drive!"

The new SUV screeches over the lot's old pavement and then we speed away from the scene. The vehicle is nice, and will definitely be missed, but it's going to be a while before that lot is reopened and the owner realizes the vehicle isn't slag, or present. By then, we'll be south of Mexico City, assuming I don't get pulled over for speeding...which seems even less likely in post-Draun Mexico.

It's twenty minutes before anyone speaks, and it's Jess who breaks the silence, telling me to get on Route 101.

After making the turn onto the four-lane highway, which we seem to have all to ourselves, our new friend decides to play nice.

"Okay, okay, despite your claims sounding, frankly, dumb, let's say that you are allies of Praxion, and that you are, in fact, the god damn Axiom, which I'm certain isn't a real thing BT-Dubs. Who are you? Like, really?"

"Micah," I tell her. "Micah Taylor. Former Army Ranger. Now part of the very small resistance working against the Draun and the Visionary."

The pug's wrinkled face falls flat. "Excuse me?"

"The Visionary is here," I say. "On Earth. Has been for a while. Lumen Sok."

"Lumen..." She mutters. "Makes sense, I guess. Who else would be able to—"

"He had help," Jess says.

"Oh, I'm sure he did. You humans are easily manipulated. You will believe *anything*, and I mean the dumbest shit imaginable, so long as it's repeated enough times with conviction. And once you embrace that thing, you hold onto it like it's your baby. Like you birthed the idea from your own vagina and have nursed it into a young concept you're so proud of...even though it's stupid as shit. Even when someone shows you the truth, proves it with science, confirms it as fact or even a universal truth written in the fabric of the cosmos, you will cling to the pitiful, malformed turd of a fetal idea implanted into your mental uterus by anyone with fewer brain cells than the skin tag that this bitch—" She hitches her thumb toward Jess. "—has dangling from her perineum." She turns to Jess. "That's the little patch of skin between your anus and—"

"I know what it is," Jess says. Despite being the target of the pug's verbal attacks, Jess is amused more than anything else. "Just like I know you're a medic."

"That so?" the pug says.

"You have a Lancer," Jess says. "They're deadly, but they also can save lives. We've both seen it. And only people with medical backgrounds call it a perinium."

"What do other people call it?" the pug asks.

"Taint," I say.

"Taint," she says, trying the word on for size. "*Taint.* Kind of captures the repulsive location that little patch of skin finds itself in, eh? Taint. New word. Thanks."

"I'm Jess, by the way, not that you were asking or care, and I'm not a soldier. I just wait around for people to save me and shake my tits when the mood needs lightening."

The pug grins, and I can tell she's trying not to laugh. She pulls herself together and says, "That's good. It's important for people to understand their place in the world. Now, help me understand why you have regulators and gauntlets without me needing to clean your liquified brains off the floor."

I spend the next fifteen minutes giving her a breakdown of everything that happened since the Kynolari literally dropped into our lives. Despite her penchant for wordiness, she listens without saying anything. Just occasionally gives a nod when something makes sense or fits what she knows about Earth, or her own people.

"And that's why we were crossing the border," I say, finishing the tale. "How about you?"

"How about me?" she repeats. "Me, me, me. Well, I was in the Kyno Corps, like your friends, hence the—" She holds up her gauntlet. "We were attacked during a deep space insertion—that's when leap nodes are deployed a light year away, rather than in orbit."

"Like a HALO drop," I say.

She nods. "Except faster than the speed of light, and when things go FUBAR traveling the gravity web…well, I pinballed around the galaxy, unable to navigate. I wound up touching down on this undiscovered—I thought—world. It was hard, at first, knowing that I'd found the Lost Tribe, and that they were primitive ninnyhammers. I tried living as one of them, but hate walking on all fours, won't let anyone own me, puke at the smell of kibble, and no one wants a dog with electronics on its arm and head. So, I've been living in the shadows, studying their ways, learning their language, reading fiction and non-fiction—"

That's why she knows terms like HALO jump and FUBAR, I realize.

"—and eventually, their history. I pieced together what I could from a distance, but it's not like I can travel to Egypt, you know? I recently figured out the Mexico connection as well—Anbu being Xolotl. It was a shot in the dark, but I was a lone Kyno on a planet increasingly populated by the enemy. Wouldn't have been long until I was discovered."

She takes a deep breath and then sighs. "They were smart. Making friends with humans."

"They didn't have much of a choice," I say.

"Could have killed you."

"Could have *tried*," I say with a smile.

She grins.

"I guess I see the appeal. With you. Not her." She motions to Jess with her head, and then gives me a wink like we're both in on teasing her. "Point is, if I'd trusted even a single human, I'd have known about the transmission you mentioned. I knew the Draun were increasing their numbers, but not how. Can smell them, you know. Evil smells like eggplant, I shit you not. Heading south in search of Anbu was a last-ditch effort. I was going to find a way to contact home or die trying."

"That's the way we do it," I say.

She gives me a funny look, like my statement was borderline offensive, and says, "We?"

I pull up my sleeve revealing the Kyno Corps brand, still red and raised.

"No shit," she says. "You're really not fucking with me." She spins around toward Jess. "Don't tell me you have one, too?"

Jess smiles and lifts her sleeve, revealing the brand.

"Well... God damn. Maybe I misjudged you. A little bit." She turns back to me. "So, what's the plan? Anbu has a ship right? Can we just blow up this planet and be done with it? Please say we can blow it up. I am so tired of reality TV. Honestly, civilizations have been wiped out for far less."

"Our plan," I say, "isn't much different than yours..."

She sags.

"Except we have people in Egypt, searching for Anbu's supposed tomb, which we discovered as raw knowledge implanted within the DNA of every member of the Lost Tribe on the planet."

"Sneaky bastard," she says, "but he didn't die in Egypt."

"Which is why the rest of our team is in Mexico already," I say, "looking for a connection…for some kind of hope. If we don't find it, we're screwed. Sorry I don't have more good news for you."

"Buddy, I've been alone for so long that I'd even settle for a chit chat with this bitch." She motions to Jess.

"Aww," Jess says. "Makes one of us." They share a laugh, and Jess continues. "So, little miss, what's your name?"

"First, if you call me, 'little miss' again, I will vaporize you. Second, strangers call me Popzillo, and the first one of you that makes a Godzilla joke loses an ear, you get me?" She points at Jess, and then at me. "You feelin' me, bro?"

I can't help but laugh. Popzillo is a handful, but all her bravado is for the sake of humor. Okay, not all of it. Pretty sure she meant the ear thing.

"And what do your friends call you?" Jess asks.

"Are you? My friends?" Her little pug face looks at each of us. It's hard to not giggle and tickle her wrinkled cheeks.

"We are friends to all Kynolari," I say.

"Guess that means you haven't met Anbu yet," she says, and then holds up a fist. "Fist bump for friendship."

She bumps fists with Jess first and then lifts her little hand toward me.

We pound fists and she makes a little explosion noise. "Okay. Now you can call me Poppy."

"Poppy," I say. "Awesome. Now…what did you mean about Anbu? That we hadn't met him yet?"

"Right, yeah," she says. "I've been on Earth for a while, and despite being a badass, I also have a brain that requires mental sustenance. They make the smartest of us medics, you know. Spent a lot of time in libraries. Stole more than a few phones to access the Internet. Studied the history of dogs. Made the whole Anbu-Anubis connection. Studied the Earth lore around him. Knowing he was Kynolari, I saw this guy for what he was, a megalomaniac asshole. But…sometimes that's what you need to win a war, right?"

30

CHIRK

"This supposed to happen?" I ask, looking at Gruunlokar's twitching body.

"I've never done this before," Citlali admits. "He is our first candidate."

"Candidate?" I ask. "For a DNA test?"

I suppose that makes sense since we're the first Kynolari to visit this world, but it's a weird way to phrase it. And I'm getting a whiff of something rotten. A change in the air. It's subtle, possibly disguised, but it's not good.

"Candidate," she says, enunciating the word slowly, "to awaken the mighty judge of life and death. To return his unflappable presence to this world, as has been done since the days of old."

"And how's that done? Do we need to shake him awake? Ring a bell? Clang some symbols? And please don't tell me there's a whole ritual to complete, because they're generally a waste of time."

"No rituals," she says, looking over Gruunlokar as his shaking subsides. She pets his head, like she can comfort him while he's unconscious. "But we will need to relocate to the Chamber of Holy Transference."

"Sounds...religious," I say.

She looks at me like I've got human pubes for whiskers. "Of *course* it's religious. Xolotl *is* a god. It is a basic truth revealed to his beloved twin cultures divided by an ocean. Only he has power over death. Only he can grant it and take it away. When we leave this mortal vessel—" She motions to her body. "—it is he I will stand before. He who will weigh the goodness of my life, and if I'm found pure and light, I will live for eternity by his side. If not...well, I don't think about it much. After Xolotl's resurrection by my hand, I will have nothing to fear from death."

"Okay," I say. "Huh. You know, in the future, you might want to start talking all culty *before* you invite people inside a secret lab. Because I'm not sure we'd have agreed to anything if we knew you were, as my good friend puts it, 'Cray cray in the brain gray.' Now, I know what you're thinking. What kind of moron says, 'cray cray in the brain gray?' I thought the same thing, too, so I won't hold that against you. But then I learned about *gray* matter in human brains. It's all up in the brain and spinal cord. Bunch of neuronal cells, and dendrites, and glial cells. Really boring shit. And what happens in that gooey gray stuff? Neuronal synapsis. I shit you not. I did not make that up, and this is so far out of my wheelhouse I'm personally shocked that I remembered the words. And in case you didn't know—"

"What are you doing?" Citlali asks.

"Explaining gray matter," I say, "so you don't think Sean is as dumb as he makes people think he is."

She shakes her head. "You're wasting time."

"You have someplace else to be while Gruunlokar is passed out?"

She squints at me.

"Didn't think so. I mean, I could tell you about my adventures in Bacon."

"*In* bacon?"

"Bacon," I say, "Capital B."

Citlali scoffs and turns around to the counter, fiddling with something. "You really are a dog, aren't you?"

"Woof," I say, taking three very quiet steps to the left.

"Well, let me tell you a story," she says. "When I was a little girl, living in this village, my father grew ill. Something he picked up from backpackers who insisted on taking photos with us. Since our mission has always been to stay without drawing attention, we allowed the interaction…and paid for it. Nine died, and my father appeared to be next in line. And that is when *he* returned—Xolotl—old and wizened, as I am now. His last act on this planet, more than fifty years ago, was to cure my father and preserve our legacy. That legacy belongs to me now, as it will to my son, and then his children. We are the chosen of Xolotl, and we preserve him as he does us."

"And how do you preserve him?" I ask. "Exactly?"

She spins around and fires a pistol at hip level. She's quick for her age and practiced. If I hadn't stepped to the side, the operating table behind me would have been spattered with *my* gray matter.

Before she can adjust her aim, I raise a mini-railgun and fire two rounds. The first one knocks her weapon away—in pieces. The second removes her trigger finger, because you only get one god damn chance to shoot me.

She shouts in pain and stumbles back, clutching her wounded hand.

"You dare molest an acolyte of the sovereign?"

"Whoa, whoa, whoa," I say. "*Molest?* If I molested you, you'd—you know what—I don't think I can say that on this planet, and I'm not about to let you spin this so I'm the little pervert."

"Oh!" she says, acting as though wounded. "He kept calling me Bacon. Oh, the things he did." She breaks character to smile at me. "I will let Xolotl weigh your heart."

"I got news for you, lady. The Holy Transference is on hold." I point my mini-railgun at her head.

"You wouldn't dare," she hisses. "You need my Lord more than anyone else. You are lost without him. You—"

"Will have access to all of the computer systems in this ancient bucket of bolts ten minutes after Harth sets foot…" Her slowly spreading grin stumbles me. "What did you do to Harth?"

I lower my weapon and stalk toward her. The plan is to leap up and pistol-whip the side of her head. Show her culty ass that I mean business. You mess with the Kyno Corps, you get messed with—even if you're loosely associated with one of the most well-known and highly respected Kynolari in the universe, who might have single handedly saved the Lost Tribe on this world and might possess a solution for defeating the Draun.

An alarm sounds, dropping me to my knees. I let the mini-railgun in my hand fall to the floor and cover my ears. It's deafening. Painful. And has no effect on Citlali. Because she can't hear it. The frequency is higher than feeble human ears can detect. It's a low blow, but it also means that either Citlali or even Xolotl foresaw a future in which a Kynolari might oppose him.

A door opens, allowing two men, wearing what looks like handmade body armor, to enter. They've probably been monitoring the conversation. Know that I'm now hellbent on disrupting their little transference, because I'm now sure that means replacing Gruunlokar's consciousness with Xolotl's.

And that ain't happening.

I put on a show of my own, huddled up and quivering like I've seen the chihuahuas of this world do. Might buy me a few seconds of pity, which is all I need to navigate my regulator's systems and reduce the frequency of sound they allow in. With a blink, my hearing reduces to that of a human's. It's disorienting, like half of the world has just gone silent, but the noise—and the pain—are gone.

"Last chance," I shout, still feigning pain and deafness. "Walk out of here now and let us go, or I'm going to unzip each and every one of you, Xolotl be damned."

Apparently, 'Xolotl be damned,' was not the right phrase to choose.

Citlali wails a hideously high-pitched sound that is nearly as aggravating as the alarm. Her two heavies reel back in shock, glance at each other, and then charge me with murder in their eyes.

Seems that being Kynolari means nothing to these people.

I'm not even sure their brainwaves would match, pack of dogs or not. All they care about is their crazed devotion to a false god they met when they were children.

Before the men reach me, I crank up the shards per second to its maximum. Then I dive roll away, get back to my feet and draw my remaining mini-railgun.

I pull and hold the trigger as my hand comes up, unleashing a stream of tungsten shards that might as well be a solid line.

They trace a path straight up the middle of the closest thug, from crotch to cranium.

He makes a high-pitched hiccup and then topples to the side. When his body collides with a countertop, the two halves slip apart and fall to the floor with an explosion of blood under pressure that isn't quite as dramatic as Sean's animes, but it has the profound effect I was going for.

The second thug screams in horror. Aside from roasting a pig or other farm animal, he's probably never seen anything like it—a man sliced in half down the middle. Come to think of it, neither have I, and it's far worse than I'd imagined.

I look down at the two slabs of meat. "Okay, show of hands! How many of us were expecting to see *green* inside this guy?" I look up. "Anyone?"

The second thug turns tail and runs away, screaming as he enters a hallway, screaming as he turns down a second, his voice fading, but still screaming, turn after turn, until he falls silent somewhere in the distance.

I turn the mini-railgun toward Citlali and her hands snap up in the air. More like it. "Okay, you, Clitoris. Wake him up." I motion to Gruunlokar with my head. "And if you try anything, I will unzip you faster than a Claudite Sewer Whore."

She has a hard time navigating past the body. She's shaking, and I don't think it's just fear. When you find yourself facing death for the first time, most people take stock of their life with a newfound stunning clarity. She's probably asking herself, *how did this happen? How did I get here? Am I going to die like this piece of shit on the floor who's got god damn* green *in him?* It's a shock to the system, especially when your life has been spent in service to a deity that is no more divine than the seminiferous tubules of my left testicle.

She removes the headset from Gruunlokar's head and then steps back.

"That it?" I ask.

"It's done," she says. "He'll—"

"Jenna!" Gruunlokar shouts, standing from the chair. He spins one way and then the other, looking for a threat that doesn't exist.

"Jenna?" I ask. "Man, you need to get past that—"

His head whips toward me, eyes wide. "Is this real?"

I motion to the dead man on the floor. "Exhibit one. This guy is, for real, very dead, courtesy of yours truly." I bend down and recover my other mini-railgun from the floor. "Exhibit two: this bitch was going to erase you and implant Xolotl's consciousness into your mind. That's how he's managed to live so long. He's body-swapping."

Gruunlokar stumbles a step. Catches himself.

"What's wrong with you?" I ask. "Little snooze and you're—"

"I wasn't alone," he says.

"That Flood chick?"

"She left a message hidden in my mind," he says, and then looks me in the eyes. "I know how to kill the Visionary."

31

PRAXION

"Fascinating," Baarfolir says, scuttling ahead to look at the next batch of brightly colored Egyptian hieroglyphs chronicling Anbu's time on this world. In fact, every panel seems to be focused on Anbu, his accomplishments, his many wives, and how he was worshipped. The narrative is heavy on the weighing of souls and the result of his judgment.

It's a little out of character. Anbu was a man of science and logic. But these pictographs tell a story of religion, death, and the afterlife. I want to think that this demonstrates Anbu's willingness to take part in this world's culture. Him being a god to them was inevitable—coming from space, his advanced technology, not to mention his vastly extended life.

But the more I see, the more I think Anbu introduced the early Egyptians to the idea of deities. As a means of control. Directing the masses and giving them a common guiding force. A vast manipulation, the likes of which is forbidden by the Kynolari dating back to before the migration.

Before he arrived on this world.

Desperation forces people to reevaluate their values, but I would never stoop so low. I am a member of the Kyno Corps. Suffering is my business. A scientist and thinker like Anbu might lack the resolve—or unflappable personal code—that prevents me from entertaining morally questionable solutions to complex problems.

"I don't know if fascinating is the right word," Torel says. While we can't read the walls like Baarfolir, it's not hard to get a sense of what's happening.

"Mm, yes," the little historian says, waddling along, hands clasped behind his back like he's giving a museum tour. "Some of his methods are a bit—"

"Cruel?" Torel says. "Lacking morality?"

"Well, I wouldn't—"

"He became a con artist," she says. "All this time, we've been looking up to a Kyno renowned for his intellect and teachings, but when things got rough, he didn't find solutions through resolve—as is our way—he changed an entire culture to fit his needs. Two, if we include the Aztecs."

"Yes, well, that is regrettable," he says, "but as you know, many of our heroes of old made scores of mistakes. They were murderers, adulterers, thieves. And then—"

"Exactly," Torel says. "They were bad, and reforged by hardship, became admirable men and women. Anbu appears to have walked that path in the wrong direction."

Baarfolir sighs. This is not what he was hoping to find. It will be a shame to all Kynolari if he records these findings honestly, which I'm sure he will. But there is another option.

"We can keep all of this to ourselves," I say. "As far as I'm concerned, this is just an empty tunnel."

"No," Baarfolir insists. "I will not entertain such a thing. History is history, even when it brings shame. It can still be learned from. The missteps of our ancestors guide us to better paths. I will tell this story, in its entirety. Assuming we survive, of course." He turns to Grover, walking beside him. "You've been quiet. Any thoughts?"

"Anbu...bad?" Grover asks.

"Bad is too simple a term," Baarfolir says.

"Anbu...help?"

Baarfolir thinks on it for a moment and then nods. "Yes, yes, of course. Anbu was clearly self-serving, but he went to great lengths to preserve the Kynolari on this world, and to send that message through your DNA that brought us here. His motivation might very well have been the preservation of self, but in this case, that means preserving the Kynolari as a whole. Our paths are aligned for the moment."

Despite all of Grover's progress, I doubt the dog understood half of what Baarfolir just said. But he says, "Okay," anyway, and keeps trotting along, more interested in what his nose is sniffing than the images on the walls. I take a deep breath through my nose. It's faint, but I can smell the ancient blood and sweat that went into building this tunnel. Death, too.

I focus on that scent for a moment, following its path down through the segmented floor.

They're beneath us, I realize. The workers who died constructing this tunnel were discarded beneath the following section. It's a desecration.

Reprehensible.

If Anbu still lives, we are going to have words.

Torel takes my hand in hers. "You smell them, too."

I nod.

"He does not," she whispers, motioning to Baarfolir, ten feet ahead, lost in the story playing out around us. "And I think we should keep it that way."

"Mm," I say. I would like to spare our small friend from the discomfort, but, I say, "The truth shouldn't be hidden."

"Not hidden," she says, "just...delayed."

"I'm not sure how long that will last," I say, motioning to Grover, whose tail and ears hang low. "He has smelled them since we arrived."

Torel frowns. "I'm afraid we are stealing his innocence."

"Not us," I remind her. "But...we can distract him." I pat my knees. "Grover!"

The dog reels around, ears perked, woes momentarily forgotten. I hold out my arms and say, "Come!"

He races toward me, leaping up onto my knee and then into my arms. I'm showered with licks that I would normally shy away from but endure because he's just getting out his nervous energy. I hold him against me, and he slowly calms in my arms, mouth parted, tongue out, panting happily.

I find Torel smiling at me. "He could be your son, you know. Such a handsome pair." She pets Grover's head, which he loves, and then mine.

It's a pleasant moment followed by an, "Oh, dear."

Up ahead, Baarfolir has stopped walking to carefully inspect a panel of pictographs. "Oh my... This is..."

He looks back at us, horrified and confused.

"Looks like he figured it out on his own," she says.

I point to the wall that's stopped him. "I think he had help."

The pictograph is a graphic representation of this very tunnel's construction and, just like we suspected, those who died from the work were entombed beneath this hall. It wasn't just a convenience, it was part of the plan, to drive home Anbu's dominance over death.

"The walkway of death," Baarfolir says, tracing his finger along several symbols. "Those who walk it will perish and face judgment."

"Look," Torel says, pointing to several human men wearing Anubis masks, holding whips and swords, driving others to work. "They were slaves."

"This world has a long history of slavery," Baarfolir says. "In fact, it is still a common practice today. There are more enslaved people on this planet than when these megaliths were built, but they're just better at disguising the practice. It is a shame of the human race...and now a greater shame of ours." He looks up at us, sadness in his eyes. "I am beginning to suspect that, before we defeat the Visionary, we may very well be required to defeat Anbu."

"Let's hope time did that for us," I say. "For now, judgment awaits."

"Unlikely," Baarfolir says, continuing on without looking at the walls. "Bold statements like that are generally meant to frighten off grave robbers. And they generally fail as mankind's greed usually exceeds their fear. That this tunnel remains intact and unlooted likely has more to do with—"

Baarfolir stumbles to a stop.

"You know, I am getting really tired of being wrong."

I place Grover down and step ahead of the group. There is someone ahead, lying on the floor, dressed in strange metal clothing. After charging my Sonizer, I step closer.

Doesn't take long to realize it's a corpse.

And it's not alone. The hallway ahead is littered with the dead.

Grover leaps into Torel's arms and we tiptoe between the bodies. Some are intact. Others have been torn apart, strewn through the hallway that is spattered with ancient blood. The floor, walls, and ceiling are covered with it. A reddish dust puffs out from beneath my feet, generations of dried blood piled up like the dunes overhead.

"Look at them," Baarfolir says. "These bodies represent thousands of years of human history. The clothing, the artifacts..." He bends down to pick up a curved sword. "This is called a scimitar. And look here—" He crouches beside a mummified body wearing tan clothing that appears to be modern, or close to it. He digs into a pocket and retrieves a coin.

He turns it around and blinks. "Oh. Oh my."

He stands and holds the coin out to me. The first thing I see is a date. 1942. Then I spot the familiar symbol, one of many in human history, that represents an evil time in human civilization's development. This one fairly recent. A swastika.

"He's a Nazi," Baarfolir says, rotating the dead man's arm to reveal a red band adorned with the same symbol. "It would appear the tomb was discovered many times."

"And not one heeded the warning," Torel says.

"Perhaps we should be the first?" Baarfolir asks. I raise an eyebrow at him. "Yes, yes. Of course. A silly idea."

"Just stay close." I glance back at Torel. "And be ready for a fight. Something *not dead* killed these men."

"Copy that," she says, powering up her Lancer while still holding Grover.

Twenty more corpses litter the hallway, which ends at a flat wall. When I reach out to touch the stone, it shifts away from my hand and then slides to the side without a sound. Air hisses through the opening and then spills back out into the hallway, warm and fetid like something horrible and massive is breathing inside the room. I step inside, ready to fire.

"We must be directly beneath the Great Pyramid," Baarfolir says, his voice booming and echoing. The chamber is large.

"Torel," I say. "Light it up."

She places Grover on the ground, adjusts her Lancer, and unleashes a brilliant orb of ball lightning. The luminous plasma floats upward until it reaches the center of the domed ceiling, lighting the space like a miniature sun.

I take a step back and nearly fire at what's revealed.

"Well," Baarfolir says, "I guess we know what killed all those men."

32

MICAH

The rest stop looks closed, but the owner sits behind the counter, despite the electricity being out. A thick cigar hangs from his mouth beneath a prodigious mustache. Everything is dusty, inside and out, lit only by the fading sun. The snacks look like they've been sitting here since the seventies.

Jess picks up a bag of Lays chips and waves a hand in front of her face as a cloud of dust slips away to dance in a beam of sunlight.

"You know," Poppy says, strutting along on two legs, looking honestly adorable in her onesie and jeans, though I'd never say that aloud. "That dust is mostly human skin cells. Breathe it deep. Nothing like a lung full of old human."

Jess takes a long sniff with her nose. "Nacho cheese flavored."

"Whoa, whoa, whoa, was that racist? Are you allowed to be racist? Because..." She motions to Jess up and down.

"Because I'm black," Jess says. "Anyone can be racist. Even dogs that can talk."

"Okay, touché, but that *was* racist, right?"

"More like a stereotype," Jess says. "Would have been racist if I didn't love nacho cheese."

"Let's save the great nacho cheese racism debate for later," I say. "Find some food we can eat without getting sick. Bottled water is at the top of the list. Just...check expiration dates. I'll take care of the gas."

They nod in unison and then give each other an annoyed glance for it, which results in both of them rolling their eyes and throwing up their hands. "Woman," Poppy says, "if you don't stop copying me, I'm gonna—"

"You're copying me," Jess says.

I leave them arguing like a couple of sisters and head for the checkout counter. The man lets out a puff of cigar smoke just as I arrive, concealing his face before lifting a newspaper in front of his face.

Maybe he's an introvert? I wonder. Weird job for someone that doesn't like talking to people, though.

"Gasoline?" I ask and the language services installed in my regulators flips a switch in my brain so that I actually say, "Gasolina?"

"Generator in the back," he says in Spanish, which I hear as perfect English. "Turn it on. Fill your tank. Shut it off. Tell me how much you spent and then pay for it."

"You don't need to see the amount for yourself?" I ask.

He lowers the top of his newspaper and gives me the stink eye. "There a reason I shouldn't trust you?"

"No, sir," I say, backing away. "Thank you."

I double time it out of the store and back out into the late afternoon heat. Nearby trees shush in wind. Dust and grit swirls through the air. This whole place is a stereotype. I head for the back and find the generator. It's older than the food inside, but roars to life with a single yank on the starter cord. Inside the store, the lights glow to life. I head for the car, uncap the fuel tank, and start pumping the one and only grade of gasoline available. Not that I'm worried about giving our stolen vehicle the very best.

The store's bell rings, announcing the return of Jess and Poppy.

They're laughing and carrying two bags full of questionable snacks and several water bottles.

"Good news," Jess says. "He takes U.S. dollars, though I'm pretty sure he's overcharging."

That he's taking any money, or is even open, is a small miracle. "Got it," I say, taking out the SUV's key fob and holding the button to open the tailgate. The door beeps and glides up as Jess and Poppy walk around to the back. They're oddly silent for a moment.

When a bag of water bottles drops to the ground, I turn my attention to the back. "You guys okay back there?"

"Depends on your definition of okay," Jess says.

"If your definition includes the sudden realization that we're fucked, then yeah, we're fine and Jim-dandy."

The pumps clicks to the stop. Tank full, I close up the cap, take note of the dollar amount on the pump, and round it up. Then I head for the back, wondering which bag of chips has a rat in it.

Jess points inside the SUV's back without saying a word. Whatever it is will be self-evid—

Holy shit.

The tailgate's contents were hidden beneath a tarp that made them invisible from the outside. But with the hatchback up, the horrible truth is revealed.

Cocaine.

A lot of cocaine.

"Oh, shit."

"We stole a cartel's vehicle," Jess says. "They're tracking us, right? Probably be here soon?"

Poppy gives her Lancer a flick and a blade extends from the end.

It's thin and sharp, serving a double purpose, just like its ability to deliver electric shocks. She stabs it into one of the twenty tightly wrapped bricks lining the back. And there are rows more.

She withdraws the blade and gives the white powder a flick with her tongue. Her already large eyes bulge a little further. "Whoo, yeah, that's the good stuff. No way they're going to let this go. Tits Magoo over here is right. We won't have long before someone tracks us down."

"Everyone in," I say, but Poppy takes hold of my leg.

"Think it through, grasshopper," she says. "There are what? Two hundred-ish bricks of cocaine in this trunk? That's a god-damned fortune. And there is no way in hell this SUV doesn't have some kind of high-tech tracking system. They're going to catch up with us, and we're going to fight them. The question is—will it be on our terms, or theirs?"

I look down at the little Kynolari. She might be small, but she's a fighter. And she's right. We need to make a stand, here and now. "You have a plan?"

"Yeah," Poppy says, and motions to Jess. "She's going to do all the work."

Jess and I look at each other and start laughing.

"Funny," Jess says.

"I ain't joking," Poppy says. "That gauntlet—and brand—on your arm means you're part of the Kyno Corps. Means you represent the rest of us. What we can do. How much respect we're owed. This one knows how to kill." She motions to me. "Can see the mental scars in his eyes." She turns back to Jess, "But I don't see much of that in you. And if you want me to trust you, in battle, with my life, I better see some god-damned psychological scarring in your gaze, you feel me?"

"I don't think—"

She shushes me by snapping a hand in my direction and pinching her index finger and thumb.

"I've been practicing," Jess says.

"Sure, you have." Poppy heads toward the dirt road framed by thick foliage on either side.

"I exploded a guy," she says.

"You do that to save this guy?" Poppy asks. When Jess doesn't answer, she continues. "Look, you're nice. I like you. And sure, you might come through in a pinch, but I want to know you will be ready to unleash hell when the time comes. That you are willing to go down in a blaze of glory, if that's what it takes."

"I *am*," Jess says.

Poppy whips around, locking her bulbous eyes on Jess's.

"Then *prove* it."

"How?" I ask.

"The highway is back that way," Poppy says, pointing back the way we came. "They'll come from there. Mr. Hot to Trot Axiom here will stand in the road, maybe dumping out the cocaine. Get them frothing mad, and then you..." Poppy walks toward the road. "You follow me."

Jess follows but looks back to me for guidance. I give a shrug, but follow it up with, "I'll have your back."

A minute later, Jess is hidden inside a bush on the side of the road. Poppy is at the end of the road, two hundred feet away, keeping watch. And after running inside to pay for our gas and convincing the shop owner to hightail it out the back, I'm standing in plain view, holding two bags of cocaine, feeling like I'm living in a Talking Heads song, wondering, *How did I get here?*

Before I have time to ruminate on the series of extremely unlikely events that led me to this ridiculous scenario, I hear a dog barking. I almost tune it out at first. Barking dogs don't annoy me. They're just kind of background noise. But then I remember Poppy.

They're coming, I think, and then hear them.

Sounds like two—no—three vehicles. Big ones. Moving fast.

They come into view a moment later. SUVs just like ours. The third vehicle is a black pickup truck with a machine gun mounted in the bed—what we in the business call a Technical. But that's not the worst of it. Hovering above them is a ridiculous looking white man wearing a Mariachi costume with a broad sombrero.

Then I remember where I've seen this particular costume before: *The Three Amigos* movie.

"Okay," I say to myself, "*that* might be racist."

I throw the cocaine to the ground. Neither break open so I make a show of stomping on them while charging my gauntlets. The engines roar, charging toward me like a conga line of elephants. But my eyes stay locked on the Draun man—who must be leading them, and maybe even took over the cartel. He wasn't part of Jess's impromptu training plan, so he's fair game.

Though I have no intention of fighting fair.

"Okay, Ned Nederlander, let's see what you got..."

33

CHIRK

"As much as I'd like to hear the machinations of a dead, lying Draun, we need to find Harth."

"Your friend is—"

"Quiet, Clitoris!" I shake a mini-railgun at her and she clamps her mouth shut. "This place isn't the Kynolari safe-haven we thought. They're a *cult*, and they're willing to do anything to bring Anbu back, including killing you."

Citlali scoffs. "He wouldn't really have been de—"

I pull the trigger on my mini-railgun, putting a single, neat round through her forehead. She crumples to the floor.

Gruunlokar doesn't even notice. His eyes are clenched shut. Showing pain isn't really his style, so it must be bad, or his mind was really screwed up by Jenna.

I put my hand on his thigh, which is awkward, but it's as high as I can reach. "Whatever you're going through looks like it sucks, but if we don't get out of here, like now, I'm not sure what will happen to Harth. Sean and Gemma are basically helpless. Pull yourself together, swallow the pain and whatever else is irking you, and save it for when our people are safe. You got me?"

When he doesn't reply, I haul back and punch his leg. Probably hurts my hand more than his leg, but I'll never show it. "You got me?!"

He clenches his eyes and snarls, showing his canines. "Got you," he growls.

With a twist of his neck, he crushes it all down into that dark place we've all got, just waiting to spill out on the day we retire.

"I'm good," he says.

"Great," I say. "Now, assuming the door we came through is locked, can you—"

He raises his 1H1K Void Sniper gauntlet toward the container through which we entered the lab. A single, powerful rail shard snaps out of the weapon and punches a hole through the metal lock.

"Oook," I say. "You know there could have been someone on the other side of that, right?"

He grumbles.

When the door swings open, allowing a sliver of sunlight inside, he motions toward it. "Go," he says. "Find Harth. I'll search the computers."

"Harth can do that better—"

"Not if he's dead," he says.

I point a finger at him. "Excellent point. You good?"

"Fucking fantastic," he says, forcing a toothy grin.

I don't like leaving him behind in his current condition, but if he's well enough to put a hole through a lock, at the end of a dark hallway, without looking, then he's good enough to take care of any cult members who grow a hairy sack and come calling.

The shipping crate opens smoothly to a village devoid of people.

Any people. Including Sean and Gemma.

I draw both mini-railguns and step into the open. No trap. No noise. Can't even smell anyone nearby—and Sean is easy to sniff out.

With a thought, I attempt to activate my comms. "Talon-One, Talon-Four, you copy?" I wait for diagnostics to see if I'm sending and receiving okay. "Talon-one, Talon-Four, are you—"

Comms report comes back quickly. Never a good thing.

As I feared, comms are still out, and have been since we left New Hampshire. Means we're under a global comms blockade thanks to Lumen Sok. It's a classic tactic. An enemy that can't communicate, can't coordinate. Leads to chaos on the battlefield, and chaos is where the Draun feel the most at home.

Also means we need to stay here in Mexico until the others arrive.

I walk uphill through the village, aiming my mini-railguns at each and every doorway. But no one emerges, and there is no one inside. Did they hear about the grand unzippering and head for the hills? Or are they preparing some kind of ritual for Anbu's reincarnation inside Gruunlokar's mind?

The wind shifts, rolling downhill instead of across it.

A scent tickles my nose.

Harth.

I double time my uphill search, wary for traps, but concerned about Harth's wellbeing.

Until I hear him. Grunting. Laughing. Having a grand old time. Got to give him credit, the guy knows how to rub one out. But we don't have time for Captain Pent-Up to unleash his years' worth of unfettered man-jam. Not with Sean and Gemma still unaccounted for.

His voice is muffled. Behind a solid wall. So, not one of the ramshackle huts. When a second shipping container comes into view behind two huts, I sprint between them, and slide beneath a fallen tree, bounding up on the far side into a flip before landing back on my feet, aiming the mini-railguns to the left and right. Had there been anyone to shoot on the other end, they'd have been thrilled about being killed in such an amazing way.

I move in on the closed container, noting that there are holes drilled in the walls, and an air conditioner mounted on one side. No idea where it's getting power from, but if there's a large amount of Kynolari tech littering the area, it's likely that Xolotl found a power cell or two—maybe more—to power his immortality efforts.

The handle to open the container is out of reach. I sigh, mutter a curse, and then leap up, letting my body weight tug the handle down. I'm not heavy, so it takes a while. During that time, a waft of cool air spills out of the ventilation holes above me. The cool air falls like a curtain, covering me with a pungent stench of not just Harth.

Despite my best effort to avoid dissecting the smell, my Kynolari mind performs the task in an instant, separating scents into various categories. Male and female. A plethora of pheromones. A cascade of hormones. And a river of unmentionable fluids.

"What in Kyno..." The latch drops. The door swings open with me still clinging to the handle. I catch a slow-motion view of the interior as the sun's fading light illuminates the scene. The details stab my eyeballs, one at a time.

Harth, buck naked and spread eagle on a mound of broad, red pillows.

His flagpole dick.

His head lolled back, mouth open, tongue hanging out, moaning in ecstasy.

Because he's not alone. He's attended to by a harem...

...of naked, writhing, licking, *chihuahuas*.

It's an offense to all that is natural. Breeds cross. It happens. I'm all for it. But there are biological challenges that prevent the largest Kyno from mating with the smallest. Of all the species in the universe, ours is one of the most diverse, especially when it comes to size, and some combinations were just not meant to happen.

I admit, part of my revulsion is that it's not me lying on the sex scented pillows, but he knows better. Or at least *knew* better. We've all done things out of character since arriving on Earth, but this is Harth's first major breach of protocol since he farted during a barracks inspection when we were cadets. Wasn't his fault. I put laxatives in his lunch. Lucky he didn't shit all over the place.

"Hey!" I bark. "Put your clothes on, asshole. We're knee deep in the shit. Your knees, not mine."

"Hey!" he says right back, leaning his head up to look at me. "Ch-Chirk. My man. What are you—hoo!"

One of the bitches all but dive-tackles his dick.

I grit my teeth. "Harth! Get a fucking grip. This place, it's a god damn thirst trap, for your...seed, and Gruunlokar's body."

"Huh?" he says, still grinning.

"What the hell, man, are you—" Shit. The pieces fall into place. Harth would never do this, a lifetime of Earth air or not. It's just not him. He's noble and pure and all the other proud Kynolari things he loves. "Are you drugged?"

"I don't think so," he says like he's floating in slow motion.

"Definitely drugged." I take a deep breath and do something that goes against my nature. I bare my teeth, bulge my eyes, and dive into the crate, biting and snapping, growling and barking, going full Earth dog, which is the only language these bitches understand.

As Harth sits up, laughing hysterically, I have to dodge his rigid love muscle—twice.

Takes a full minute to clear the ladies and send them running, yipping as they go. They can't talk, but I think they were as drugged as Harth.

In fact, I'm starting to feel a little funny, too.

It's the air, I realize. Not Earth's air. The air conditioner.

I grab his finger with both hands and say, "C'mon, man! Get your clothes and let's get out!"

"Got another finger you can take," he says, and rotates his hips.

I know what he's doing. I see it coming. But I'm so in shock I don't have time to move. I'm struck in the side and sent sprawling to the floor. It's beyond embarrassing—for both of us—and I won't stand for this bullshit for another second.

"Harth!" I scream, leaping up.

I take hold of his scruff, planting my feet against his chest and then slapping the shit out of him three times.

And he laughs.

"Laugh at this," I grumble, and then drop back down. I crouch and spin when I land, extending my small foot, sliding beneath his meat rod, and kicking his prodigious testes.

He howls in pain.

Sobers him up just long enough for him to sprawl onto his hands and knees, crawling his naked ass out of the container and onto the ground, ass and tail in the wind.

I grab his shed clothing and join him outside.

Catching my breath, I sit down beside him.

"Thank...you..." he mumbles.

"I own your ass now," I say.

"I know..." he says and drops his head against the ground. He's big enough that the effects shouldn't take too long to wear off. If he's lucky, some of his memories will go with it.

"I'm giving you sixty seconds," I say, standing up. "If you're not dressed and on your feet by the time I get back, I will write your biography and title it 'The Day My Friend Fucked a Gaggle of—'"

He grumbles and reaches out for his gear.

"You're damn fuckin' right," I say, getting to my feet and then going to look for Sean and Gemma. "Sixty seconds!"

34

PRAXION

"It's a pile of scrap metal?" Torel asks. It's a fair assessment. There are thousands of metal parts lying in a mound, topped with a metal Anubis head. But this isn't a simple trash heap.

"It wasn't always," I say. "Look at the components. Put them together in your mind."

Baarfolir gasps. "It's a MagniFrame."

"With some modifications," I say.

"There is one at the Great Museum, but it's incomplete," Baarfolir says.

"Manufacturing and construction changed with the discovery of anti-gravity propulsion," I say. "But their parts were still useful."

"What's the human expression?" Baarfolir asks. "The one Jess is fond of when there is left over food?"

"'Waste not, want not,'" Torel says.

"The head is unique," I say. "I didn't know there was a model with a head fashioned like Anbu."

"There wasn't," Baarfolir says. "This model was either unique, one of Anbu's personal collection, or—as I believe—it was constructed, or adapted, after his arrival on this world, perhaps for the sole purpose of protecting this burial site."

He crouches down and motions to a blade poking out of the rubble. It's coated in dry blood and nicks from where it struck metal and bone. "Which, it appears it did, quite efficiently, for some time."

A red light flicks to life at the center of the Anubis head. Baarfolir stumbles back, trips over himself, and falls onto his backside. Luckily for him, it's not far to fall.

"I'm okay." He stands, brushing himself off. "The light startled me."

"Startled all of us," I say, lowering my Sonizer.

The small red light expands into an oval. Above it, five more red lights blink to life from within the dusty black skull.

"It's a thumb scanner," Torel says. "Really old tech, but they were used to confirm identities. In this case..."

She leans in close.

"I suspect it is meant to analyze DNA."

"And if you fail the test..." Baarfolir says, looking back at the hallway full of dead humans. "Though I doubt most of these poor souls would have understood the function of a DNA scanner."

"That's what the countdown is for," I say, after one of the five red dots disappear.

"What happens after the countdown finishes?" Baarfolir asks.

I glance back to the dead. "I don't think we want to find out."

"I'll do it." Torel steps toward the head and reaches her hand out to the thumb-shaped red pad.

I catch her wrist. Shake my head. "My team, my risk."

She rolls her eyes. "Don't pull that bullshit with me. You know, just because we're..." She glances down at Baarfolir. "Just because you have feelings for me."

"For each other," I add, smiling.

Another eyeroll. "Doesn't diminish my role on this team. If you try to—"

"Baarfolir," I say.

He waves his hands in the air. "Oh, no. I want no part in a lovers quarrel."

"That's not what this is," I say. "*Listen.* Both of you."

They wait in silence, which is good, because we're down to three red dots.

"Baarfolir," I say, "please tell Torel about my lineage."

"Your linea—oh! Oh, I see. Yes, yes, yes." He turns to his one-person audience. "Torel, Praxion comes from the longest line of unmixed ancestral DNA. From his parents, back down through countless generations, Praxion's family have maintained at least one line of pure breeding. There has been very little variation, even since the time of Anbu. I believe, what Praxion is suggesting, is that the DNA of modern Kynolari might not be fully compatible with whatever markers this is looking for. With his pure blood—in a historical context, not any kind of superiority—his DNA is most like that of the Kynolari from Anbu's time. In conclusion, his argument is actually one of logic, rather than—"

"Thank you," I say. "One dot."

Without any argument or resistance, I reach out and place my thumb against the red oval. There is a prick of pain, enough to make my hand snap back.

"Not the toughest DNA, though," Torel says with a smirk. She takes my hand and gives my thumb a look. "Thirty-seven thousand years is a long time for a needle to remain sharp." She sprays a med-seal from her gauntlet. It closes the small wound while disinfecting it. "All better."

When she smiles at me, I forget all about the old MagniFrame. The bodies. The countdown. There's just Torel, and her eyes. Baarfolir was telling the truth about my lineage. It is one of the purest lines on all of Kyno, but I do not value such things as highly as others in my family. I will no doubt alienate many, should we survive, return home, and continue our relationship, but I have no concern of what others think—not after playing a major role in saving the universe from the Draun scourge, and now, again, for a second time. I hope.

Baarfolir clears his throat. "Ahem. The results are in."

My eyes flick to the skull. Orange. We're good.

"Sweep the chamber," I say. "Look for anything that stands out, but don't touch anything." I look down at Grover, who's been standing by my side, slowly wagging his tail. "Grover."

"Love Praxion," he says, and I can see he's just warming up for several more declarations of adoration.

"Hold on, buddy," I say, sounding more like Micah than my old self. "Just wait. Sit and listen."

He plunks down on this backside, eyes wide and staring into mine, ears perked.

"Good boy," I say, and his tail wags faster. "I need you to stay. Right here. Without moving. Can you do that?"

"I do," he says. "I do."

"You're sure?" I ask. "It's an important job. Standing guard. Making sure no one comes down that tunnel."

His head snaps to the hall of death. "Yes, yes, yes. Grover brave."

"Yes, you are." I pet his head and repeat myself one more time, holding my hands out like I'm trying to magically restrain him. "Stay. Here."

"Yes, yes, yes."

"Good boy," Torel says, and she gives him a pat on the head, too. Then we break up and head deeper into the chamber still brightly exposed by the ball of plasma crackling against the ceiling. We'll have about five minutes until its energy is spent and the space goes dark again. Until then, the tomb is lit better than an operating table.

To my surprise, the chamber beyond the pile of metal parts is mostly empty. There is a sarcophagus at the center. Shards of what must have been pots litter the floor around it. Massive painted carvings cover the walls and ceiling. Each one of them is less of a story and more of a tribute to Anbu's greatness.

"Anbu the magnificent," Baarfolir says, wandering around the opposite side of the chamber. "Anbu the generous. Anbu, master over death. If he oversaw the creation of this chamber and the tunnel leading toward it, I'd say Anbu was rather fond of himself."

"Less so of the Lost Tribe," Torel says, pointing to a mural of Anbu standing upright, atop a pyramid, looking out over a sea of Earth dogs, all seated and looking toward his radiant form. "I think he wanted the Lost Tribe to worship him."

"And when they didn't," Baarfolir says, motioning to another panel, "he chose to become one of humanity's gods. For a time, at least."

"Look at the ceiling," I say. The art bends around the dome but shows a single image. On one side is Anbu, standing once again atop a pyramid. He is clothed in ancient Egyptian garb, radiating light. All around is an impressive recreation of the surrounding region as it looked thousands of years ago, but it is full of rigid people, on their hands and knees, heads bowed in supplication.

"Another display of grand self-exaltation," Baarfolir says. "I'm afraid I do not care for Anbu very much, no matter what he left behind in this chamber."

"About that," I say. "Look at what he's holding."

Anbu's arms are lifted up. He clutches a radiant blue disc with eight metal prongs wrapped around the front, like a set jewel.

"Is...is that—"

"Power cell," Torel says. "An old one, but they're built to last. If it's not damaged, it could still be working even now."

"I think it's more than that," I say, pointing. "Look there. The red lines protruding from the bottom, running down the center of the pyramid." We gather together, following the red lines, down to the wall, where they wind their way down to a small, almost unnoticeable portion of the overall epic scaled artwork.

Despite its size, the small image of yet another pyramid nearly knocks me over. "Is that..?"

"Aztec," Baarfolir says. "I believe...hidden within all the grandeur are instructions. We need to take that—" He points to the old power cell on the ceiling. "—to Mexico."

"For what purpose?" Torel asks.

Baarfolir gasps, walking around the chamber, taking in the larger mural once more. He rubs his furry chin, scratches the top of his head, and then takes a deep breath as his jaw drops. "They're not bowing. Look! Look at them!"

Torel and I wander back out into the chamber, eyes up.

"Look at how they're sitting," he says.

"They're bowing," Torel says.

"No, no, no," Baarfolir says, shaking his head. "They're sitting...*like dogs*."

I see it all at once. The power source. The people posed as sitting dogs. "This is how we do it. This is the answer. We can't change their bodies, but maybe, like the Visionary did—we can change their minds. Like all these people on the wall. Kynolari—like Micah."

"But we still need to find the power cell," Baarfolir says.

"Do we?" I ask, smiling at Torel.

She nods. "Together on three. One, two—"

We both put our hands on the sarcophagus's lid and shove. Takes an effort, even with the two of us, but it gives way and slides smoothly away, falling to the floor where it shatters.

"This...this is highly unorthodox," Baarfolir says. "I don't think we should—"

I reach inside, take hold of the lone object within, and then hold it up for him to see. "You were saying?"

His eyes go wide at the sight of the ancient power cell. His mouth opens to speak, but he never gets the chance.

Grover whines, which is unusual, and asks, "Grover move?"

He has my instant attention, and when I see what has him worried, I shout, "Grover! Move!"

35

MICAH

I'm not sure if Jess is going to follow through on the plan. The people inside the trucks might be a drug running cartel, but they're still human beings. And Jess is not a killer. I understand Poppy's motive—it *is* hard to trust someone on the battlefield if they're not capable of, or willing to, take a life. But this is...extreme.

Then again, they will definitely kill us if we don't take care of business, and fast.

When Jess's grappling hook fires from within the bush she's hiding in, I'm both surprised and proud. She's stepping up. I'm also sad, because taking a life, even of a bad guy, is never easy. At least she won't have to see the bodies.

The grapple punches through a wooden fence on the far side of the road. The thin, unbreakable wire snaps tight across the dirt road. If it were a normal cable, Jess would be yanked out of the bush, dragged into the road, and run over by the second SUV. But the moment she superheats that line, it will slide through metal and flesh as easily as air. She won't even feel a tug.

When she ignites it.

Seconds away from impact, I redirect my aim toward the front car. If I can blow up the engine it might bounce up and over the line. But the second vehicle will—

The line glows hot orange in the blink of an eye. *She was waiting for the last moment,* I realize, *so they didn't see it coming.*

As expected, the SUV drives straight into and *through* the Stinger's white-hot line. But Jess's aim is off. The plan was to aim high. Turn the vehicles into convertibles and remove the heads of those inside. Quick deaths. Wouldn't even know what hit them.

Instead, she's aimed low. Very low.

The line cuts through the bumper, through the tires and out the back. I think this was Jess's idea of mercy. Take out the vehicles, maybe knock them unconscious, and we sneak away.

That's not the way it plays out. Not even close.

She cuts through the gas tank, which goes up in an explosive blast that launches Jess back out of the bush. The Stinger's grappling hook retracts, and she's able to fire it into a nearby tree, slowing her fall and saving herself.

But the vehicle…

Oh my god.

The top section flies up and back, trailing a curtain of fire, like a woman emerging from water and flinging her hair back in front of an orange sunset. Beautiful for a moment…

Then it turns horrific.

The top half of the SUV crashes down on the second, crushing the men inside and setting fire to the vehicle. Four men spill from the first SUV, screaming and on fire, running on stumpy legs, their feet missing thanks to Jess's low cut.

One by one, they fall to the ground, succumbing to the heat, smoking and crackling.

I look up to Ned Nederlander. He's floating twenty feet up, partially obscured by smoke, but visible enough to see the look of horror on his face. Since he gained his Draun abilities, he's likely been the one doling out death and destruction. It's a shock to the system the first time a battle goes sideways from the get-go.

Somewhere in the distance, I hear the Technical spraying dirt as it retreats. There's a brief booming of a machine gun, followed by the high-pitched screams of men realizing they're about to be cut down by an adorable pug.

The Draun man takes it all in and thinks twice about continuing the confrontation. But I'm not in the merciful mood. As he turns to fly away, I take aim and unleash a narrow beam of laser light that punches into a small portion of his body—and out the other side.

He drops like a fly that's been broadsided by a burst of pesticide.

I round the burning vehicles, giving them a wide berth. Glancing to the side, I find Jess sitting, arms wrapped around her knees, a frown on her face. She's going to need a pep talk at the very least, but I can't do that until I'm sure the danger has passed.

I find the Draun in a fetal position, both hands cupping his crotch. And… he's crying.

The moment I get close enough to really see his face, I understand. He's a kid. Can't be older than eighteen.

Doesn't mean this isn't a ruse, though. He wouldn't be the first young person to find himself in the middle of a war. I keep the Hell Hounds fully charged. If he makes a move, it will be his last. I kick his foot. "Hey!"

He flails onto his back, and I nearly cut him in half, but he's not a threat. He's been undone, weeping openly. "You shot me in the fucking nuts, bro!"

"I didn't shoot you," I say. "If I had, there wouldn't be anything left of your nether regions. I put a neat little hole through a nut. Singular. You can still have kids…if I don't kill you."

"Fuck you, man." He's blond. Clean cut. Doesn't look like he's worked a job in his life. Accent is distinctly Southern Californian. "You can't just kill people like that."

"You came at us with three vehicles, including a Technical armed with a machine gun, chasing down a stack of cocaine. What was your plan?"

"I don't know, man! Most people just run away when they see me flying around."

Huh...

"So, you haven't killed anyone?"

"What? No, man!" He wipes snot from his nose.

"But you're Draun," I say, not trusting him for a second.

"Yeah, obviously," he says, somehow oblivious to the fact that everything he says is paving a path toward two possible futures—one where he is alive, and one where he is dead. "Then why haven't you killed anyone? Why aren't you in Japan?"

"I don't know, man. I just...didn't feel like it, you know. I don't give a shit about space dogs or whatever. It's like that scene in that movie... with Tom Hanks. On the island. And Wilson...uhh..."

"*Cast Away*," I say.

"Yeah, that. It's like, yeah, the coconuts are falling on the sand, but who's *throwing* the coconuts? They never show who's in the trees. Doesn't make any sense."

"Riiight," I say, realizing that this Bro-Draun might be too stupid to fully make the change into a nefarious, maniacal killing machine bent on world domination. Or maybe his entire phone-addicted generation is immune to the signal's full effect—a portion of their minds already kidnapped and controlled. "And the drugs? The cartel vehicles?"

"I was already one of those guys," he says.

"A Draun."

"Yeah, man. What is this, a frikken pop quiz? Anyway, I'm hanging with Santos."

"Santos?"

"Billy Santos, man. And our crew." He starts ticking off fingers as he names his 'crew.' "Jacob Garcia. Freddy Torres. Jessi Muniz, Fenix Vaquez, Genario Martinez."

"Your crew was all—"

"Mexican, man, yeah. What are you, racist or something?"

I sigh. "And *your* name?"

"Austin Woodbury."

"Okay, Austin with all the Mexican pals—"

"Descended from Mexicans is a better way to put it, I guess. We're all originally from San Fernando."

Shocker.

"Why do you have cartel vehicles and drugs?"

"We just found them, dude. On the side of the road. Everyone gone…except some bodies nearby. Figured dead guys can't drive, so we took them and headed south to avoid being busted."

"Wait, you headed south, through that insane border, to avoid being arrested?"

"Well, yeah, man. It's Mexico."

"And if they'd searched your vehicle?"

He stares at me, unsure of what I'm implying.

"You know what? Never mind. That's a coconut question, I guess."

"Whatever, dude," he says, offended once more. "Why aren't you questioning the others, man? We were all doing this together. You put holes in all their dicks, too? I mean, *Jessi* didn't have a—"

"You hit your head when you fell?" I ask, looking him over.

His brow furrows.

That supercomputing machine he has for a brain is over-clocking as he reassembles his memories.

"Wait. No. *Shit.*" He whips around, looking from one vehicle to the next. "They're *dead*?! *They're all dead*?! You *killed* them?!"

"You got them killed," I say. "What was the plan? Wait. Nevermind. You didn't have a plan beyond, what? Sell a few hundred million worth of cocaine…to who?"

"I don't know, man!" he shouts, crying his eyes out as the weight of his own stupidity crashes down on him. I actually feel bad for the kid. He didn't ask to be a Draun. Could have lived out his days in the valley, not really contributing to society, but not fucking with cartels or Kynolari.

Poppy emerges from the brush at the side of the road, dive rolling to my side and standing with her hands pre-thrust at Austin. "What the hell is this shit-show about? Cut his head off and be done with it."

Austin wails and scrambles away, face soaked with tears. "Stay away! Stay back. My father is a lawyer, man. He'll sue your asses."

Poppy stares at him for a moment and then bursts out laughing, slapping her little knees. "Oh, this is rich! A Draun, crying? Seriously, what the hell, Micah? This isn't supposed to happen."

"Fuck you, dog lady!" Austin is still scrambling, but not really making much progress.

"Can I kill him?" Poppy asks.

I shake my head. "He's a Draun…but he's also not. He's connected, but not controlled."

"Prisoner then. Right." Her eyes light up. "Can I interrogate him?"

"That will be up to Praxion," I say, hoping that our plan to meet the others in a national forest south of Mexico City turns out better than Austin's cocaine cartel non-plan.

"Grumble, grumble," she says. "He's going to be less fun than you, right?"

"Oh, yeah," I say.

"Can I at least knock him out?" she asks.

I motion to Austin with both hands. "He's all yours."

She springs into a flip, doing a double cartwheel and saying, "Hoo!" "Ha!" and "Heh," with each bound. She springs up at the end, performing a double flip over Austin. Above his head, she opens her arms and legs, making him flinch. Then she smiles and unleashes a bolt of electricity that flows into and through his body. Poppy lands as he spasms for a few seconds and then falls still. She smiles. "Hell, yes. I still got it."

"What about the others?" I ask.

"The ones trying to get away?" she asks, and then quickly follows up with, "Yeah, they're all *kkk*." She draws a hand across her throat. "You know this thing has a blade, right?"

"I know," I say.

"Looks like our girl came through," she says, looking at the two halves of the still burning SUVs.

"Yeah," I say, looking back for Jess. I'm expecting to see her still sitting in the grass, but she's just a few feet away, looking around at the destruction she created. She doesn't look broken. Doesn't look sad. But she's definitely not happy. I'd be worried if she was.

"He's just a kid," she says, looking down at Austin.

"A *Draun*," Poppy says. "Second you underestimate them is the second you die. But you did good. Happy to have you on my team."

"*Your* team?" Jess aims her Stinger toward Austin. The grapple fires and wraps around his leg. "This is *my* team now." She turns to pull Austin to our car. Would have been a dramatic exit. Instead, she makes it a few inches before his weight stops her. She looks back at us. "Well, don't just stand there, help me lug his ass back to the SUV before someone shows up. The Draun are attracted to chaos, right? Well..." She motions to the column of black smoke rising high into the sky.

"Boss lady has a point," Poppy says, giving Jess a wink.

"Boss lady needs to learn about mass, gravity, and friction," I say, picking Austin up and throwing him over my shoulder. "Battlefield Timesaving 101. Don't drag bodies."

36

CHIRK

"Okay, you big sunuvabitch," I say, pulling on Harth's unconscious body with everything I've got. He doesn't budge. Doesn't even shift in his body armor. At least he managed to get his gear on before passing out.

I throw my hands up. "Sixty seconds! I was gone for sixty seconds and now your giant ass is out cold. Fantastic, just...fantastic."

A wooden wagon full of some kind of funky root, or fruit—hell if I know—sits beside a nearby ramshackle hut. "That could work."

I leap into the wagon and disgorge its contents, each of which weighs more than I do. I'm panting by the time I'm done. "Fuck's sake..." With a kick, the wagon's handle swings up and wobbles at the top of its arc. It's about to fall back toward me, so I jump up and give the thing a swift spinning kick. It's a little extreme, but I've got just a few pent-up frustrations that need releasing, and I don't have a damn harem to help me out.

The wagon is nearly as heavy as Harth, and when I pull it, the thing just wobbles a little.

I clench my fists, center myself, and then walk the wagon's perimeter in search of the problem. I find it on the second rear wheel. Some genius decided to put a locking mechanism on it—probably to keep it from rolling down the village's slope, but I still curse them to an unheard of hell, destined to have their insides gnawed on by Garamthic Anal Leeches.

Back at the wagon's front, I pick up the handle and pull again. It rolls forward, but not smoothly. Dirt grinds from wheels. Clumps of old mud make each rotation a lumpy thumpfest. I'm exhausted after just a few feet of pulling. I fuel my effort by unleashing a string of curses beneath my breath. It's the kind of stuff I don't even say around the team. It's so offensive and twisted that I might be kicked from the Corp for even thinking it.

To make matters worse, Harth is sprawled out on the ground uphill from my position. I hold the handle with both hands, my legs shaking as I pull it slowly toward Harth.

When I'm nearly at his position, I realize that I still need to haul his ass up and into the wagon...which, thankfully, has a brake. Anal leeches might have been too extreme a curse. Whatever.

But then...then I need to pull this wagon with Harth inside it?

Ain't going to happen. I might as well just—

"What are you doing?"

I tilt my head back to find Gruunlokar looking down at me. "Gruun. Thank God. We just need to—"

A figure steps up beside Gruunlokar.

It's Harth, awake and alert, looking down with an apologetic smile.

"You know what?" I release the wagon. Gravity yanks it downhill. It bounces, nearly tips over twice, and builds speed until it strikes one of the huts and bursts through the shoddily built wall. "Three points." I turn around to my teammates. "And fuck you both." Then I start up the village's central pathway, my thighs shaking with exhaustion.

"What did I miss?" Gruunlokar asks.

I throw my hands up. "Ask Captain Sausage Loaf here!"

"Who is Captain Sausage Loaf?" Gruunlokar asks.

Harth plays dumb. "*What* is a sausage loaf?"

"Both of you, just follow me," I grumble, walking as fast as I can, which isn't very fast, thanks to my shaky, very short, legs. They have no trouble catching up.

"How do you know where to—hold on." Gruunlokar lifts his nose and sniffs the air. "I got him, too."

The 'him' in question is Sean, and his pungent pot smell is easy to find in most circumstances, even hours later. His trail leads uphill, following the winding dirt path. The village fades, replaced by short trees and brush on either side.

Ten minutes later, my legs have limbered up and I'm moving faster, leaping between rocks, pausing to sniff the air. I've been at it long enough to pick out different scents now. Gemma is still with Sean. Her shampoo has a strong chemical sweetness to it. There are three others. Two men and a woman. I'm not picking up any stress hormones, so the village hasn't shown their true colors to them yet.

I glance back at Gruunlokar. "What did you find in the database?"

"A lot of information about the Lost Tribe. Chronicles of their lives here. Generations of stories. But I didn't see any scientific data beyond vital statistics for the Kynolari that lived on this world. Looks like they monitored the transformation from Kyno to Earth dog for a few thousand years, until they no longer had the mental capacity to understand the technology. By that time, Xolotl must have become Anbu, and didn't return for a very long time. There was a massive gap in the data until a burst several hundred years ago, and then a slow trickle since, presumably from the humans he recruited to maintain the site in his absence. It's worth collecting for historical preservation, but I wouldn't call it high on our list of priorities."

"It is fascinating, though," Harth says. "Thirty-seven thousand years of unknown Kynolari history and evolution on an alien world."

"Fascinating as the lumps in my shit this morning," I say, leaping ahead.

"Something happen I don't know about?" Gruunlokar asks Harth under his breath. I don't hear a response, so I assume Harth plays dumb and gives a shrug. Big dummy.

Big *lucky* dummy.

I hate feeling jealous, especially about something so trivial. No, no. You know what? It's not trivial. He stole my *dream*. Pillaged the little bodies of my simpleton brethren. Okay, fine. That's a little too far. From what I saw, the pillaging was being performed by them, but still, he should have insisted it be me. And, to make matters worse, that particular fantasy of mine is ruined for all time, because every time I even think about a bevy of little bitches descending on me with orgasmic intent, I'll get a mental image of Harth's pink log swinging toward me.

A shiver runs through my body, shaking my angst away. I pause to sniff. The smell shifts with the trail, fading as the path leads downhill. I don't waste time discussing what to do next. The answer is obvious. I bound down the hillside, descending into the unknown, ready to level every single culty *pendejo* who dares to show their face.

The jungle around us grows lush and wet. Large leaves line the path. The trees are a mix of pines and leafy, like in New Hampshire, but much shorter. It's not long before the jungle grows over the path, dropping us into deep shadow, blocking out the majority of the setting sun's orange light.

The path levels out, winding toward a tall cliffside ascending a thousand feet straight up. That must be where the path ends.

"Okay, boys, time to make a plan. Go in hot or run recon first?" Before either of them can respond, I do it for them. "Great. Going in hot. Glad we all agree."

"I'm not sure—"

I cut off Harth with a shouted, "Going in hot, Great Pink Hope!"

He sighs and follows my lead. We're not barging into a Draun den. Our enemy is a handful of backwoods assholes worshiping a sham who might also have some kind of something that could maybe help defeat the Visionary and his new recruits, not to mention the army of biologics he's been building. The worst-case scenario is also the best case—we kill them all.

I smell water ahead. Hear it, too. A waterfall. When it comes into view, I slide to a stop and take cover behind a boulder. No guards. And the path leads around the back side of the waterfall.

"Kind of cliché," Gruunlokar says. "A secret base behind a waterfall. It's a common element in Earth stories."

"Clichés start somewhere," Harth says. "This has been here since long before the human race started publishing stories or had any concept of what a cliché was. So, this waterfall protecting the entrance to a secret lair pre-dates the very meaning of cliché. Thus, it cannot be what didn't exist at the time of its creation."

"What kind of bullshit..." I shake my head. "Is it also cliché to run in, guns a' blazing and kill every human that isn't Sean or Gemma?"

"Well," Harth says, "*John Wick*—"

"That was rhetorical. This ain't a book club."

"*John Wick* was a movie," Gruunlokar says. "The one with the Earth dog. That was killed."

"Right," I say, remembering the man who would have been a great hero to the Kynolari—had he been real. "Charge your gauntlets, boys. We're about to Baba Yaga gun-fu the shit out of these assholes."

I slip out from behind the boulder and charge the waterfall—just as I spot a Draun hovering above the pool of water. It's a woman. Unusually large and dressed in clothing more than a few sizes too small. She's using her telekinesis to part the water, revealing a horrific temple, at the base of which stand a very confused looking Sean and Gemma.

37

PRAXION

Instinct guides my arm as I lift my Sonizer and unleash a narrow beam of compressed soundwaves. The blast strikes my target, but only manages to stumble it.

Thankfully, it's enough.

Grover manages to dash away just before the MagniFrame's metal fist pounds—and cracks—the solid stone floor where the dog had been standing. What was a pile of scrap before, now somehow magnetized, has snapped back into its humanoid form, with heavy metal hands powerful enough to tear apart anything made of flesh and bone. It's both bulky and sleek, built for hard labor, but upgraded to look regal. Covered in armor, including a helm that looks like Anubis himself, with glowing orange eyes.

"Oh my!" Baarfolir says, staggering back.

I crouch and hold out the power cell. "Protect this with your life. No matter what happens here, you need to make sure the others get this. Do you understand what I'm asking you to do?"

"R-Run?" he asks.

I nod. "And take Grover with you..." I look back to the MagniFrame, holding its ground in front of the entrance. This is not the mindless automaton the ancients used for construction. It has been redesigned and programmed to guard this chamber. It allowed us in because of my blood, but now I believe it is testing our mettle, ensuring that whoever claims this prize is capable of fulfilling the task spelled out on the walls.

That doesn't mean it won't listen to orders. I stand and in my most commanding voice, say, "I am Commander Praxion of the Kynolari Corps. I order you to cease all hostilities and—"

The robot raises its arms and fires a spray of metal debris from within its body. We take cover behind the sarcophagus. The projectiles pound the far side, shattering stone.

"Oh!" Baarfolir shouts, hugging the fuel cell to his chest. "Don't let it destroy all this history!"

"You want to explain the historical significance of all this to the killing machine," Torel says, "be my guest." She rolls to the side, fires a bolt of electricity, and then rolls back. "No effect. It just absorbed the energy."

"I'll draw its attention away from the exit," I tell Baarfolir. "Be swift. Be silent."

"Swift and silent," he repeats. "First time for everything, I suppose."

I stand and raise my arms. "I surrender."

The MagniFrame fires another volley, breaking through the sarcophagus's far side as I duck back down.

"I surrender?" Torel says. "I *surrender*?! That's not how you distract an enemy."

"It could work," I say.

She rolls her eyes and looks at Baarfolir. "Move when I move, understand?"

He nods, but it's not enough. I grab hold of his body armor and give him a shake. "Do you understand?!"

"Yes!" he shouts. "I'm ready."

He climbs up onto his little legs and tugs on Grover's collar. "We need to run, boy."

"We run," Grover says. "Run away."

"Yes," Baarfolir says. "Run fast."

"Grover am fast," the dog says.

"Go!" Torel says, dive rolling to the right.

Baarfolir obeys, but Grover is faster by far. He takes off running with Baarfolir still clutching his collar. The historian is yanked off his feet and dragged toward the exit, clutching the power cell, and shouting the whole way.

At least they got the fast part right, I think, and then I lean up to support Torel.

She unleashes a crackling wave of electricity that isn't very concentrated or powerful but *is* bright and very distracting.

The MagniFrame swings its large arm toward the luminous web, passing straight through the electric field without taking any damage. With its attention on Torel, I'm able to get a good look at it.

The machine, while familiar, isn't constructed like the ancient MagniFrames. Most of its body might have come from spare parts, but I can't see what's holding it together, or even begin to guess at how it took this form after being a pile of scrap. I activate my heads-up display and then shift through electromagnetic spectrums. Visible light. Infrared. Ultraviolet. Nothing reveals anything unusual. I check for Gamma rays, X-rays, and radio waves. Nothing. I can't detect any kind of energy radiating from the robot.

But it can detect me. While still focused on Torel, one of its arms rises toward me, unleashing another spray of debris. I leap to the side, roll across the floor, and come to my feet in a sprint. With a leap, I bound up the wall, ten feet above the floor, where I dig in my feet and shove away. I sail up and over the robot, unleashing a full power blast of sonic energy into its head.

It would be enough to liquify the insides of anything living. All I manage to do is knock it down to one knee, for just a moment. But during that moment, Grover manages to sprint into the tunnel, dragging Baarfolir and the power cell with him.

Good boy, I think, and then land on my feet. "I have an idea."

"By all means," Torel says, diving to the side. She lands behind the sarcophagus again, and I join her as the MagniFrame reduces what remains of the stone tomb to rubble.

"Tungsten isn't magnetic."

"Okay," Torel says. "Thanks for the info, but how is that going to help?"

"Tungsten is *paramagnetic.*" I wait for the 'ooh' of realization, but it doesn't come. Torel is a medic. Trivial information about rare metals is not part of her knowledge base. "If that thing is using magnetism to hold itself together, it should be generating a violently fluctuating magnetic field. And that, will either attract tungsten, or repel it violently."

A fresh barrage of scrap metal reduces our cover to a short, crumbling wall of limestone.

I draw my side-arm, a recently constructed railgun of Harth's design. He calls it a Slapper. Micah thought it was a funny name and told us not to use it in the United Kingdom. Never did find out what it meant. Unlike Chirk's mini-railguns, I have no control over the rounds fired per second. But what the Slapper lacks in customizations, it makes up for with raw power. Less than Gruunlokar's 1H1K Void, but Harth claimed it could kill an Earth dinosaur—if they weren't extinct.

I lean up from behind our little wall and take aim—just to the side of the MagniFrame. I fire a single round, knowing exactly where it should strike. It hits the wall ten feet to the right. Repelled. Anbu somehow used the magnetism the unit once used to move heavy ship parts to hold the body together, making it capable of reassembling itself, no matter how much firepower we manage to hit it with.

I lie back down.

"So?" Torel asks.

"It's held together with magnetism," I say. "I'm not sure how we can—"

"I got it," she says. I can sense her intention through our regulator connection, but I lack the knowledge to understand.

Happily, she explains.

"While I don't know exactly what a MagniFrame is made from, if it's magnetic, a good portion of it must be iron, the atoms of which oscillate at 300 gigahertz. All I need to do is generate the right electrical field and I can deactivate the magnetism."

"Oh, is that all?" I say, laying on the sarcasm.

"It's not hard," she says, "but…it's similar to how your Sonizer can duplicate the resonant frequency of materials."

I frown. "You need to touch it."

"Preferably before it touches us." Her statement is punctuated by the last of our cover coming apart under heavy fire.

"Go!" I say, rising to my feet, giving the machine a target. It tracks my progress around the room, but when Torel stands and heads in the opposite direction, the Anubis head splits down the middle, watching us both.

Then it opens fire.

We've both been under fire with nowhere to hide. The key to survival is to keep moving. Even if you're—

"Ahh!" I shout, when the back of my planted leg is hit. I go down in a rolling heap, already planning my next evasive maneuver.

It's also not the first time I've been shot. Won't be the last.

Torel runs up and along the wall, chased by a stream of metallic rounds that punch into the stone wall—and then snap back into the body.

It will never run out of ammunition.

As I roll back to my feet, she springs away from the wall, reaching out her hand toward the Anubis head. She makes contact, and vaults away, twisting her body like a pen in the hands of an artist. She lands facing the robot, and bounces straight back toward me, Lancer raised toward the MagniFrame.

Her power level drops from full to nothing as a burst of electric blue light fills the room from floor to ceiling and wall to wall, leaving the robot no place to hide. It travels at the speed of light, striking and demagnetizing the machine a moment after it's unleashed.

But the MagniFrame is far quicker than any living thing, and in that second it took Torel to fire, it unleashes a blast of metal shrapnel that's impossible to avoid.

The result…

Torel falls into my arms at the same moment Anbu's robot clatters to the floor in a heap.

I stumble back a step from the impact, and then lay her down on the floor. She's been struck, several times. Wounds on her legs. Her torso. One to the side of her head. Blood pulses from the wounds.

"No," I say, emotion already hiccupping from deep within.

With shaking hands, I take out my cannister of KynoSeal. One by one, I shove the nozzle into Torel's wounds, plugging them with a liquid coagulant. In seconds, the cavities fill with expanding foam that will keep her from bleeding out. I flip her over, looking for exit wounds and find none. "Damn it. God fucking damn it!"

I shove the KynoSeal into the hole in my leg and fill it.

I grunt as the foam expands and hardens. Then I stand with Torel's unconscious body in my arms and head down the tunnel.

Despite the pain, I move quicker than I ever have before. Desperation is a powerful motivator. I've never felt it before this moment. I do not like it.

Tears matte the fur beneath my eyes. Because I've seen wounds like this before. Sometimes they're survived. More often, they're not. And without Torel to guide the MedBay's systems, the odds are not in her favor.

And that's if we make it back to the *Prowler*.

I emerge from the cavern into the bright light of morning and stagger to a stop. More than thirty people stand outside our excavated secret entrance. All of them staring.

"What is this?" I ask, ready to unleash a Sonizer blast that will loosen their bowels and send them running.

Baarfolir places a hand on my gauntlet. "They're children."

I scan the crowd again. Baarfolir is right. Every one of the gathered people are children. And they're not alone. Earth Dogs scurry among them, tails wagging.

A rough looking dog emerges from the crowd and greets Grover. They sniff each other for a moment, tails wagging. Then Grover looks back. "They help. Good Boys."

A boy steps forward, smiling. In awe. He places his hand over his heart and says a single word I don't need translation services to understand, "Kynolari."

I repeat the gesture and his word. "Kynolari."

The crowd parts as a small vehicle buzzes toward us. It slides to a stop at the sand's edge. The boy motions toward it, saying, "Tuk tuk! Come! Hurry!"

I lay Torel down in the vehicle and climb in beside her as Grover and Baarfolir cram into the small front seat with the boy, who turns around, and with a combination of elation and concern for Torel, asks, "Where to, boss?"

38

CHIRK

"What the–" is all I get out before the girthy Draun's cackle drowns out all noise in the area, including the waterfall.

Is she amplifying her voice? I wonder.

Then she shouts, "Kynolari scum! Your day of judgment is...*at hand!*" With a surge of power, the waterfall bursts out to the sides, revealing the Xolotl cultists. They're armed with Earth weapons. Mostly shotguns. And they're not afraid to use them–despite it being a waste of time and ammo.

The weapons boom, over and over, unloading torrents of buckshot toward the floating woman. Not a single pellet connects. Instead, they form a cloud of metal, hovering in space where the waterfall should be.

Sean and Gemma duck, and I have to admit it, I feel proud when Sean shields her with his body. The defensive posture saves both of their lives as the pellets reverse course and are returned from whence they came. Every single one of the cultists are shredded and dropped to the ground, coming apart in bursts of gore that make no logical sense...until you consider the possibility that the Draun still has control of the pellets, swirling them around the temple cave, striking the bodies over and over, laughing the entire time.

This is a sick one. Probably was already very Draun-like before the signal was broadcast around the world.

"Yeyah!" she shouts, pumping both her fists, flapping waves of loose skin beneath her arms. "Uh! Uh! Uh!"

"My eyes," Harth says, wincing as the woman thrusts her prodigious pelvis.

"Your eyes?" I ask. "This is nothing."

I turn toward Gruunlokar. "Take the–"

He's gone.

And way ahead of me. Now that I'm focused on him, I can sense him moving through the brush and trees, heading up the concealed mountainside to get a better view.

"Okay," I say. "Gruun's on task, at least."

"I think we should–"

"I don't care what you think, today," I say. "Prax put me in charge, and you put me in therapy."

Harth grumbles. "You know I was intoxicated. What happened back there… It will shame me for the rest of my life."

"Shame you?" I scoff and shake my head. "It's a god-damned badge of honor."

"Not for me," he says, and I know he means it. Not everyone has the same appetites, and Harth…the big noble bastard will be tortured by what happened. Which sucks because *I'll* feel shitty every time I make *him* feel shitty about it. Which means I can't tease him anymore, because I'm a nice friggin' guy, a good teammate, *and* I don't like feeling shitty. Doesn't mean I can't take advantage of the situation, though.

"I'll make you a deal," I say. "We do this my way. No arguments… I'll never bring it up again. Like it never happened. Memory erased…"

"Deal," he says without thinking about it.

"Great," I say, "now throw me."

"Excuse me?" he says.

"You heard what I said, assmonkey. Throw. Me." I point to the obese woman turning her attention to Sean and Gemma. "We both know that a Draun's telekinetic field isn't attuned to flesh and blood if they don't know it's coming. If we open fire, she'll shield up. I need to get up close and personal. Get her to drop her shields and give Gruun the chance he needs to erase her head."

"But your clothing," Harth says. "Your weapons."

When he looks back down at me, I'm already half naked. "Some of us don't mind showing off the goods."

He smiles and shakes his head.

"We were born with weapons," I say. "We just forgot how to use them. Now throw me like the Earth footballers and toss me the fuck up to there before that Belusian Sky Flarp kills our friends!"

Without another word, Harth picks me up in his hand, which is its own kind of humiliating. Then he hauls back and launches me into the air. Feels like I'm flying for a moment, like I could just keep on going right up into the sky, but then I reach the top of my arc and start falling.

At least he's got good aim. Looks like I'll come down on the lady's bulging neck. I'll just latch on and go savage.

As I descend toward the woman, I get a good view of her outfit. The pink tights are lost up the black hole that is her ass crack. She's wearing a white tank top that's slid up over the lowest of her back rolls. The image on the back is of a muscular man wearing sunglasses and an American flag cut off shirt with the words, 'This Bitch Knows How to Please a Man.'

Takes a supreme effort to not laugh at her. She's a caricature that I'd like to say was uncommon in the United States. But I've seen enough of this world, in person and online, to know this woman isn't an endangered species. Plenty more where she came from.

Her permed blonde hair quivers as she laughs, opening her arms wide.

Inside the temple, I see the bloody pellets separate into two floating masses. When she brings those hands together, my best friend and the only woman he might actually stand a chance with, will be reduced to ground beef.

I will myself to fall faster. There is nothing I can do about it, though.

But there is a way I can stop her…

A way to save Sean and Gemma.

But it's going to cost me. No way to know how much. But Sean's my man. I'm his dog. Like Grover and Micah.

The woman's arms swing toward each other.

The buckshot shoots toward the cave's center.

Learning from Grover's example, I shout, "Hey, Thickums!"

The woman reels around toward me.

I catch sight of the pellets falling to the cave floor.

Then I'm face-to-face with Thickums, arms and legs spread wide, snarling, eyes bulging. I let out a savage bark.

"Glack!" the woman shouts in surprise. Might be because no one would expect a dog to be way the hell up here. Might be because I'm about to slap her nose with my cock. Doesn't really matter. Her response would be the same either way.

While she recoils in surprise, her telekinesis follows her subconscious desire to be shielded from my attack.

So instead of latching onto her face, biting her ear, and shaking like Micah's unbalanced washing machine, I hit the top side of her spherical shield. Then I slowly slide down its surface, staring her in the eyes.

She recovers from her shock and sneers in revulsion upon seeing me. Doubly so when she sees my stretched-out dick, dragging along the invisible surface. I give her two middle fingers as I approach the side—

—and fall away.

Don't bother screaming. There's no point, and I won't give her the satisfaction.

I glance to the side and see Sean, standing at the temple's edge, watching through the open curtain of water as I fall from the air. While keeping one middle finger extended toward Thickums, I raise a fist to Sean and extend my thumb.

"No!" he screams over the waterfall's roar, and he does something I'd never have guessed he was capable of.

He jumps.

Dives really.

Arms outstretched.

It's a dumbass move, but I'm proud of him for it.

Even prouder that he's clearly paid attention to the lessons I've been giving him—in how to fight, how to pick up women, and how to be a sneaky-ass-motherfucker. Because when he leaps out over potential death, throwing his body at the Draun, he keeps his mouth shut and doesn't make a sound.

Thickums, still focused on me as I splash down into the water, doesn't bother extending her shield all the way around her body.

When I kick back to the surface and look up into her eyes, she pays the price.

Sean slams into her from behind, wrapping his arms...part way around her stomach.

He missed her head, which is where you really want to aim when squaring off against a Draun at close range. Knocking them silly, or unconscious, is the only real chance you get.

But Sean...

Thickums spins around from the impact, and I get a look at Sean, face planted between the giantess's ass cheeks, nose deep in a skid mark.

"Uagh!" I shout, reeling back.

Behind me, on shore, Harth winces and says, "Ohh!"

And then—it gets worse. For everyone.

Sean scrabbles for a grip, finds one, and lets it hold his weight. The result? He plummets toward the pool of water while holding onto Thickums's waistband. The hot pink tights slide down the woman's legs, inverting as they go. They snag at her feet, but Sean holds tight and fully 'depants' the woman before tumbling away, trailing the god-forsaken pink fabric.

Thickums notices the breeze and looks down toward her lady parts but can't seem to spot them. She bends back and forth, twisting around, and then thinks to pat her hips. The slap of skin on skin reverberates over the pool. It's followed by a scream of horror.

She's gone in a blur, up into the sky and out of sight.

Well, I think, *that's one way to do it.*

Sean swims over to me and spits out water. "Lord Sean Huempfner, one. Draun, zero."

"You're an idiot," I say, climbing onto his back, "but...you did good. She's going to be pissed when she returns, though."

"We better hurry then," he says, swimming for shore as the waterfall zips itself back together and crashes down behind us, kicking up a wave that helps propel us toward the riverbank, where Harth is waiting, a smile on his face.

"There seems to be an above average amount of...nudity today." He holds up my gear as I shake the water from my body. "Hopefully, that is the last of it."

39

CHIRK

"You ever feel like the universe is paying extra attention to you?" I ask Sean as he leads us along the path to the hidden, now blood-soaked temple. "Like, if there was a god, or some kind of cosmic architect, he might occasionally stay focused on you longer than usual?"

"When I'm blazed," Sean says, "maybe. But normally? Naw, man, I don't think so. But it sounds awesome. My parents barely even paid attention to me."

"I was coddled," Harth says. "Count yourself lucky."

"The grass is always greener," Gemma says, after she'd come down the path to meet us.

"An Earth saying?" Harth asks.

Gemma nods. "People envy what other people have, even if they already have better. It's part of the human condition, to want—almost need—everything."

"That's the Draun in you," I say. "That craving to take…everything, whether you need it or not. It's evil. Resist it."

"Most of us do," Sean says. "Like, all the time. Well, until the signal, I guess. I think it got harder for a lot of people."

"Agreed," Harth says. "Sometimes people—even Kynolari—find themselves in circumstances beyond their control, in which they do things they would never previously do."

"All that is fascinating," I say, "but can we get back to me, please? Any of you ever feel that way? Like a sense of a lingering attention."

Gemma shakes her head.

Harth looks down on me. "Perhaps it is Gruunlokar, keeping an eye on us."

"It's not a regulator connection," I say. "Feels bigger." A shiver runs through my body. "Honestly, it feels ominous. Like shit's about to go down and I'm the target."

"Instinct," Gemma says. "Earth dogs are known for it."

"They're not the only ones," I grumble, "but that's not it."

The waterfall's roar cuts the conversation short, which is just as well because the feeling is starting to freak me out. I nearly forget about it when the smell of blood overwhelms my other senses.

A cavern opens up behind the sheet of falling water.

The deep orange sun filters through, making the interior appear to be on fire. When I look up at the hidden temple, dancing in the light, almost alive, I think that this was the time of day it was meant to be seen—because it brings the twenty-foot-tall visage of Xolotl to life, creating the illusion that his eyes are shifting about, watching everyone from beyond the grave.

While the style is Aztec, the face and ears match the Egyptian Anubis. There's no doubt he was here and left his mark on the people here, not to mention their undying—well, now very dead—devotion. But did he leave anything behind that will help?

Other than a copy of his consciousness. Because I'd rather not bring the guy back. Strikes me as a douche canoe. He might have saved the Lost Tribe, but he just rubs me the wrong way. And maybe we don't even need him now. Gruunlokar had another mental powwow with that Flood chick. Said he knew how to kill the Visionary. Didn't *share* that information, but what more can a long dead, waiting to be resurrected, Kynolari sham of a god, give us?

Only one way to find out, I suppose.

I approach the temple. It's a step pyramid, hidden inside a large cavern. The place has been kept clean over the years. Not a trace of growth on its surface. I stop in front of Xolotl's face, looking up at his big eyes. I lift my hands to the sides. "Hey, asshole. I'm not in the mood to figure out where your hidden door is, and in case you missed it, your people are paste."

I glance back at the mess. The floor, already wet with water, is coated in globs of organs, sheets of skin, clumps of coagulated blood, and a scattering of bones, like a pup came through and messed up a puzzle that used to be people.

"Paste might be too kind of a word," I say.

"Slurry," Harth says.

Sean chimes in with, "Chum."

"Seriously?" Gemma says, shirt pulled up over her nose. "It's obviously grume."

"Grume?" Sean asks. "You made that up."

"Sounds fake to me," Harth says.

"Fine," Gemma says, "how about splorch? There's splorch all over the place."

"Splorch?" Sean says. "Gross."

"Yeah, that's too far," I say, and am about to continue when the glint of orange coming from the eyes is a little brighter than the sun's diffuse glow. "Uhh, guys. I think—"

An orange light beams out of the eyes, striking me and scanning down my body.

Then it flicks off.

"What was that?" Gemma asks.

"Body scan," Harth says. "Used to determine species, sex, age, and other attributes. Even individual identities."

"Hope it didn't need to be one of the splorch dudes," Sean says.

"They wouldn't have been alive, when this was put in place," Harth says. "Let's hope that—"

A grinding rumble sends a quiver through the stone floor, and the water behind us. Xolotl's mouth drops open, lowering until a ramp up into a tunnel is formed. Looking up at the altered face, I ask, "Is it just me or does he look really surprised to see us now?"

Harth nudges me from behind.

"Yeah, yeah. I'm going. I'm going." I walk up the blocky staircase tongue and step inside the temple.

Lights wink to life as I enter, illuminating a white corridor. It's old. Ancient really. But the stylings of Kynolari design—the smooth flow of the walls, ceiling, and floor—are easy to spot. There won't be any poly-organic doors opening at our approach, but this is an old Kynolari space cruiser.

Part of one, anyway.

"Chirk..." Harth says, sounding astonished.

"I know," I say. Kynolari don't indulge in things like 'sacred ground,' but if we did, this would be it. The passage winds past several closed doors that have been welded shut. Could have been done after the crash. Could have been before, if there was a hull breach they were trying to seal off. Might be what ultimately brought them down. But that feels off, mostly because of the dark red X painted over each sealed door.

It's old. I crouch beside one of the doors and scratch at the X.

Give it a sniff. "Blood," I say.

"Kind of figured that, bro," Sean says.

"Wise ass," I say and give the blood a second sniff. I flick it off my nail, stand up, and say, "Human."

"Awesome," Gemma says, sounding nervous. "Seems to be a lot of human blood wherever there are Kynolari."

She ain't wrong about that. I give her a wink. "Just stay on our good side and you'll be fine."

"Like my uncle," she says. "You didn't forget about him, right?"

Uncle... Uncle... Shit.

"We would not forget Haruto or his predicament," Harth says, "but we cannot charge into a nation of Draun and expect to return alive, let alone with your uncle and those in hiding with him. What we are doing now... What you are *helping* us do..."

Help is kind of a strong word for Gemma's contribution, but I guess she can get a participation award. Sean says they're common on this world, which is just...sad. Do they get a ribbon every time they take a shit? I'd need a warehouse just for my shit awards. I participate in every single one.

"...is your uncle's best chance at survival."

"You can trust them," Sean says, placing his hand on her shoulder. "They have our backs. Like...all our backs."

She nods and smiles. Looks a little uncomfortable with the attention suddenly being on her. Good news for Gemma, I step out of the hallway and into a large chamber that makes me forget all about her uncle again. The chamber is shaped like half an egg. Part of the smooth arching walls and ceiling are original to the ship. The far side was carved out of the mountain's interior, polished to a smooth shine.

But the size and structure only make an impression for a moment. It's quickly replaced by decorations mounted around the room. Decorations isn't really the right word. I don't think they're meant to look pretty, but like a good piece of art, they invoke a lot of questions, starting with—

"Why are there dead bodies hung around the room?" Sean asks.

"And what kind of bodies are they?" Gemma asks, moving toward the nearest corpse. "It has canine features, but look here, and here..." She motions to the rib cage and spine. "The ribs are too broad. And the spine is built to support weight vertically, not horizontally. It's like a cross breed, between Kynolari and...well, dogs."

"It's *not* a cross breed," I grumble. "This is more like a transitional species, somewhere during the middle of the Lost Tribe's devolution into dogs."

"Yes," Gemma says, nodding. "It's fascinating."

"It's unnatural," I say.

"Not on this planet, dude," Sean says. "We know how to go primal."

I smile. "Yeah, you do. And it looks like Xolotl knew how to go native, too." I point to the body displayed two to my left. It's mostly skeletal, but there are tattered remains of clothing hanging from it.

"It's *human*," Gemma says, moving over to the body. "Based on its skeletal structure...I'd say this was a woman."

"He was ahead of his time," Sean says.

Gemma laughs. "By five hundred years."

"Thing is," I say, "this kind of physical manipulation, transplanting your mind into another Kynolari, into another *species*...it's beyond forbidden by every civilized culture in the universe."

"His punishment would be unfathomable," Harth says. "And justified. How long have our people revered Anbu? And now, to find out *this?* That he was a monster?" Harth clenches his fists and walks away, reining in his anger like only he can.

It's impressive because he's crushed. Kynolari history is important to him, not because he's interested in old shit, but because he's proud of where we come from, of who we are as a species. Anbu, Anubis, Xolotl, whatever you want to call him, has just shattered the foundation of what makes Harth...well, Harth.

"Okay," Sean says. "So, we know he lived a really, really long time, possibly by using these dead people, and Kynolari, as vessels or whatever. And assuming they lived an average life span—"

"Which would have been much shorter, even just a hundred years ago," Gemma adds.

"That would be what?" Sean asks, attempting to calculate the number in his head. His eyebrows do a funny kind of dance as the few brain cells he's got left under that crazy mop of hair attempt to stand up for the first time in weeks, only to find their legs asleep.

"Somewhere between five hundred and seven hundred hosts," Harth says, sparing Sean from the embarrassment of giving up. "And I think I just found out how." He steps to the side and points to the far side of the room, where every cable, pipe, and corpse converges.

40

CHIRK

"Okay, someone please tell me they feel that," I say.

"A weight," Harth says, searching the chamber. "As though we are being watched."

"Like we're doing something important," Sean says.

"Oh, thank God," I say. "I thought I was going crazy."

"I don't feel anything," Gemma says. "Except a little nausea still from what happened to those people."

"It's a dog thing," Sean says. "Must be. Heightened senses. Maybe the regulators, since, you know, I'm not actually a Kynolari."

I turn to Harth. "Any ideas?"

He looks down at me. "The feeling began when we reached the temple. Could be an electric or magnetic field. A security system. Perhaps something stranger, but without a way to determine which, I suggest we ignore it. Our mission is too important to be distracted by who or what might be observing us."

"Copy that," I say, and force myself to ignore the increasing feeling of being watched. Then, I focus my attention on the contraption mounted to the wall at which all of the corpses' heads are turned. The device is molded for a biped—a head, torso, two arms and legs, but there aren't any features that would suggest it was for a human, Kynolari, or any other particular species.

"This is what he's using," Harth says. "To transfer his consciousness into a host."

He glances at a series of tubes up from what looks like a helmet full of electrodes, sensors, and sharp things. He follows it to the right, where an ancient database is hidden behind one of the corpses.

"I never thought I'd see one," Harth says, shaking his head, "and still functioning." He turns to me, grinning. "It's a K-13 508 Zeffer system."

"That like a Commodore 64 for people?" Sean asks and then waves his hands like he's erasing the comment. "Never mind, you won't know what that—"

"Commodore 64 was an early 8-bit computer introduced in 1982 and used in people's homes until game systems, Macintosh, and PCs dominated the markets in the late 1980s." He winks at Sean. "I've had time to read about Earth's technological growth. And you're not wrong, it's a fair comparison—"

"*Fair* comparison?" I say. "You said it was 8-bit! *Eight*! Did people lobotomize computers before releasing them?"

"A comparison between this system—" He motions to the Zeffer. "And our current systems. There is no worthwhile comparison to make between human technology and Kynolari."

"The heat of an insect fart and a white dwarf star," I say.

Gemma crosses her arms. "Bombardier beetles use stomach fluids to create a chemical reaction that's been measured at 212 degrees. Fahrenheit."

"Thank you for proving my point," I say. "White Dwarfs tend to radiate heat somewhere in the range of a hundred eighty thousand degrees. Fahrenheit."

"Okay," Sean says. "But two hundred and twelve degrees is just thirteen degrees shy of the perfect temperature for slow cooking ribs."

We slow turn toward him as a group.

"Wow," I say, and give Sean a pat on the arm. "That's a great point, Sean. Really, your logic is beyond comprehension."

Gemma cups her mouth to hide a laugh as I turn Sean away from the conversation, before he destroys his chances with the woman. "Okay. So. We have a Zeffer. Which is what? Where Xolotl stores his consciousness?"

"And controls the transference to a new host," Harth says. "That's what this whole chamber is for, except it's missing something." He points to the wall above the Zeffer.

"An empty power cell node," I say, squinting. "But there is power in this part of the ship. There must be a functioning node somewhere—"

"Agreed," Harth says, "but this appears to require a dedicated power source."

"But isn't it just like moving data from one hard drive to another?" Sean asks. "Even a Commodore 64 could do that."

"The Commodore 64 did not have a hard drive," Harth says. "It used what humans called 'floppy disks.'"

"Floppy dicks?" I say with a chuckle.

"Yo!" Sean says, laughing. "I used to call them the same thing!"

"I don't think you appreciate the enormity of a conscious mind reduced to bytes," Harth says.

"Educate me, my man," Sean says, as enthusiastic about this geek stuff as he is about everything else—not that he'll retain the information. But Harth obliges, probably because it's rare that someone will actually listen when he blathers about technical topics.

"How many megabytes does your computer have?" Harth asks.

"Don't have one, bro."

"Mmm. Not surprising."

Harth ponders for a moment. "How about your phone?"

"Oh!" Sean says. "Sixty-four gigs."

Harth turns to Gemma. "And you?"

"One twenty-eight in the phone. Eight terabytes in the computer."

"*Eight* terabytes?" Sean says, mouth dropping open.

"I have a lot of nature videos," she says. "And games. I might be a gamer."

"So cool," Sean says. "You're not a streamer, are you?"

She's about to answer when Harth holds up his large hand. "Your eight-terabyte hard drive would only be capable of holding point three-two percent of a human consciousness."

"A human being's mind contains two point five *million* gigabytes of data?" Gemma says, truly enthusiastic about the information.

He glances at Sean. "Some more than others."

Sean snaps out of a thought that had pulled him out of the conversation. "Huh?"

"And now consider this," Harth says to Gemma. "A Kynolari mind, adapted to life among the stars, to dealing with complex calculations, to pondering science beyond your comprehension, and engaging with the social structures of vast civilizations spread throughout the cosmos? A Kynolari mind is closer to one hundred petabytes of data, all of which is stored in there—" He points to the Zeffer, "and will be transferred into a flesh and blood host, strapped to the Neuro-Port." He points to the biped shaped device on the wall.

"NeuroPort?" I ask.

He shrugs. "Sounded good to me."

"Wait, wait, wait," Sean says, "we just get to name things we find?"

"Just when you think he's not paying attention," Harth says.

"PsyJumper," Sean says and then gasps. "The *Brain* Bridge."

Before he can pitch any more ideas, a high-pitched buzz sings through the chamber, entering and exiting in a blink. If Harth and I didn't know what it meant, we might have just written it off. Instead, Harth charges his Incinerator and I draw both mini-railguns.

"Uhh," Sean says. "What'd I miss?"

"You hear that buzz a second ago?" I ask.

"I heard something."

"It's a warning-disc, fired by a rail gun. Spins so fast it creates a buzz that's easy to hear."

"What does it mean?" Gemma asks.

"Trouble," Harth says, heading for the hallway.

I follow the big man and turn back to Sean. "You two stay here."

"But we can help," Sean says.

"Someone needs to guard the Zeffer," I say. "And the lady."

His eyes widen. Tries to hide his grin. "Right. Yeah. Of course. I'll keep watch until you get back."

"Good boy," I say, and then enter the tunnel. The moment we're out of sight, we break into a run. With comms out, the warning-disc is the only way Gruunlokar has to communicate with us, and he wouldn't do that unless the circumstances were dire.

Meaning we're not about to exit the giant Xolotl head to find more cultists.

Best case scenario, Thickums is back.

We can handle one Draun.

We exit the mouth-ramp to an empty cavern, a liquid gore slick, and the roaring waterfall separating us from the world outside.

Then the water parts.

Thickums...

She lowers into view, still dressed in her god-awful tank top, now accompanied by a mass of large leaves forming a skirt that I think must be held together telekinetically.

"Fools!" she shouts, going full-Draun. "Now you will feel the wrath of a goddess!"

I look up at Harth. "Divide and conquer?"

He gives a nod.

Draun, especially those new to the business of world domination, can have one track minds. It's how Sean managed to depants her earlier. But neither of us think we'll reach her this time. She'll be ready for the dual attack.

What she won't be ready for is the third, from Gruunlokar.

Just when I think we've got this in the bag, a figure steps through the water that's been shifted to our right. It's low to the ground, featureless black, and prowling. A Hound. A biologic Hound. And it's not alone. Several more step through the water, joined by two Furies. Multiple Straub hunt squads...recreated in biologic form from the very real ones we duked it out with in New Hampshire.

Well, that's not good, but the close confines of the cave will allow Harth to make short work of the newcomers.

Then the water splits again, dividing the waterfall into four columns, around three gaps, in which float two more Draun. The first is a skinny man. Shirtless. Covered in tattoos. Has a lit cigarette hanging from his lips. The second is what Sean might call a bombshell. Very tan. Short jean shorts. A bikini top. Problem is, her face looks like she fell from a Toranian Sputum Throp and hit every Chambling on the way down. Actually, she looks a lot like Thickums might have thirty years ago.

They're her children, I realize.

Which could work to our advantage, if there's any humanity left in them. If not, they'll turn on each other if it advances their status.

Harth and I retreat toward each other.

"Ideas?" I ask.

"Stand still," he says. "Don't move."

"You know they're not Tyrannosaurs and that *Jurassic Park* wasn't real, right?"

He grins at me. Then glances up.

I follow his gaze and understand the plan. Then I pat my knees toward the nearest hunch-backed, jet-black Fury and call it like an Earth dog. "C'mere! C'mere boy. Want to get fucked up? Of course you do. Cuz you're a good boy, aren't you?"

41

CHIRK

My head snaps up toward Harth. He looks down at me, confused. He nods and says, "I felt it. The weight. The attention. Strange."

And that's all we get to say about it, because the Hounds and Furies have us surrounded. They've formed an ever tightening half circle around us. I've seen what a Fury can do to a living thing. It's like every part of their black body is sharp, from their long teeth to the jagged spikes along their arched backs, to their god-damned armpits. They can just run into a person and dismember them from the impact.

But I ain't afraid.

Of them.

The Draun floating behind them, waiting patiently in the gaps between waterfalls, are the real problem.

The nearest Fury crouches low as it stalks closer, preparing to pounce.

"All right, big guy," I say to Xolotl, looking up at his big face. "Time to come through for your peeps."

As though hearing my prayer, orange beams of light shoot from the ancient Kynolari's eyes, scanning the nearest Fury. When it's done, the light quickly scans each and every member of the hunt squad. They flinch at the sudden light display sliding over their bodies, top to bottom. They don't understand it, and don't have the angle to see the brief flicker of purple at the end of each scan.

But we see it.

I relax my guard and wait.

The nearest Fury prepares to pounce again, opening its broad, toothy mouth and letting out a drooly hiss. When the last member of the hunt squad is scanned, I smile and say, "Bye, bye."

An alarm sounds, deep and rumbling. Not sure it's supposed to sound like that, but considering it's thirty-seven thousand years old, I'd say the thing is working spectacularly.

Four compartments on Xolotl's cheeks snap open, extending two-barreled auto-turrets. They're old school weapons, closer to Earth tech than current Kynolari weaponry. But they'll work just fine against biologics, and most other things in the universe.

One by one, the cannons fire, their barrels snapping back, firing four fat rounds per second, tracking their targets with lasers.

Four of the Hounds burst into pieces before the rest—or the Furies—have time to even think about reacting.

I cackle with laughter as the cannons sweep back and forth, unleashing waves of concussive force, shattering bodies, sending limbs flying, and adding layers of biologic gore to the human splorch littering the cave floor.

It's absolute, one-sided carnage.

Not one of them makes it two steps in any direction before they're just…dismembered.

When the cannon fire finishes, just ten seconds after it began, I'm on the ground, laughing. Just letting it all out. I don't even register that the fight is over until Harth nudges me with his big foot. "Chirk!"

I get to my feet, wiping my eyes. "I'm sorry." I hold a hand out to the three Draun still floating by the waterfall. "Sorry. It's just…wooh…the way they came apart. Was like the human fourth of July in—*hck*!"

An invisible force grabs my throat and slams me against Xolotl's chin.

I glance up at Harth to find him fighting against the Draun's telekinetic vice grip. For a moment, he actually resists it, his body and force of will fending off Thickums's attack. Then the siblings join in, shoving him back as easily as they did me.

"Okay," I manage to say while choking. "What…now?"

The metal between us clangs. We both glance toward the sound. There's a familiar looking hole just a foot from my head. A rail round fired from a sniper rifle is the only thing that creates a hole like that. Gruunlokar took a shot, and it ricocheted off the shield protecting whatever Draun he was aiming for. Nearly erased my head.

"Ssshit," I croak, but I know he won't try that again. He'll be closing the distance now, trying something different, but I can't think of anything that will work against three of these bastards.

Harth grunts beside me.

He's growling, teeth bared, still fighting against all three Draun. When his hand pulls away from the wall, I try to gasp, but air isn't moving in or out of my lungs, and a pressure is building inside my head.

Harth leans forward, peeling his back away.

Then his other arm.

Outside, Thickums guffaws, shrieks, and extends both hands toward Harth. He's slammed back so hard that the wall behind him is indented. He clenches his eyes shut, grinds his teeth, and howls.

We're about to pop.

I've seen it.

I've been in this position before.

But never against these odds.

Explosions pound the Draun from the right, over and over. Gruunlokar is closing the distance, unleashing explosive rounds as he moves. But with their shields up and united, there is nothing he can do. And if he gets too close, he'll wind up just like us.

The sound of the waterfall distorts, like I'm listening through a tube that's growing longer. My vision narrows. The pain beneath my skull builds, but I'm almost unaware of it. Because in a moment, I will cease to exist.

My fight will be over.

And I will regret...

...nothing...

A barrage of fresh explosions pounds the Draun. They're followed by a series of high-power laser blasts and a shower of shards. A powerful Draun can deflect most any projectile or energy weapon, but they all have limits. It's why we developed weapons that don't—if you ignore the recharge time. But these three haven't been Draun long enough to fend off the multi-pronged attack from above.

I drop to the floor, gasping for air. Before I can recover, I'm scooped up, tightly secured, and being shouted at by a man whose breath is both familiar and smells of sauerkraut—a delicacy on this world, or at least to Sean.

"Don't you ever leave me behind when you might get whacked, bro," he says, expressing rare anger. "If you're going down, I'm going with you. Got it?"

"Okay," I moan. "Okay. Just—"

A second round of explosions slaps us back. Sean drops to one knee but remains upright. The BabyBjörn carrier keeps me snug against him and free to watch what's happening outside.

A fresh round of ship killer shards pounds against the telekinetic shield and breaks through above the son. A moment later, he's just...evaporated, pulled down by the waterfall that closes over him.

Thickums shrieks and turns her full attention toward the sky, reaching out for her enemy.

But the daughter? She sets her heavily eye-shadowed eyes on us. Seething, she slides into the cave, letting the waterfall close like a curtain.

"Might get your wish sooner than later," I tell Sean.

"Stay back!" Gemma shouts, stepping between us and the daughter. She's got her fists clenched and has assumed some kind of fighting stance, but she doesn't stand a chance. And I think she knows it. Guess that makes her brave instead of stupid.

"I mean it!" Gemma shouts, taking a step away from the daughter as she hovers toward us, hair whipping about in a telekinetic breeze.

"Ready?" I ask Harth.

"Charged and ready," he says. "Not my first last stand."

"Not your last," I say.

He grins and nods, but before either of us can act, a very furry human baby flips through the air, bouncing between clean spots on the floor with a, "Hoo! Ha! Hef!" At the crest of its somersault that takes the creature in between us and the daughter, it springs open and unleashes a cascade of lightning that wraps around the telekinetic barrier, searching for a way through and keeping the Draun's attention off us.

"The fuck was that?" I ask, and then I spot the familiar wrinkles of a bitch pug.

"A Lancer," Harth says, identifying the weapon, but not the carrier.

Another newcomer swings into view, crashing through the waterfall, rolling to his feet, and sliding across the splorchy floor. This one I recognize.

"Praxion!" Sean shouts, bouncing with both hands in the air.

He's so fucking noble and composed it nearly brings a tear to my eye, and his return gives me a whole lot of hope. There's nothing to see, but I know he's firing the Sonizer at the daughter, helping to weaken the defensive field.

But it's not enough...

Until another weapon is fired.

Bright orange light illuminates the entire temple complex.

A beam of laser light strikes the daughter's shield, forcing her to put all her energy into blocking it.

The moment she does that, electricity snaps down and through her body while Praxion's sonic wave strikes her full on. Several things happen at once, and not one of them is pleasant.

First, she shits herself. Praxion unleashed the brown note. The violent expulsion sprays from the sides of her too-tight short-shorts. Next, her hair, which must be full of chemicals, catches on fire. Last...as her consciousness and telekinetic shield fades, she is launched back by the laser light and slammed into the cave's stone wall at something close to the speed of light.

While some of her paints the wall, most of her body is turned to mist, drifting away in the breeze, into the waterfall and pulled away.

Thickums must have felt the connection to her daughter break because her shrieking turns back in our direction.

Before she can do anything about it, a single shard punches through her shield, striking the back of her leg—which comes apart at the kneecap. She wails in pain, spinning around before falling flat on her back—shield gone.

Harth stomps over to the woman, his Incinerator charged. He's about to drop a white-hot ball of plasma on her chest when I shout, "Stop!"

He looks back at me, outraged.

"We need her," I say, "alive." I glance back toward the open mouth of Xolotl and then back to him.

His eyes widen with understanding. A smile spreads. And then with a hefty punch, he knocks the pain-blinded Draun woman unconscious.

42

PRAXION

"Okay," Chirk says, leaning back, feet propped up on the table of the *Prowler*'s ops center. "So, we all agree, Xolotl/Anbu/Anubis, is kind of a slow roasted, dry-aged douche nugget, yes?"

"Couldn't tell you," Micah says. "We just got here."

Chirk cocks his head to the side and looks at me. "He is not the Kynolari we imagined him to be."

Then he waves his hand at me. "You don't have to be diplomatic. It's just the three of us. Team captains. We need to be honest with each other."

"While I'm not sure douche can actually form nuggets," Micah says, "I'm with him. No reason to filter yourself with us."

I sigh. "The Anbu we found in Egypt was a megalomaniac asshole who might have remained loyal to the Kynolari as a people, but who betrayed our code by forcing a lesser species—" I turn to Micah. "No offense—to worship him as a god."

"And by sacrificing hundreds of people and Kynolari in his quest for immortality," Chirk says.

"Sounds like 'asshole' might be too kind a term," Micah says.

A low growl sneaks up out of my throat as my thoughts linger on Anbu. "He will answer for what he's done."

"Oh *shit*," Chirk says. He points at Micah. "If you ever hear your name come out of his mouth sounding like that, your days are numbered, my friend." He lets out a laugh, unfazed by my roiling anger.

"Why are you so relaxed?" I ask.

"Gee, let's think. Gruunlokar nearly had his mind erased, but I killed those bitches. I got in a fight with a wagon—long story. I rescued a drugged-out Harth from...torture. My boy, Sean, defeated Thickums—that's the Draun bitch we got on lockdown. We found Xolotl's secret chamber of nightmares. And when we were faced with two hunt squads and three Draun, Harth and I showed them what the Kynolari are made of. You all just came in at the end to sweep up the crumbs. But the weirdest part—I felt watched the whole time, like more than usual. I felt all this pressure. Not a fan of the spotlight, you know?"

Not sure what he means by that, but the story I've heard from Chirk, Harth, and Gruunlokar is...harrowing to say the least.

That they all survived is a testament to their skill.

The end of *my* mission has me questioning my ability to lead our resistance.

"Don't do that to yourself," Micah says. "Doesn't help anyone."

"Do what?" I ask, pretending to have my head in the game.

"I can feel your self-loathing," Micah says, tilting his head to the side and tapping his regulator. "Look, we've both lost people before, and I know that Torel—"

"Don't speak of her like she's dead," I say.

Micah holds up his hands. "Not dead. But out of the fight."

"She fights for every breath," I say.

"Okay," Chirk says. "The bossman's a little stressed, so maybe we should wait until—"

"No," I say. "We need a plan, and we need it now."

"You're distracted," Chirk says.

My anger peaks. "I *love* her."

Silence follows the statement. Then Chirk lowers his feet and swivels his chair toward me. Leans his elbows on the table. "Listen. Prax. I get it. She took your virginity. Makes you feel all warm and cuddly inside. You wish it was you fighting for your life in the med-bay. But here's the deal… I love *you*, man. I love Gruun, Torel. Hell, even Harth. We're a family. Can't not be, after wading through so many unmentionable nightmares together. I might not be mounting the bounty that is Torel, but that doesn't mean I'm not feeling terrified for her. All of us are. But there is nothing we can do for her, and the rest of us can't finish this mission without you."

I'm about to respond when Chirk pounds the table with his fist. "You get me?"

I blink in surprise.

Chirk gets to his feet, standing on the chair, leaning forward, hands on the table. "You *get* me?!"

His eyes pierce through my worry and scramble it all up. He's been tested, too. He's changed as a result. Stronger. I'm proud of him for it.

I sigh and let the stress deflate out of me. "I get you."

He sits back down. "You're damn fucking right you do." He smiles at me. "Now, tell me about this Poppy bitch. Who, how, and why?"

We both turn to Micah, and he launches into a detailed story of how he and Jess escaped the battlefield in New Hampshire. Their journey south. Encounters with a Draun and how he dealt with it. And then finally their encounter at the border, meeting with the Kynolari named Poppy, and her story of being marooned on this world for eight years. It's a believable story. We all know the risk of being knocked off course during a Leap Node insertion. If I'm honest, her misfortune is a blessing for us.

Poppy, like Torel, is a field medic. And she knew Torel by name upon seeing her unconscious form. She immediately sprang into action, taking over Torel's treatment from Baarfolir, barking orders, and frantically trying to save her old friend's life. Micah finishes his story with a tale of another Draun—who had his powers but declined to join them and instead turned to a life of delinquency. Now, the Draun man who Micah calls both 'Ned Nederlander' and 'Austin the Racist Bro' lies unconscious alongside the woman Chirk insists we call 'Thickums.' Jess says it's an offensive name. Chirk countered with, 'That's the point,' and it stuck.

"Fun story," Chirk says, "but since your addition to our current situation is a Draun wannabe cartel boss and a hyperactive bouncy pug—"

"Who is helping save Torel," Micah adds.

"A pug," Chirk says. "Of all the breeds..." He shakes his head.

Micah turns to me, raised eyebrows asking for an explanation.

"Chirk was in a relationship with a pug," I tell him.

"A relationship?" Chirk says, exaggerating his feelings. "A relationship?! She stole my heart, man. Would have given up everything just to be with her." He turns to Micah. "And you know what she did with my heart? She skewered it with Gongoloid Flosh Quil. Ripped it out of my chest. Gnawed on it and shit it back into my chest, before throwing me into a pit filled with horny Flishing Fonderscamps. Those are parasites that crawl up your anus, set up camp for a month eating your feces, before spawning a thousand hunger grubs that chew their way through your body and emerge from your dick. It's not fatal, but most people die from the shock and horror of it. What Befna did to me was worse. Left me a broken shell for...what?" He looks at me for the answer.

"Days," I say.

"Days! Entire days! Five, at least."

"Doesn't sound like you ever got over her," Micah says. "Befna must have been something special."

He shrugs. "She was a pug. Have you seen their chubby folds of skin? That curl in the tail?" He shudders. "I just can't..." He turns to me. "Promise me you won't deploy Poppy under me. See! I can't even speak without imagining her under me. God damn this planet and its erection-inducing atmosphere."

"Okay," Micah says. "Glad we got that out of the way. Can we get back to the plan?"

I nod. "We recovered a power cell from the tomb beneath the Great Pyramid. From what I've heard, the device inside the temple requires one. Our path forward seems clear to me."

"Except," Micah says, "we have to sacrifice a person to bring Xolotl back to life. Which is just...out-there bananas... And then what? Interrogate him? I get the impression he's going to be uncooperative when he finds out he's not in charge."

"You're kidding, right? They're Draun," Chirk adds.

"Unless we figure out how to undo what's been done," Micah says. "They *could* still be saved."

"Okay," Chirk says, lifting his hands. "Okay, okay, okay. How about this? Thickums goes first. She's missing a leg and she's all-in Draun. Her future is precarious at best. Ned Nederlander can wait. Plan B. If he's not going along with the Draun agenda, he might not be a threat."

"Agreed," I say, not giving Micah a chance to argue. His willingness to give people a chance at redemption is admirable, but when it comes to the Draun, I'm not sure it's possible.

"Great," Chirk says, and I'm impressed with how he's taking charge. He's always been bossy, but this is a new side of him. The events of the past day seem to have changed him. He folds his hands together and leans forward. Very serious. "Question. What is the only known thing in the universe that can brute force its way through a Draun shield?"

"Dual Hell Hounds," Micah says, clanging his gauntlets together.

Chirk shakes his head. "Uh-uh. Wearing a Draun out isn't the same as punching through an active telekinetic shield. It's impressive, but it's not the same."

He looks at me, waiting for the answer.

"A greater telekinetic force," I say. It's an answer we all know. "Why?"

"Thickums's leg," Chirk says.

"What about it?" I ask.

"Gruunlokar took it off with a single shard," he says.

"That's not unusual—"

"Her shield was still up," he says. "All the way around. His shard passed straight through like it was wrapped in its own telekinetic shell."

"What are you getting at?" I ask. Never been a fan of guessing games.

"He's been talking to her," Chirk says. "Jenna Flood. In his head. But..." He looks uncomfortable when he drops the hammer. "...maybe it's not...just in his head."

43

MICAH

"Ubbaduvablechabiblebupumunjiabubuaba!" Thickums screams, shaking her head and body all about, sending waves of flesh rolling around like a crowd of Chinese people in a wave pool. She's a nightmare to watch. Hair burned away. Too tight clothing scorched in inconvenient places. And she is seething, out-of-her-head enraged in a way that is very much not human.

She is a Draun, with her powers dampened by the mental restraints attached to the sides of her head. Harth says they're like regulators, but their sole purpose is to reduce a Draun's telekinetic abilities. And they don't work on the most powerful Draun. Thankfully, Thickums isn't the most powerful. Like most of the converted living in Japan, she is new to the game, but strong enough to be sent after us.

Which begs the question— *How were we found?*

I'd like to interrogate her, but she's already strapped to the human-shaped receptacle on the chamber's wall. I look away from her horrible, one-legged form, but the view in every direction isn't much better. We're surrounded by the dead. Xolotl's previous vessels, both Kynolari and human, all of them forced to give up their lives in service to a single consciousness. To all these people, he was a god. Doesn't justify their sacrifices, though.

"Grraawww!" Thickums shouts. "I am going to flay your skin from your bones and suck the marrow—"

"Ain't a lot of marrow in these bones," Chirk says, held up by Sean, checking the wiring attached to the Brain Zapper—Sean's name for the machine that might bring Xolotl back to the land of the living.

"What is your name?" Harth asks the woman.

"Oh, you wish you knew!" she shouts.

Harth's brow furrows. "I have no personal desire to know your name. I simply wanted to know if you had any family you'd like us to inform about your…passing."

"Ha! The High Lord was right about ya'll! World destroying, race purging aliens from another planet. How long will it be before you're flooding our land with your useless, pitiful little dog bodies? You belong in cages! You belong in the dirt. Bunch of genocidal murderers, all of you." She attempts to spit at Harth, but her mouth is too dry. Tries three more times before giving up.

Harth isn't disturbed by the display. He just turns away and says, "Suit yourself."

"Aren't you interested? Hmmm? In how we found you?"

That piques *my* interest, but I don't bite.

"Oh, c'mon, you *must* be wondering." She giggles. "Which one of you betrayed the others? Which one of you fucked up? Personally, I don't think you should trust the negro."

Jess stands up. She's been sitting beside me, patiently waiting for the show to start. "*Excuse* me?"

"Mmm, you've always been a dog, though," Thickums says. "Begging for everything you've ever gotten. Living off the scraps from better people. You... Descended from Cain. Marked with the sign of—oof!"

Harth takes a step back, withdrawing his fist from within her loose folds of skin. His powerful punch managed to get past her thick hide and knock the wind out of her.

Thickums gasps for air as her face turns red.

"Silence, Draun," Harth says, "I will not suffer your vile words."

"Thanks," Jess says, smiling up at Harth.

He gives a nod. "Draun are masters at sowing division and blinding people with rage. If we don't ignore her, she will convince us to kill her."

"Kill her?" Jess asks.

"She understands that we have a use for her," Harth says. "She might not understand what it is, but if she is useful to us alive, she will attempt to bring about the opposite—her own death. The irony is that we will soon be granting her desire, just not in the way she thinks."

Praxion enters the chamber. "We are clear for the time being, but we should assume that there are more Draun en route. Best if we recover Xolotl and fall back before that happens. How are we looking?"

"Near as we can tell," Chirk says, from Sean's baby carrier, "everything is good to go. Just need to pop that battery into place. There aren't any settings to mess with. Just 'off' and 'on.'"

Praxion nods, stops beside me, and crosses his arms. "Do it."

Harth lifts the ancient battery that still somehow holds power and fits it into place in a wall-mounted socket. The fit is perfect. He starts closing the eight clips that will hold it in place.

"How is Torel?" I ask Praxion.

"Stable, thanks to Poppy," he says. "Thank you for finding her."

"Wish I could take credit, but you'll have to thank fate for that."

"Fate," he says with a chuckle. "Fate seems to have a grudge against me."

"I hear that," I say. "You seen Grover?"

"He hasn't left Torel's side," Praxion says. "He told me, 'Torel help save Grover, Grover help save Torel.'"

"He said all of that?"

Praxion nods. "He is learning quickly, and not just how to speak using the regulators. His intelligence is increasing as well. Baarfolir thinks he might eventually be able to read. He'll be limited by his physiology, but—"

"Do you know what's causing it?" I ask. I don't have a problem with Grover being smart. I've always thought he was smarter than the average Golden Retriever, not that that's saying a lot. But I'm not a fan of mysteries.

"Best guess," Praxion says, "it's a result of his connection with you. You're connected through the regulators. It's like an information highway between the two of you. Just as you can see through his eyes and experience his senses, he is able to learn skills from you."

"Huh…" Not sure what else to say about it. In a world that rarely makes sense anymore, my connection with Grover is the one thing I can rely on to ground me—whether it's a quick snug, or a simple conversation. He's still my main man.

"What about Gruunlokar?" I ask. "Were you able to speak with him?"

Praxion shakes his head. "Not yet. I have him back at the *Prowler*, guarding the others."

"How'd he feel about that?"

"Strangely obliging." He frowns. "The idea of Gruunlokar being influenced by a Draun is disconcerting. But what Chirk described…it would have to be more than influence. Gruunlokar would have to be a conduit. Not a Draun himself, but a willing vessel for a Draun's power. Such a thing is forbidden, clearly, but—"

"He did use it to…" I motion to Thickums's severed leg, now cauterized thanks to Harth's Incinerator blade.

"Which is why I have decided to entrust him with the defense of the others. But we cannot risk this process…which we know so little about. My hope is that he will come to me about the matter."

"And Ned?" I ask. "The kid?"

"Secured and unconscious," he says. "Watched by Gemma and Baarfolir. He shouldn't be a prob—"

A buzz fills the chamber. Bolts of electricity arc up and over the walls.

Harth backs away, hands raised. "Just finished connecting the battery."

"I didn't flip the switch," Chirk says.

Sean raises his hands in the air like he's being held up. "Yo, I didn't touch anything."

Chirk reaches up and pats Sean's face.

"We know that, dingus. We know." Then he turns to Praxion. "I'm guessing someone left the switch on."

No one gets a chance to respond. The electricity jumping along the walls flows down toward the floor all around us. We back into the center of the space, wary of what will happen when it reaches the floor.

"Give me the word and I will melt this machine to slag," Harth says.

"Hold," Praxion says, watching the electricity, but I can tell he's close to giving the order. Xolotl's life, for all his accomplishments and bravado, isn't more valuable than our own.

With a bright flash, the electricity surges into the corpses mounted around us. They come to life, twitching and flailing, their bodies animated by ancient alien power.

"Owee, owee, owee, owee!" Thickums screams, her body shaking with spasms of electric blue washing over her. Pink ethereal light flows between the machine and her head. Eyes rolled back, teeth clenched, she does the truffle shuffle at double speed. Froth sprays from her mouth. Blood from her eyes.

It's a ghastly sight and leaves me uncomfortable. We're the good guys. There is no doubt. But this... If I had known it would be this horrible, this torturous, I would have thought twice before approving it. But only twice. All of humanity is at stake. I'll sacrifice some of my own to save the rest.

"Oh my god," Jess says, looking away.

The rest of us watch. Harth remains stoic. Probably making mental notes about how everything works. Chirk's jaw has dropped, and I think he might be amused. Sean is disturbed, though. Maybe even close to tears. And Praxion...he's questioning this decision, same as me. We share a look, communicating nothing beyond mutual discomfort with how this machine works...and what it did to six hundred people and Kynolari before our arrival.

Thickums's high scream lowers in volume and pitch.

And then all at once, the dancing corpses fall still. The chamber goes dark. For a moment, I'm blind. Then we start switching on our body-lamps and powering gauntlets. The light is warm and orange, most of it focused on Thickums's limp body.

She hangs there, still.

Her chest isn't rising or falling.

"Is...is she dead?" Chirk asks, as Sean moves them closer. Chirk raises a finger to poke her cheek, but the pair flail back when Thickums snaps her head back and takes a raspy smoker's deep breath. Sounds like a broken foghorn.

Then she leans forward and with all the air in her lungs, unleashes a torrent of bellowing laughter, screaming, "Alive! Ahaha! Your god has returned. Drop to your knees! UhahahHA! Bow to your master!"

44

CHIRK

"No," Praxion says, his voice deep and authoritative.

"Eh?" Xolotl in Thickums's form says, cocking his head to the side. "Who dares?!"

Can't see yet. Found his voice pretty damn quick, but he's having trouble with his senses and bodily control.

"I was created at the spark of creation! I am the scales of life and death given form! You will stand before me when your life ebbs, and I alone will determine whether your life's reward will be eternal light, or darkness. Now, bow!"

"Dude drank his own Kool-Aid," Sean whispers in my ear.

I lean my snout up and reply. "I don't know what Kool-Aid is."

"Means he believed his own hype," he says.

"Okay, I got *that*, but what is Kool-Aid?"

"Ohh. It's like a fruity drink that these cult dudes drank in a mass suicide. So, if he's drinking his own Kool-Aid—"

"I get it, I get it." I pat his cheek. "Good, Captain Beefcake."

"Stop speaking!" Xolotl shrieks. "Show respect to your master and drop to your knees, or I will—"

"Do nothing," Praxion says.

Xolotl's hairless head snaps toward Praxion, eyes squinting, struggling to see. He sneers and hisses. "You! Come closer, that I might gaze upon the face of the first to be sacrificed—"

Praxion closes the distance between them with one long stride.

Xolotl's eyes go wide and his head snaps back. "You…you are—"

"Kynolari," Praxion says.

"H-how?" The ancient god's bravado has fled. He seems more nervous and fearful. Because he knows what he has done. He knows his acts are shameful to our people.

"I am Praxion of the Kyno Corps. My team and I are on a mission to find the Lost Tribe."

"That's what you call us, eh? *Lost?* Feh!"

"It has been thirty-seven thousand years since your people were separated from the other migrant ships," Praxion says. "There is no one else alive for you to hold a grudge against."

"Thirty-seven thousand years," he says with a creepy smile. "And yet, here you are, with the same bravado as your predecessors, commanding others to do your bidding, believing yourselves the moral authority of the cosmos."

"He's projecting," Sean whispers. "It's what some people do when they get busted behaving badly. They accuse the other person of what they did, which puts the other person on the defensive."

"Won't work with Prax," I whisper back.

And it doesn't.

"We know the horrors you have carried out on this world. Have been to the tomb in Egypt. Have seen the dead there, and here. Your sacrifices, both human and Kynolari. All in the name of self-preservation. Afraid of death."

"I have died countless times," Xolotl says. "I do not fear oblivion."

"You will this time," Harth says, stepping forward, Incinerator blade extended and glowing orange. The big man's patience is waning.

Xolotl whips Thickums's head around, flinging sweat from his forehead. He eyes Harth for a moment, looking him up and down. "I have defeated entire armies, controlled continents, and influenced this world more than any other deity—"

"Jesus," Sean says.

"*What?*" Xolotl's full and rather nasty gaze falls upon the two of us. "You dare?!"

"Well, I mean, it's not like there are Xolotl potlucks anywhere. We kind of know who Anubis is, but Anbu? Xolotl? It's like, naw, man. No one knows who you are. I have this one friend, Alexander…uh…last name starts with M. Not important. Anyway, every time I talk to him, it's like, 'Jesus this,' and 'Jesus that.' The dude's obsessed. Honestly, I'm not sure he has a single thought that doesn't run through his religion filter. But no one, and I mean, like, no one in the whole universe, even remembers you, dude."

My jaw is open.

Sean just verbally eviscerated one of the most revered Kynolari heroes in history, and every single word he said was true.

Xolotl just stares, eyes twitching.

Sean gives it back, eyebrows perched high, challenging Xolotl to prove him wrong.

Instead, the ancient god behaves like a child. He throws his head back and screams. He arches his back, shoving out his bulbous core. The sudden motion snaps him free from the device, which of course he knows how to free himself from. He stabs a finger at Sean. "You will be the first to feel my wrath!"

He leaps down.

All Thickums's weight compresses her remaining leg. The knee buckles and Xolotl topples to the side with a yelp of surprise.

"What have you done?!" he screams. "My leg! It's broken. My other leg! *Missing?!* And this form! I reject this body."

He flails onto his back, kicking and pounding his fists. "As lord of life and death, I refuse to dwell in this abomination!" He screams again, high-pitched. His voice reverberates against the walls. "I reject it! I refuse it. And I remove myself from it!"

His scream builds in volume. A vibration moves through the air. Pain stabs my head, right between the eyes. *Is he accidentally accessing Thickums's Draun telekinesis? Or is this something different?*

There's an audible crack and then blood fills Thickums's eyes and her body goes still.

"Did he just..." My voice trails off.

He's definitely dead.

It's Jess who laughs first, pitching forward in a series of guffaws that brings tears to her eyes. Within a few seconds we're all laughing.

"That guy is ridiculous!" Sean says.

Even Praxion is chuckling. "We will not speak of this to anyone outside this room."

"I don't know, boss," I say. "First, this story will make me a hit at parties. Second...it's a lesson worth learning. Kynolari might not be as great as we like to think we are. Might be a little more human than we'd like to admit."

"You insult your own people?" Harth asks.

Jess points to her chest. "I think he was insulting us."

"Not trying to insult anyone, you touchy sunzabitches," I say. "Just think that we can learn from his mistakes."

"Chirk is right," Praxion says. "Hubris made a hero into a monster."

"Not sure he was the hero you all think he was," Micah says. He has our undivided attention. "He spoke poorly of your predecessors. Implied that they were domineering and claimed moral superiority...which is somewhat believable."

"Hey," Harth says.

Micah holds up his hand and continues, "He also took exception to the idea of being lost. What if Xolotl was never lost? What if he brought the Lost Tribe here on purpose? What if they *all* came on purpose?"

"Harumph." Harth crosses his arms. "What are you suggesting?"

"That the Lost Tribe wasn't lost," Micah says, turning to Praxion. "They were a rebel faction. They fled to Earth. Maybe because of moral persecution. Maybe because they were controlled by a megalomaniac. Who's to say, but I don't think he—" Micah points to Thickums. "—is a friend."

Praxion grunts.

It flies in the face of everything we've been taught. But it wouldn't be the first historical embarrassment swept under the rug by changing the narrative.

"I think he's right," I say. "Everything about this guy stinks. We've been thinking that he's different or changed since arriving on this world, but what if he was like this from day one? He's not acting like an Earth dog. He might be delusional, but his mind, passed down from one host to another, is just like it was during this fucker's first life."

"And maybe it *wasn't* his first life," Sean adds. "What if this is the reason they rebelled? Or were chased off?"

"If there is any truth to this, we need to kill him," Harth says. "For good."

"Not yet," Praxion says. "We still need answers."

"That guy's not going to talk to us," Jess says.

"Will he remember any of this?" Praxion asks Harth.

Harth ponders the question for a moment. Shakes his head. "Memories were implanted. There is nothing to suggest that his consciousness was being recorded once he was awakened. I believe a reverse process would be required. If he were to be awakened again, he would have no memory of his brief time with us." He motions to the body. "This version of him is dead forever."

Praxion nods. "Then perhaps there is a chance." He turns to me and Sean. "Collect Ned Nederlander."

He turns to Micah. "Are you okay with Grover helping us?"

Micah frowns. "Grover?"

"We're going to put on a show," Praxion says. "Grover will be the star."

"I'm not leaving him," Micah says.

"I would never ask such a thing. We will all be with him. But he will need to do the talking for us."

"Grover?" Jess says, sounding as dubious as I feel. "You want him to have a *conversation* with that psycho nut bag."

"A short one," Praxion says. "We will struggle to hide our revulsion."

"Hey, I took improv," Jess says. "If I can convince this guy—" She points her thumb toward Micah. "—that I have feelings for him—"

"Hey!" Micah gives her a playful shove. Real lovey-dovey-like. Yuck.

"—then I can convince some ancient asshole that I'm a faithful servant. That's what you want, right? For us to stroke his ego? Extract the info without confrontation? That about right?"

"Very well," Praxion says. "You *and* Grover will communicate with him, while the rest of us bow in supplication."

"But why Grover?" Micah asks. "What do you need him to do?"

"What he does best," Praxion says. "Be excited to greet someone new."

45

GRUUNLOKAR

"I know you are there," I whisper, eyes closed, sitting crosslegged on the floor of the *Prowler*'s armory. Most of the weapons and ammunition here are for the *Prowler* and Chirk. His Ridgeback battle suit, both sleek and hulking, takes up a quarter of the space. It's the definition of 'overkill,' but like Sean says about his marijuana, 'Better to have it and not need it, than need it and not have it.'

Which, I suppose, is why he always has it.

With the others using energy-based gauntlets, they have little need for ammunition, aside from the side-arms they sometimes carry as a backup. Most of the shards are used by Chirk—who uses them in excess, and by me, who uses them sparingly, and with greater effect.

I smile, imagining Chirk's response to my thoughts.

The smell of metal—oxium and tungsten mostly—relaxes me. The padded cases containing the armaments are also nice sound barriers. When I meditate here, I am well and truly alone.

But not anymore.

Now there is a voice in the back of my head.

It doesn't say much, but I can feel it squirming around. Gestating. Growing. Influencing.

When I took that last shot at...Thickums—what a horrible name—I remember aiming. And pulling the trigger. And thinking I was wasting a round because the Draun's shield would just deflect it as it had done before. But in that fraction of a moment when the rail magnets accelerated the shard, I felt a flow of energy slide down my arm, and into the gauntlet, wrapping around the shard.

The result was immediate.

The shard pierced through the Draun's telekinetic shield, just as Jenna promised it would, removing the horrible woman's limb.

But it wasn't me.

For that moment, I was not at the helm of my mind or body. Jenna took control, and her Draun energy flowed through, and out of me.

She lied to me. There is more of her tucked away in the recesses of my mind than she led me to believe.

And if I am not careful, she might wrest control.

So, I am attempting contact, in search of answers before I debrief Praxion on the situation. I believe he already suspects, hence my being put on guard duty, but he will understand my desire to provide answers rather than questions.

I slip into a liminal space, inside my mind, but also separate from it. There is a gap between the conscious and unconscious, an endless void just microns across. It's the perfect place for a compressed, or incomplete, consciousness to hide.

I'm alone in a white room with twisting organic walls. Humans would be intrigued by the space, but the patterns formed by the twisted bands of white oxium are as plain as Kynolari architecture gets.

I walk through the open doorway and into a winding hallway.

There are rooms to either side, some leading to more rooms, some leading to more hallways. Doesn't matter which direction I choose. It all leads nowhere, and everywhere.

It's the perfect escape from the stresses, pressure, and volume of the real world. It's also a convenient place to hide—and stay hidden.

I won't be able to find her here.

She's going to have to reveal herself.

"Show yourself, Jenna," I say. "I am not here to harm you or remove you from this place. But I do have questions. And I deserve answers."

Silence.

"Taking control of a body that is not your own is forbidden on my world, and in most of the civilized peoples throughout the universe. Only Draun would stoop so low."

That's not true, of course. We know now that Kynolari are also capable of great evil. I take consolation in the fact that Xolotl was the product of a bygone era, but his actions have peeled away my belief in our species' inherent goodness.

"I didn't mean to," a voice says.

It is Jenna, but also not.

"You lied to me," I say.

"I don't *know* you," she says, sounding genuinely confused. "Or where the hell I am."

She's afraid. Sounds...young.

"You're nowhere," I tell her. Not exactly comforting, but I don't want her to be comfortable. I want her answering questions.

"I don't understand," she says.

"Your name."

"Jenna."

"Jenna..."

"Flood. Jenna Flood. Where *are* you?"

I take a random left and keep walking through the liminal world between my thoughts, memories, and knowledge.

"I can't see you," she says.

"I'm not sure you should," I say.

"You some kind of freaky monster?" she asks.

"Depends on who you are," I say.

"Not comforting. But you should know, I'm not defenseless."

"Telekinetic?" I ask.

"Huh?"

"The ability to affect the physical world without interacting with it physically."

"Like psychic stuff? Is that what this place is?"

"In a sense," I say, and decide to open up a bit. "We are inside my mind."

"Cool." Heavy on the sarcasm, trying to hide her fear. "Cooool. Wait a second. Hold up. Telekinesis. I *do* know what that is. Well, not really know it. Feel it, I guess. And I remember… Did I help you? Are you… Are you a sniper? Did we shoot someone? I thought that was a dream. Or a hallucination. But…I was seeing through your eyes, wasn't I? And we shot her. And…she was flying. And her leg… Oh my god."

"Stay calm," I say, sensing her shift toward panic. "You are safe here."

"Easy for you to say. It's your brain. Which makes me what?"

"I'm not sure," I admit.

"Can I leave this place?" she asks. "I don't like it."

"I think that would be…unwise," I say, and don't bother telling her about my regulators. The moment a wisp of her consciousness hidden here escapes, all traces of her will be eradicated. Except…she already did. When she imparted telekinetic energy to my shard.

"Here is the truth," I say. "I do not fully understand why you are here, but I believe your…former self left you here to help me…in case she failed her mission."

"Wait. I'm *dead?*"

"Yes," I say.

"Who killed me?" she asks.

"Lumen Sok," I say. It's not exactly the truth, but not really a lie. Depends on your perspective.

"Don't know who that is, either," she says.

I stop short of the next doorway when I catch a scent that isn't mine. She's standing in a room, slowly spinning around, looking at the twisted walls. And she looks different. Younger.

Innocent.

There is no trace of Draun in this version of Jenna Flood.

Standing outside the room, I ask, "What year is it?"

"2015," she says. "I'm from Key West, Florida. Do you need my social security number, too?"

She's off by nearly a decade. Jenna—the one I knew, and helped kill—left behind her former self, the one that existed before she came into contact with the signal that transformed her into a Draun. And she gifted her younger self with the knowledge and ability of telekinesis, but none of the brainwashing that came with it. The moment I said her name, because of that damn duck, this version of her was unlocked, and the previous erased.

A moving sacrifice.

"Wait, what year do *you* think it is?"

"Not important," I say.

Fear turns to anger. "Hey! You don't get to decide what's important and what's not!"

"We *are* in my mind," I remind her.

"I don't want to *be* in your mind. I want to be...in me."

I sigh. "Scale of one to ten, how good are you at handling the brutal truth?"

She's silent for a moment. I watch her around the corner, fists clenched, eyes on the floor. She tightens her jaw, purses her lips, and says, "Ten. Just...tell me. Rip off the Band-Aid."

"We are ten years in your future. During the time you cannot remember, you came into contact with an alien signal, awakening ancient knowledge contained in your DNA, granting you powerful telekinetic abilities and a hatred for my species. Your former self aligned herself with evil, but some small part of her wished to be the person you are. She left you behind, in my mind, in case she died."

"Why?" The question is a whisper.

"To help me kill Lumen Sok."

"That's...wow. You know, I don't know why, but...I think I trust you."

"Then you should know the whole truth. I was part of the team that killed you."

Her body sags, more sad than angry.

"Was I really that bad?" she asks.

"Could have been worse."

A slight smile creeps onto her face. "You said, 'my species.'"

"I am not human, though we are now allied with several humans. My people are called Kynolari. Our enemy, currently trying to overthrow the Earth—"

"Narf!" she says.

"What?"

"Never mind. Who are the bad guys?"

"The Draun."

"Am I wrong to be freaking out right now?" she asks.

"Not at all," I admit. "But I think we should trust that your former self had the best intentions for you. And I think we should trust each other."

"You're not like some freaky lizard person or something, right? Like from *V*?"

"Based on typical human responses to my people's appearance, I believe you will be...pleasantly surprised."

"Okay," she says. "My father always told me to listen to my gut, and to make up my own damn mind. Honestly, I'm not sure what that means. Should my gut or brain guide me? But *both* are telling me to trust you."

I step around the corner, into the room. "Over here."

She turns. Sees me. Her eyes widen and a smile spreads. "Awwww."

I hold up my hand and say, "I am an elite sniper in the Kyno Corps and my breed is one of the oldest and most noble among my people. Do not, 'awww' me. Save that for Chirk when...if you meet him."

"Chirk. He's like you?" she asks, looking me over. "A...dog?"

"What your people call a chihuahua," I say. I hold out my hand in a human gesture of peace. "I am Gruunlokar."

She shakes my hand. "Jenna Flood."

46

PRAXION

"Aaaargghh!" Ned Nederlander shakes as bright blue arcs of electricity flow into his body, from the dancing corpses around us. I see now that they are also meant to serve as a welcoming party, their movements akin to fearful servants. Everything about this macabre display is revolting and shameful.

I watch the scene from under my hood. Grover sits before the returning false god but is oblivious to the horrors playing out before him. Micah, also dressed in a hooded cloak, is covering the dog's ears, while Jess covers his eyes. Grover sits patiently, tail wagging, wondering what wonderful surprise awaits him.

Pink energy flows from the machine, seeping into Ned's head. His face turns up, eyes rolling back. Froth spews like a geyser.

The sight makes me uncomfortable. Unlike the female Draun, Ned wasn't violent and lacked a desire to join Lumen Sok. According to Micah and Jess, he isn't what anyone would call a 'good person,' but he isn't our enemy, either. The fact that he agreed to this says a lot about his underlying character. We promised to attempt recovering his consciousness and failed to mention how painful the process would be, but this is horribly necessary.

The dancing bodies jangle to a stop.

Darkness envelopes us.

Ned hangs limp.

Then his fingers twitch.

A smile spreads across his face, as fiendish as any Draun's.

He sucks in a deep, hoarse breath, and lets out a booming laugh before screaming the same thing he did when last he woke from his slumber. "Alive! Ahaha! Your god has returned. Drop to your knees! UhahahHA! Bow to your master!"

And this time, we do. All of us in cloaks, faces hidden in shadow. Micah and Jess release Grover, moving to their positions and bowing with the rest of us.

I feel a surge of confused emotions, and they're not mine. The regulators connect us in sometimes strange ways, giving us an instinct about what each other is up to, but most of what I'm feeling now—a mix of confusion, fear, and excitement—comes from Grover. Even though he missed the grotesque display leading up to this moment, the transformed and clearly mad Ned is a challenge for even Grover to accept.

"We bow to your excellency," Jess says, leaning forward. The rest of us bow as well. "We praise you, oh god of death, mighty adjudicator, immortal savior of your people."

"Savior?" he says. "That is not something I have been called before. Show me your face."

I lean up out of my bow and am glad to see the others do the same. Standing out would have been a mistake. But if Xolotl tries anything, I want to see it coming.

Xolotl, now in full command of Ned's body, arches his back and pops himself free from the device, just as Thickums did. This time, he lands on his feet, and sighs in satisfaction. He holds out his arms and inspects them. Tugs at the T-shirt Ned was wearing. He frowns but doesn't address it. Instead, he squeezes his fists and nods in approval. "A worthy host. Young. Strong. And strangely powerful."

He can sense the Draun power within him, but does not know how to use it, which is a very good thing.

His bare feet slap against the cool floor as he approaches Jess, not giving the rest of us a second glance, or even a first, including Grover who is still sitting like a good boy, tail wagging in expectation. Any non-Draun human would have instantly headed for his happy face.

He stands over her, confident and radiating self-aggrandizing machismo. He taps Jess's hood with his finger. "Your face."

"Yes, my lord." She pulls back the hood and looks up. Her face is painted in dripping red, giving her the appearance of some kind of tribal priestess. In some ways, she resembles members of the cult who were slain, but it has been a long time since Xolotl has walked the Earth. He is likely accustomed to waking to a new time, with new faces, and changed traditions.

"Intriguing," he says. "You are of the African continent?"

"I am," she says.

"And yet, your language is that of the Northern white men."

"The world is a changed place, my Lord, and your presence is desperately needed."

"I'm afraid there are some things I desperately need before we discuss anything more." He places his hand beneath her chin and lifts her face until they're looking into each other's eyes. "Or have the rituals of awakening been forgotten?"

Micah tenses but manages to control himself. We will not allow any harm to come to Jess, but we must let this progress far past our comforts if need be.

"Of course, my lord, but—"

"I will not be long," he says, offering a sickening smile. "In fact, I will—"

"Hello," Grover says, tail wagging madly.

Xolotl closes his eyes. Slow turns his head toward Grover.

He squints upon seeing him. "This...dog? Did it speak?"

"Yes, my lord, I have been trying to—"

Xolotl holds his hand up, silencing her. His full attention is on Grover now. He crouches down in front of the dog, not reaching out for him as a human would. "How do you speak?"

Grover turns his head to the side, revealing the regulator. The technology did not exist in his time, but that will not matter.

"Humanity has evolved since my last awakening."

"Yes, my lord," Jess says. "Technology has greatly advanced in the past hundred years."

"One hundred years, from living like savages, to *this?*" He motions to Grover's regulators.

"Several hundred years," she says, "for you. But most advanced technologies were developed in the past hundred years, yes. You will be so proud of what your people have done in your absence, all thanks to your guidance and tutelage."

"Hrm... And you still live in close contact with my descendants?" He places his hand on Grover's head. When Grover starts licking Xolotl's hand, he sneers and pulls it away. "They might be simpletons, but they are still my brethren."

"Best friends," Grover says. "Jess is best friend. Micah is best friend. Tor—"

"Do not bore our master with such details," Jess says, stopping the dog before he was able to speak a Kynolari name.

Grover throws his head back shaking his ears around in an excited expression of playful desperation. "Master be best friend?"

"More loyal than I remember," he says. "Perhaps because when last I walked the Earth, Kynolari could not speak."

"Abiding benefactor of all humanity, I apologize with the most emphatic desperation I can—"

"Get on with it," Xolotl says. "Tell me what you must, but then my loins will be satisfied."

"Of course," she says with another bow. Then she looks him in the eyes and says, "We have been invaded."

"You are human," he says. "War is in your nature." He leans down to her like she is a mindless baby. "How much of your technology was developed during and after a time of war? It is a palate cleanser for this world, tipping the scales of judgment toward the strongest, as it has always been and should be. But you know that already. My teachings make it clear that—"

"The invaders—"

"You dare speak over me?" he hisses.

"They are from beyond the planet!" she shouts.

He snaps to a stop.

"Beyond our solar system. Beyond our galaxy."

He doesn't seem surprised by the news. "These invaders...do they have a name?"

Jess nods. "The Draun."

"Have they been awakened?"

She nods again.

"When?"

"Months ago, my lord, but..."

"It did not affect everyone," he says. "As was my design. Tell, me, what are their numbers?"

"Two hundred and fifty million," she says, not holding any information back. "More by now."

"More by now...what do you mean?"

"Those who were not changed right away are becoming Draun over time, except for—"

"Those in close proximity to my people," he says. "I know. And what are *their* numbers?"

"Five hundred million," she says.

"These numbers...they are much larger than expected. What is the planet's total population?"

"Eight...*billion*."

He staggers back a step.

"Also mostly in the past hundred years," she says.

"We must act quickly, then," he says.

"Yes, my lord. A wise choice. Tell us what needs to be done, and we will carry it out—"

He looks between Jess and Grover, evaluating the pair. From what I've seen and heard, Jess has been convincing. But there's no way to know if we didn't perform some kind of ritual upon his awakening. I suspect such things change over time, though, and her news has captured his full attention.

He nods. "The time has come. We must reset humanity."

47

MICAH

"Amazing," Harth says, breaking his silence. He keeps his head down, snout hidden in shadow. "Only a marvelous intellect such as yours could conceive of such a bold plan. Please, before we start, regale us with the science of how such a thing might be accomplished."

Xolotl's attention snaps to Harth. "I almost missed you there, so silent and stoic." He turns toward me, and then Praxion, and finally Sean, who still has Chirk strapped to his chest, no doubt getting stuffy beneath that cloak. "Is it possible that you have progressed enough to understand?"

"If anyone on this world could comprehend your genius, sire, it is me."

Careful, I think. I have little doubt that Harth's knowledge of science far outweighs Xolotl's but resetting the minds of an entire world—and what that means exactly—aren't really part of his wheelhouse.

Xolotl wanders toward Harth, who wisely bows even farther.

"He tells the truth," Jess says, pulling the dog-god's attention back to her. "He is one of our most brilliant scientists. We were fortunate to recruit him to our cause after the Draun invaded. When the time comes, he will be the one assisting you."

"I like science," Grover says.

Jess shushes him.

"Love Jess."

Can't help but smile at that guy. Fate of the world hangs in the balance and he's still just a love machine.

Xolotl's pacing lands him in front of Grover. Looking down.

Grove just wags his tail, looking up with wide eyes, tongue hanging from the side of his mouth. When a look of disgust twists onto Xolotl's face, I brace myself for action. He will not strike my dog, fate of the world be damned.

"New friend?" Grover asks.

Xolotl sighs and shakes his head. "How far you have fallen." He turns away, looking back at the machine that's kept him alive in new bodies for so long. "Very well, but I will not explain this twice."

"There will be no need," Harth says.

Xolotl nods and grins. He likes Harth's confidence.

"Are you familiar with quantum mechanics?" Xolotl asks.

"Yes," Harth says. "The atomic and subatomic behavior of matter and light have always intrigued me."

"Very good," Xolotl says, sounding impressed now. "We will need to construct a device capable of targeting the quantum properties of DNA molecules. You see, every molecule has a unique quantum resonance frequency. Call it a 'molecular fingerprint.' And it can be influenced, at the quantum level, by external stimuli."

"Fascinating," Harth says, and I can't tell if he's being genuine or condescending.

Xolotl doesn't debate the matter. He's bought into the idea that the people here with him are true devotees. After thirty seven thousand years, why would he doubt it?

"After connecting to my satellite system, we will be able to achieve a state of quantum entanglement with a specific strand of DNA in every person on this world." Xolotl pauses. "Do you know what quantum entanglement is?"

"Yes, my lord," Harth says.

He nods and continues. "Our connection to the DNA of everyone on this world will be instantaneous. And before you ask how I know this will work, how do you imagine I altered the genes of two entire species, all at once? This will not be the first time I have achieved wonders."

"Praise Xolotl," Sean says.

The dog-god chuckles. "Indeed." He begins pacing again, and I get a sense that our science lesson is far from over. "Using the satellites, we will broadcast a highly sophisticated signal at a frequency that resonates with the quantum state of human DNA. Once resonance is achieved..." He grins. "...the signal alters the wave function of the DNA's quantum state."

Oh. My god. I hope Harth is catching all this because I'm already struggling to hold off a yawn. I distract myself with thoughts of the past. Of that amazing first date with Jess. Of our time playing in the field with Grover. The connection was fast and powerful. Has only grown since. I picture her face behind that hood, trying not to yawn. I nearly chuckle, and it snaps me back to the lecture.

"...at the quantum level cascades into a macroscopic alteration in the DNA structure. Essentially, the signal doesn't just *send* information, it actively modifies the quantum probability field of specific genes!"

He's getting fired up now, like a preacher at a Southern corn field revival. Sean senses it, too, unleashing another, "Praise Xolotl."

"With precise control, we will alter gene expressions by triggering DNA switches, essentially deactivating the Draun genes in humanity, all at once. Those who are Draun will become human once more, and those not yet affected, will be protected."

"And you will ascend to your throne once more!" Sean adds.

Xolotl looks toward Sean with a crooked grin. He addresses Jess, the only face he can see, and says, "I like this one."

"And we need a satellite network to achieve your goals," Harth says.

"It is of no consequence," Xolotl says. "My satellites have been orbiting this world since our ship first arrived."

"Uh," I say.

His attention snaps to me. "Speak."

"I served in the modern world's most advanced military force," I say. "And we have thousands of satellites in orbit now. More than ten thousand. If you had anything up there, we'd know about it."

"What are you suggesting?" he asks, growing irritated.

"That yours, somehow, are gone."

He lets out a low growl and then addresses Harth. "And yet, you claim there are thousands of satellites in orbit...placed there by humanity?"

"Indeed, my lord," Harth says. "And I believe they will be sufficient enough to carry out your plan."

"Very well," Xolotl says.

"We have everything we need," Harth says.

A rush of emotions fills me, projecting a feeling of impending action. It's powerful, and yet vague, shifting like waves. I can feel Grover. See what he's planning. And the others, all of us mobile and moving. Quickly, all at once. It's a plan, I realize, being pushed to us by Praxion.

Harth's last words—*We have everything we need*—weren't meant for Xolotl. Regulators are weird, let's be honest. I'm still not thrilled about having these things on the sides of my head. But at times like this, when they provide a massive tactical advantage, I'm on board.

"Now, my acolytes, go out and—yeaih!"

We rise up all at once, shedding our cloaks and rushing Xolotl. Chirk emerges from beneath Sean's cloak, stabbing his finger toward the dog-god. "Get 'im!"

Grover runs behind Xolotl and lies down. I plant my hands on his chest and give him a shove. He trips over the pooch and flails backward. He lands hard on his back, the air knocked from his lungs, and he struggles to catch a breath when Sean and Jess slam down atop him, straddling his body, pinning his arms and legs.

I charge my gauntlets and point them toward his head.

"Ha!" Chirk says, laughing. "What a sucker! Just like every other self-loving motherfucker in the universe. Stroke their ego's dick for a minute and they'll just blab to keep you going." He leans in close to Xolotl's face and says, "You brought shame to your people. Now it's time to go bye-bye."

Xolotl gasps, both in surprise and to catch his breath. His voice comes out raspy. "Impossible. It's been so long..."

"Not nearly long enough," Chirk says.

"Almost ready?" I ask, looking back to Harth and Praxion.

The big guy is working on Prax's gauntlet, changing settings quickly despite his meaty fingers. With a swipe, he exits the display and snaps the small latch back in place. He nods to Praxion. "Should operate as usual, but it's been calibrated to detect the resonant frequency of things at a molecular level. Combined with our database of Draun DNA, locating the strands in question should be as easy as finding the resonant frequency of wood. A simple burst directed at the target will instantly affect all quantum-entangled DNA strands, making the change system-wide, and immediate."

With that, Harth turns toward Xolotl and says, "Your technology is both ingenious and antiquated, foreign to us only because it is both reprehensible and forbidden."

Xolotl sneers and attempts to wriggle free. "Heathens! Kynolari scum! Traitorous Horgoths! I will hump the marrow from your bones—"

"Eww," Chirk says. "Guy. What's wrong with you?"

"I will...I..." His eyes widen for a moment, and then squint. He stops struggling. "Whose body is this? What have you done?"

"Uhh, bossman," Chirk says, "make it snappy!"

Praxion rounds the group and crouches beside Xolotl's head. "For crimes against your people, and those of Earth, you are hereby sentenced...to non-existence."

He places the hand of his gauntlet on Xolotl's forehead. The display screen flows with numbers and code for a moment, and then flashes orange. He stands up and aims his Sonizer toward Xolotl. "On my go."

We all nod, ready to dive away.

"No," Xolotl whispers. "It can't be."

For a moment, I think he's talking about his impending demise, but then realize he's still focused on the body he's inhabiting. Ned Nederlander's.

The Draun's.

"But it is," he says. "I can feel it. I can *access* it!"

"Praxion!" I yell.

"Go!" he shouts.

All at once, we start moving away from the supine man. But before anyone can get clear, we are lifted and thrown away, scattered around the chamber. I soar twenty feet before landing and rolling through one of the ancient dead bodies. It shatters and falls atop me. Dust of the dead gets in my mouth. My body aches from the impact, but I push myself up quickly, spitting as I get back to my feet and spin around toward the chamber's core, where Xolotl hovers five feet above the floor, surrounded by swirling power.

He turns his head to the ceiling and cackles with laughter.

48

CHIRK

"In all my time on this pitiful world, I have never met a group more foolish than you lot! You seek to usurp my power! Control me as a pawn! To end my life. My life! Eeeeeahahahaa. You cannot end what is eternal. You cannot defeat he who, with a word, can take your life!"

Never thought I'd see this.

A Kynolari become Draun. He was already a power-hungry ambitious asshole who'd done more than drink his own Kool-Aid. Now he's guzzling the stuff, his desire for power increasing along with the realization that he's inhabiting a Draun and has full access to all the power that comes with it. Maybe even more than Ned did.

I unclip myself from the baby carrier and slip out, down to the floor. Xolotl has his back to us, making a slow spin, inspecting the others for life. Some of them are moving—Micah and Harth—but they're not going anywhere fast. Praxion is out cold. Jess, too.

I give Sean's cheek a swat. "Yo, Sean! Eyes open, bitch!"

Doesn't smile. Doesn't flinch.

I press my hand against his neck. There's a pulse, but he's out cold. Being strapped to his chest protected me from the impact with the floor. Which means, it's just me and Xolotl Nederlander. Helps that he's still dressed in that ridiculous costume. Hard to take him seriously, so it's hard to envision him taking me in a fight. That said, I'm also fully aware that he just kicked our collective asses in the total duration of one of Sean's epic sneezes.

Xolotl continues his victory spin, floating at the center of the chamber, surrounded by the team and the ancient dead, most of whom have also toppled to the floor. "Who would like to face my judgment first? Hmmm?"

I slip to the side, ducking and rolling between heaps of bodies once worn by the ancient Kynolari psychopath. I'm small enough to take cover behind them, or beneath their rag clothing. I manage to remain behind him as he turns his attention to Sean.

"I will start with you," he says. "The buffoon who feigned adoration." Xolotl floats closer to Sean. "No words for me, whelp?"

The air inside the chamber begins to swirl.

I'm not sure Xolotl has any idea what the Draun are capable of, or what he's really doing, but he seems to be acting on an instinctual level, feeling a moldable world all around him.

He thrusts both hands toward Sean, seizing his body in a telekinetic vise grip. Sean floats up, limbs hanging down, head lolled back.

I take aim with both mini-railguns. Need to aim carefully or the shards could slide through both Xolotl and Sean. Wouldn't be much of a rescue. I direct my aim toward the back of Xolotl's head. From my angle on the floor, I should be able to put a shot up through the back of his skull, with the exit wound at the top of his forehead. It will be inches from Sean's head but should pass by and into the ceiling.

I focus on the railgun in my right hand. No need to spray. One shard will get the job done.

Just...

One...

I pull the trigger, just as Xolotl senses my presence and snaps his head around to look at me. The single shard nicks his ear, removing a clear circle, but does nothing else.

He casts Sean aside, holds one hand to his ear and lets out a sneer. "So puny. I can feel your fragility from here. It is a wonder they allow your pitifully small breed to leave your new home world. Where is that, by the way? Perhaps I will overthrow the Draun here, take their forces as my own, and finish what I started thirty seven thousand years ago."

"Why would you want to finish getting your ass kicked?" I ask. "That's why you fled here. Tail tucked and pissing yourself, you came here with your believers because the alternative was to die for your crimes."

"For our beliefs!" he shouts. "In the eternal. In sacrificial love. In—"

"Licking your own balls?" I ask. "In sniffing each other's assholes? Because I've seen the Lost Tribe for myself. Your beliefs reduced your followers to...to dogs." I smile at the thought of them. He doesn't know it, but I think they're amazing now. In some ways, they are the best of Kynolari. But I'm not about to tell this proboscis skin tag anything like that.

He glides down to the floor and just for the hell of it, I fire a dozen shards toward his chest. They're deflected into the air. He hasn't erected a full shield, but there is a telekinetic force protecting him from projectiles now.

I glance toward Harth. He's still on his back, dazed.

Micah is on his side, eyes widening and narrowing like he's having trouble focusing.

Sean is out cold still. Jess, too. Praxion, who was flung the furthest hasn't moved at all, and I'm starting to fear the worst.

Looks like this is between me and a thirty-seven-thousand year old legend turned asshole megalomaniac enemy of Kynolari with Draun abilities...that *we* gave him.

Awesome.

"Say what you will about the Kynolari on this world," Xolotl says, walking toward me, "but they are exactly how I designed them to be. Subservient. Incapable of rebellion, of profound thought. They do as they are told, they worship without cause, they bow to any will more superior than theirs. And I am superior to all."

"You designed... You made the Lost Tribe devolve into Earth dogs?"

"Surely you have noticed the changes in yourself," he says. "The longer you breathe this world's air, the more your genetic code will change. Generations from now, your descendants will be as inept and loyal as the dogs you discovered on this world."

"You did something to the air," I grumble.

"Far beyond your ability to comprehend," he says. "But there are other ways to make someone useless."

He reaches out a hand. Despite the ten feet still between us, he grasps my arm with telekinetic force. With a twist of his hand, he wrenches the top of my forearm a hundred and eighty degrees while keeping the low half stationary. The break is sudden, excruciating, and clean.

The mini-railgun falls from my hand.

He releases me, and I drop to my knees.

"Yeargh!" I shout, firing my second mini-railgun from the hip. My aim is true, but he's still defending himself. The fusillade of shards deflects upward, shredding the ceiling.

"You're a coward," I tell him. "How about this, I'll put down my railgun and you drop the shield. I'll beat your ass with one broken arm and—argh!"

My left arm twists and cracks, my last weapon falling to the floor.

"Mother*fucker!*" I climb to my feet and face off with him. "I will kill you with my god-damned feet if I need to."

He chuckles. "I have no desire to fight fairly. This is too much fun."

He lifts his hand toward me again, and this time I feel the pressure in my neck. *Shit. This is it. This is how I die.* Killed by the greatest abomination in Kynolari history. Suppose that will get my name in the history books, but it's not really the reason I was hoping for. Finding the Lost Tribe. Reuniting them with Kynolari. That would have been something special.

"There it is," he says, angling his head to the side as he looks in my eyes. "The fear. The reflection. 'What have I done with my life?' 'Why am I going to die like this?' Have no fear, mongrel, I will make sure no one remembers you at all."

The pressure increases in time with his maniacal laugh, "Eeahahaha—ohh!"

My neck is released.

"What?!" Xolotl shouts, looking down at the gyrating blur of golden majesty dry humping his leg. Grover is latched on tight, slapping his dick against the dog-god's leg, jaws gripping the side of his frilly blue coat. "You dare?!"

Just as Xolotl is about to turn his telekinetic power on the dog, he's tackled from behind by Sean.

"All you assholes with gauntlets on better wake your asses up!" I shout. "Right fuckin' now!"

A single groan is the only reply. Not sure who it was from.

Xolotl topples over under Sean's weight.

My man gets in two cheap shots to the kidneys before being flung away by a telekinetic burst that sends Grover sliding across the floor, too.

"This ends now!" Xolotl says, floating upright like some demon possessed girl in one of Sean's horror movies. He lifts his arms up, gripping the air. Everyone in the chamber, conscious or not, is lifted up and slammed back to the ground. Sean grunts. Grover yelps. I'm filled with rage, but there is no way to do anything.

We start floating up for a second brutalization.

"Put them down."

The voice is calm and confident.

"Gemma?" Sean says, leaning up.

She enters the chamber and looks around. "Intriguing." She struts toward the dog-god. "What should I call you before killing you? Anbu? Anubis? Xolotl? Pitiful? A Kynolari wishing to be Draun." She scoffs.

If she's putting on a show to distract him, she's doing a fantastic job, but whatever the next part of the plan is, it better be quick, because Xolotl isn't known for his patience.

"You can call me 'Master!'" He thrusts both hands toward her, kicking up a telekinetic wind that sends the rest of us, and all the dead bodies, tumbling across the floor until we slam into the back wall.

But not Gemma.

She stands in the middle of the storm, smiling. Not even her hair is moving.

Because she's protected.

Shielded.

Realization churns my guts.

She is how the Draun tracked us here.

Because *Gemma...is* Draun.

"Ahh, shit."

49

PRAXION

I wake to the sound of Xolotl screaming at someone, telling them to call him 'Master.' I feel groggy, like I spent the night getting drunk on Haddrillian ale. Whole body hurts. Eyes don't want to open.

I'm slapped fully conscious by a roaring telekinetic wind. I'm too weak to fight it and find myself sliding across the floor. Bodies of the long dead crash into me, shattering and cascading away. As I spin, I spot a blurry but familiar shape inching toward me.

Chirk. He's awake and crawling while watching whatever is happening at the chamber's center. Xolotl is there, floating above the floor. But I can't make out who is standing before him—resisting his powerful attack.

I hit the far wall, crushing long dead bones beneath me, and I'm once again dazed. Chirk lands against my stomach, knocking the air from my lungs. I can't move. Can't breathe. Can barely think.

But I can hear.

"Ahh, shit," Chirk says, voice full of apocalyptic dread.

I manage to catch a breath and squeak out a single word. "Chirk."

Grunting in pain, he manages to sit up and turn toward me. Over the raging wind, he says, "Bossman, you okay?"

"Head is...screwed up," I say, taking a deeper breath. "Vision is blurry. You okay?"

"Well," he says, "my radius and ulna are broken, in both limbs, so that hurts like a Maddernian sphincter beak clamped down on my arms. Other than that, we're basically all fucked. How's your day going?"

I tilt my head toward the scene playing out before us. "What's happening?"

"Short version," he says. "Xolotl kicked our collective asses. Nearly killed me. Would have, if it wasn't for Grover and Sean. If a new challenger hadn't entered the ring, we'd all be dead."

I lift my head, trying to see. I can feel my regulator sorting things out, but my vision won't be restored until all the work is done. "New challenger?"

"A Draun," he says.

The way he says it is different than the usual disgust he puts into the word 'Draun.' There's conflict in his voice.

Because he knows this Draun.

"Who is it?" I ask.

"Gemma."

That's why he is conflicted. While he might not have strong feelings for the woman, Sean certainly does. And now...well, now we need to kill her. Though that seems unlikely at the moment.

"Sitrep on the others?" I ask.

"All down," he says. "Micah was starting to wake up before we got bitch-slapped against this wall. Harth is out cold. Sean and Grover are down after that last blast. Haven't seen Jess. Near as I can tell, it's just you and me, Prax, and I don't have any weapons...or working arms."

There's a loud *thwip* sound in my ears, and just like that, all my senses are returned and functioning normally. My body is still a wreck, but at least I can think clearly.

Not that there is much I can do right now, other than watch.

Xolotl is putting everything he has into his attack on Gemma. She just stands her ground, waiting for him to wear himself out. He appears powerful but has no experience with telekinesis. Has no real idea about how to use it effectively. Honed by a creative and concentrated mind, it is the most powerful natural force in the universe.

Which Gemma displays by clapping her hands together. A repelling wind cancels out Xolotl's. The room falls still. The force pinning me against the wall disappears.

I start to move, but Chirk stops me with a whispered, "The hell you doing?"

"I have a plan," I say.

"Getting killed ain't a plan," he says.

"You have any ideas, you let me know."

He grimaces but doesn't speak.

"Keep an eye on the others. Anyone comes to, we'll adapt. If not, I don't see any other way to play this out."

He sighs and slides to the side, giving me room to push myself past him and out of the tangle of corpses.

My muscles quiver with every movement, but I'm able to drag myself free. I make it a few feet before being frozen in place by what happens next.

Xolotl, frustrated by his impotent powers, screams in frustration as he pours everything he has into the attack. But his telekinesis is being contained. He's powerless, perhaps for the first time in his long life.

Gemma tents her fingers in front of her. Casual. Then, as though conducting a gentle melody, she pulls them apart.

Xolotl's scream goes high pitched, just for a moment.

And then…he just comes apart.

I've seen enemies and friends get vaporized before. Turned to dust. Burst apart. Carved into a hundred pieces. But I have never witnessed something as horrific as this.

Xolotl…he's pulled apart into his various components. His skin peels away. His vascular system snakes out from his musculature, which separates from his bones. Every strand of his nervous system is pulled from its place. His organs slide out of his gut and chest cavity, entrails twisting around him like living things.

And yet…

He is not dead.

His heart continues to pump. Lungs expand and contract. Muscles twitch.

Xolotl has been reduced to his various pieces, but they are all still attached. Not a drop of blood has been spilled.

I cannot imagine the agony and fear he must be feeling. And if I could, I'm not sure I would mind. But when I look at him, like this, I know two things for a fact.

Gemma is our enemy.

And we are next.

"Where is your bravado now?" Gemma asks the dismantled body. "C'mon, oh ancient one, pull yourself together!" She has a laugh at his expense. "To think, you were these rebels' last hope. A beast long past his prime, ready to be put down. When I'm done playing with you, of course. I was told to make all of you suffer, but I'm going to start with you…you who attempted to usurp our claim on this world and its people. You who sought to take what is Draun and make it yours."

She twists her hands and the thin strands of his nervous system knot up. Every part of him quivers in pain, unable to scream. With a snap of her thumbs, a dozen bones break.

How long can she prolong his death?

How long can a consciousness sustain such horrors before it loses sanity?

She maneuvers his eye out and around, trailing long strands that keep him connected to his skull and the brain still inside. He can see everything that's happening to him.

And, he can see me, dragging myself toward her along the floor.

His teeth chatter. Is he trying to speak? To warn her?

When his eyes roll away from me, and she laughs, I understand.

He's keeping her distracted. I hope he's not suddenly in search of redemption, because he won't find that here. But I *will* end his torture. What she is doing to him is barbaric.

She's consumed with her task, oblivious to the rest of us, fully engrossed in the dissection already in progress. Xolotl's bones break. Muscles tear. Nerve endings are crushed.

And yet, through it all, he lives.

Thirty-seven thousand years, and now he probably can't think of anything other than the mercy of death.

Almost there, I think, pulling myself along. I'm just feet from her now. Three more heaves and I'll be close enough.

One...

Two...

"You think you're so sneaky," Gemma says. "Crawling along like a slug. What is your plan, Praxion? Your Sonizer will have no effect. Your shard-firing side arm? Useless. Perhaps you'll go feral, like your Lost Tribe, and bite my foot?"

"Just wanted to get close enough..." I say, pulling myself forward one last time. I flop onto my back beneath her. "...to spit on you."

"The brave and noble Praxion, reduced to a dog."

"Dogs spit on people?" I ask, pretending that I'm spent, arms relaxed by my side.

She rolls her eyes and motions to Xolotl, a net of flesh, bones, and organs hovering behind her like a living shroud. "Not much of a god, after all, huh?"

"End his suffering," I say.

"Don't be in such a hurry," she says. "You are next. I'll leave the others for my friends. They should be here soon. Perhaps you would prefer I kill you alongside your love, hmm? I think I can arrange that."

She answered the question nagging at the back of my mind. Torel still lives. But for how long? We are in no shape to take on more Draun. Hell, even Gemma is too much.

Unless...

"How could you?" It's Sean, standing at the back of the chamber, bloodied and clutching his arm. Unlike the rest of us, he wasn't flung against the back wall.

"Poor pitiful Sean," she says, rotating toward him.

While she's distracted, I make my move, raising my hand and gently placing it on the skin between her casual socks and black tights.

"I don't want to kill you," she says, and then grins. "You really should do that yourself. Without you, all of this would never have been possible. Your rush to affection and the weeb desires for a Japanese face made you an easy target. And the moment I had you, I had them."

"No," Sean says, staggering from the revelation. But he is not to blame. We all accepted her the moment she said she'd been sent by Haruto.

And I'm not the only one who realizes that his fate might be more dire than she told us.

"What of Haruto?" It's Micah. He's barely standing. Neither of his gauntlets show signs of power. We make momentary eye contact. He glances to my hand and turns his attention back to Gemma. "Where is he, really?"

"A guest of the Visionary, held in the Imperial Palace's spacious dungeons. Tortured? Perhaps. Dead?" She shrugs. "In pieces?" She smiles up at Xolotl. "One can hope. But he gave all of you up. Can you blame him? The moment you see your body disassembled before your eyes, you'll give up your own mother."

Xolotl's vascular system tears down the middle, unleashing a violent spray of blood. She releases his body, and it falls to the floor, dissected and still, never to rise again.

"Hey!" Sean screams. "Fucking bitch!" He's got one of Chirk's mini-railguns in his hand, aimed at her head.

"Sean, no!" Chirk shouts. But with his arms broken, all he can do is watch.

Sean pulls the trigger, unleashing a storm of shards that deflect into the ceiling.

She lifts her hands toward him. "You ridiculous little man..."

Sean lifts off the ground and starts screaming when his skin begins to stretch.

50

MICAH

Despite Sean's obvious pain, I hold my fire. We'll probably only get one chance at this...and I'm not sure what *this* is. All I know is that Praxion was holding his hand against Gemma's leg the same way that he does when he's detecting a resonant frequency.

He's got a plan; of that I have no doubt. I just hope it doesn't take very long. Sean has seconds at best.

His scream breaks my heart, not just because he's in pain, but because of who is doing it to him. He had real feelings for Gemma, and I don't blame him for it. She was supportive of him. Laughed at his jokes. And she's beautiful. I can't imagine what it would feel like if Jess turned out to be a Draun.

In that sense, he's already been torn apart.

Would be nice if we could stop him from literally being torn apart.

I watch Praxion. He's focused on his gauntlet, waiting for whatever calculation is being worked out by whatever the hell these things have in them for computing power. Each one probably puts the best of Earth's computer's power to shame.

His eyes snap to me, and he gives a sharp nod.

Show time.

Both of my gauntlets charge to full, and I concentrate all of it into a tight beam of laser light. Yes, she's protected. She's clearly an experienced, or very talented Draun. But there's no harm in trying something new.

The laser's impact on the back of her shield gets her instant and full attention. Sean drops to the floor, groaning in pain, but alive. She increases the power of her shield while I force-of-will power my gauntlet, creating a beam far more intense than anything I have before.

The chamber glows orange.

Waves of heat warble through the air. Feels ten degrees hotter in here already. I'm going to cook us if this goes on too long.

She expands her shield, pushing back against my power. Her eyes are manic. She's smiling. Laughing. I wonder if true Draun power comes from insanity. Then I push back against it. The laser beam splits in a thousand different directions at once, wrapping around her sphere and continuing past her on the far side, slicing through the chamber wall and the mountain beyond.

She alters the shape of her shield, bending my laser light to her will. She carves a trough up through the ceiling. When water starts pouring in, I realize what she's up to. She's going to flood the chamber using the river above.

"Any day now!" I shout.

"Hit her hard!" Praxion shouts back.

I switch tactics and dump as much energy as I can muster into the beam, which is now like a battering ram and less like a scalpel.

The beam is simultaneously deflected into the ceiling and strikes with enough force to fling Gemma back against the wall. She hits hard and falls to the floor on her hands and knees. It's at that moment that the river above pours through the open ceiling.

Before the water strikes the floor, Praxion gets to his feet, takes aim with his Sonizer, and pulls the trigger. I can't hear a thing, but I can see a mild distortion in the air where his pulse crosses the chamber and strikes Gemma just before the water does.

There's a flicker of horror in her eyes, and then nothing at all.

The water slams down atop her, sweeps over Sean, and races toward the rest of us. I spin around and unleash a second massive beam of power that carves through the back wall and anything beyond it—hopefully nothing and no one important.

I'm knocked off my feet and carried out of the room, surrounded by the floating remains of the dead, including a mass that looks like old seaweed, but is actually Xolotl's separated body parts.

The moment we exit the room, the slight downward angle I carved pulls us toward the pool. We're dumped out into daylight far lower than we would have been if we'd just shot straight out.

The fall isn't bad—if you're conscious, and don't have broken arms. I'm beaten by the dead, thumping down atop me in the froth of falling water. I kick away from the white mist and start looking for the team. Praxion surfaces with Chirk on his head, coughing and cursing. Beyond them, I spot a dog-paddling pooch who looks thrilled to be helping. He's got Jess's shirt in his mouth, slowly dragging her toward shore. She's awake but dazed.

Night has fallen, but the full moon above provides enough light to see by.

I spot Harth face down and swim to him. I roll him over and am relieved to find his eyes open.

"Is there anyone left to kill?" he asks.

"Don't think so," I say.

"Good," he says. "Just let me drift away, please."

"Not today, big guy."

I grab hold of his armor, which is conveniently buoyant, and kick for shore. I spot Praxion again, ahead of me. Chirk is still on his head. He's speaking to Sean's limp body being pulled along. Hard to tell if Sean is alive or not.

I keep up a steady, one-armed side stroke. Harth might not be sinking, but his broad shoulders create a lot of drag. Going to take a minute to reach shore, especially with all the debris in the river. Bodies. Equipment. Rolling chunks of stone.

Along the way, I bump into a body I mistake for the dead, shoving it away. As I pass, I see it for what it is: Gemma. She's floating on her back, unconscious, but alive.

My debate is brief, but in the end all sides of my consciousness are in agreement. I take hold of her with my free hand, lean back, and drag both Gemma and Harth toward shore. By the time we reach the riverbank, my legs are rubber. While Praxion pulls Harth out of the water, I drag Gemma just halfway out and then collapse beside her.

Praxion, hands on knees beside me, out of breath, says, "Everyone is alive and accounted for." He glances at Gemma. "And her?"

"Out cold," I say. "But alive. Think we should do something about that?"

"Might not be necessary," he says.

"What did you hit her with?"

"Reset switch."

"Reset—you did it?"

"Xolotl's science was ingenious only in that we lacked the creativity to conceive of such a thing and lacked the knowledge of what he'd truly done to the DNA of humans and Kynolari living on this world. Once I knew what could be done, it was easy enough to apply to my Sonizer."

"Then we can do it?" I ask. "Reset the world?"

He gives a slow nod. "Perhaps." He looks to Gemma. "I'm not sure what's left of the original Gemma. If she gave herself to the Draun fully, there might not be anything left. That would mean—"

"We'd be killing more than two hundred and fifty million people," I say, feeling sick.

"To save billions," he says. "It is the heaviest of burdens to carry, and I will understand if you do not want to—"

"I'm in," I say. "Ned—" I chuckle. "You know I can't remember his real name now... He chose to not go full Draun. Even Jenna fought against it to a degree. Being powerful doesn't inherently make someone evil. That's a choice. And there are consequences for that choice, especially when you're trying to take over my damn planet. Yeah, I'm in."

Sean coughs and sits up suddenly. He pats his hands over his body. "Am I all here? Are all my pieces still attached?" His search ends at his crotch. "Oh, thank God."

"Bout time," Chirk says, giving Sean a playful kick. "Get off your ass and carry me to the med-bay."

I turn around and am happy to see the *Prowler* parked nearby, hatch already open, where they left it upon arrival.

Harth rolls over and pushes himself up with a grunt. He looks down at Gemma. "We should kill her."

Praxion shakes his head. "We need to know. If it worked. If she wakes up at all, and some Draun remains in her, then we will kill her. Until then, we'll watch her."

Harth grunts. "Well, then you can carry her back." He follows after Sean and Chirk. When Praxion drags Gemma away, he reveals Jess lying on her back not far away. She's looking up at the sky. Grover sits beside her, ever attentive.

"Hey," I say.

"Always wanted to visit Mexico," she says. "Not exactly how I pictured it."

"Same," I say. "No me gusta."

She laughs and then grunts.

"You okay?" I ask.

"Bruised ribs, I think. Head is pounding. You?"

"Bruised a lot of things," I say. "Nothing broken."

"So, that was insane," she says. "What did I miss?"

"You mean when you were napping?"

She smiles.

"I'll fill you in later, when we're not eating."

"That gross?"

"Beyond gross." I push myself up and tilt my chin up toward Grover. He pants and lets his tongue hang out but doesn't abandon his post by Jess's side. "Good boy."

I work the kinks out of my back and then hold out a hand for Jess. "We better get inside. Sounded like we had more trouble inbound." I pull her up and into my arms. During our quick embrace, Grover slides between our legs.

"Love you, guys," he says, tail wagging slowly. Then he goes rigid. I look down to find him staring at the sand in front of us, the hackles on his back raised. I follow his gaze and find four long shadows stretched out on the beach.

"Are those people on horses?" Jess asks, looking at the shadows.

I turn around and look up toward the dry top of the original waterfall, now flowing out of the middle of the cliff. Standing atop it are four horses. Seated atop each one is a rider, silhouetted by the moon behind them.

The opening to Johnny Cash's "The Man Comes Around" plays through my head. I think he might be quoting the Bible, but I really have no idea.

And I heard, as it were, the noise of thunder. One of the four beasts sang, 'Come and see,' and I saw. And behold, a white horse...

There are four horses standing above us, their colors hard to make out.

But their riders...are Draun. I know because the horses aren't actually standing, they're floating.

The final lines from Cash's masterpiece come to mind, punctuating the scene.

And I heard a voice in the midst of the four beasts, and I looked, and behold a pale horse. And his name that sat on him was death, and hell followed with him.

"On three," I say. "Run."

51

MICAH

Before I reach the end of, 'one,' Grover and Jess bolt.

"What the—hey!" I don't bother following them. Someone needs to watch their backs as they run for the ship.

"Sorry, babe!" Jess shouts. "Only one of us is the Axiom!"

She's not wrong about that. She's got some skills now. Is growing accustomed to war and the horrors that come with it. But these guys look like they mean business, and she's not afraid to admit when she's out of her league.

Question is, am I out of *my* league?

Almost certainly.

Sure, I might have some untapped power and tricks left to uncover, but *four* Draun? One is bad enough. And getting past their telekinetic shields is a pain in the ass.

I wait on the beach, watching the Draun above us. *The hell are they doing?* Maybe they're just here to watch and report? Doesn't make sense. The point of recon is to figure out the enemy's movements *without* them knowing. But these guys stand out like truck nuts in a Lilith Fair parking lot.

"Any movement?" Praxion asks, stepping up beside me.

"They're just watching. Just us?" We're both beat up pretty good, but not nearly as bad as the others.

"Not quite," says a small and familiar voice. I glance back to find Poppy cracking her neck one way and the other. "You know, I'm out of practice, but I'm itching for a fight. Jess and Grover are manning the med-bay. Sean and Chirk are out of the fight for now." She looks up at Praxion. "No change in Torel's condition, but that's not bad. Not really good, either, but sometimes 'not bad' is the best we can hope for."

Praxion gives her a nod. "Harth is moving...slowly...to the *Prowler*'s weapons systems. MIMIR is already keeping watch on us, but Harth doesn't trust the A.I.'s aim."

"So, what's the plan?" I ask. "I'm guessing retreat? Before more show up."

"Yes..."

"But?" I ask.

"With four of them, we might not be able to escape."

"Okay," I say. "We reduce their numbers by, what, two? And then make a run for it?"

"Yes," Praxion says.

"Can you 'reset switch' them from here?" I ask.

"They're out of range," he says.

"I can't reach them from here, either," Poppy says.

"We just need to wait," Praxion says. "The strongest of them will lose patience. Will want to show his superiority. And will not fear the three of us. They do not know what happened to Gemma."

"And if they don't lose their patience?" I ask.

"They're Draun," Poppy says. "If they don't lose patience, they'll get ambitious and want to claim our deaths. Raise their status. Position themselves to someday overthrow the Visionary and rule in his place."

"How the hell do they function as a species, let alone one strong enough to threaten the entire universe?" I ask.

"Raw power," Praxion says, "and the Visionary's strength. He has been challenged thousands of times and dispatched them all with a thought. He's probably been challenged on Earth a few times already, and with every kill, his influence of the Draun grows in unison with their own cravings. It is a difficult balance, but the Visionary has maintained it long enough to unify the Draun into an army with a solitary goal—even if they disagree over which of them should be in charge."

"Look alive, bitches," Poppy says, hopping from one foot to another, "here comes the first sucker."

The horse and rider to our left float up and away from the top of the cliff. The horse whinnies and moves its legs but can't go anywhere. It's probably out-of-its-mind terrified. Far as I know, horses can't become Draun, which means this guy has been hovering through the sky, who knows how far, or how fast.

I smile at Poppy.

"You have no idea."

"I miss something?" Poppy asks.

"Maybe a few things," Praxion says, charging his Sonizer.

"Any way you can make it look like we didn't do anything?" I ask.

He taps his gauntlet. "Should minimize visual distortions, but out here in the dark, it would be hard to see."

"Seriously," Poppy says. "Please tell me you have this handled."

"The first one," Praxion says. "Hopefully. The others...only if I find time to recharge."

"Right," Poppy says. "For a second there, I was starting to think I wouldn't get to kick some ass."

Horse and rider settle down in the river, but don't get wet. The water flows around the invisible telekinetic shield, already raised.

I imagine the Visionary has probably learned how to *sleep* fully shielded.

"Kynolari," the rider says, his voice electronically modified. His face is hidden behind some kind of Japanese anime cat mask. Its eyes and ears, along with a pattern on its face, glow red from thin lines of LEDs that look like neon tubes.

"It's not bad enough that they're Draun, but now they're wearing cat masks?!" Poppy's gauntlet crackles with power.

"What is wrong with cats?" Praxion asks. "They are simple-minded creatures of instinct. Like aggressive rabbits."

"Spend nearly a decade on this world and your opinion will change," Poppy says.

"Kynolari!" The man repeats louder, annoyed that instead of cowering, we've had a conversation.

"Oh, right," Poppy says. "*He's* here. Well, what do you want Hello Kitty? We got places to be and worlds to save. You know how it is."

The glowing mask turns down to Poppy. The man behind it chuckles, then turns his attention to Praxion. "Why do you persist? You must know this feeble crew of yours is no match for—"

The man sits still and silent for a moment. Then the horse drops the last inch to the ground. The jolt knocks the man off balance, and he slides to the side, toppling off the horse and faceplanting in the sand, one foot hooked in a stirrup.

Freed from the man's telekinetic grip, the horse rears up, lets out a loud neigh, and then slams back down before charging off into the night. The limp Draun man is dragged along beside it, bouncing off every bump, rock, and stump on the way.

I glance down at Praxion's now powerless gauntlet and grin. "Subtle."

"Holy shit!" Poppy says. "The hell was that?"

"Reset button," I say.

"My Sonizer is set to the resonant frequency of the DNA strand which activates the Draun segment of the human genome. I can turn it off, removing the Draun energy from their bodies."

"Looked like you lobotomized the guy," she says.

"When someone is fully Draun," Praxion says, "there is nothing left of their former selves."

"Aha. I get it," she says. "But I don't think they do." She points to the three remaining horsemen. They're looking down at us still but are clearly debating about what to do next.

I motion to Praxion's Sonizer. "How much time to recharge?"

"Thirty seconds left."

"So, we just need them to come down one at a time, every sixty—never mind."

All three Draun float away from the cliff and descend. They land in the river, a little farther away than the first. They're being careful, and they've united their shields into a single wall, diverting the river far behind them. Each one of them are wearing the silly cat masks, each with a different color scheme. Green, pink, and orange.

"Hey," I say. "Guys. Can we clear something up before you get all intimidating and shit? I'm just curious about the masks. Are they supposed to be frightening? Or adorable? Because I'm having trouble figuring out what you're going for."

They glance at each other, and then Green Mask says, "Both. Frightening *because* they're adorable. Like Poppy Playtime."

I glance down at Poppy.

She shrugs. "No idea."

"Next question," I say. "How old are you?"

"Old enough!" Orange Mask shouts. "We have wasted enough time! The Master wants the human alive. Filet the r—"

Orange Mask sags in defeat and falls forward onto his horse's neck.

I nearly laugh.

"What did you guys eat for diner?" Poppy asks. "Seriously."

"J-just sushi," Pink Mask says. Sounds like the youngest of the bunch. Possibly a girl. I hate the fact that we might be facing off against teenagers here, but they're not even human anymore. The best they have to offer the world is death, greed, envy, and destruction. Erasing the evil in them is a mercy to their original selves, and every other person on this planet. Not to mention the universe beyond. The stakes are the highest I've ever faced.

"It's *not* the sushi," Green says, looking down at Praxion's recharging gauntlet. With a flick of his head, he sends Praxion flying back. Before he hits the ground, Green flies up and off his horse, before flinging it after Praxion.

What an asshole, I think, and then hit him with a beam powerful enough to knock him a hundred feet back, into the cliff that once had a river flowing over it.

Pink, on her own now, just kind of sits on her horse, still protected by a shield, but unsure about what to do.

I swing around, tracking the airborne horse. It's going to land on Praxion, and it's going to hit hard. I aim with my gauntlets, but never have to fire. The *Prowler*'s weapon systems hum to life. A trio of rockets twist out of hidden pods and connect with the equine target one at a time, reducing it by a third with each explosion. The only thing that strikes Praxion is a slight red mist.

"Oh my god," Pink whispers.

"How old are you?" Poppy asks her.

"Sixteen," Pink responds.

"How long you been with these guys?"

"Few days."

Poppy tilts her head to the side. "Get the fuck out of here."

The girl glances back to the cliffside which I debossed with Green. He's not visible behind all the rock dust filling the air around the impact.

"We'll tell him what's left of the horse is you," Poppy says. "Last chance."

Pink nods her cat face, turns her horse away, and gallops—on the ground—off into the night.

Honestly, wasn't expecting mercy from Poppy.

"That was…nice," I say.

"Good deed for the year," she says. "Won't happen again."

A scream turns our attention back to the cliff. An earthquake rolls beneath us. Then the cliff face shatters and slides down, kicking up a roiling dust.

"Well," Poppy said. "He just woke up."

"Woke up?" I ask.

"Draun go through stages of growth. The last one awakens their full power. Can be triggered by anything really, but pain is the most common instigator. Good news is, you hurt him. Bad news, we're about to get squashed, unless Praxion—" We look back together and spot Praxion flat on his back, breathing but not moving. If there is a tomorrow, we are all going to be in a lot of pain. "Yup, squashed it is."

52

GRUUNLOKAR

I'm angry. Mostly at myself. If I hadn't been struggling, I would have been with the team. Might have been able to prevent the injuries I've seen. Harth is dazed. Sean is wracked with pain from nearly having his body peeled apart. Gemma is unconscious. And Chirk... His arms are broken.

I don't normally want to shoot anyone. It's what makes me a good sniper. Considering the weight and importance of what I'm about to do before pulling the trigger helps me maintain peace and ensures I never take a life in vain. But right now...I'm struggling to follow orders.

Especially when they come from a pug medic I don't know, who's been off grid and out of the fight for eight years. I outrank her, but protocol says that inside a med-bay, the medic on duty holds a temporary command position. Meaning, she's the boss. After setting Chirk's arms and getting him medi-cuffed, she checked on Sean and Harth, deeming them both non-critical. She didn't bother with Gemma at all, which confused me. Before I could ask why, she told me to 'stay,' the way a human would to a dog, and headed for the door.

When I asked why, she said, "There are four Draun outside and your head is not in the game! I don't know what your deal is, but you better sort it the fuck out, pronto."

Now she leaps into the hallway, where she barks, "You two!"

"Whoa," Jess says. "Dial it back, little miss."

"*Excuse* me?" Poppy says.

"Sorry," Jess says. "Just dazed."

"Grover dazed, too," the dog says. "Me am tired."

"Aww, I'm so sad for you both," Poppy says. Doesn't mean a word of it. "Know how to operate the *Prowler*'s weapon systems?"

"I've been shown," Jess says, "but—"

"Well, you're on your feet, so you'll do. With me, now." I listen to their footsteps fade.

"She is a handful," Baarfolir says.

I nod. "And capable."

"While my language might not be as colorful as our new friend's," Baarfolir says. "You do not seem yourself."

Their dual diagnosis weighs on me. Perhaps Jenna isn't in my head? Maybe I'm infected. Or mind-controlled without realizing. I sit down, and content myself with watching over the wounded, ignorant to what is happening outside.

My attention turns to Torel, stable, but still in a coma. She spent a lot of her time during the war in a room just like this. Removing limbs. Sometimes attaching them. Saving lives and calling the time of death. With her warrior's heart it must have been a struggle to not leave.

"So," Baarfolir says, sitting beside me. "What is happening to you?"

"Not sure history is going to help me much," I say.

"Just answer the damn question," Chirk says, his voice weak, not from his injuries, but from the pain killers coursing through his system while the medi-braces stitch his bones back together.

"Speak," Harth says, lying on his back, two cots to the left.

"Yeah, dude," Sean says, grunting. "We're like a band of brothers, right? No secrets, except for what we do in the bathroom. No one needs to know what Harth gets up to in there."

Harth chuckles and winces.

"Trust me," Chirk says. "It's not something you wanna see."

"Hey," Harth says, a warning.

Chirk rolls his sleepy eyes. "Yeah, yeah. I know."

I sigh and lean back. Of all the things I am good at in this world, talking to a bunch of injured comrades is not one of them. I don't generally like speaking at all. So, I give them the short and sweet version. "Before we killed Jenna Flood, she gained access to my mind. Without me knowing, she deposited a duplicate of her consciousness in my head, just in case she died."

"That's how you blew off Thickums's leg," Chirk says. "Your shard was wrapped with a telekinetic shield of its own."

"Wait," Baarfolir says. "You have telekinetic abilities?"

"Sick," Sean says.

"Will you all be quiet? Please. Let me finish." After a moment of silence, I continue. "I do not have control over the telekinesis. That is still Jenna, from within my mind."

"But the regulators—" Harth starts.

"She is hidden inside a liminal space I created while meditating. She is out of my regulators' reach. For now."

Harth pushes himself up with a grunt. He sits on the side of his cot. "A quick adjustment should—"

"She's not the Jenna Flood we fought," I say. "Not the woman we killed. This copy of her is from long ago, *before* she became Draun. She retains the knowledge of how to access and use her telekinetic abilities but has no hatred of the Kynolari. No memory of her misdeeds. She is not Draun, and she is not our enemy. Were she not trapped in my mind, I believe she would be an ally."

"Man," Sean says. "Must be weird having a chick in your head. I definitely wouldn't want a female wading through my mess."

I shake my head. "The liminal space is empty of everything aside from endless, plain rooms and hallways. She could wander forever and never encounter a single part of my consciousness unless I visit that place."

"Okay, so, like, can she come out? Like that Xolotl dude? He made a backup of himself over and over again. So maybe we can put her in a computer, right?" Sean lifts a hand and points it toward Harth. "This guy said that Xolotl's tech was creative, but not advanced, which I think means he could recreate it."

"It is forbidden," Harth says.

"Screw forbidden," Sean says. "It's not against the law on Earth. And even if it was, laws change all the time. For all you know, it's been made...*pro*bidden while you've been gone."

Baarfolir raising a finger. "I don't think 'probidden'—"

"I made it up," Sean says, waving him off and wincing from the movement. "People do that all the time, too. Look, my dudes, you're rocking with the human race now, and we are all about breaking rules and pushing boundaries. Pot used to be illegal in my neck of the woods. Now it ain't. And you've been living in New Hampshire, my dudes. You know the state motto, right? 'Live free or die.'"

I grin. "Inspiring, but—"

"Hold on," Chirk says. "Hold on. Please tell me I'm not the only one thinking it, because I'm going to feel like an asshole if I am." He looks at each of us, one at a time, studying our faces.

"Bro, what did I miss?" Sean asks.

Chirk faces him. "You were almost there. But not quite."

Sean's brow furrows and he looks around the room, freezing when his gaze lands on Gemma. We're all looking at her now. The solution.

"Look," Chirk says to Sean, "buddy. She was important to you, but—"

"She was a lying bitch who used my heart, broke it, and tried to kill my friends and destroy the human race," Sean says. "Fuck her. Bros before hoes, anyway, right?"

"Bros before hoes," Chirk says, giggling. "The stuff you say, man."

"Goes the other way, too," Sean says. "Chicks before dicks."

He gets us all laughing to some degree.

"Great," Chirk says. "Then we all agree. We put the Jenna chick into Gemma's empty husk of a mind, try like hell to not mix up their remarkably similar names, and see if we can't pull off Xolotl's body-snatching trick."

"After which we must destroy all knowledge and technology used during the transfer," Harth says.

"Agreed," Baarfolir says.

All eyes turn to me. I give a nod and say, "Let's get her out of my head."

A minute later, we've managed to hobble, roll, and limp our way from the infirmary to the workshop. This is where Harth spends most of his time, repairing, building, and maintaining weapons systems and electronics. Baarfolir is the last to arrive, pushing Gemma in on a hovering stretcher that he's set to its lowest level, a foot above the ground, allowing someone of his short stature to maneuver it.

Chirk would normally be the one to aid Harth with the finer details of electronics work. His dainty fingers make him an expert at handling small things, something he does at least once a day. I nearly say all this aloud but decide to give the little man a break, on account of his arms already being broken. He'll heal, but I can see he's still in pain. Might not have been the best idea to move out of the med-bay, but he'd never let us do this without him.

"Okay," Baarfolir says. "Best of luck to you all. I'm, ahh, I'm going to maintain my watch on Torel."

"Good thinking," Chirk says. "The bossman and her—"

"Oh, I know," Baarfolir says, shaking his head. "I know."

Chirk calls after him as he leaves the workshop. "Whoa, whoa, wait. I'm sensing a story there. Baar, c'mon, man!" Our historian wisely keeps walking. "Bah. I want to punch something."

"Right here," Harth says, pointing to a little switch on the interior of the regulator he's peeled open. He's split an ambient energy arc with two resistor nodes, giving us access to the normally hidden switch. I reach in with a long, thin metal rod, aware that touching the arc might be enough to add my name to the list of wounded. With a gentle push, the switch moves upward a tick. I withdraw the rod and Harth releases the arc. He holds out his hands. "That's it. Hardware and software safeguards have been updated. It's not going to outright kill her for not being Kynolari, but the danger is still significant."

"Great," Chirk says. "But that's only *if* we can transfer her data, or whatever you'd call it—"

"Her *essence*," Sean says with a flourish.

Chirk looks at him in silence for a moment.

"Weird, but sure."

He's about to continue when the ship shakes from whatever is happening outside. Feels like a trio of rockets exploding at close proximity. He turns to Sean. "Do me a favor?"

"Of course, my dog," Sean says.

"Help Jess…and *Grover*…with the guns. You know what, if Grover *is* manning a gunner's seat, please replace him. You have a clear shot on anything about to hurt our people, you take 'em out."

Sean's eyes widen. He stands up straighter. Gives a salute, and then without a word limp-sprints out of the room.

When he's gone, Chirk turns back to me. "Now, any ideas on how to get her out of there—" He points to my head. "—and into there?" He motions to Gemma's still form.

Harth hands me a connection node and I plug it into the side of my regulator.

"I'm going to ask her," I say.

"This will be similar to the experience Grover and Micah had when their minds were merged, but she will be exiting a mind she doesn't remember entering, and moving her entire being into a body that is not her own," Harth says.

"Should be fun," I say, and plug myself in.

I don't feel myself lose consciousness, or fall, or anything like that. I flicker from the real world and back into my twisted, white, liminal space.

"Hello?" I say, and when no one replies, I start walking.

53

MICAH

"Get to Praxion," I tell Poppy. "See if you can wake him up."

"Not leaving the fight," she says.

"You're a *medic*."

She frowns her little pug face up at me. I nearly melt. She's adorable.

"Fuck you, asshole."

"What?" I ask. "You *are* a medic, right?"

"For looking at me like that. You know how many times people have come up to me, grabbed my face, and spoke gobbledygook at me with their horrible breath? I got mental scars, man. And all of them looked just like you did a second ago. Knock that shit off."

"Sorry," I say. "My grandmother had a pug. 'Pugsly.'"

"Amazingly creative name," she says, and then sighs. "But you're right. Praxion is our solution, and he's out cold. So, have fun dying." She motions to Praxion. "I'll be over there."

She bounds away, taking cover beneath the *Prowler* with the Kynolari's unconscious leader. And now I'm standing alone as Green floats away from the cliff face, a swirl of stone and dust following him. He's got his hands out to either side, partially clenched. Can't see his smile behind the luminous Japanese cat mask, but I'm sensing a shit-eating-grin. Things are about to get all melodramatic.

Which is fine by me. The Draun seem like talkers. Like comic book villains who like to monologue before a fight kicks off. Probably an ego thing, or maybe a self-confidence booster. This might be Green's first real fight, so it makes sense that his confidence might need a—

"Oof!"

I'm struck from the side by what feels like a runaway yak. I spiral through the air, catching sight of the ground in time to unleash a few pulses of laser light, leveling myself out and allowing me to land in a crouch.

"Okay," I say to myself. "This guy isn't a talker."

He hovers over to me. His last attack came with no warning. No flick of the wrist. If his eyes were a tell, I'd never know. Can't see them behind the damn mask, which is not cute-scary.

It's cute-dumb.

Rather than wait for another sneak attack, I create a laser shield around myself. No idea if it will deflect a telekinetic attack, but I'm guessing he doesn't know either.

This time, I see his finger twitch. Right hand. Index finger. Attack is coming from my left, again. Powerful, but not creative.

I launch myself into the air with a blast of energy that carves a hole in the earth beneath me. His attack scours the ground where I'd been standing. An invisible katana-blade weed whacker buzzes through foliage and hacks down a tree.

Okay, he might be a little creative.

I maintain the downward laser blast, slowly but surely carving a hole toward the Earth's core. I wonder what will happen when I reach magma.

We hover thirty feet across from each other.

Can't tell if he's confused by me or not. Fucking mask. But I roll the dice on him not fully understanding what's going on, and that his lack of monologue is a barely contained urge.

"You don't stand a chance," I tell him.

He chuckles.

"That's it?" I ask. "No wild claims? No bravado? What kind of Draun are you?"

"I..." he says, all tentative. "I-I-I h-have a st-st-st...*stutter*."

Oh, for fuck's sake.

I don't want to kill a guy with a stutter. I mean, yeah, it's just a speech impediment. I went to speech therapy for a lisp when I was younger. Doesn't mean he can't be evil incarnate. I bet a bunch of Nazis had trouble with h-h-heiling Hitler. Ugh, I'm going to hell. *Whatever*, I decide. Him first.

"Okay, let me lay this out for you, then."

He waits.

"You...are nobody. I don't know your name. In my head, you're just 'Green' because of your mask. You're new to your power. Probably haven't killed anyone yet. Now, you are Draun. Which means you've got some pretty badass telekinetic abilities and more than a dozen frat boys worth of ego and ambition bouncing around in that skull. But that does not make you strong, ruthless, or brave. But me...I'm a U.S. Army Ranger. I've killed people. I've killed *Draun*. People who did have names, who weren't new to their power, who even you might have known."

"B-b-bullshit."

"Jenna Flood," I say. "She's dead, you know. Because of me." Us, really, but I'm trying to intimidate the guy, shake his confidence. He doesn't need to know it was a team effort.

"And I can do the same to you."

He just stares.

"Do I look familiar?" I ask. "Maybe Lumen Sok imprinted my face on your consciousness while he blinded you to the truth that you are simply a replaceable cog in his machine? Or maybe you know my name?"

"Axiom," he says, almost a whisper.

"See? Now we're on the same page. Now you know that Lumen Sok is afraid of me. And now—"

He cackles with manic laughter. "And now my mind's eye has seen the glory of my ascension to the throne. With the Axiom's head on my belt, even the Visionary will bend a knee!"

"How are you going to get my head on your belt?" I ask. "I mean, I get that you can rip it off, but my hair isn't long enough to tie, and have you ever *tried* tying hair? Impossible. Can you sew? Oh, maybe duct tape? Probably your best bet."

"You...talk...s-s-so much!" He screams and swats his hand toward me. I stop firing lasers into the ground and plummet toward it. A strong breeze flows past where I'd been. A near miss. But I only manage to prolong my beating by a second, because his next swing is straight up.

My protective laser sphere manages to shield my body from the impact, but I'm launched skyward like a tennis ball pitched to Babe Ruth. Green and the *Prowler* shrink away beneath me.

As I topple through the sky, I turn off my shield to hide myself. Then I take a brief moment to look up at the stars. With no light pollution in this part of the world, the Milky Way glows like I've never seen it before. Coupled with the knowledge that it is teeming with life, wonderous and horrible, makes it that much more impressive. Then my view shifts to the moon. For a moment, I think there's something wrong with my vision. There's some kind of distortion in front of it.

Movement.

My eyes focus, and I manage to understand what I'm seeing.

The blurs are people.

Draun to be precise. A squadron of them flying overhead. But not toward me. Not engaging in this fight. They're headed out into the world, like the three little pigs seeking their fortunes.

We're too late.

I don't remember my perilous position until I'm fifty feet from finding out what it's like to crash through a dozen tree branches before impacting the ground at terminal velocity.

With a burst of orange light, I fire my lasers into the ground and slow my descent. Someone cooler than me might have been able to swoop back up all in one motion, but I'm barely able to Iron Man this shit back to *terra firma* without faceplanting. Once my feet are on the ground, I turn toward the orange glow left behind by my long blast into the ground and launch myself through the air. Takes a few laser leaps, but I make my way back just as Green turns his attention to Praxion.

It's at that moment when whoever is behind the *Prowler*'s weapon system unleashes everything they've got. Lasers, shards, rockets. The storm of shock and awe armaments pound into Green, concealing him in a blossom of light and fire, the heat of which I can feel from fifty feet away. It's like the thumping finale of a Fourth of July fireworks display, rumbling for miles in every direction.

But it's not working. Between explosions I catch sight of Green, casually waiting out the storm.

So, I attack before he can see it coming.

I launch myself closer, until the heat is nearly unbearable. I land in a rolling dive that ends with me on my stomach, facing Green. Arms angled upward, I unleash a broad laser blast that strikes, wraps around, and then propels the telekinetic sphere—and man within it—skyward at something close to the speed of light.

I have a vision of him striking his shield so hard that he turns to paste and is then vaporized as the shield falls away.

But that's all it is.

A vision.

When my light fades and the last of the rockets explode, Green remains, unharmed, unmoved, and unimpressed.

I underestimated him.

Maybe that was the mask's true purpose? To make me see a child. To assume he was immature. To lower our guard.

When he reaches out his hands and a vice grip around my body lifts me off the ground, I'm sure of it. I unleash a laser blast straight into the ground beneath me. Give it everything I can. But I'm held in place, unable to move.

Praxion is lifted next, along with Poppy. He's still unconscious, and she is pissed.

"Some Axiom you turned out to be!" she shouts at me.

I ignore the comment and try to slip a solidified laser light between myself and the telekinetic grip. If I can, I might be able to force it open far enough for me to—

"Hrk!"

The grip tightens.

I float to within a few feet of Green, and he turns toward me. "Good news. I've decided against taking just your head."

I attempt to think of something witty, but I'm all out of quips. I'm tired, hurting, and pissed off that I couldn't even handle this one asshole that's new to his power.

"I'm going to bring you all," Green says. "T-T-That will be enough to ensure my s-station among the most high and put me within striking distance of a command p-position."

He turns his attention to the others. "The Axiom. The infamous P-Praxion." He looks at Poppy. "Whoever you are." He glances at the *Prowler*. "And a genuine Kynolari *spacecraft* capable of reaching the s-stars—of *returning* the Draun to the stars. Where we belong."

When we start lifting higher into the air, and the *Prowler* joins us, I fight harder against my bonds, unleashing all the power I can muster. But it's no use. This man is too powerful for me alone. And the team... I look to Praxion. We were so close to a solution. But now... Now we are the prisoners of a Japanese cat-mask wearing asshole.

And there is nothing I can do about it.

"Hey!"

Our collective attention turns toward the booming feminine voice.

I'm surprised to find Gemma standing in the *Prowler*'s open hatch. We erased her mind. There shouldn't be anything left.

Green thrusts a hand out toward her while maintaining control of the rest of us. But nothing happens. Gemma doesn't even show a sign of resisting him. He grunts and tries again.

Still nothing.

Then Gemma steps out into the air and calmly glides up toward us. She stops in front of Green, who recognizes her as a fellow Draun, but probably not his superior, given the fact that he's now hell bent on usurping Lumen Sok.

"Let them go," she says, and then glances at Poppy and says, "Oh my god. So cute."

Poppy and I look at each other, confused by the development.

Green is thrown off, too. "I-I-I will n-not."

"Okay," she says, cracking her knuckles. "Last chance."

He cocks his head. "W-Who are you?"

Gemma lifts her hand, positioned to snap her fingers. She lets the tension build for a moment and then snaps. The cord is cut from Green's power, and he plummets to the ground.

The rest of us, including the *Prowler*, begin to fall, but are quickly caught by a much gentler telekinetic force, and lowered to the ground. We stand behind Gemma as she touches down between us and Green. She crouches beside the man, who is not long for this world after falling fifty feet.

She peels off his mask, revealing a young Japanese man. Blood gurgles from his mouth. "My name," she says, "is Jenna Flood."

"Jenna?" I say, staggering back a step.

She turns to face me. "Have we met?"

"Briefly," I say. "Are you…"

She raises her hands. "A friend. Yes. Well, now I am, I guess. Long story."

"I bet…"

Praxion shifts. "Ugh…" We crouch down beside him.

"Easy," Poppy says, supporting his head with both of her hands.

Gemma…or *Jenna* now, I guess—that's going to confuse the shit out of me—joins us. "Will he be okay?"

Praxion opens his eyes. Blinks twice. "Did we win?"

I chuckle. "For the moment." I nod to Jenna. "Thanks to her."

Praxion looks to Jenna. His brow furrows. "How long—"

"Micah!" I've never heard my man so worried. "Micah, Micah, Micah!" Grover sounds excited instead of worried when he sees me. He arrives by my side, circling and nudging me with his nose until he's under my arm, wagging his tail fast enough to kick up a breeze. "Love Micah."

I lean down and place my head against his. We've been apart too much lately, and I'm thrilled to be with him again. "Love Grover."

"Grover shot *rockets*," he says. "Exploded horse. Was gross."

I can't help but laugh.

I give his coat a rough shake.

"You did good. Saved Praxion."

"Mm," he says in quick agreement, moving on to the next order of business. "No more away. Always with Micah."

I nod, our foreheads rubbing. "Always."

"Always Jess, too?" Grover asks. He leans back and looks me in the eyes, very serious now. "Grover love Jess."

Motion draws my eyes up. Jess is standing over us now, beleaguered, but smiling. "Yes," I tell Grover. "Micah loves Jess, too."

"Okay," Poppy says. "Did I die and wake up in a Hallmark movie? Is this hell?"

Grover turns his attention to Praxion. "Praxion okay?"

"Improving," he says with a grunt.

"Yes!" Grover says. "Torel better, too."

"She's awake," Jess says, laying on some reality before anyone gets their hopes up. "Hasn't spoken yet."

"But it's a good sign," Poppy says. Gives Praxion's shoulder a punch.

He looks up at her. Pretty sure he's intending to thank her. But then his brow furrows and his jaw sets. He's looking past her, toward the sky above. Toward the moon, where the Draun fly past, eyes on other targets. "They're attacking."

Jenna looks up and sees her former brethren soaring past. "Attacking what?"
"The world," Poppy says.
I nod and add, "The whole damn world."

TO BE CONTINUED IN

GOOD BOYS: THE VISIONARY

AUTHOR'S NOTE

When I started writing the first *Good Boys,* I was planning on it being a standalone novel. About halfway through, I was having so much fun with the characters and world that I decided it required a sequel. About ten chapters into writing the second *Good Boys,* I decided it needed to be a trilogy, written and released back-to-back, which is something I've never done before. I usually need a break from a story so I can come back excited, but I'm about to start writing Book Three and I'm just as excited to get back to these characters. They've become some of my favorites. Hopefully yours, too!

I wrote Book Two with the actual Grover by my side. I am always inspired by his adoration and shenanigans. (It is difficult to write with a big Golden Retriever resting his chin on your hand.) It's kind of a magical experience, writing a trilogy featuring my dog during his first year of life, adding his personality into the book as he grows and changes, and our bond becomes more and more like Micah's and the fictional Grover's. Just the other day, ten-month-old Grover defended my wife, Hilaree, from two angry dogs that rushed them while on a walk. He taught them a lesson, sent them home yelping, and revealed that he is just as brave as our fictional good boy.

If you're enjoying the series, it would be amazing if you could help spread the word. I have no idea how a series about space dogs will sell, but writing an entire trilogy with no sense of sales is a big gamble. I'll be done with Book Three by the time the first is released, so no matter what happens, all three will come out. But let's set our sights higher! A TV series! A movie trilogy! Sky is the limit, but as an indie author, I need help getting the word out. If you want to help spread the news, please post a review on Amazon and Audible. Or post it on your socials. Start a *Good Boys* book group and invite me for a Q&A!

If you want to be sure you don't miss the final book, all the novels to follow, and news about upcoming comic books, movies, TV series, etc., you can visit bewareofmonsters.com and sign up for the newsletter. You can also join the Tribe at facebook.com/groups/JR.Tribe. It's an amazing group of fans, and it's the first place that cool stuff gets announced. Also, we give away free stuff every week!

Hope to see you there and thank you so much for reading and supporting the books. Let's make a deal: You keep reading my crazy novels, and I'll keep writing them.

—Jeremy Robinson

ACKNOWLEDGMENTS

Once again, I need to thank Alex Maddern for the idea that became *Good Boys*. His taste is generally questionable—he loves Fortnite, can't get enough of it—but this time he managed to come up with enough material that I was able to spin it into gold. Just call me Rumpelstiltskin, and Al is like a nice pile of hay. Wink emoji.

Thanks to Kane Gilmour, editor extraordinaire, who helps me turn first drafts into finely tuned, entertaining word machines. He might be the actual Rumpelstiltskin. Maybe I'm the loom. As always, big thanks to our army of proofreaders: Adrian Brooke, Julie Carter, Elizabeth Cooper, Cynthia Gregory, Gavin Gregory, Deanna Haddrill, Matt Ingram, Marcy Jaqua, Andre Jenkin, Scott Kehoe, Rebecca Laurent, Janis Levonitis, Stefanie Maubach, Kyle Mohr, Jessica Otterstål, Jeff Sexton, and Courtney Westendorf. You all help conceal the fact that I'm just as bad at typing as I am at spelling.

Big thanks to Tom Taylorson for lending his voice talents to such a strange trilogy of sci-fi books, and to Podium for agreeing to publish this insanity. And that's only possible because of you crazy readers coming along with me on this weird ride through indie publishing, where the corporate gatekeepers can't filter my imagination. Viva La Indie Revolución! Thank you!

—Jeremy

ABOUT THE AUTHOR

Jeremy Robinson is the *New York Times* and #1 Audible bestselling author of over seventy novels and novellas, including *Infinite, The Others,* and *The Dark,* as well as the Jack Sigler thriller series, and *Project Nemesis,* the highest selling, original kaiju novel of all time (which is in development for TV with Chad Stahelski, director of John Wick). Robinson is known for mixing elements of science, history, and mythology, which has earned him the #1 spot in Science Fiction and Action-Adventure, and secured him as the top creature feature author. Many of his novels have been adapted into comic books, optioned for film and TV, and translated into fourteen languages. He lives in New Hampshire with his wife and three children.

Visit him at www.bewareofmonsters.com.

Printed in Great Britain
by Amazon

48928754R00179